Ralphkern1980@gmail.com

Cover art by Tom Edwards
Editing by Shay VanZwoll

Acknowledgements

Caroline, for helping me come up with the concept for this book, and for her patience in putting up with a writer. I can't imagine how frustrating we must be!

Shay, for her wonderful editorial input.

Tom, for the amazing cover. He really is one of the greatest digital painters on the planet. See more of his work here:

www.tomedwardsdesign.com

Nathan Hystad, Josh Hayes, Robert M. Campbell, Scott Moon, Jacob Cooper, Andy L, Isaac Hooke – without your support, this wouldn't have been possible.

The brave men and women of our armed forces, who make sacrifices for us all.

The many beta readers who have given invaluable feedback for this novel.

The indie community as a whole.

And finally, my biggest thanks is to you, the reader.

Please subscribe to my mailing list here:

https://www.scifiexplorations.com

Or email / add me to Facebook here:

Ralphkern1980@gmail.com

ISBN 9781519037954

UNFATHOMED

Prologue

The mainsail had been ripped away in a storm a week before, leaving no respite from the unrelenting sun.

Eric could have gone below deck, he supposed, but why? The shade wouldn't save him. It hadn't saved Lucy, whose decaying body even now lay on a bunk within the sloop.

No, a dehydrated buzzing filled Eric's head, *the heat will soon take me. Maybe I'll just drift off to sleep and not wake up.*

He felt strangely restless, wanting to give up but also to move his body. Perhaps it was the knowledge that soon, the ability would be beyond him. He twisted weakly on the sun lounger, wanting a better view of the turquoise ocean beyond the low rail surrounding the sloop's white hull.

He gave a bitter, croaking chuckle. Miles away he could see storm clouds on the horizon shedding dark columns of rain down to the surface. The winds already carried them away from the sloop. If only they'd thought to store some of the water from the last deluge which had pounded the boat. But then, they'd still held the vain hope that rescue would come.

Giving a slow shake of his head, Eric let his heavy eyelids close and sleep take him...

...To be awakened by a noise. Eric cracked open his crusted eyes. How many hours later was it? Night had fallen and stars dusted the blackness. He could feel a presence on the sloop, moving around. A figure appeared in his line of sight, silhouetted against the stars.

"He's dead, leave him. Let's see what salvage we can take."

With a grunt, the person standing over him moved away and Eric heard the sound of the hatch leading below decks creaking open.

"Este es un barco hermoso. ¿Cree que podemos mantenerlo?" someone out of Eric's view said.

"You wish. The boss will want the boat for himself." A gagging noise came from below. "Jesus, what the hell is that smell?"

"He…" Eric croaked, the word catching in his parched mouth. "Help."

"He's alive!" The silhouette reappeared, then was joined by another.

"Really? That shrivelled corpse? More than can be said for the chick below deck." The figure turned and barked, "Boss, we've got a live one."

"Wat… water," Eric gasped dryly.

"Let's see what the man says first, shall we."

Eric's brain was slow and sluggish, but surely, these people should be helping him? He heard the sound of footsteps and he let his head loll to the side. A third figure, an athletic man stepped into Eric's line of sight and hunkered down next to the lounger. He cocked his head, giving the

impression of intensely scrutinizing Eric.

"What do you reckon, Urbano?" one of the other figures asked.

The man, Urbano, looked in Eric's eyes for a long moment before standing.

"Toss him overboard."

"Wait," Eric gasped. What the hell was going on?

He felt himself being pulled out of the lounger, his body a dead weight held in a firm grip. They began half-dragging, half-carrying the confused Eric to the side of the ship.

"Money. Have money," Eric rasped.

"Money don't mean shit to us." a straining voice said as Eric found himself forced double over the railing.

Eric gripped the railing as he felt hands move down his torso, their intention obvious — to lift him over and let him plunge into the dark sea. The adrenaline that seeped through his system was starting to activate his body, giving strength where seconds earlier there was none.

"What do... you want?" Eric grated out, kicking at the arms.

"I want a lot of things, friend. But I doubt you can give them." The hands grasped at his thighs, inexorably lifting him.

"I... can give." Eric's voice rose in volume, becoming firmer as he twisted around in his struggles.

"Stop." The leader — what was his name? Urbano? — held up his hand. "There is more life

to this one than I thought." Urbano stepped closer. "How?"

"What?" Eric asked.

"How will you give us all we want?" Urbano's eyes flicked down toward the dark lapping water below. "And talk fast."

Synapses in Eric's brain which had previously started shutting down began sputtering, then firing again.

"I make things happen," Eric croaked. His

instincts, which had gotten him so far in life as a senior executive of Fenton Oil, kicked in. He met Urbano's eyes. He knew it was vital he put just the right intonation into his next few words. It couldn't be a plea; it had to be a promise. "Trust me and I can help your organization, whatever it may be."

Urbano glanced left and right at the figures on either side of Eric before theatrically raising his arm and looking at his watch. "You have precisely two minutes to convince me."

Chapter 1 - Day 1

"Four billion dollars' worth of ship and equipment, and we're lost," Walter Grissom muttered.

On hearing the exasperation in the young officer's voice, Staff Captain Liam Kendricks lowered his tablet and looked over at him. Grissom stared at the monitor with an expression matching his tone. The bright touchscreen displays lit his clean-shaven face, contrasting it with the low lighting of the rest of the bridge. "What's up, Walt?"

"I've lost our positioning fix, sir." The officer began jabbing at the screens which made up his workstation. "I'm showing the GPS system is completely down."

Placing his tablet on top of his own console, Kendricks stood from his leather command seat and walked across *Atlantica's* dimly lit bridge to the navigator's station.

"It'll probably come up in a moment, son." Kendricks looked over the young man's shoulder at the mapping display. Stubbornly in the center of the blue expanse, a stylized satellite icon with a line struck through blinked, indicating they had lost the

GPS lock.

"The whole system is down. We can lose one or two satellite links and it just degrades our positional accuracy. We've lost every last one of 'em. I'm getting nothing," Grissom continued tapping ineffectually at the screen in a vain attempt to work around the problem.

"Okay…" Kendricks looked out of the bridge's huge windows, as if he could divine what had happened to the satellite link by mere sight.

One of Kendricks's least favorite jobs as the executive officer of the M/S Atlantica was mentoring young-in-service officers. He found it frustrating, although he did admit to himself at times, also satisfying when he found someone with potential and helped develop them into a valuable part of the crew.

Grissom was one of those, for the most part. But like the Captain, he didn't like it when things went off-piste and was quick to show his annoyance.

Still, this could be a training opportunity, Kendricks thought. "If we've lost all the NAVSTAR GNSS satellite locks, what does that suggest to you, son?"

"That the problem is probably at our end, sir," Grissom responded quickly, as he should with such a basic issue.

"Good, and in the interest of bringing your staff captain solutions and not problems, what's the SOP for this situation?" Kendricks said, wanting to gently tease the answer from Grissom.

"We perform a self-diagnostic following a reset on the NAVSTAR program. If that doesn't show any errors, then we should do a full restart of the system itself with a level two diagnostic," Grissom replied, as if reading from a checklist.

Kendricks nodded, and gave Grissom a light pat on the shoulder before walking back to his seat. "Sounds simple enough to me. Get to it. And in the future, Walt, when I'm in the chair, don't wait for permission on the basics. My expectation is that you will go ahead and fix the problem, then inform me."

Reclining back in his chair, Kendricks looked out of the window. Far ahead of the bow of the vast cruise ship, *Atlantica,* he could see flashing electrical forks of lightning lancing down through the dark mass of cloud obscuring the stars off the port bow. He couldn't recall seeing any storm warnings on the meteorological report, but it wouldn't be the first time it had been wrong. *We have the most high tech cruise ship in the world, yet we can't even maintain a GPS lock and we miss a goddamn storm.* It was far enough off their heading they would easily avoid it, but still...

"Sir, I've reset the NAVSTAR. Still nothing." Grissom looked at Kendricks.

"Very well." Kendricks rolled his eyes; this problem had just become more irritating, but it was still minor enough that Grissom really should have sorted it out and then let him know. He was far beyond the point where he needed to have his hand held through every stage of a problem. Captain Solberg was not nearly as easygoing as he was, and would likely tear a strip off the young man. Publicly. "Go to the level two diagnostic and be so good as to pull up the notifications feed, too. Let's see if an unexpected service outage has been announced."

"Already done. The coms link is down, too." Grissom gave a grunt as the vast ship nosed over a wave, plummeting down the other side.

Kendricks was a seasoned seafarer and more than used to rough weather, but the drop felt extreme, even to him. He wondered if it was the harbinger of choppier water due to the storm system ahead. When a second wave didn't come, he refocused his attention on the problem at hand.

"Okay." Kendricks released his grip on the console's edge. "Switch to LORAN Radio Direction Finding. We still have places to be and a schedule to keep. Captain Solberg will shit if we wander off course."

"RDF…" Grissom said hesitantly as he stared at his console, "is down, too."

"Say what?" Kendricks exclaimed. The ship had multiple means of navigating the seas, but the two main ones being offline at the same time was a hell of a coincidence. "Very well, I presume we're not picking up the land-based radar-nav towers this far out to sea. Let's get old fashioned about this. We'll go off simple dead reckoning and get IT to do a full-fault find."

If anything, Grissom's expression became even more confused.

"Walt, can you wake up, please?"

Grissom gestured helplessly at his screen, before looking across at Kendricks. "Sir, the compass?"

Kendricks frowned at the digital compass displayed on his command screen. Standing again, he walked to the front of the bridge and squinted at the old-fashioned brass compass situated on a pedestal. The antique device was a vestigial part of a modern cruise ship's navigation suite, although this device in particular was more an ornament than ever actually having been intended for use. It was showing west-south-west. An almost perfect opposite of *Atlantica's* original heading.

"I think it's time to interrupt the captain's dinner," Kendricks said slowly.

***

"She is certainly a most beautiful ship," Rear Admiral Sir John Reynolds, Retired, said, his deep voice richly cultured. "Or at least she shows up my former seagoing experiences."

The gentle clink and murmur from around the wood-paneled, traditionally appointed dining room had resumed after the wave had briefly upset the sedentary atmosphere. The ten people who had been invited to dine at the Captain's Table were dressed in their finest clothing – tuxedos for the men and glorious evening gowns for the women were the standard.

"Thank you, Admiral." Captain Lars Solberg nodded, his Norwegian accent giving his voice a singsong lilt. "I would certainly hope our accommodation is somewhat better than a warship, even one of His Majesty's Royal Navy vessels."

"There was nothing nice about your old quarters, daddy." Laurie Reynolds flashed a smile to her father. "I was horrified at that floating metal shoebox you called a home away from home."

"Quite." Reynolds nodded. "I must admit to being somewhat jealous when one of my former colleagues decided to jump ship and join the lines. Although, not quite jealous enough to have ever made that jump myself."

The waiter quickly and efficiently served the appetizer, a salmon roulade, his presence near unnoticed by the chatting diners of the stately room. The chamber was large, and the murmur of conversation washed out from the three tiers of tables and chairs which created an amphitheater surrounding the round Captain's Table in the center. It was one of the few spaces on the ship that had a quaint appearance, with brass fittings and beautiful maritime-inspired watercolors adorning the walls — a stark contrast to the rest of the advanced vessel.

One of the roles of the passenger service director was to go through the passenger manifest and assign seating based on age, an old tactic of the cruise lines to ensure people got along and bonded, forming a community for the short time they would be guests on a vessel.

The Captain's Table was different, though. To be seated there was by invitation only. Different captains had different criteria. Some chose their fellow diners randomly and some by lottery. Captain Solberg chose his dinner companions with consideration to networking and what was in it for him. A former admiral and his daughter, a town mayor and his wife, a couple who were investment bankers, and a rather attractive pair of young ladies who were traveling together were among Solberg's choice for this meal.

"I always wondered," Denise Heller, one of the young ladies, said as she gestured with an open hand encompassing the whole of the tiered dining room, "what one of these things actually costs."

"The *Atlantica*," Captain Solberg steepled his hands over the appetizer, "didn't come cheap, my dear, and that's before her not inconsiderable running costs. I'm sure you can imagine, filling her up costs a pretty penny, too."

"And what's the return on investment?" Brett Jenson asked, before giving a theatrical "Ouch" as his wife playfully punched him in the side.

"Not tonight, sweetie," Miranda said. "I'm sure Captain Solberg doesn't want to talk shop."

"Oh, I don't mind." Solberg smiled, and indeed he didn't. Maritime affairs and ships were as much a passion for him as young women, and of those ships, none more so than the *Atlantica*, the new flagship of Crystal Ocean lines. "But yes, it does take more than a few years of operation to recoup the line's costs."

The impeccably dressed headwaiter, Mister Santino, stepped into Captain Solberg's line of sight and casually scratched his nose with his right index finger. The captain's eyes met Mister Santino's and he gave a near-imperceptible nod.

"If you'll excuse me, ladies and gentlemen. Duty calls. I'll be back shortly."

Drawing his chair back, Captain Solberg stood and placed his napkin next to his as yet-uneaten appetizer before making his way around the table to the tuxedoed waiter.

"Sir, Mister Kendricks is requesting you on the bridge," Santino whispered discreetly.

"Is he now?" Solberg said irritably. He was about to give a cutting remark to Santino to express his annoyance at having his dinner interrupted, but instead he took a deep breath and said, "Thank you, Mister Santino."

The captain walked out of the dining room, giving polite nods to the passengers who were enjoying their meals. Approaching the palatial entrance foyer, the glass doors slid apart and he walked onto the glorious atrium at the stern end of the long promenade. It was like passing into an entirely different ship, switching with a step from quaint and classic to cosmopolitan and high tech. Glass elevators shot up and down the huge space, twelve-decks high. The mind could barely comprehend such a structure was moving at nearly twenty knots across the sea. Solberg briefly considered taking one of the passenger elevators, but disregarded the idea. Trying to get from one place to another on a cruise ship was a nightmare for a captain. Everyone seemed to want to stop for a chat, thinking he had nothing better to do than engage in idle conversation.

Atlantica wasn't the biggest cruise ship in the world, although she was comfortably in the top ten. She was, however, certainly the most modern. In her gargantuan hull she had every modern convenience it was possible to put inside a vessel. From theaters to nightclubs, to cinemas and even an ice rink—it was all packed efficiently into the vast hull.

The promenade stretched nearly two hundred and fifty meters along the length of the ship, dotted on either side by bars, restaurants, and shops. It was truly a high street, in which hundreds of people were visible milling around, some in their finest evening wear—after all, tonight was the ship's formal night. Others hadn't bothered and were still wandering around in shorts and flip-flops. Solberg gave a frown. Back when he'd started on the lines nearly three decades ago, dressing for formal night was a requirement, not an option.

Quickly ducking into a staff-only entrance before

anyone could corner him, Solberg entered one of the sparse, whitewashed crew corridors that riddled the hull. These out-of-bounds spaces allowed the ship's business to be conducted without breaking the illusion for the passengers that maintenance still needed to happen, bars needed to be refilled, and crew had to get around without being interrupted.

Reaching an elevator, he pressed the button and waited. Pulling his smartphone out of his pocket, he idly flicked through the notifications feed showing him the status of his command.

That'll be the problem then, he thought as he saw the message giving a brief update that all the communication and navigation equipment was down.

Stepping into the elevator, it raced toward deck twelve, where the bridge was nestled beneath the ship's gym and solarium.

He still had a long walk ahead of him to reach the bow, and it took him a couple of minutes to pace along the crew access corridor, nodding in greeting at the bustling hospitality staff who drew themselves into some semblance of attention as he swept past them.

The door to the bridge was an imposing metal hatch, as secure as that of a bank vault. Pressing his index finger to the print-reader, he waited for it to give a bleep before entering his passcode.

With a rumble, the heavy doors slid open, revealing the low-lit bridge and its banks of touchscreen consoles.

"What do you have for me, Liam?" Captain Solberg said as he strode onto the bridge. He shrugged out of his spotless white dress jacket and carefully draped it over the back of his command chair.

"Apologies for disturbing your dinner, Captain," Kendricks said from where he was stood next to the chart table with Walt Grissom. "We are having a major malfunction in, well, every piece of communications and navigation equipment we have. And that includes the compass."

"The compass?" Solberg said in a confused tone as walked over to them. "Have you isolated the issue?"

"We haven't even nailed down whether it's a hardware or software fault yet. IT has been running diagnostics and they're saying our end is fine."

Captain Solberg glanced down at the chart table with its blinking "signal lost" symbol in the center of the interactive display. The map had frozen, showing *Atlantica* as being almost half-way between Nassau and her next destination, Bermuda.

"I presume inertial navigation is still dead-reckoning our position?" the captain said as he slipped off his glasses and cleaned the lenses with his handkerchief before replacing them.

"Negative, sir." Kendricks and Grissom exchanged looks. "The inertial system feeds off speed and heading. We haven't even got a heading."

Frowning, Solberg tried to divine meaning from the error message. "But the speed and heading are entirely based on on-board equipment. Even if we have a glitch in the communications array, which is what I am suspecting right now, we should still have that."

"Aye, but our last heading was roughly east-north-east after leaving Nassau. Now look." Kendricks pointed at the simplest piece of equipment they had — the compass, something they never seriously thought they would ever use. It was showing west-south-west.

"Liam," Solberg replaced his glasses. "I presume you haven't put my ship into a handbrake turn, because that is damn near the opposite of the way we should be heading."

"Sir," Grissom said. "I've taken the liberty of pulling up the raw data control logs. We're not showing the slightest drift on the commands to the rudder or maneuvering thrusters."

Pinching his nose, Solberg nodded, his mind whirling. His ship didn't know where it was, or even which way it was pointing.

"Talk to me about communications," Solberg said finally. "What do we have there?"

"Nothing." Kendricks opened his hands like he was supplicating to the captain. "We have nothing on VHF or sat-link. Even the automatic maintenance upload channels to Crystal Ocean are down."

"I think it's time to get our heads together on this one. I want all department leads in the bridge conference room in fifteen minutes."

"Aye aye, sir."

Chapter 2 – Day 2

"We're ready. The reset from the backup partition is good to go." The head of IT, Tricia Farelly, looked intently at her tablet.

"Very well, Tricia. Let's do this," Solberg said.

The conference room was filled with *Atlantica's* senior staff. Manuals, coffee mugs, and half-eaten pastries covered the table. They had spent the last few hours trying everything short of a full reset of the navigation systems. Each attempt resulted in an accusing "signal lost" message blinking from the screen.

"You sure about this, sir? I've not tried a hard reset while at sea," Farelly's tone had a hint of nervousness to it.

Leaning back in his chair, Captain Solberg gave a long sigh. "Well, we can't exactly be any more lost, can we? Go for it."

"Aye, sir. We'll be down for around three minutes while the systems boot up again."

"Very well. Liam, send a ship-net message, if you please. Give a ten-minute window from…" Captain Solberg glanced at his expensive silver watch. "0410 hours. That'll give people a few minutes to sort themselves out before we get a systems outage."

Kendricks gave a nod and quickly tapped out a text on his smartphone.

Fortunately, the major mechanical departments, as

well as engineering and a host of other departments were headed by the people in the airy conference room, so most of the crew were expecting the outage. Still, it would be highly irritating for any staff who were doing a stock count after a long night in one of the ship's many bars to find they had lost their work.

"Sending it now," Kendricks said. In the room, every officer's phone gave a beep as they all received the message in unison.

There will be a systems outage from 0410 until 0420. Please save any work now.

Taking a sip of his tepid coffee and grimacing, Captain Solberg watched the numbers on the digital clock advance toward the appointed time. Seeing the 0409 blink to 0410, he nodded at Farelly. "Do it."

"Resetting," Farelly responded. Tapping her screen, the lights in the conference room shut down. The room went pitch black other than luminous strips outlining the door. A second later, the reserve power kicked in and the room returned to its well-lit former self, and the only thing missing was the purr of the engines from deep within the ship.

The screen at the head of the table illuminated to show a graphic of a blue bar inching across as the ship's primary computer systems slowly rebooted.

"Fingers crossed that we'll be back on our way with no one the wiser," Kendricks muttered.

Solberg gave a smile and held up his hand, his fingers crossed.

The blue bar appeared to race across the screen at some points, at other places it crawled. It seemed to take far longer than the three minutes Farelly had told them it would, but finally a message appeared.

Systems Rebooted

"Right." Solberg clapped his hands together and rubbed his palms as if he was warming them. He cocked his head and gave a satisfied nod as he heard the low hum of the engines starting up again. "Bring navigation up."

Farelly tapped on the tabletop touchscreen, opening up the desired display.

Signal Lost

"Goddamnit!" Solberg barked, causing several of the people in the room to start. "Communications?"

Farelly gave a shake of her head.

"Very well." Solberg took a deep breath, calming himself before giving a resigned sigh. "We cannot continue on like this. Executive decision time. We will come about and head back to Nassau."

The officers glanced at each other, all undoubtedly doing the calculations in their heads of how much that would cost the cruise line.

"People, I know what you're thinking, but we can…" Solberg's voice trailed off. What he was seeing was surely impossible. He stood up and moved around the table to the curved window overlooking the ocean. The other officers' eyes tracked him. "What time is sunrise supposed to be?"

"It is… 0537 today, sir," Kendricks said, glancing at his tablet that had come back online with the ship's other systems.

"Then will someone mind telling me why the sun is rising now?"

The other officers stood and joined Solberg at the window, watching the first light of dawn begin to creep over the horizon dead ahead of them.

"Liam," Solberg's voice was low. "Turn us back

toward Nassau."

"Sir, we don't even have the compa—" Kendricks began.

"Mister Kendricks, as far as I'm aware, the sun rises in the east. Put it to our stern."

Chapter 3 – Day 2

"Home, Steel Actual. We are in contact with ten plus dismounted and two technicals." Sergeant Jack Cohen flinched away from the rounds impacting the dry sandstone wall he was hunkered against. The whole wall seemed to rock with the thudding strikes of the heavy 7.62 ammunition the ISIL remnant's AK-47s sprayed out. Flecks and chunks of the wall flew in every direction.

In a brief lull in the deluge of fire coming from the shattered remnants of the two-story school in which ISIL had set up their Forward Operating Base, Jack dared a glance over the bullet hole-riddled wall. The opposing sides were less than fifty meters away from each other, separated by an urban waste ground of smashed buildings and sandy open space.

"Sergeant, I've got Melton's bleeding stopped, but he ain't looking so good." The marines already had a man down from this ambush and the squad's medic was frantically working on his injury. He'd caught a round right in the armpit. It had sliced between the plates of armor and had done horrendous damage to the young Marine's chest. Melton lay on the dusty ground, body armor sliced open and splayed wide to expose the damage as blood pooled around him.

"Steel, Home. Thunder will be over you in two mikes. Prepare for fire mission."

"Home, Steel Actual. That's a roger. Status on the 9-

line?" Jack shouted into the radio over the cacophony of gunfire.

"Right on Thunder's tail."

Goddamn it, they better be! Jack thought. Their top cover and casualty evacuation chopper should have been available in a hell of a lot less time than its taken Thunder to get their asses over here.

"Marines, we have two minutes," Jack held up two fingers as he called up the line to the next man, who in turn passed it further up the chain.

Giving another glance over the wall, Jack saw a militant break cover, firing his rifle on rapid-fire from the hip, attempting to leapfrog closer to the marines' position. Bringing his own rifle to bear, Jack sighted the militant through the ACOG sight and gently squeezed the trigger of his M4A1 carbine in a smooth measured rhythm.

The weapon gave a loud popping noise, and the bearded man pirouetted before hitting the dirt. The return fire from his comrades was savage and unrelenting. The stream of bullets from the .50 caliber machine gun bolted on the back of one of the technicals, a dirty red battered pickup truck, slammed into his cover. Jack could feel the wall disintegrating under the onslaught. The dust and dirt sprayed over Jack as he hunkered down as low as he could go, feeling and hearing the hiss of rounds penetrating the wall all around him.

A loud "thunk" came from one of the Marine's underslung M203 launchers. The grenade impacted the cabin of the truck, giving pause to the cannon behind. Whether the operator was killed, stunned, or had merely ran out of ammunition, Jack didn't care. The fire had stopped and he was very happy about that fact. He glanced down, checking himself over, almost in disbelief that he had not been hit.

"Steel, Thunder. We are thirty seconds away. We have

your beacons. Begin your designation, over," the voice on the radio crackled.

Through the ringing of his ears from the exchange of fire, Jack could hear the dull beat of helicopter blades. Looking to the east, he saw two specks in the intensely bright mid-day sky. The AH-64E Apache gunships, their top-cover, had arrived.

"Thunder, Steel Actual. Your mission is the building fifty meters due west of our position. Looks like an old school. Identifying marker is a playground to its due north. We have ten plus in and around that location and one effective technical. We are danger close, I repeat danger closer," Jack shouted into his radio.

"Roger that, you are danger close, Steel. Fifty meters puts you inside our minimum safe target box."

"I hear you, Thunder, but I need to get one urgent surgical out ASAP. I have no opportunity to disengage at this time. I need that position servicing and now," Jack called.

"Roger that, I have the school. Stay down."

Jack slouched so low he was lying on his back as the two ugly olive-green helicopters roared overhead, the downdraft covering him with even more dirt and debris. The fire from the enemy eased on Jack's squad as the militants began firing into the air, hoping to bring down the heavily armed and armored war machines, a trophy they undoubtedly thought would earn them seventy-two virgins if it cost them their lives.

"Servicing your targets. Guns, guns, guns," the calm Texas accent of the pilot announced.

A stream of bullets surged out of the cannon slung below the nose of the helicopter, slamming into the one remaining technical, tearing it into bullet-riddled shreds.

"Guns," the call came again as the Apache circled laterally, wheeling around the target area, keeping its fire *heading away from the beleaguered marine squad. A wall two militants had been ducking behind simply disintegrated in a cloud of sand-colored debris and red mist.*

"Guns." The lower floor of the long-abandoned school seemed to erupt as the heavy 30mm cannon rounds ripped through the building.

"Guns, guns, guns."

Jack closed his eyes, hunkering down as far as he could away from the fury of the devastating vengeance the Apaches were wreaking on the insurgents.

"Steel, Thunder. I see no further movement. Confirm, over."

Glancing back over the wall, Jack could see the bloody remnants of the group that had ambushed them. Nothing appeared to be alive. Jack couldn't even believe that anything could be alive after the pummeling Thunder had given out.

"Thunder, Steel Actual. Can't confirm but looks clear."

"Steel, Thunder. We are providing over-watch. Looks like your rides here. Out."

"Thank you, Thunder," Jack breathed. He would be able to buy the pilots a beer later, but for now brevity meant the radio net had to be kept clear of such pleasantries.

The thumping noise of the UH-60 Black Hawk helicopter began to drown out the engines of the more distant orbiting Apaches as it got closer. Settling down in a clear area in the devastated urban waste ground a hundred meters back from their position, the loadmaster, dimly visible through the cloud of dust the rotor blades kicked up, began waving them over.

"Marines, back to the Hawk. Melton first," Jack shouted over the noise.

His squad gave a chorus of "affirmatives" and began

retreating back to the safety of their ride out of the hellhole they were fighting in.

Jack kept his position, listening as each of his men confirmed they were aboard. Looking through the telescopic ACOG sight of his rifle, he gave a last sweep of the building before picking himself up and starting to turn toward the waiting Black Hawk.

The corner of his eye caught a movement in one of the upper windows of the school. The bright light of the Syrian sun contrasted with the darkness inside the structure. Jack began bringing his rifle to bear on the window.

"Thunder, Steel. I ha — "

The RPG round lanced out of the building, a trail of smoke behind it. It seemed to travel in slow motion straight toward him, the whoosh noise of the rocket washing ahead of the grenade itself.

Jack began to react, his muscles moving slower than the spear of the RPG round racing toward him. He dove, striving to reach the safety of the ground. The lance streaked closer and closer as he felt himself falling to the dirt. Time moved slower and slower. A race between him reaching the sandy dirt and the grenade striking.

He wasn't quick enough.

The world washed out in an explosion of noise and pain before fading into darkness.

With a cry, Jack sat bolt upright on the bed, sweat pouring off his body, heart racing and his chest heaving. He looked around, panicked. Slowly the nightmare faded as reality took over.

Giving a deep breath, Jack lowered his head, pinching his nose, taking a moment to calm himself. He was long since used to the dream and how to shake it off. He'd had it nearly every night for the last six months, after all.

Shaking his head, trying to clear out the cobwebs, he slid a finger in his ear, wiggling it in a vain attempt to clear the tinnitus he'd had ever since Syria. *At least that's clearing up,* he thought to himself. It had slowly eased in the last few months. The incessant buzzing noise had gone from crippling to merely annoying, which at least allowed him to hear people talk now.

Jack lay back and let the thudding of his racing heart fade back to normal as he gazed out of the large round porthole at the blue ocean racing by outside.

Jack briefly considered trying to go back to sleep, but the thought that the dream would greet him again proved too much.

With a sigh, Jack pulled the sweat-soaked bedsheets off his body and swung himself around into a seated position on the bed. He took a moment to wipe the crusted sleep from his eyes before leaning down and reaching for his prosthetic leg, which was propped against the bedside cabinet.

The prosthetic that had replaced the lower half of the left leg he'd had taken from him on the war-torn battlefields of Syria.

Chapter 4 – Day 2

Laurie gritted her teeth in frustration. The sea breeze caused the pages of her notebook to whip over unless she held it open, while the bright sunlight washed out the view on her laptop. The noise of the dozens of children splashing around the *Atlantica's* central pool wasn't helping her concentration, either. The screams of delight as they flung themselves down the waterslides and the hustle and bustle were nice to watch, but difficult to work next to.

Finally giving up on the idea of topping up her tan while doing her work, she closed the laptop and stuffed it, along with her notebook, into her rucksack before standing from the sun lounger. Making her way down the stairs away from the pool to the side of the ship, she saw most of the seating areas were also busy, filled with an older crowd gathered around the tables chatting away, playing cards, or just watching the world go by.

Laurie spotted one table which seemed empty apart from a lone man, seated at one corner of a table quietly gazing at an E-reader, a half-empty bottle of beer in front of him.

"Excuse me?" Laurie said as she approached the man from behind.

The man looked at her, his eyes hidden behind his

mirrored aviator sunglasses. He was dressed casually and the lower part of an indistinct tattoo was just visible on his muscular right arm beneath the hem of the tan short-sleeve shirt. Oddly, he was wearing a pair of chinos in the mid-day heat.

"Are any of these seats taken?" Laurie gestured toward the other end of the table.

"Err no," the man croaked. It sounded like the voice of a person had who hadn't spoken to anyone else all day, his unused vocal chords activating for the first time. It was surprising—it was noon, after all. He gestured at the empty chairs. "Please, feel free."

"Thanks." Laurie pulled her laptop back out of her bag and opened it up on the table as the man's attention went back to whatever he was reading. She lowered herself into the seat and powered up the computer, finding the lesson plan she had been working on.

She begrudged working on her holiday, but the simple fact was these things needed to be done. Still, she wasn't going to turn down her father's offer of an all-expenses-paid Caribbean cruise, even if that did mean she would have to spend the odd day tapping away at a keyboard, generating classes and lectures for the sixth formers due to start their A-levels in September.

She began filling out a spreadsheet in the school's required format for lesson plans, populating the cells with little notes. She had thirty weeks of physics classes to fill, and that started with the basics.

Out of the corner of her eye, she spotted the man take a long swig on his bottle before slowly and deliberately setting it down.

Now, that will help, Laurie thought to herself. In the center of the table was a touchscreen used to order drinks and she tapped on it, requesting a glass of house white. She glanced at the man, wondering whether to interrupt him. *Why not? It would be nice to strike up a conversation with someone who is my side of forty.*

"Hello again," Laurie called to the man, who looked over to her and cocked his head, his aviator sunglasses reflecting a distorted image of herself. "I'm just ordering a drink; want me to request one for you, too?"

The man seemed to watch her, taking a long moment to respond. "Sure, thanks, why not? Bottle of beer, please."

"Coming right up." Laurie smiled and tapped the screen, requesting a bottle of Budweiser, the brand he was drinking. Laurie presented her wristband to the small sensor next to the touchscreen. It bleeped in response, completing her order, and the screen flashed to say someone would be over with the drinks.

"I'm Laurie," she stuck her hand out. The man reached over the couple of seats that separated them and shook it.

"Hello, Laurie. I'm Jack."

His grip was cool and his hand calloused. He was obviously no stranger to manual labor.

"Pleased to meet you, Jack."

"Likewise."

"I love this table service," Laurie said, wanting to strike up some kind of polite conversation with the near-monosyllabic Jack as they waited for the harried-looking waiter to bring their drinks over.

"Very high tech, and sure as hell beats waiting at the bar."

"Yeah," Jack replied, seeming to be striving for words. "It's good."

Laurie nodded at him. He seemed to not really want to talk. *Well, I have work to be getting on with anyway,* she thought with a mental shrug, and looked back down at the laptop screen.

"What are you working on?" Jack asked after a few moments.

"Homework, unfortunately. It has to be done, even on the high seas."

"Poor you." Jack finally smiled. "And what is it you do that requires homework to be done?"

"I'm a teacher, for my sins. Physics. I have to start getting next term's lessons all arranged. I've had weeks to do it already, which I mostly spent procrastinating. Hence why I have to do it on my holiday."

"That sucks." Jack nodded sagely. It was curious… whenever he was listening to her, his head was cocked like he was paying rapt attention to every word she said.

"What about you? What do you do back in reality?" Laurie asked.

"I'm kinda between jobs at the moment. You know, re-evaluating stuff."

"We all do that at some point, I guess. Who are you on holiday with?"

"I just came on my own. I came into a bit of money recently and thought I'd treat myself."

"Very wise. You can't take it with you." Laurie smiled. "My dad brought me along to keep him company. He insisted on it, in fact. But if he wants to bankroll me, who am I to turn him down?"

"That's a generous father you have," Jack said.

"Yes, he is."

They both looked up as the waiter brought their drinks over and set them on the table. They thanked the well-presented young man as he cleared away Jack's now empty bottle.

Jack is rather good looking, Laurie thought as she took a sip on the wine and looked at him. *A bit rougher than my normal type, and he clearly doesn't believe in going clean-shaven, but a girl has her needs. Pity I doubt I'd be able to sneak away from daddy. C'est la vie. Very curious he's wearing a pair of trousers on the deck, though.*

"Sunburn?" Laurie gestured as Jack's legs.

"What? Oh, yeah something like that," Jack replied as he realized she was indicating to his lower half.

"It's a bitch. I've managed to avoid it. I've got some great after-sun. Here, let me get it for you."

"I'm okay, thanks."

"No, I insist. It's in here somewhere." Laurie rummaged in her rucksack. Pulling out the small blue bottle of cream, she presented it to Jack. "Go on. Go put some on; it's far too hot to be wandering around in a pair of trousers."

Jack held his hands up. "I'm fine, honestly."

"You shouldn't suffer, bless you. Here, take it." Laurie thrust the bottle into his hands.

"Okay." Jack took the bottle and turned it over in his hands. "I'll... I'll go put it on."

Jack started to get to his feet, staggering slightly as he stood up.

"Had a few already?" Laurie winked as she saw

him totter.

Jack gave a sharp intake of breath, before standing silently for a long moment. "I'll go put some on. Be back soon."

"Hey, it's always happy hour somewhere in the world," Laurie called teasingly after him as he walked away.

***

"Goddamn it." Jack gritted his teeth as he concentrated on walking. Over the last few months he'd strived hard to hide his injury, and for the most part succeeded. He didn't think anyone would even notice if they didn't already know, but sometimes it caught him out and he forgot himself. *Calm down, she was just trying to be friendly.*

The glass doors leading into the interior of the ship slid open and he found himself in the plush stairwell. Without even thinking, he ignored the glass elevators racing between the lower bowels of the liner and the top deck and started down the stairs. He'd long since made it a personal policy not to use elevators. Despite it being ten decks down to his cabin, he was keeping to that policy. Practice made perfect, after all.

The only concession Jack made to his disability was occasionally clutching the banister as he walked down the stairs. Finally reaching deck four where his stateroom was, he set off down the long corridor that ran down the portside length of the ship. Reaching his door, he pressed his wristband against the lock and it clicked open.

Slumping on the sofa in the small cabin, he rested,

gazing into space for a long moment. His mind was whirling. He couldn't be sure, but the girl on the deck had seemed to be hitting on him. But she didn't know... and if she did, she'd run a mile.

If Jack had responded, reciprocating that hint of interest, once she found out she would reject him. As far as he was concerned, it was better if he didn't put her in a position where she would have to find some excuse to ditch him.

Rotating the blue bottle in his hands, he looked at it again before gently setting it down on the glass coffee table.

I think I'll eat lunch in here, Jack thought. *Again.*

Without prompting, the large LED TV embedded in the wall came alive and the captain appeared, backdropped by the bustle of the bridge.

"Ladies and Gentlemen. As you are aware, *Atlantica* is a brand-new ship and, as expected with any maiden voyage, there is always the possibility of glitches in the ship's systems," Solberg said in a calm reassuring tone. "We have, unfortunately had a slight problem. You may have noticed already some disturbances to your internet and phone access."

Jack rubbed his false leg, cocking his head as he listened to the captain speak, picking his voice out through the ringing in his ears.

"In the early hours of the morning, we set our course back to Nassau. We will be traveling at our best speed. I can assure you, there is plenty of slack in the itinerary. Over the next week, I envisage we will make up for any lost time. As of now, we are not anticipating any lost time on any of our island stops and you will not lose out on any excursions.

Well that explains the breeziness, if the ship was

hauling ass. Jack thought back to the windiness of the deck.

"I emphasize, there are no safety concerns. If you have any questions, our staff will be more than happy to help. Enjoy your voyage."

Jack reclined back into the soft couch as the screen went dark again. Finally, he reached across to the phone and picked it up.

"Hi, can I order a ham and cheese panini? Thanks... no, no fries, salad please."

Chapter 5 – Day 2

Karl Grayson never thought he'd get bored of his favorite movie, but after at least the twentieth time, it was finally starting to drag.

Still, the tired, tight, cluttered cabin of the tiny yacht was not exactly filled with all the mod-cons. The small portable DVD player he had was about as exciting as it got. Hitting the pause button, Grayson pulled himself off the bunk and made his way across the cabin to the cabinet which contained his stash of cigarettes. He was down to his last few packets, and as determined as he was to make them last, right now, he felt the urge for one.

Plucking one out of its pack and grabbing his lighter off the shelf, he climbed the four steps to the deck, lighting up as he went and taking a long, deep drag on the cigarette. He felt the smoke wash down into his lungs, filling them in a most satisfying way. They were a treat for him which he could mostly take or leave, especially when his wife, Kristen, was around to give him a disapproving glare. Sometimes though, he just fancied one, and right now was one of those times. Moving to the rail overlooking the deep blue sea, he leaned over, idly flicking the ash overboard between drags.

Giving a loud yawn, Grayson figured it was about time for his second nap of the day. He'd noticed in the days he'd been stuck on the boat, he had steadily become more and more inactive — wanting to doze or sleep just so time would go by that little bit faster. It was only his sense of self-discipline, rather than desire, which allowed him to keep his fitness regimen. He ensured he spent at least an hour a day doing body weight exercises.

Flicking the cigarette stub overboard, Grayson looked out to sea. A dark speck dotted the horizon, far away. Maybe it was little more than his imagination, but it was the most interesting thing he'd seen in a while. Squinting, he tried to see if it was merely a mirage or something more solid.

Giving up on simple eyesight, he grabbed his binoculars from the where they were stowed by the helm and focused on the speck. It was definitely there. Something big, something real.

Grinning to himself, Grayson opened the lockbox and pulled out the flare gun. He loaded it with a cartridge.

Finally, he thought, as he scrambled for the radio set he already had tuned in to VHF Channel 16, the channel for giving a distress call.

***

"I have a Mayday on 16. A yacht with one soul on board." Kelly Maine, one of the bridge officers, pressed a hand to her headset earphone.

Solberg glanced up from his console. "Position?"

"Flare, sir," Staff Captain Kendricks interrupted

Maine's response, the binoculars against his eyes as he watched the burning red point of light slowly descend toward the sea.

"Thank you, Mister Kendricks," Captain Solberg replied calmly from his command seat. "Is anyone closer to the distressed answering?"

"That's a negative, sir," Maine responded.

"Very well. Mister Kendricks, you know our obligations. Lay in a course, best possible speed."

"Aye aye, sir." Kendricks lowered the binoculars and called over to the helmsman. "Lay in a course on a heading for the distressed vessel, best speed."

"Aye aye, sir." The helmsman glanced at his console, seeing the heading pop up on his display. "Best speed."

"Ms. Kelly, if you would kindly inform the distressed we are en route. We are…'

"An hour out, Captain." Kendricks consulted his display.

"An hour out. And Mister Kendricks?"

"Sir?"

"Prep for rescue and recovery."

Ponderously, the glistening white *Atlantica* came about and the mammoth ship began accelerating to her emergency speed of twenty-five knots, striving to reach the distressed vessel.

***

She is a beauty! Grayson thought as he looked at the clean lines of the cruise ship, the name *Atlantica* proudly emblazoned on her pristine white bow. Blue solar panels studded her flank. She was easily three hundred and fifty meters long and had twelve decks visible which, from Grayson's knowledge, meant that she had at least several more hidden in the hull itself. It was clear she was a floating palace, full of amusements and frills that would keep her occupants in the lap of luxury. From the rail, high above him, he could see hundreds of tiny figures looking down on him, curious at what the *Atlantica* would undoubtedly be considering a rescue operation.

Low down on the hull, a cargo bay was already gaping open, the hatch lowered to provide a platform upon which several people were gathered. Even the lower edge was high above the deck of Grayson's diminutive *Mayfly*.

"Do you require medical assistance?" a man shouted down.

"No, no thank you," Grayson called back from the deck of his yacht. "I'm running low on supplies and have malfunctioning navigation and coms equipment."

"Okay, we'll be right down."

A rope ladder dropped from the platform and Grayson took the dangling bottom rung and fastened the tie to an eyelet on the deck, securing the link between the ship and yacht. Three figures carefully began climbing down the ladder to the *Mayfly*, taking their time to reach the deck on the writhing ladder.

A kindly looking bespectacled middle-aged man arrived first and approached Karl, looking him up and down.

"Hello, I am Doctor Abeo Emodi, from the *Atlantica*," the man said in a deep Nigerian accent. "I appreciate you have said you are well and the reason for your distress call is technical, but would you mind if I give you a once-over?"

"Ah, I'm fine, Doc." Grayson replied, hearing the contrast between his own Southern accent and Dr. Emodi's.

Smiling, Dr. Emodi held out his hands in a placating gesture. "I understand that, but please. Let me just give you a quick check."

"It's been awhile since my last check-up, Doc, so if you must. This doesn't affect my health insurance though, does it?"

"No, no." The paternal-seeming doctor laughed as he reached up and pulled Grayson's eyelids apart and looked intently in them. "Any dizziness? Headaches, tiredness?"

"No, no, and no, Doc."

"Good, have you been having sufficient food and water?"

"I've been surrounded by water for days. Of course I've been drinking enough." Grayson saw a look of concern cross Dr. Emodi's face. "But I've had my own stores. Don't worry, I haven't been drinking ocean water. Honestly, I'm fine. It's a bit embarrassing but this is an equipment failure, not a medical situation."

"Very well, Mister...?"

"Karl, Karl Grayson."

"Well, Karl. Let's get you up to the ship. I'm sure our staff captain, Liam Kendricks, will want to have a chat with you, but I'll give you a full medical exam, courtesy of the *Atlantica,* before he does so."

Shrugging his rucksack on his back. Karl grinned back at the rescue party. "That'll be much appreciated. I'm already packed if you want to get me the hell off this spam can."

***

"Staff Captain Kendricks, XO of the *Atlantica*," the man said, extending his hand. Grayson grasped it and shook it enthusiastically. "Captain Solberg extends his compliments. Unfortunately, he's indisposed at the moment."

After his check-up by Dr. Emodi, Grayson had been given a small curtained cubical in one corner of *Atlantica's* well-equipped clinic. He was sitting in the plastic chair, flicking through a magazine one of the nurses had brought him, when Kendricks walked in. On the bed was his rucksack, already checked by the ship's security team.

"That's fine, Captain Kendricks. Tell him thanks when you see him next."

"I'll be sure to," Kendricks nodded as he propped himself against the crisply sheeted bed. "So you've been having navigation and communications difficulties? How long for?"

"That's right... started a couple of days ago. I've heard nothing from no one. I was starting to get a little worried."

"Quite," Kendricks nodded. "I hope you don't mind, but we had a look over the... what's she called? The *Mayfly*?"

Grayson gave nod.

"The *Mayfly*. You were running pretty low on supplies there, buddy. What are you doing all the way out here?"

"Yeah, I was just doing a bit of fishing out of Dunmore. They were biting and thought, why not? I'll stay out. I didn't expect my coms and nav to fail.

The goddamn compass was even ass-backwards. Kept saying the sun was rising in the west and setting in the east. How screwed up is that?"

"Pretty screwed up," Kendricks nodded in agreement. "And you say all this started a couple of days ago?

"Give or take. It could've happened overnight and I'd not noticed."

Kendricks reached into his pocket and pulled out the CB radio that the security team had taken out of Grayson's rucksack when he'd come on board. It had been the only thing of any note they'd found among the sailor's belongings, which had mostly comprised of clothes which looked as if they'd been worn a few too many times. "What's with the CB?"

"Just a backup I'd had on me. I use it to speak to a few buddies when close to port. You know, tell hoary old sea dog tales."

Kendricks turned the volume nob, switching it on. As when he had checked it before, nothing came through other than the soft crackle of static. Kendricks lifted it to his mouth. "Testing one, two, three?"

As expected, there was no answer. Grayson looked curiously at Kendricks. "If it had worked, I wouldn't need you to save my ass."

"Pity it doesn't. Mister Grayson—"

"Karl, please."

"Karl, the thing is, we've been having the same problems. GPS, RDF, everything is down at the moment. We can't even raise anyone on the radio. And like you, our compass has even gone haywire."

"Well… shit," Grayson said.

"Yeah. Either way, we're heading back the

direction we think Nassau is. But without nav equipment, we're going on the best heading. We're navigating by the sun, that's how low tech we've had to get."

"Okay… How long 'til we get back to Nassau?"

"A day. Without accurate nav data, we'll probably approach the coast a little away from the port. If so, it'll be a bit longer as we figure out where we are." Kendricks pushed himself off the bed. "We'll keep you posted."

"Thanks," Grayson said. "Hey, can I have my CB back?"

Looking at the small device in his hand, Kendricks asked, "Why? No one's on the other end."

"Those things are expensive, man." Grayson smiled. "I can keep trying for you. If I get anyone on it, I'll let you know."

"You do that. Get some rest," Kendricks said as he placed the handheld CB radio on the bed. Reaching into his pocket again, he pulled out a ship's wristband. "When you get hungry, this wristband is loaded with some ship's credit. You can use it in any of the complimentary restaurants."

"Thanks. Can I ask, will this get me any booze?"

"Ha, I'm sure someone will comp you a beer," Kendricks said as he slid open the curtains and stepped out of the cubical.

***

Captain Solberg removed his glasses and gently laid them on his walnut desk before reclining back in his plush leather chair. His office, just off the bridge, was well appointed, although minimalistic. The captain hated clutter with a passion. The only decoration was a large painting of the *Atlantica*, backdropped by a sunny tropical island on the wall behind him.

"So he can't help at all?"

"Nope." Kendricks took a sip of coffee from his steaming mug. "He did say something curious, though. He reckoned he's had the same technical troubles we've been having, only his have been going on for a couple of days."

"I see. So whatever has affected us, has him, too, just for longer," Solberg said. "Interesting. This isn't making any sense at all, Liam."

"I agree, but I'm sure we'll find out what's going on when we get back to civilization."

Chapter 6 – Day 2

The two-lane all-weather running track circumnavigated the deck of *Atlantica*. It was mostly empty at 9:30 pm other than the occasional couple strolling the deck, who were easily avoided. The majority of people left top side were clustered near the neon-lit bars by the pools, thumping music washing out from the oases of revelry.

Jack concentrated hard as he ran, one foot in front of the prosthetic other. His pace would have put most people to shame, but for him it was a mere shadow of his former top physical ability. Long months recuperating in Walter Reed Army Medical Center had helped; they had an okay fitness regime in there, but it wasn't up to Marine Force Recon standards by any stretch.

His step was heavy as he thudded his way along the track, the rail to his left. Darkness had set in, with just the light from the bars, stars, and the waning moon illuminating the deck. He'd finally switched to shorts, having snuck up one of the lesser-used stairwells so as few people as possible could see his… Problem.

As he rounded the flow rider and mini golf course

at the stern of the ship, he could see another figure running the opposite way toward him. Jack looked down at the tan asphalt, not wanting to make eye contact.

"Hey," a familiar voice called out as he sensed the figure approaching him.

Oh, for god's sake! It was her. Jack looked up to see Laurie's lycra-clad athletic body.

"Oh, hi," Jack said as both came to a halt on the fresh, breezy deck. Laurie lightly jogged on the spot, her exposed skin glistened with perspiration.

"You never came back." Laurie raised an eyebrow at Jack.

"Yeah, I kinda got distracted with something."

"Something?" Laurie's eyes were twinkling with reflected light. "Something that caused you not to return a girl's precious after-sun lotion. Which was sorely needed, I might add."

"About that…" Jack said, feeling sheepish he'd effectively ran off with a lady's belongings. "I'm sorry."

"It's okay. I guess you saw the Captain's announcement, too. Back to Nassau, huh? Well, it was beautiful. I certainly don't mind a second look at the place."

The breeze, annoying when trying to sunbathe and refreshing when jogging, was now freezing on their sweat-slickened bodies.

"I'm getting cold. Want some company for your run?" Laurie asked, still bouncing from one foot to the other.

Jack desperately tried to think of an excuse, but none was forthcoming.

"Come on," Laurie punched Jack playfully in the

chest. "I'll try not to leave you in the dust."

Without giving him the opportunity to refuse, she turned and set off in the direction he had been running.

Giving a sigh, Jack set off after her, struggling to keep up. One foot in front of the other.

Sensing his slightly slower pace, Laurie slowed down, allowing Jack to catch up.

"I take it you're more of a gym rat than a CV bunny," she said, barely panting.

"I'm a bit of both," he said, not panting either. His cardiovascular system wasn't the problem, mobility was.

The two dropped into companionable silence, completing lap after lap.

Jack started to wander if she was ever going to give up. He could feel his leg, in the cup where it met the prosthetic below the knee, starting to chafe. He would pay hell for this tomorrow, but the pragmatic side to him said he had to wear himself in. The only way he'd get used to running again was to keep trying.

Finally, they ambled to a stop. Laurie leaned over and began stretching out one hamstring while Jack did his best to ignore her shapely backside.

"You did well," Laurie said as she swapped legs. "So, how long has it been? If you don't mind me asking."

That's it, she's seen. I won't see her again now. She'll just make her excuses and disappear. "This?" Jack glanced down at his left leg. Below the knee was little more than a metal rod until it met the false trainer-clad foot. "Six months."

"Was it an accident?" Laurie stood, interlocked

her fingers and pressed her arms upwards.

Her directness was almost refreshing. So many people skirted around the subject. Or ignored it completely. The problem was, Jack hadn't figured out which approach he preferred yet.

"No," Jack said. "I was in the marines. It... happened in the Vortex... Syria, I mean."

"I don't mean to pry." She smiled briefly, before getting serious again, an earnest look to her gaze. "Look, I'm sorry for the crack about you being drunk earlier. I didn't realize."

"It's okay. I don't exactly advertise it," Jack said, finally meeting her gaze.

"If you want to prove I'm forgiven, why don't you come join me for a nightcap? My father is up in the Platinum Lounge," Laurie said.

"Nah, no thank you." Once again, a direct excuse was eluding him. "I wouldn't want to cramp your style."

"Don't make me beg, Jack. Up there is a bunch of stuffy old men and women who frankly bore my tits off." Her cultured British accent contrasted with the crudity of her words, causing Jack to raise an eyebrow. "Let's join them for a drink, then go hit one of the nightclubs. Come on, I'm a damsel in distress here."

Jack got the impression Laurie would take it as a mortal insult if he were to refuse. She was pushy, but in a way which, despite himself, he found welcoming. Jack finally came to a decision and smiled at the woman. "I'm guessing you'll let me go grab a shower first?"

Putting on a poor imitation of his accent she grinned back at him. "You guess right."

***

Every lounge on *Atlantica* was richly appointed, but the Platinum Lounge took opulence to whole new levels. Leather armchairs and couches were dotted around the highest bar on the ship. The panoramic windows had a near 360-degree view of the deck, dark seas, and star-dusted night sky. The elevators and small service area alongside the bar provided the only obstructions to the view. The only area open to passengers higher was the sky chapel.

Black and white tuxedoed wait staff served the drinks—missing was the tablet-ordering system that permeated the other bars; here it was only the personal touch for the Platinum Lounge customers.

The doors of the elevator slid open and Jack stepped out. He looked around the room and spotted Laurie standing among a group of several men and women. He gave a low whistle under his breath. She was wearing a black dress, demure enough to be just below knee-length, yet showing her sun-bronzed calves. She looked simply stunning.

Glancing toward the elevator, she gave a little wave to Jack and gestured him over to the group. Suddenly he felt very underdressed for the occasion. He'd dug a shirt and trousers out of his luggage, but the blazers the men were wearing probably cost as much as his entire wardrobe.

"Jack." Laurie air-kissed him just off each cheek, giving a theatrical "Mwah" as she did so. "Thank you so much for coming. Daddy, this is Jack, my new friend I was telling you about."

"Pleased to meet you, Jack," John Reynolds said

while shaking Jack's hand, his grip strong.

"And you, sir," Jack said.

"And Jack this is my father, John."

Jack quickly took in the late middle-aged man's bearing. A back that was ramrod straight, physically still fit, and with an air of calmness he knew well. He flicked his eyes at the flash of silver on John's tie, a tie slide with a small crown in it.

"I'll save you the trouble of having to find an excuse to look closer." John Reynold's eyes had a twinkle to them. "I'm formally of the Royal Navy."

"Ah." Jack nodded. "Your daughter didn't say, but you can take the man out of the Navy — "

"But not the Navy out of the man," John finished with a smile. "Laurie tells me you used to be in the military yourself. U.S., I take it?"

"Yes, sir." The man's cultured tones and the confident calm demeanor gave Jack the distinct impression this man had either been an officer or senior NCO. Either way, he felt a hell of a lot safer calling him "sir". "United States Marines, Force Recon."

"Hmm, Force Recon," John said appreciatively. "A unit with a reputation as excellent as it is deserved. I did some work with them alongside our own Royal Marines back in the second Gulf War. Even our own SBS boys said good things, and let me tell you, they're notoriously difficult to impress. Please, let me get you a drink."

Gesturing with one hand, Reynolds called a waiter over. "I appreciate it's probably not your normal fare, but I have a bottle of Harlan Estate behind the bar. A glass if you please, my good man."

The waiter nodded and returned to the bar as

Reynolds turned to the others. "I am being rude, Jack. As much as I would love to talk shop to you, we best include the others. This is Miranda and Brett Jenson, Martha and Wayne Cahill..."

Jack shook hands with the men and air-kissed the women as he was introduced. The waiter brought his glass over and he took a long gulp of it. The flavor was delicious. It was velvety and warm with a hint of fruit to it. It was, by far, the best wine he had ever tasted.

"Wow, this is good stuff. I might have to get me some when I get back stateside."

"I can set you up with a good supplier," Brett grinned. The slight condescending tone to his voice wasn't lost on Jack. "I could probably get you some for a steal. Around $700 a bottle."

Jack's eyes bulged out, but he quickly suppressed it. Looking Brett straight back in the eye, he said, "That would be real good of you. Thank you."

The interplay wasn't lost on Reynolds and his daughter, who rolled her eyes not so subtly.

"Personally," John said, giving a wink as he extended the glass to Jack in a mock salute, "I think you can't beat a good beer, but sometimes you just have to slum it."

"Roger that," Jack said, clinking his glass on the side of Reynolds's and taking a more restrained sip.

"So, Admiral," Brett said, changing the subject, but putting an emphasis on the older man's rank in a clear attempt to put the younger man back in his place. "As a man of the sea, what's your take on the course reversal?"

Jack mouthed "Admiral?" at Laurie as Reynolds looked over at Brett. She gave a little shrug, as if to say, "And?"

"It's nothing too concerning," Reynolds said with his own shrug. "Every new ship has bugs that need to be worked out. If Captain Solberg feels the need to reverse course, then he reverses course."

"But you don't believe it to be anything dangerous?"

"Son, if it was dangerous, I'd be wandering around in a life jacket right now. I had one hurting ship under me in the Falklands War as a fresh-faced middy. I can assure you, *Atlantica* doesn't feel like a hurting ship. At the most, this is an inconvenience but undoubtedly they will make up the time, if for no other reason than they don't want to pay any compensation."

"Hmm, quite. Well, as long as we don't lose any time in Bermuda I suppose. I, for one, was looking forwards to a spot of SCUBA diving out there." Brett took a sip of his wine. "So James— "

"Jack," Laurie cut in.

"Jack, my apologies," Brett waved his free hand dismissively. "How's your suite?

"Just fine," Jack was getting irritated at the man's condescending tone. He had gone for the cheapest option available when he'd surfed the internet. Although it was hardly steerage, his small stateroom certainly looked nothing like the huge, palatial suites which could be bought. "Nothing too fancy."

"Nothing too fancy?" Laurie repeated with a mischievous grin. "You should see it, Brett. Jack here has one of those simply gorgeous ones. It's bigger than my apartment back home. Why you felt you needed your own dining room, I'll never know. It's plain old simple excess."

"Yeah, well, you need the basics," Jack not so smoothly segued into her act.

"Oh, you've seen it then?" Reynolds raised an eyebrow at Jack, his lips pursed slightly.

"I... dropped by." Laurie gave her father an opportunistic fleeting wink as Brett cleared his throat and regarded the glass in his hand, swirling the wine around. He had a disappointed look on his face, despite the fact his wife was standing next to him.

Reynolds nodded nearly imperceptibly at the wink, the twinkle back in his eye and clearly catching on to Laurie's mischief. "I'm glad to see you're making friends."

"To new friends." Laurie raised her glass for the others to toast against.

Chapter 7 – Day 3

"We should have sight of land by now. So where the hell is it?" Captain Solberg growled to Kendricks. They both stood at the very front of the bridge by the huge floor-to-ceiling windows, out of earshot of the bridge crew. The two senior officers didn't want to show their concern to the others.

"Without a solid heading, we could have slipped between Eleuthera and Great Abaco. But yeah, agreed, it's worrying we didn't see either," Kendricks murmured back. The two long, thin Bahamian islands should have created a barrier stretching across their course. "The question is; do we mess around trying to find Nassau or the Andros Islands?"

Pinching the bridge of his nose underneath his glasses, Solberg's mind raced. If they lost any more time, they would never be able to catch up with their itinerary and that carried all kinds of financial implications in terms of compensating the passengers. It was not a decision which Solberg would take lightly.

"No, whatever's going on is a major malfunction. We can't even count on our clocks telling the right time. I'm half-tempted to call a pan-pan." Solberg looked at his reflection in the window. His face was tired and drawn from only taking the shortest of catnaps over the last couple of days. If he called a pan-pan, and it was found to be inappropriate, at best he would face some hard questions. At worst, his long, and thus far illustrious career would be over. Still, as master of the *Atlantica,* if he was found to have put his passengers and crew in even the slightest danger, he was damn sure Crystal Ocean Lines wouldn't think twice about hanging him out to dry. After a few moments' consideration, Solberg finally said, "Let's push on back to Fort Lauderdale. We can get a technical crew out to us who might be able to solve this problem while we head back east to at least try to make up our timeline."

"We wouldn't be able to stop, sir. We'd have to get there, pick 'em up, and get underway while they're fixing us. But I agree, sir. We might miss Nassau, but we sure as hell aren't going to be missing Florida."

"Hopefully they could fly someone out to us by helicopter and meet us off the coast." Captain Solberg continued gazing through the window. Beyond his own reflection he saw the twinkle of stars in the sky. Seeing the distant points of light, a thought occurred to him. "Liam, are any of your staff good at navigating by stars?

"You can be damn sure I can't remember how to do it; it's been years since I've had a go. We need someone fresh out of training." Kendricks turned to look at Grissom, who was yawning at his console. "Walt? Over here, please."

"Sir?" The young officer started, then stood and

walked around his console to them.

"We want to confirm our heading. What's your celestial navigation like?" Kendricks asked.

"Err." Grissom frowned. "It's passable, I guess."

"Good enough," Kendricks said, nodding. "Get somewhere you can get a sighting on the stars and see whether you can get us a location."

"I might need to, you know, brush up a bit," Grissom swallowed as his gaze flicked between the two senior officers.

"Understood. It's not like you're able to do much here with the system's outage anyway." Kendricks smiled reassuringly at the young officer. "Hand your station over to Kelly. Do whatever you need to do to get yourself up to speed and go see if you can give us some kind of position report."

"Aye aye, sir." Grissom hustled out of the room, grabbing his fleece from the rack by the hatch on the way out.

"Celestial navigation? I can't believe it has come down to this," Solberg grumbled.

***

There weren't many areas on the ship's deck to get away from the light pollution that spilled off the *Atlantica* in every direction, but the muster stations where the bulbous gaudy orange mega lifeboats were situated was the closest Grissom could think of.

He walked past the boats toward the stern of the ship, where he knew the lower lighting from the sports facilities above wouldn't wash out the stars— as much, anyway.

The art of celestial navigation was nearly a lost

one when it came to the average sailor, and Grissom was little better than most. On the way down he'd grabbed a small brass sextant and taken the opportunity to go by the ship's library to see if there were any books on the subject… which there weren't. Fortunately, when he had checked the ship's intranet, he'd seen that someone had, at some point, viewed a website on the subject and it was still in the ship's cache.

Finally reaching the stern, he saw he wasn't alone. Standing in the center facing out to sea was a male figure, dimly illuminated in the low LED lighting.

"Hey there," Grissom said as he approached the man from behind. He gave a start and turned, moving his hands behind him to keep something out of Grissom's view.

"Oh, hi," the man said, glancing around the deck before focusing on the young officer.

"What are you up to?" Grissom was mindful to keep his tone lighthearted. This area wasn't off limits to passengers, it was just that it wasn't exactly visited often being far more utilitarian in layout than the majority of the ship.

"Just getting a bit of me time away from the crowds, you know how it is." The man smiled.

"How about yourself?"

"Working, I'm afraid. Hey, aren't you the guy we pulled off that boat?"

"Yeah, you folks saved my bacon. I'd be starting to lose a bit of weight in a couple of days if it weren't for you," Grayson said.

"Ha, you're welcome. I'm not sure how much better off you are with us though right now."

"What do you mean?"

Realizing he'd said too much, Grissom changed the subject. "Don't suppose you know too much about celestial navigation?"

"Celestial navigation? Not a clue. Why?" Grayson cocked his head.

"Nothing."

A crackle came from behind Grayson and a tinny voice. "Karl, did you get my last?"

"What? Who the hell are you talk—" That was all Grissom could manage before Karl Grayson was on him. The athletic man clubbed the young officer on the temple with the base of his CB radio which he'd had hidden behind his back, dazing Grissom and causing the young officer to drop to his knees.

Grayson grabbed Grissom's head and smashed it into the railings again and again, knocking him clean out. Going limp, Grissom slumped to the deck, blood bubbling out of the gash on his head.

Glancing around to ensure no one else was present, Grayson whispered calmly into his radio, "Standby, just dealing with something."

Putting the radio into his jacket pocket, he knelt down next to the unconscious officer and wrapped his hands around Grissom's neck and began to squeeze.

For the briefest moment, Grissom came to. He gave a gargling choke and kicked frantically at the railing while making a weak effort to pull the much stronger man's hands off him. It was to no avail… within seconds, the life had left him.

Grunting in effort, Grayson picked up the dead weight of the corpse and heaved it overboard. With a distant splash, Grissom's body disappeared into the white frothy trail emanating from the ship's engines.

His chest heaving and his body trembling with adrenaline, Grayson looked around again, satisfying himself that no one was around.

Pulling the radio out of his pocket again, he pressed the talk button. "I'm back with you but we might need to speed things up. How long until you can overtake us?"

The radio crackled briefly before a heavily accented and authoritative voice on the other end said. "We'll be with you in ten hours."

Chapter 8 – Day 3

The pumping bass erupted from the speakers with a force that Jack could feel physically pounding his body, yet the warm glow of the alcohol in his system turned it from an annoyance into a pleasure. Even better, the music drowned out the constant ringing of the tinnitus in his ears.

Laurie and Jack were in the middle of the dance floor of Buccaneers. This was the younger and hipper of the ship's two nightclubs, and was nestled deep in the bowels of the hull away from the passenger cabins. Strobe lighting and lasers washed over their sweat-slicked, gyrating bodies and the crush of others around them pushed them closer together.

Jack's dancing had not been great even before Syria. Now it had descended to new depths of awfulness, but right now, he didn't care. He was drunk, dancing with a beautiful woman, and for the first time in six months, felt alive again.

The music smoothly segued from a dance track to a slower beat and with a hiss, smoke was pumped out onto the dance floor, creating a misty, surreal place with strobes flashing in time to the beat. Around them couples pressed together, some kissing, some just cuddling up.

The distance between Jack and Laurie began to reduce even more. Their bodies began to press closer, eyes locked together.

No, Jack thought. He stepped back slightly. *She's drunk, she'll just regret it. She'll have to find an excuse. No. If she does this, she needs to do it sober.*

Jack couldn't believe he was cockblocking himself. His first chance at any action in a year—including the time he had spent deployed in Syria.

"I'm thirsty," Jack shouted to be heard over the music as he made a drinking gesture with his hand. "Want one?"

A quickly suppressed flash of disappointment crossed Laurie's face. Giving a nod and smile, she followed him off the dance floor, both heading to the bar.

***

"Sergeant Jack," Laurie slurred. "It has a nice ring to it. I think that's what Captain America's real name should be."

"Actually," Jack said pointedly, staggering slightly as they wandered up the near-deserted promenade. "I think you'll find Captain America's real name was Steve."

"Really?" Laurie frowned, cocking her head in the look of abject concentration which only a drunken person could give before saying decisively. "Well, I prefer Sergeant Jack."

"Well, I'm sure your father would prefer an officer and a gentleman," Jack replied as they reached the glass elevators. "You know I have a policy, I only use the stairs."

Laurie looked up at the vast atrium space and squinted. "I think you're on your own there, Sergeant Jack. I'm on deck ten."

"Yeah, you may have a point. That's a long way." Jack frowned; it did indeed look a long way up. "I'm only on deck four."

"That," Laurie laughed loudly, causing one of the crew whirring by on a motorized floor polisher to start and look at them, "is the worst line I've heard in a long time."

"No, no I didn't mean it like that!" Jack held his hands up as if he were warding off the accusation. "What I meant was—"

"Don't worry about it," Laurie continued, chuckling. "You can walk me back to my cabin like a good gentleman and then you can go back to your palatial suite."

"Yes, ma'am." Jack nodded.

"Because the last thing we'd want is for you to take advantage of a drunken lady and my father have to castrate you."

"No, ma'am." Jack winced.

Chapter 9 – Day 3

"That radar return is firming up. We definitely have a ship out there," Kelly Maine said from Grissom's usual station.

For the last few hours as dawn had set in, again far earlier than expected, they had been picking up something seeming to be trailing them. It had slowly gone from being an intermittent blinking smudge to a solid spot of light on the radar display as it steadily overtook them.

"Understood. Let's try signaling her again. Now we've established they actually exist, hopefully someone is now in the mood to talk over there," Captain Solberg said.

"She's definitely closing in on us, Captain. Her speed has jumped to around thirty knots."

Solberg glanced at Kendricks who stood next to his chair. "Thoughts?"

"I'm not liking this." Kendricks frowned. "She's been messing around at the limits of our radar perception, and suddenly she jumps to thirty knots. She's not talking, and we've already figured out our radio is transmitting and receiving just fine. If she's having the same problems as us she should, frankly, be begging to talk."

"Indeed." Captain Solberg began lightly drumming his fingertips on the arm of his chair.

"She could just be nervous if she is sharing our navigation difficulties. Send another message; reiterate to them we wish to offer assistance."

"Aye aye." Kendricks reached for the mic, lifted it to his lips and paused. "Shall we come to a stop? Let her catch up?"

Solberg looked at the radar return on the screen above his head, trying to divine some kind of sense from the speck of light that seemed to be silently stalking them.

"No, maintain course. If she's not requesting assistance then I don't want to burn fuel and time stopping for her," Solberg said after a few moments. "How long until she overtakes us?"

"We're looking at around four hours, sir."

"And how long until we sight land, or at least should, anyway?"

"Five, Captain," Maine called out.

Kendricks frown took a more pronounced turn. "That sounds a little too convenient timing to me."

"Yes… yes it does." Solberg agreed. He continued drumming his fingers on the arm of his chair for a long moment. "Send out another broadcast. If she doesn't answer keep putting it out every thirty minutes, but maintain course and heading."

***

With a groan, Jack lifted his head from the couch cushion onto which he'd fallen face first.

Pushing himself into a sitting position, he wiped

the corner of his mouth where some dried drool had formed a crisp film.

Taking in a deep breath, Jack made an abortive effort to stand up, getting about halfway before the alcohol-induced dizziness and pain in his head caused him to slump back down into a seated position.

Resting his head in his hands for a moment, he desperately fought the temptation to lie back down on the couch and slip back into blissful unconsciousness.

Come on, man. Buck up and get up. You know what you need to do. With a groan, he stood himself up and stumbled into the toilet. Taking a deep breath, he stuck a finger down his throat, feeling it tickle.

Without much more incentive, he vomited, feeling his stomach heave painfully.

Panting from the effort, Jack grabbed the shaving glass and filled it with water. Rinsing out his mouth, he spat into the toilet after the remains of the previous night's excess. Fumbling in his wash bag, he took out a tub of aspirin and gulped down four of them, washing down the pills with more water.

Peeling off the previous night's shirt and trousers, he turned the nozzle on the shower and stepped in for the next stage of "Operation Feel Human Again."

***

The surfing simulator, a blue sloping surface with water roaring down it was, as ever, surrounded by laughing and cheering people. The grinning young woman on it was performing well. She had been on for at least thirty seconds as she zigzagged through the surf.

The attendant, who couldn't have been out of his teens gave a shout, "Who wants to see her plant?"

The crowd roared an affirmative and the attendant turned up the flow. The running water became a bubbling white torrent. The woman managed to resist for a few more seconds before flying off and tumbling gracelessly into the netted catch area.

The attendant pulled the laughing woman out of the water and gave her a quick once-over before turning back to the crowd. "Next!"

Kendricks had made his way around the periphery of the crowd, nodding and exchanging pleasantries with the more nervous passengers who were hanging back.

With one final, "If you'll excuse me," he reached the stern and lifted the binoculars hanging around his neck to his eyes.

The tiny black speck behind the *Atlantica* came into focus. A white shape, twin hulls joined by a boxy cross-section, powering through the blue sea in pursuit of them.

Kendricks pressed the screen on his smart phone, selecting the Captain's number. "Sir, looks like she's a catamaran ferry. Probably a Caribbean island hopper."

"At least it's not a goddamn pirate ship. Is she displaying any flags?" Solberg replied.

Squinting, Kendricks looked through the binoculars again. From this distance, the flag was minute, but just visible. A red cross on a white background — the international sign of a ship requiring assistance.

"Sir, I'm seeing a Victor flag," Kendricks said.

"A Victor? Stand by, Liam."

"Standing by."

***

"She's talking, sir." Maine pressed the headphone into her ear.

Lowering himself into his chair and composing himself, Solberg said, "We'll, let's hear what she has to say."

"Aye, sir." Maine touched her console.

" —say again, I require assistance." The voice through the speaker had a Spanish or Hispanic lilt to it.

Maine glanced over her shoulder at Solberg. The captain gave a nod and she turned back to her console. "Unidentified vessel, this is the *M/S Atlantica*. We stand ready to assist. Please state the nature of your emergency."

"Thank you *Atlantica*. I am the *Liliana*. We have a number of casualties on board from a ship's fire.

Any assistance you can offer would be gratefully received, *Atlantica*."

"Goddamn it, is this stretch of the fucking sea cursed?" Solberg muttered, before saying more loudly. "Helm, come about and make back toward the *Liliana*."

"Aye aye, sir," the helmsman called out.

"Engine room, this is the bridge. Prepare to go to emergency dash. Again."

The ship began to turn ponderously. The only thing to show her changing heading was the sun moving slowly across the sky.

"Liam, get back up here. Looks like we have more casualties on board that ship who need rescuing."

***

The pain in Jack's head had subsided to a dull ache and his stomach had settled now that he had filled it with scrambled eggs and toast.

The breakfast and lunch buffet room, Beachcombers, was high on the stern of the *Atlantica*, directly above the main dining hall. A vast panoramic window curved around the room, showing the ocean behind. Extending into the distance was the foamy wake of the ship, a white road on the azure blue water.

As Jack watched, he saw the road begin to curve to the left. Dabbing his napkin to his lips, he leaned against the straight-backed chair. Why the hell were they adjusting course again? Apparently they were heading back to Nassau.

Maybe they had fixed what they needed to fix and were resuming their original course?

***

"No, Doctor, I haven't managed to get a straight answer out of them about the number and nature of the casualties yet other than it's the result of some kind of fire." Solberg was frustrated. The *Liliana's* master was just being plain obtuse when it was coming to giving them any kind of information. At the moment, Solberg was putting that down to language difficulties, but he sure as hell would be writing a long and strongly worded letter to whoever her owners were.

"Understood. We will prepare as best we can for multiple burns and smoke inhalation," Dr. Emodi replied.

Disconnecting the call, Solberg placed his phone on the console and gave an exasperated sigh.

Solberg's sixth sense was telling him something was wrong about the situation. *Well, even more wrong than it already fucking is.*

The *Liliana* was dead ahead. Soon *Atlantica* would have to cut engines to make a rendezvous with her. A cruise ship didn't exactly stop on a dime—she would need a good couple of miles to come to a halt relative to the ferry.

"Mister Kendricks?" Captain Solberg said, his nervousness causing him to be more formal than the norm with the closest thing he had to a friend on board. "Bring her along our port side mid-ship loading hatch and prepare for rescue and recovery."

"Aye aye, sir."

"And Mister Kendricks, make sure we have a security detail at the station."

"Yes, sir. And the LRAD?" Kendricks asked.

"Yes." Solberg nodded. "Get that manned, too."

Plucking his phone out of his pocket, Kendricks dialed the head of security. "Mister Singh, meet me down in the security center. And bring along a detail." He paused as he listened to the response. "Yes, a full team. And bring your key."

***

The utilitarian security center was deep in the bowels of the ship, just off of one of the main crew corridors, affectionately called "Route 66". The walls were adorned with everything from white boards displaying rosters scribbled in marker to posters warning the crew to be aware of suspicious packages and people.

The nine men and women of the security team were primarily of South Asian or Eastern European descent, attracted to the life on a cruise ship for the relatively high wages despite the relentless working hours imposed upon them. All were well trained and many had some kind of military experience.

"Ladies and gentlemen," Liam Kendricks briefed them. "We are about to engage in rescue and recovery operations on a distressed ferry. We have an unknown number of casualties on board."

Pulling a keychain from around his neck, Kendricks caught a confused look in Haroon Singh's eyes. "Something doesn't feel right about this. The distressed ship has been late in communicating with us, evasive in its communications when it finally did, and suspicious in its maneuvering. Hopefully this is going to be exactly like it appears, but we are not going to take any chances with the four thousand passengers and two thousand crew on board."

Kendricks nodded at Singh and the two men went to an innocuous bulkhead hatch. There were two locks on it, and each of them had a key for one of those locks. Only Captain Solberg had both keys to open the door on his own.

Looking in Kendricks's eyes, Haroon Singh said formally and for the benefit of the CCTV which recorded the access to the hatch. "Staff Captain Kendricks, do you have the real and honestly held belief that the ship may be under threat?"

"I do," Kendricks replied, equally formally.

"I concur. I note the time to be 1247 hours and I am using my key on the armory." Singh slipped the key into one of the locks and turned it, before stepping aside for Kendricks to do the same.

"I note the time to be 1247 hours, and I am using my key on the armory," Kendricks repeated, slipping his own key into the second lock.

Grunting with effort, Kendricks swung the heavy door open and stepped inside the room which was little bigger than a walk-in closet. Inside, racks of handguns and several shotguns rested against the bulkhead.

Picking a Heckler and Koch HK45 off the rack, Kendricks turned to the solid-looking red metal bullet catcher tube angled against one wall. Checking that the safety catch was on and there was no magazine in the handle, he drew back on the black slide and released it three times before locking it back and looking into the chamber, ensuring there were no rounds within.

Gesturing with his free hand for one of the security officers to join him, Kendricks tilted the handgun to show the empty chamber and said, "Clear."

"That is clear," the woman said and took the weapon from him. Taking a magazine from the shelf, she slid it into the grey handle of the gun and pressed the release catch. With a thunk, the slide locked forward.

"Take four spare magazines and a Taser," Kendricks said before reaching for another handgun. "Next."

Chapter 10 – Day 3

The breakfast had sorted Jack out and he decided to skip lunch. Instead he was seated at a table in Art Deco, a café on the promenade. As its name suggested, it was inspired by the 1930s. Gaudy paintings were intermingled with stylish cityscapes of buildings and ships of the period. The decorations were something that would have been lost on Jack, other than the fact he was flicking through the ship's magazine which explained all of this.

Taking a sip on his coffee, he heard the bing-bong chime of a ship's announcement. One of the cityscapes, showing a black and white image of the Chrysler Building, revealed itself to be a TV screen with the captain now on it.

"Ladies and gentlemen, as you may be aware, we have performed another maneuver. This is to effect rescue operations on a distressed ferry we have encountered. There is no cause for alarm, so please enjoy your day."

The screen blinked off, reverting to the image of the Chrysler Building.

Two rescue operations in as many days? Jack's mind whirled. *There has got to be something bigger going on here. We've had no contact with the outside world in days, and have now encountered two distressed ships.*

Downing his lukewarm coffee, he stood and made his way out onto the promenade, heading for the elevators which would take him to the deck, forgetting for the moment his resolution to only use the stairs.

***

The squat *Liliana*, as large as she was, was dwarfed by the vast bulk of *Atlantica*. The two ships were approaching head to head, offset slightly so they would draw parallel with each other.

Liliana's hundred-meter-long double catamaran hull was painted white, her name emblazoned on the side in multi-colored lettering. Nestled on top of the twin hulls was the passenger section, three enclosed decks with small portholes along the side, and a bridge window visible at the front. Structurally, she seemed new; an advanced catamaran of a type which many of the sailors on board the *Atlantica* recognized as only having been plying the Caribbean for a few months.

Her paintwork told a different story — it was faded and discolored by sea spray and the sun. Rust was visible around her ports, giving all the signs of long years of service.

***

"Open the loading hatch," Kendricks called out.

There was none of the refinement of the passenger sections of the ship down in the working decks. The walls were metal bulkheads and exposed piping, and the only adornments to them were safety notices and posters. The room they were in was nearly fifty meters long and twenty deep, full of pallets of supplies. The tons of dry goods that went into providing for six thousand people were stored in ten similar bays nestled in the ship's hull. Everything from flour to dishwashing powder was stored in such chambers.

With a loud whine, the massive cargo doors rumbled open, exposing the glistening blue ocean and ferry beyond. The crewman on the control panel pulled another lever and a platform extended from under the cargo bay doors, locking into place with a mechanical "thunk".

Kendricks and the security detail were wearing long wax raincoats to hide the fact they had shoulder holsters containing handguns and Tasers. Dr. Emodi and his medical team were waiting to one side, along with a dozen wheeled stretchers they had already brought down in anticipation of casualties.

Kendricks stepped out onto the platform, exposing himself fully to the scorching hot midday sun. He was already sweating and mopped the perspiration from his brow with the back of his hand. The hatch to the top deck of the

Liliana was nearly flush with the platform.

Kendricks waved over a couple of crew members who, carrying a gangplank between them like a ladder, jogged over and fastened one end to the eye bolts on the edge of the platform.

The hatch on the flank of the Liliana opened, two figures visible within. They waved to *Atlantica's* crewmen, who lowered the gangplank, letting it drop neatly into the open hatchway. *Liliana's* crew fussed over the end of it, securing it to the door, creating a bridge between the two ships.

One of *Liliana's* crew, a muscular Hispanic man in his thirties, wearing a black t-shirt and faded blue jeans, walked across to the platform, extending out his hand as he did.

"Good afternoon," Kendricks shook the man's hand. "Staff Captain Liam Kendricks, executive officer of the *M/S Atlantica*, and you are, sir?"

"I am Urbano Bautista, master of the *Liliana*. My sincere thank you for your assistance, Staff Captain."

"We understand you have casualties," Kendricks said, cutting to the chase. "Our medical facility is at your disposal."

Bautista gave a nod. "If we may get them across as soon as possible?"

"By all means." Kendricks stepped aside, gesturing toward the entrance of the bay.

Bautista turned and shouted back at the gently rocking *Liliana*, "Llevarlas, rapidamente."

A parade of men and women emerged from the hatch of the ferry, carrying a stretcher between each pair. Kendricks stood to one side, letting them pass. "Take them into the cargo bay, we have a triage facility set up there." *And our security team,* Kendricks thought to himself.

There were six stretchers in all, each with a moaning man or woman on them, specks of blood visible on the faces, the rest of their bodies covered by green woolen sheets tucked up around their necks.

"What happened, Captain?" Kendricks stood next to Bautista as the stretchers and bearers passed them.

"A fire, below decks." Bautista shrugged. "Probably a cigarette? Who knows, our priority is their medical condition rather than investigation."

"Fair enough," Kendricks had to agree with the sentiment. Apportioning blame could come later. "Okay, that's enough. Let my medical teams process them. Then we can take more on board if need be."

Bautista gave a nod. "As you wish."

Kendricks and the Latino man walked back into the cargo bay as the stretcher-bearers laid the first of the casualties down on the red-painted floor.

"You'll forgive us if our security officers just perform a routine check?" Kendricks asked.

Bautista paused for a moment. "Of course, by all means."

A security officer approached one of the prone figures and hunkered down next to him. With a quick motion, he pulled aside the sheet. On the stretcher alongside the casualty lay a pair of automatic rifles.

The "sick" man's eyes flashed open and he lifted the handgun already in his hand, and fired it twice into the security officer's chest. Blood splatters blossomed on his white shirt and the security officer looked down, a confused expression on his face before falling backward. The man on the stretcher sprang upwards, firing wildly as his comrades dived for the rifles.

The security team had been ready, knowing this was the moment in which if anything were to happen, it would. They drew their handguns from their holsters.

Haroon Singh fired twice into the man who had shot his security officer. The man fell to the deck with a cry.

Bautista turned and drew a small pistol from his waistband where it had been hidden. Smoothly he drew a bead on Kendricks and opened fire.

The staff captain was already twisting away as he heard the first shots. He was fast, but not fast enough. He felt a sharp lance of agonizing pain in his left shoulder. Drawing his own sidearm, he fired wildly toward Bautista as he stumbled back toward the cover of a cargo pallet. Every shot missed, but it did succeed in forcing the man back behind the cover of a crate.

The first exchange of fire was brutal at such a close range. The dead and wounded dropped to the deck and puddles of blood spread around them. What was left of the security team dove behind whatever cover they could find while the medical team bolted toward the exits. Then the automatic fire of the boarder's rifles began. Bullets ripped through the cargo crates, turning the hold into a maelstrom of burning hot lead.

Hunkering behind a support stanchion, keeping his right hand on the gun, Kendricks reached into his pocket with his left. His arm felt weak and trembled as blood trickled down it.

Pressing the bridge speed dial on the screen of his phone, Kendricks barked into it, "Terrorists, they're fucking terrorists!"

***

"Terrorists, they're fucking terrorists!" Kendricks's voice bellowed out of the bridge's speakers.

"What the hell?" Solberg whispered. The CCTV from the cargo bay had been piped up to the bridge and the officers watched events unfold with shocking rapidity.

"Sir? Orders?" Maine called out.

"Fucking terrorists?" Solberg growled, repeating Kendricks. His shock turned to a burning anger. Terrorists, on his fucking ship! "Maine, send out a Mayday. Announce we are under attack."

"Yes, sir," she replied. Hunkering over her

console, she began to call into her mic, "Mayday, Mayday, Mayday. We are under attack. I am a cruise ship with an unknown number of threats boarding us."

"Helmsmen, flank speed. Get us away from that ferry. Now, damn it!" Solberg barked.

"Aye aye, sir." The helmsman pushed the rarely used manual throttle lever wide open. The engine noise rose from silent, through a purr to a deep rumble, creating a vibration throughout the whole ship.

"Get any other security we have to the armory. Tell one of them to pick up my keys on the way!" Solberg called out.

**

Atlantica slowly began to accelerate as more boarders ran across the gangplank. The structure gave a sound of tortured metal being warped and twisted before the end sprang from the eyebolts on the *Liliana.* Along with a screaming person, the gangplank plunged into the ocean with a splash.

The two ships bounced off each other, grating and

sparking as *Liliana* began to grind backward along the *Atlantica's* hull.

***

"Jesus," Jack muttered as he heard the unmistakable sound of gunshots and the rattle of automatic weapons from amidships. Leaning over the side, he saw the ferry that had pulled alongside bounce repeatedly into *Atlantica's* hull, slowly pirouetting as the cruise ship's greater mass pulled it around.

All around him were cries of panic from the other passengers. Some were running away from the sound of the shooting; others were frozen in fear.

"Charlie, Charlie, Charlie. All hands, Charlie, Charlie, Charlie," A panicked voice shouted from the ship's PA system.

Looking around, Jack caught sight of a young woman, dressed in the polo shirt and shorts of one of the children's play workers running by him.

He just managed to catch hold of her arm, stopping her and twisting her around.

"Hey, hey," he said. "Listen, I'm ex-Marines. I can help. Can you take me to the security office?"

"No, I have to get to the children. That's my job when there's a Charlie." The girl's eyes were wide in fear and her voice had an edge showing she was on the verge of tears. "I have to look after them if something like this happens."

"Okay, that's good," Jack glanced at her nametag. "Clarice. You get to your station. But I need you to tell me what deck the security office is on?"

"It's on Route 66-B," Clarice tried to tug her arm free. "That's crew deck two."

"Got it." Jack released her arm and in his slight limping run, headed for the stairs.

Chapter 11 – Day 3

The battle in the cargo bay had quickly turned into one of bloody attrition. It was a battle the heavily armed and more numerous terrorists were winning with their military-grade weaponry.

"I'm down to two mags," Singh called from where he was hunkered down next to Kendricks. "We aren't going to win this."

Kendricks leaned around the cargo pallet and fired two shots toward a terrorist who had stood and began running toward a yellow forklift truck that would have given him a better angle to attack the beleaguered security team.

The man skidded to a halt and ran back, spraying his AK-47 wildly toward Kendricks. Rounds pinged into the bulkhead behind him, one bouncing back into the pallet that he was crouched behind, narrowly missing Kendricks's head.

"Are all the medics and crew out?" Kendricks shouted, his voice twisted with the pain of his injured shoulder.

"From what I can see," Singh called back.

"Good. Let's withdraw, we can try and bottle them up in the corridor."

***

Panting from the exertion, Jack had managed to descend fourteen decks. He had had to weave his limping way past dozens of screaming, panicking people, but now he was in the crew sections where the sound of the gunfire was audible as a metallic, echoing roar.

"The security room?" he said breathlessly as he grabbed a waiter who was running down the corridor.

"Down there, it's signed." The man didn't even question who he was, merely pointing down Route 66 before continuing his blind escape from danger.

Jack set off at a run, glancing left and right at the bulkhead doors as he passed them, looking for the right room.

Finally, he reached it, the hatch door already half open. Inside were five scared looking men and women.

"I'm here to help," he panted, trying to catch his breath.

"Please, sir, go back to your rooms," a young terrified-looking Sri Lankan man said.

"Listen, you're being boarded. I'm military. Give me a gun and let me help," Jack said.

"Me too," A panting voice said from behind Jack. Turning, he saw a man in his late thirties wheezing, his hands on his thighs. Taking a deep breath, he stood up. "I'm Major Leonard. U.S. Army."

"Major, I'm Sergeant Cohen. Marines."

"Are you infantry?" Leonard asked, his eyes were wide with fear.

"Yeah, Force Recon. And you, Major?"

"Logistics Branch."

Shit, Jack thought. "Okay, sir. You mind if I take operational command in that case?"

"With pleasure," Leonard snorted.

"Guys, we can either mess around," Jack said, addressing the security officers, "or you can accept the help of two trained soldiers." *Well, one trained soldier and one guy who has probably shot a gun less than your average Texan housewife.*

"Okay, okay," said the man who had first responded to Jack, who seemed to be the closest thing to a leader of the remnants of the security team. He pointed at the open armory door. "Take what you need."

Jack stepped in and pulled a handgun off the rack.

***

"Go, go, go!" Kendricks shouted. The three surviving security and the staff captain broke cover and ran at the open door.

A deluge of fire followed them, striking one of the security in the back, knocking her onto her front. She lay silent, a puddle of red expanding around her.

Ducking into the corridor, Kendricks slammed the hatch shut. There was no way to secure it, but it at least stopped the terrorists firing after them.

"Okay, back to Route 66-C," Kendricks said. He flicked his phone out and wiped the blood-covered touchscreen on his trousers. "Captain, have we got any reinforcements coming?"

"Yes. We're mustering them up. You have a few more on the way."

"We've withdrawn to lateral twenty-seven. We'll

try and hold them here."

***

"Bring us back onto our original course," Solberg called out, then pressed a button on his armrest. "Engine room, we require full speed. Go to emergency dash as soon as you can."

"Aye aye, sir," the tinny voice from the speakers announced.

"Terrorists? This close to American waters? They have to be ballsy." Solberg shook his head in disbelief at the situation that was occurring below decks.

***

The *Atlantica* began turning in a wide arc back toward what her compass showed as east. Her engines, designed to go up to twenty-five knots, screamed in protest as they were redlined pushing her up to twenty-seven.

The *Liliana* had stopped twisting and regained control. The much faster and nimbler ferry came about and set off with a roar of engines and spray in pursuit of the cumbersome cruise ship.

***

"Is there any way we can flank them or get behind?" Jack asked. He had taken two handguns— one in a thigh safari holster and the other tucked in his waistband. In his hands he held a Mossberg 500 twelve-gauge shotgun.

"If we can get to one of the other cargo bays on the port side, we can head through to the loading bay," one of the young security officers said.

"Okay, let's do that. You," he pointed at the spokesman of the small security detail. "Lead the way, and you," he pointed at another, "take as many magazines as you can carry and resupply the other team. Questions? No? Let's move."

***

The *Atlantica* could not match the top speed nor acceleration of the *Liliana*, but she did have one defensive weapon she could use.

"Come on, quickly, get it mounted!" Josef shouted at his crewmates.

Together, they hoisted the heavy LRAD up and clamped it to the rail on the stern of the ship near the flowrider.

The LRAD, or Long Range Acoustic Device, was *Atlantica's* non-lethal anti-boarding weapon. It looked like a black hexagonal radar dish with clips on the bottom to fix it to the railing.

"Okay, boys. We'll fire at two hundred meters," Josef said.

The *Liliana* started toward them, barreling through the tumultuous foam wake of the cruise ship, gaining on them at a relative speed of five knots. Through his binoculars, Josef could see crew gathered on the deck of the ferry, making no efforts to hide the fact they had weapons.

Liliana shifted to one side, striving to get out of the turbulence of *Atlantica's* propeller screw wash. Reaching the crystalline blue sea she began to follow again, gaining even more speed.

"What is she doing?" Josef muttered.

Springing into sight from between the *Liliana's* hulls, four speedboats raced toward them.

"Shit," Josef barked. "Focus on the lead boat."

Josef waited until the boat was two hundred meters away, the heavily armed men hunkered low against the spray within.

"Fire!" Josef shouted as the speedboat reached what he judged to be the LRAD's maximum effective range.

The crewman who had the control box for the LRAD pressed the big red button on it.

Josef heard a low-pitched hum coming from the device. Beyond the daylong training course he had taken on the device, he had never seen, or more accurately heard, it in action. For the men on the speedboat, the noise was completely different. A deafening wall of sound smashed into them, pulsing like a car alarm, but at an incredible volume. Two men recoiled so violently they were knocked back into the churning water. The others clasped their hands to their ears in a vain attempt to block out the noise. From this range, it was likely that some of them would be permanently deafened.

The speedboat skewed to the side, striving to get away from the punishing LRAD cone of effect. The other boats, seeing what was happening, became wary and began to angle out of range.

Josef pumped his fist and cried out, "Yes, you bitches. How you like that?"

Squinting he saw a group gathering on the roof of the *Liliana*. They seemed to be working on something. Lifting his binoculars, he looked closely.

"Oh shit. Down!" Josef shouted.

The machine gun the terrorists had secured onto the roof opened fire, sending a stream of bullets toward where the crew had placed the LRAD. One crewman was torn apart by the heavy-caliber rounds, and the railing disintegrated around them.

Josef and his surviving companion ducked down, desperately crawling away from the railing to escape the hail of death coming from the *Liliana*.

"The LRAD!" Josef shouted, coming to a stop. "We must get it before they destroy it."

Crawling as low as he could back toward railing, bullets hissing overhead, Josef unclamped the LRAD stand and pulled it back down. With a thud, the heavy piece of equipment landed next to him and he started to drag it back to safety.

***

"Kendricks, is it?"

Liam looked at his phone questioningly. His security detail had reached something of an impasse with the terrorists bottled up in the loading bay. They had turned the access corridor into a kill zone for anyone who tried to get down it, still it was only a matter of time before they used one of the other exits. "To whom am I speaking?"

"I'm Sergeant Jack Cohen, one of the passengers. I have with me some of your security team. We are going to sweep through and flank them from the bow side. We're going to need you to keep them occupied. Can you do that for us?"

"Jack... Sergeant. I have three men left with me, and only one of those is uninjured and none of them are soldiers—"

"I appreciate that." Jack's voice was calm and measured coming through the phone. "But still, we're going to need to clear this area out or they will break out. If they do, we are not gonna be able to contain them. We'll lose civilians. Do you understand what I'm saying? We're it."

Kendricks looked down the access corridor to the now-open hatch. A bloody corpse of one of the terrorists was slumped in the hatchway. A hand reached from around the hatch and pulled the body out of the way.

"We'll do what it takes, Sergeant."

***

Solberg was watching in horror on the CCTV system as his crew were dying both below decks and above. Never had he even considered the prospect of his ship being attacked, yet here that nightmare scenario was happening… and within a stone throw of America's coast.

"Best estimate for our distance to land?" Solberg barked.

"Fifty nautical miles, give or take," Maine called. "I mean, we must be around that distance."

"Just keep broadcasting our Mayday and don't stop, no matter what. And engineering, keep the goddamn engines redlined."

***

"Tactics, accuracy, power, and speed is what we need, people," Jack said. His impromptu lesson in close quarters battle was being delivered at a breakneck pace. They were hunkered by the access hatch leading from one of the cargo bays into the loading area where the terrorists were holed up.

"Tactics—we are going in; you will cover the left side," Jack pointed at Major Leonard. He pointed at another security officer. "You right, and I'll be center. You, there, you will be reloading cover, don't fire until someone needs to drop a mag. Accuracy, keep your weapon up, sight picture, squeeze. Aim fast, shoot smooth. Power—we need to dominate the room, get in there fast and do not, whatever you do, hesitate. They have shown their intentions of killing us. Shoot them first and cry about it later. Use cover, but stay away from the walls. Bullets will skip straight down them and into you. You got all that?"

The scared men and woman nodded jerkily. They were trembling with fear and adrenaline. Jack knew to give them any more information would just saturate them. He needed them fast and dynamic. CQB—Close Quarters Battle—was hard and exhausting, even with trained soldiers. With these amateurs it was likely to be a slaughter. But they had to try before the terrorists managed to break out into the rest of the ship.

"Today you're going to be Marines, boys and girl. You're going fight fast, hard, and with all of your might and we will defeat those terrorists. Understood?"

Jack looked at their terrified faces. After a long moment, Major Leonard met Jack's eyes with his own and said, "Understood."

"Let's do this. Go, go, go!"

As an impressive one, Jack and the others

launched themselves through the hatch into the loading bay. Jack's shotgun was already at port arms, the butt lodged firmly in his shoulder. Two terrorists in the room covering the door were slow to react to them coming through and Jack's first shot smashed into the chest of one, knocking the man back. The second was winged by one of the shots, spinning around before she was caught by the fire from Major Leonard's shotgun.

Jack turned, racking the pump-action, and fired again at a group of four in the clear who had begun to dive for cover. Jack hit one, making a ragged mess of his chest. Leonard fired his shotgun at another group that was gathered at the opposite hatch, wounding one.

Racking his shotgun again, Jack fired at another one that was slow to get down. The rounds caught the man in the head, turning it into a tattered ruin.

"Keep moving," Jack shouted at his comrades. "Kendricks, now!"

From the access tunnel, Kendricks's ragged group charged in. A round caught Singh, knocking him down, screaming in agony.

Major Leonard gave a gasp. Jack glanced over to him, seeing the man's chest was stitched with bullet holes. He slumped to his knees before falling to his side. Jack refocused; there would be time to mourn later.

The shotgun roared again and again, a subconscious part of Jack's brain kept count of how many rounds he had fired. When the weapon emptied, he dropped it, smoothly drawing his handgun from his thigh holster, and he brought it up in a weaver stance, one foot in front of the other.

Sight picture. Jack saw a terrorist turning toward him in adrenaline-induced slow motion. The rear sight notch on the back of the handgun and blade at the front aligned on the man's center of mass. *Squeeze.* Jack smoothly pulled back on the trigger twice. The HK45 barked. The bullets caught the man in the chest. Twisting, he saw another terrorist leaning out from behind the cover of a crate, the muzzle of the AK-47 he had raising toward Jack. *Sight picture, squeeze.* He fired twice at him, catching him in the neck and arm. Turning again, he saw another man firing his pistol at one of the security, and the woman went down with a scream. *Sight picture, squeeze.* Jack avenged the fallen woman.

The ferocity of the counterattack which had at first stunned the aggressors now routed them. The few survivors turned and began sprinting toward the open cargo hatch, not even pausing before leaping out over the edge to the sea roaring underneath at more than twenty-five knots.

Panting, Jack looked around at the loading bay, slick with the blood of the dead, dying, and injured.

"Kendricks?" Jack called, turning to look at the injured officer, who stood gripping his handgun, blood running down his other arm.

"Yeah?" Kendricks said, wincing.

"Get your medical team in here. Start patching up the survivors."

Kendricks simply nodded and started speaking quickly into his phone.

Jack limped to the edge of the cargo hatch and looked out. Receding into the distance he could see dark specks, the pirate survivors taking their chances in the sea. Looking up, he saw the ferry, circling wide, prowling out of range, obviously waiting for another chance.

***

"Captain, the boarders have been repelled." Kendricks's voice was strained with pain over the speakers.

"Thank you, Liam. We still have other problems though," Solberg barked. Looking at Maine, he asked, "Distance to coastal waters?"

"Forty miles, sir."

"We should have heard something from the Coast Guard by now. That goddamn ferry is still hounding us."

The *Liliana* was maneuvering behind them, twisting and turning to run parallel near the rear of the ship. There was no way that *Atlantica* could outmaneuver the far more agile vessel, they just had to hope they didn't have any more tricks up their sleeve before the Coast Guard, Navy, or someone could respond.

"*Atlantica*," a voice emanated from the speakers. "I am a U.S. Navy Seahawk from the *USS Paul Ignatius*. We have monitored your situation. We will be on station in a few minutes. Hang on."

Finally, Captain Solberg gave a long exhalation. *The Navy was arriving.*

***

The light grey Sikorsky MH-60R Seahawk was a true workhorse of the U.S. Navy. It was a large helicopter used on just about every type of warship.

Lieutenant Grace "Mack" McNamara loved the aircraft and her job, even if over recent years life had taken a very strange turn for her.

"Hank," she called over the intercom to her weapon systems operator. "You better have been keeping the 17/A serviced. Looks like we're going to be seeing some action."

"Don't you worry, ma'am. Geraldine is locked, stocked, and ready to rock," Hank shouted back to Mack.

The Seahawk thundered over the sea at 160 mph, keeping at low level. Grace kept one eye on the fuel gauge. It was at a premium these days, and despite the fact the captain had ordered her to haul ass, she didn't want to burn one drop more than she had to.

There, Mack saw a dot on the horizon, a thin plume of smoke above it.

"*Atlantica*, this is Sierra Hotel 1-1. We have you on visual. We'll be coming in hot. Please advise what you are facing."

"We have some kind of catamaran ferry full of terrorists. We have repelled some boarders but the ferry itself is still on our ass," The thickly accented Norwegian voice answered. "They have deployed speedboats. We managed to knock one away with our LRAD but the others are still circling."

"Roger that, *Atlantica*."

The ship grew from a speck into the glistening white and blue leviathan it was. At three hundred and fifty meters long and nearly fifty wide, it was longer and bulkier than a Nimitz class aircraft carrier. It was studded all over its flanks with solar panels and windows, giving the ship one of the most futuristic appearances Mack had ever seen.

Closing, and then racing down the length of the ship, Grace climbed the Seahawk, catching sight of the low-slung ferry behind.

"What do you see, Hank?"

"Looks like an island hopper to me. I don't think we've danced before," The weapons operator drawled back. "Got a bunch of folks gathered on the top-deck and I have four speedboats. I reckon they're doing some SAR."

"We ain't gonna just buzz 'em. Weapons free and perforate 'em," Mack called.

Mack yawed the helicopter around, presenting the open side door to the ferry. A loud, rumbling drone resonated through the aircraft as Hank fired the GAU-17/A minigun. A hundred rounds of 7.62mm ammunition streaked through the ferry. The people gathered on the top dropped prone as holes appeared all around them.

One of them, braver than the others, went for the machine gun, swinging it around toward the helicopter and returned a stream of fire toward them.

Mack winced as she heard a pinging noise coming from the hull of her bird. She pushed the cyclic forward and drove the collective down, causing the helicopter to dart forward and down out of the torrent of fire.

"Hank, take out that gun."

The drone reverberated through the helicopter again and the man on the *Liliana's* machine gun disintegrated in a cloud of red mist. Under him, beneath the top deck something exploded, ripping a gaping hole in the top.

"She's turning away, ma'am. Want me to keep going?"

Below them the ferry began to angle away from the *Atlantica,* smoke billowing out of the gaping wound left by the explosion.

Mack thought about it for a moment. To kill that damn ferry would likely use up every round she had on-board. And even then not guarantee they'd sink the thing. She was begrudging not taking the time to load up on Hellfire missiles, but the extra weight would have meant more fuel burn. And they didn't have very many of the precious missiles anyway. *Besides, like it or not, there are probably non-combatants on board that ship, and I for one don't want to be responsible for killing them.*

"Negative, Hank. If she gets cocky again and turns back to the *Atlantica,* remind her she's better off anywhere else but here, but we aren't going to burn the ammo."

"Roger that." Hank's voice was disappointed.

The *Liliana* had come about to the opposite heading and began speeding away. The speedboats quickly took on the survivors from the abortive attack and raced after their hurting mothership.

"Well done, boys," Mack said to her crew as she yawed the Seahawk back toward the rapidly retreating *Atlantica.* Pressing the radio stud on her cyclic, she said, "*Atlantica,* U.S. Navy Seahawk. Looks like that ship is retreating. Request permission to land on your flight deck."

"Granted, and maybe you can tell us just what the hell is going on."

Yeah, Atlantica, if you think you're not happy now, just wait until you find out what bizarre Charlie-foxtrot you've found yourself in, Mack thought grimly as she flew back toward the massive liner.

***

Bautista clambered, soaking wet, out of the speedboat onto the platform on the inner side of the catamaran's hull. Climbing rapidly through the crowded ship, ignoring the cries of the children gathered close to their mothers and the moans of the injured, he reached the rear balcony of the ferry. Far in the distance he could see the cruise ship pulling away from them.

"What do you want us to do, Urbano?"

The lean man turned to his second in command who he had left in control of the *Liliana*. "We will return to the *Titan*, Davey. We need to tell them about what has arrived."

"He's gonna be pissed. We lost a lot of people today, not to mention burned a lot of resources."

"Yeah, but a prize like that? She's even worth risking going into the *Ignatius's* territory for." Bautista watched the *Atlantica* shrinking toward the horizon, his eyes narrowing. "She could change everything."

Chapter 12 – Day 3

"Liam, are you fit?"

Kendricks grimaced, cupping the phone awkwardly between his ear and shoulder as Dr. Emodi finished bandaging his arm. "Yeah, Captain. I took a hit, but it's only a flesh wound."

"Good," Solberg said distractedly. "Get up to the flight deck. We've got some visitors. That Navy chopper is putting down."

"Liam, I would rather you rested up. You—" Dr. Emodi started to say.

"Doctor, thank you for your concern, but I'll rest when the current crisis is over," Kendricks said, wincing as he stood from the crate the doctor had sat him on while he worked. He glanced over at Jack who was holding a drip for the medical team as they worked on a horrendously injured security officer. "What about you? You coming?"

Jack nudged one of the medics and handed the bag of saline to them before stepping toward Kendricks, nodding. "Yeah."

"Good." Kendricks gave the carnage-strewn hold a glance. As much as he wanted to stay and help, he couldn't get bogged down in first aid when he had an entire ship to consider. Even if, technically, he was one of the casualties.

Dr. Emodi finished putting Kendricks's left arm in a sling and patted him lightly on the right side. "You're good to go. Just please, no more gunfights, eh?"

With a grunt, Kendricks started walking towards the hatch. "That's for damn sure."

***

"What the hell happened?" Grayson hissed into his CB. He was in a spot not far from where he had murdered Grissom, leaning against a support stanchion for one of the orange lifeboats. "This was supposed to be a cakewalk. This is a cruise ship, not a damn warship. We've got to be well inside *Ignatius* territory. How the hell am I supposed to get back?"

"Karl, calm down. We're heading home but we'll be back soon. I suspect the boss will consider that ship worth taking on the *Ignatius* for."

"Well, let's hope you're not writing checks the boss can't cash," Karl said grimly. "I'm signing off."

"Okay. We'll have a relay boat shadowing *Atlantica*. Keep in contact once per day."

***

The helicopter's rotor blades spun down as Jack, Kendricks, and a pair of uninjured security guards approached the large grey Seahawk which had settled on the circular green landing pad on the bow of the ship.

Coming to a halt, the four men watched the

helmeted, olive flight suit-clad crew through the cockpit window as they flicked switches, shutting down the aircraft. The pilot opened up the cockpit door and stepped out, pulling off her white helmet and laying it on her seat. Kendricks nodded at Jack and the two of them stepped forward, approaching the ebony-skinned woman.

"Lieutenant Grace McNamara of the *USS Paul Ignatius*," the woman said as they approached her.

"Staff Captain Liam Kendricks of the *M/S Atlantica* and this is Jack—" Kendricks paused as he realized he had forgotten the man's last name in the confusion.

"Jack Cohen," Jack filled in for him. "Sergeant, USMC."

"What's your status, Captain? I trust there is no significant damage to the ship itself?" Mack asked, no nonsense in her tone.

"No, no. We've taken casualties, at least seven dead. A few more injured, some seriously."

"And the pirates?"

Pirates? Kendricks thought. *An odd term for terrorists.*

"We got at least ten of them, thanks to Jack here. One more is injured. He isn't going to make it.

The rest took their chances jumping over the side."

"My condolences for your losses," Mack said quietly.

"Lieutenant," Kendricks looked the pilot straight in her brown eyes. "What the hell is going on? We have had no communication for days. Our navigation systems are down, even the compass is ass-backwards and now we're being attacked by terrorist-pirates."

Mack looked down, taking a deep breath. "Staff Captain... I have a lot to tell you. Maybe it would be better if I could do so with your Captain present as well?"

Kendricks and Jack exchanged looks. Jack gave a slight nod.

"Very well. We'll take you in to the ship's conference room."

"Thank you." Mack looked back at the helicopter. "Boys, stay here. I'll be back soon."

"Lieutenant? If you wouldn't mind, ma'am?" Jack pointed at the sidearm Mack had nestled in her shoulder holster.

The pilot raised an eyebrow. "Really?"

"Ship's policy." Kendricks responded for Jack. Frankly, he agreed that right now the less people with weapons onboard, the better.

The pilot gently plucked the weapon out with her thumb and forefinger, making it clear she wasn't drawing it as a threat and proffered it to Jack, butt first. "I want that back."

"Of course," Jack said, taking the weapon and handing it to one of the security officers before gesturing toward the hatch leading inside the *Atlantica.* "After you."

Mack nodded and walked toward the entry.

"Kendricks." Jack took hold of the other man's uninjured arm and leaned in close. "Clearly we're in some kind of military situation. There is a man among the passengers who it may be worth getting briefed at the same time, a recently-retired admiral."

Kendricks nodded. "That might be an idea. Okay, go get him, then bring him up to deck twelve."

***

"Laurie, it's Jack. Open up."

Jack knocked on the door of the suite. Finally, the door opened slightly, revealing Admiral Reynolds's face.

"Jack, are you okay?"

"Yeah, how's Laurie?

"She's fine. She was holed up in here the whole time with me." Reynolds fully opened the door, revealing the spacious lounge area of the suite where Laurie stood, looking at the door anxiously.

"Glad you're okay," Jack said to her.

"I am," Laurie said. "Do you have any idea what's going on?"

"Not completely. Actually, sir, it's you I need."

Jack ignored the hurt look on Laurie's face. "We have a situation where your perspective may prove invaluable."

Reynolds glanced at his daughter, then back at the earnest-looking man in front of him. Nodding, he slipped a light linen jacket off the back of one of the dining room chairs. "Lock the door after I leave. Don't let anyone in until I come back."

***

Solberg pointedly looked at his watch as Jack and Reynolds entered the bridge's conference room. Mack was seated alone on one side of the table, her hands clasped. Solberg and Kendricks the other. The two newcomers joined Solberg's side. To Jack, it felt like he was taking part in a promotion board for the calm and composed pilot.

"Now we're all here, if we can begin?" Solberg said impatiently.

"Of course," Mack said. "I'm Lieutenant Grace McNamara, stationed on the USS *Paul Ignatius*, an *Arleigh Burke* class destroyer, formerly assigned to the Fourth Fleet."

Mack paused as Admiral Reynolds regarded her with his cool blue eyes, the question at the word "formerly" obvious in them.

"Now, as far as we can tell, we are the Fourth Fleet, in its entirety. For the last two years, we have been out of communication with Mayport, U.S. Southern Command, the Pentagon… in fact, anyone outside of our immediate sphere of influence, which you are now in."

"Lieutenant, I retired a few years ago," Reynolds said in a calm measured voice. "Whilst I am not as familiar with U.S. Navy deployments as I once was, I am very sure that a loss of communications with a major surface combatant of any navy in the world would have appeared on CNN. If you would be so kind as to start again, and this time, kindly tell the truth."

"Sir," Mack said. "I wish I could tell you the full story. We simply don't have it, though. What I am telling you is our own experience. Something happened to us, the same thing that has happened to a number of other ships and boats we have encountered throughout this vicinity. And the same thing, I presume, that is happening to you. We have found ourselves in an unknown region with no communication with the rest of the world, no satellite uplinks, nothing. Gentlemen, we aren't in Kansas anymore, and that's about all I can tell you about where we are."

"Quite, but that does not account for the two years a United States destroyer has been out of the loop." Reynolds said pointedly.

"And that is where things get strange, sir. Or at least stranger." Mack's brow furrowed and she leaned forward. "Whenever we encounter a new ship or boat, they always list the last confirmed date they were in contact with anyone else as July 12, 2024. Whether that be land or navigation uplink. For us, the *Ignatius* I mean, we are at 752 days post-event, however our last communication with anyone else was July 12, 2024 —"

"Which was three days ago," Solberg cut in irritably. "Listen. I don't know what shit you are giving us here, but frankly I don't believe it."

"Captain, I appreciate this may well be a lot to take in." Mack looked levelly at the man. "But I am not messing around. Every ship we have encountered has believed that the last external navigation data or contact they had with anyone, whether that be via GPS link or radio communication, was that day."

"Assuming what you are saying is correct, and please don't think I'm convinced by any stretch of the imagination," Reynolds said, "then that implies that somehow, you have found yourself isolated here. And other ships have appeared at different periods over the last two years, but all thinking it's the same day?

"That's about it, Admiral." Mack nodded. "However, we weren't the first. We have encountered several vessels that have been here for longer than us, including those we have just had a run in with."

"Yes, about them," Kendricks said, rubbing the arm that was lodged in the sling. "Who the hell were they, and why did they attack us?"

"They are a faction—a loose alliance I suppose—who found themselves here before we did. They now prey upon ships which come through, taking what they need."

"So they really are pirates then. Well, unless they have a bloody warship, Lieutenant, can I ask why you haven't simply blown them away?" Admiral Reynolds asked pointedly.

"Because the *Ignatius* has hardly any fuel left," Mack said. "And how do we find them? The battle scape is awfully limited when you're down to one destroyer, a single functioning helicopter, a pair of RIBs, and a few allied non-combatant boats."

"Point taken," Reynolds said as he leaned back.

"So, the big question is... where the hell is America, and for that matter anyone else?" Kendricks asked the obvious question.

"We don't know. We have explored back to where the coast should be. The most we've found is a little island, which is where we have set up base."

"Set up base?" Reynolds asked.

"Yes, sir. It's hardly big, but it has helped to support us while we're... trapped here."

"Captain, going there sounds like an option until we figure out what's going on," Kendricks said.

"Well, is it?" Solberg asked of Mack.

"Is what, Captain?"

"Is it an option?"

"Yes, Captain Slater extends her compliments,"

Mack said. "She would welcome you under the *Ignatius's* protection if you so wish."

"And if we don't wish?" Solberg replied.

"You can take your chances with the pirates." The pilot gave a shrug.

"Very well, you have given us much to think about. If you would excuse us," Solberg said, gesturing through the glass partition to one of the security officers waiting outside. "I think we need to discuss this."

"Take your time. When you come to the right decision, I'll provide you a heading."

***

"What utter bullshit," Solberg spat once the pilot had left. "She's expecting us to believe that the whole world has disappeared?"

"Some things are starting to make sense, Lars," Kendricks said quietly. "We have no contact with anyone, GPS is down, and Nassau has disappeared... and as for being attacked by pirates this close to American waters? It answers that as well."

"Don't you start." Solberg waved his hand dismissively. "We could have just missed Nassau."

"Captain, as Sir Arthur Conan Doyle said, once you have eliminated the impossible, whatever is left, no matter how improbable, must be the truth," Reynolds said.

"Admiral Reynolds. The whole damn world disappearing is impossible," Solberg pointed out. "I'd rather believe that these pirates have somehow taken out the whole of the U.S. fleet."

"Fair point. But at the moment, the evidence

suggests that the impossible is what has happened. Jack, what are your thoughts?"

Jack lightly drummed his fingers on the glass table, considering the conversation of the last few minutes. After a moment he spoke, "My first thought about the pirates was that they were some kind of terrorist cell, or drug runners. However, it has been bugging me that they were completely multinational—men and women of several ethnic backgrounds. Although it's not unheard of, neither terrorists nor runners are exactly renowned for their equal opportunity employment policies. It does support Lieutenant McNamara's story."

"Quite," Reynolds said. "How about this for a plan? Let's resume a course aiming for America. If and when we confirm that the land is gone, we return to the *Ignatius*."

"This is my ship. I make the decisions here," Solberg said in a low voice.

"Of course," Reynolds held his hands open in supplication. "I am merely here in an advisory capacity. But I would strongly recommend that course of action. If, and by that I hopefully mean when, we make contact with America, I'm sure the U.S. Admiralty will be very interested in what's going on at their door step. Not the least of which appears to be some very sophisticated jamming capability. If we don't, and the good lieutenant is telling the truth then I, for one, would rather take my chances with the *Ignatius* than pirates who have clearly shown their hostile intentions."

Solberg glanced around the table at the others. Kendricks gave a nod, Jack merely gazed back at him with calm in his eyes.

"Very well. I have decided," Solberg emphasized the I. "We will resume course toward Florida. If this bullshit turns out to be true, we will go find this Captain Slater."

Reynolds gave a nod. "Good decision."

"Captain," Kendricks shifted uncomfortably, both from his wound and what he had to bring up. "We have seventeen fatalities. Dr. Emodi tells me that's going to go up to eighteen in a matter of hours when one of the captured pirates… succumbs to his wounds."

"Jesus," Solberg said with a shake of his head.

"We have a problem. We only have ten morgue storage spaces."

"Okay," Solberg looked thoughtful for a moment. Cruises were renowned for attracting an older clientele and as such they were prepared to deal with bodies, but they still only had a limited number of spaces. "As much as I'd like to simply dump the pirates overboard, I'm guessing at some point, assuming McNamara's story is a load of crap, that Homeland Security or whoever are going to want those bodies as part of their investigation."

"I'd assume so, too," Kendricks agreed.

"Very well. Our own crew and passengers are to get the morgue spaces. I want their bodies treated with dignity. As for the pirates, run it by Dr. Emodi but I'd guess one of the food storage freezers would do the job?"

"I'll ask the question," Kendricks said.

"Just make sure the food comes out first." Solberg stood to signify the meeting was coming to a close.

"Aye aye, captain," Kendricks said, a look of distaste crossing his face.

Chapter 13 – Day 3

"What's the word, ma'am?" Hank asked. He had been guarding the Seahawk with the copilot, his HK MP7 personal defense weapon discreetly close at hand. He wasn't going to take any chances with their only operational helicopter and, if need be, the two crew would have stormed *Atlantica* themselves if Mack had been in trouble.

"The word is, they don't believe me. They're going to make for where they think the States are." Mack said approaching the Seahawk. She squinted at the bullet holes which stitched along the grey flank and winced.

"I'm not entirely sure I'd believe you either," Hank said pragmatically. "You want us to lift?"

"No," Mack scratched her fingernail over one of the holes and frowned. "I don't want to burn the fuel. They'll figure out soon enough I'm telling the truth and, if they know what's good for 'em, head straight back to the Iggy. We'll just hitch a ride."

*****

"Resume course, original heading, full speed,"

Solberg said as he lowered himself into his seat on the bridge.

"Sir, just on the off chance that pilot is telling the truth, maybe we should consider a more fuel-efficient pace?" Kendricks said.

"I don't think, Liam, that I am quite willing to accept the whole world has disappeared just yet," Solberg replied. "Full speed."

"Full speed, aye," Kendricks said, catching the frown on John Reynolds's face.

"I better address the passengers. Quiet on the bridge, please." Solberg composed himself, tugging his shirt straight before tapping his console. A red light appeared next to the webcam lens and he selected the mode which would show him on every screen throughout the ship.

"Passengers and crew, as you are aware, assailants attempted to board the *Atlantica* using lethal force." Solberg stared straight into the lens of the webcam, which was built into his console. "Our security teams successfully fended them off, but not without casualties. We now have a United States Navy helicopter to escort us, which is more than capable of protecting this ship from any further attacks. We will be making our way back to Fort Lauderdale at our best possible speed. Captain Solberg, out."

***

"This is everything they left behind." Josef gestured at the array of weapons laid out on the table in the security room. Three AK-47s, a couple of M16A4s, a shotgun that Jack didn't recognize, and a few handguns. Mingled in were a few handheld walkie-talkies and spare ammunition. "As you can see, it's quite the collection."

"Yeah." Jack picked one of the M16s. It was the latest generation of the venerable weapon system. Mounted on top of the weapon was an ACOG sight. "How are the survivors, Josef?"

"The ship's doctor says the critically injured terrorist, or pirate, whatever the hell he is, is just waiting to die," the officer said with a shrug.

"And ours?"

"Whoever's not going to make it," Josef said quietly, "has already gone."

With a nod, Jack placed the rifle gently back down again. "We're making back to the States at full speed. Hopefully, we'll make landfall in a few hours."

Josef raised an eyebrow. "Hopefully?"

"Yeah," Jack said as he walked out of the room. "Hopefully."

***

"Are you okay?" Jack asked.

"Yes, I'm fine," Laurie said, the concern evident in her face. "More importantly, are you? Daddy told me you helped defend the ship."

"I'm okay. May I?" Jack gestured at the settee.

"Sorry, of course," Laurie said, moving across on it to give him space.

With a weary sigh, Jack lowered himself down next to her. He rubbed just below his knee, where the prosthetic met flesh. "Where's your father?"

"I think he's gone up to the bridge. Jack, what's going on? The Wi-Fi and phones have been out for days, we've been answering distress calls left and right, and now the ship has been attacked by bloody terrorist-pirates! I may be understating matters a touch here… but something is not right."

"Too right it's not." Jack stopped playing with his sore leg and leaned back, resting his head on the back of the couch, closing his eyes.

"The sooner we get off this ship the better."

Jack responded with a gentle snore.

Chapter 14 – Day 3

"Even in the worst-case scenario, we should be twenty miles inland by now," Kendricks said quietly. There was nothing through the bridge window but ocean and a slowly lowering sun, turning red as it dipped closer to the horizon. The watery desolation before them was matched by the drained exhaustion Kendricks felt.

"Shit!" Solberg shouted. The other bridge crew glanced around, startled, before quickly turning back to their workstations.

"Captain," Reynolds said mildly but firmly, in a low voice only Solberg and Kendricks could hear. "For the benefit of your crew, please compose yourself."

"You are here by invitation, Mister Reynolds," Solberg emphasized the lack of rank. "Don't presume to tell me what to do on my bridge."

"Sir," Kendricks interjected in an attempt to head off an argument. "Request permission to bring the ship to steerageway. Every drop of fuel we use on this heading is another we have to use if we decide to come about."

"Yes, yes. Bring us to steerageway," Solberg said

in a resigned tone, the anger leaving him.

The ship began to slow, lowering from its top speed to the minimum it needed to maneuver.

Solberg looked around the bridge, noticing an empty workstation. "Where the hell is Grissom?"

"I haven't seen him since last night." Kendricks frowned. The whirlwind events of the last day had caused him to forget completely about the young officer. It was nearly twenty-four hours since he'd sent the man to figure out where they were. "I assume he was unsuccessful getting a position fix, forgot to check in and went back to his quarters since his watch was over. Kelly, I don't suppose you've seen Walt?"

"No, sir," Maine replied, shaking her head.

Kendricks thumbed through the contact list on his phone. Finding Grissom's number, he called it. It went straight to voicemail. "Mister Grissom, Staff Captain Kendricks here. Please report in as soon as you get this message."

"Get someone down to his cabin," Solberg said as he lowered himself into his seat. "Now's not the time to have the crew slacking off."

"Aye aye, Captain."

"And get me that pilot up here."

***

"By our best estimates, we should be sailing through the Everglades right now." Solberg pointed at the touchscreen tabletop map of Florida which was focused on Miami. "Clearly, we are not."

"I did say, Captain," Mack said from where she stood by Solberg's seat. "America is gone."

"How the hell am I supposed to explain this to the passengers?" Solberg's voice was strained, the tension showing in the tendons of his neck, choking his voice.

"That's a little above my pay grade, Captain," Mack replied.

Kendricks winced, expecting a fiery comeback from the Captain. None came. Instead, Solberg went back to pinching the bridge of his nose beneath his glasses. A posture he had adopted more and more often over the past few days.

"Captain, we have encountered ships and boats before that have pushed on. They refused to stay, wanting to continue sailing to the pre-event west. Out of those that turned back, and our own reconnaissance efforts, we've seen nothing but sea and the occasional tiny island. The others? Well, they simply never returned," Mack said quietly yet earnestly. "*Atlantica* is a vast pool of resources. If you return with me to the *Ignatius*. Perhaps we can join forces and find out what's going on. Or at least survive."

"Captain," Reynolds said gently. "I think we should take the lieutenant up on her offer."

"Sir, I agree. At the least until we can form a better plan," Kendricks concurred.

Solberg tapped on the tabletop, bringing up a graphical representation of the fuel tanks. The cylinders showed their fuel supplies were three quarters full.

"We have, at max economy cruise, nearly four thousand nautical miles worth of fuel, give or take. We can push on for another couple of thousand if necessary before we need to turn around."

"Why? If we have to turn around, then we'll be down to our last drops when we return. That would reduce our options substantially," Reynolds said levelly. "If we head to the *Ignatius* now, there is nothing to preclude us taking that option later, but for now, I strongly recommend that we meet with this Captain Slater and see what intelligence about this region she can offer."

"Lieutenant," Solberg sighed. "Please provide my helm with the best heading back toward the *Ignatius*. The rest of you, we need to figure out just what, and when to tell the passengers."

"We'll have to tell them something soon," Kendricks said. "They know we've been going back and forth for days."

"I know, Liam."

"Perhaps as a first option, we can tell them that due to the attack, we are going to rendezvous with the *Ignatius*. It wouldn't seem preposterous for us to join with a naval vessel after such an incident," Reynolds suggested.

"And if she's telling the truth?" Solberg pointed at Mack. "Then they will be even angrier we have kept them in the dark."

"And if this somehow turns out to be a load of bollocks?" Reynolds retorted. "Then we would be unnecessarily worrying them."

"Fair point." Solberg nodded before saying decisively, now that the choice had been made, "Let's just get to this destroyer."

Chapter 15 – Day 4

The island was small, little more than a drop of green and yellow in the vast turquoise ocean. A central, vegetation-clad peak lanced high into the air surrounded by more gentle, tapered hills. Visible from the *Atlantica's* bridge, the gently sloped areas had what looked to be cultivated fields. All told though, it wouldn't have accounted for more than a few square miles.

The squat grey *USS Paul Ignatius* nestled in the natural bay formed by the contours of the island. Her one hundred and fifty-five meter length had, concentrated within, a devastating array of hardware. There were no frills to her lines; every inch of her was designed to be a warship. Her boxy form was built from the keel up to be able to fight, and win against any almost any threat on, or in fact off, the planet.

On the front was a small cannon, the only clearly visible weapon. Her true weaponry was hidden in her hull. Ninety-six cells contained a variety of different missiles, each capable of dealing death and destruction on land, sea, air, and even in space.

"I still think one of our Type 45s could take her,"

Admiral Reynolds murmured as he regarded the ship through a pair of borrowed binoculars, noting the hull numbers DDG-117 painted on the bow of the warship.

"What was that?" Solberg asked, glancing over at the older man.

"Nothing, Captain." Reynolds lowered the binoculars. "At least we know your story bears out, Lieutenant. This part at least."

Mack nodded. "Don't get me wrong, sir. I appreciate that so far this is a pretty tall tale. But you tell me any way a con artist could get hold of an *Arleigh Burke* class destroyer?"

"If you're quite done," Solberg said. "Lieutenant, please provide Ms. Maine with your frequency, it's time to pay my compliments to Captain Slater."

"They'll be monitoring sixteen."

Maine, listening to the exchange nodded at Solberg. "You have the com."

"*USS Paul Ignatius,* this is Captain Solberg of the *M/S Atlantica.*"

"*M/S Atlantica, Ignatius* Actual," a firm female voice answered. "I was wondering when you would say hello. Welcome to Nest Island."

"Nest Island?" Solberg mouthed at Mack, who smiled and shrugged.

"The old American eagle had to nest somewhere."

"Thank you, *Ignatius.*" Solberg returned his attention to his console. "As you can imagine, we have a lot of questions."

"As I would expect and I will endeavor to answer as many of them as I can for you. Perhaps I could come aboard?"

Solberg looked at Reynolds, then Jack, who was

standing next to the older man. Jack gave a slight shake of his head.

"*Ignatius*, with the greatest of respect. My vessel has found itself in a rather confusing and extraordinary situation. We are, by anyone's definition, completely lost and we have been attacked by pirates. I, for one, would rather our first meeting be in a neutral place."

"That sounds very sensible, Captain," The voice on the radio replied.

"Excellent. We will send you details shortly. *Atlantica*, out.

"You do realize," Reynolds said with a slight smile. "If she had wanted to, the *Ignatius* could have smashed us to smithereens an hour ago."

***

"Wouldn't it be more appropriate if I go?" Kendricks asked as Solberg climbed up into one of seventeen-meter-long CRW55 mega lifeboats. *Atlantica* had twenty of the boats nestled into the ship's flanks, each one capable of packing in three hundred and seventy people.

"Liam, you have a giant hole in your shoulder. As appropriate as it may be, I think I'll let you recover before I put you in harm's way again."

Solberg ducked inside the hatch, followed by Jack, Reynolds, Mack, and a pair of crew who would be piloting the large craft. Deciding who would be included in the party hadn't required too much thought. Reynolds would be on hand for any naval advice while Jack would provide an element of muscle. They were all dressed in blue windbreakers, proudly emblazoned with *Atlantica's* name.

The lifeboat, designed to carry so many, seemed empty with just six on board. Settling into the gaudy orange plastic seats, Solberg plucked his phone out of his jacket and switched it to radio mode. "Lower us."

With a lurch, the lifeboat descended towards the water far below, the winch system allowing the lifeboat to be lowered directly into the water rather than having to be swung out. Gently, the boat settled into the sea. The clamps on the davit released, freeing the lifeboat from the *Atlantica.*

With a chugging noise, the motor started and the catamaran-hulled lifeboat began to power toward the island.

Before long, they saw a speedboat powering through the whitecaps toward them rapidly. The Rigid Inflatable Boat swept around them and the two Navy personnel onboard regarding them wearily, but with no weapons on show. They were clearly assessing whether the lifeboat constituted any kind of threat to them. Satisfied, the RIB slid to a halt next to the much-larger craft.

"Captain Solberg?" The same voice that had been on the radio shouted over the wash of the sea. "Permission to come aboard?"

"Granted."

A dark-haired woman in her early forties appeared in the hatchway, dressed in blue and grey camouflage trousers and jacket with a bulky life preserver over the top. On the left side of her collar was the silver leaf of a commander and on the other collar, the six-armed golden star insignia of a commander-at-sea.

Solberg stood in the confines of the lifeboat, walked to the hatch and extended his hand. The woman took it and pumped it in a firm grip. Turning the handshake into an offer of assistance, Solberg guided her down the three steps to the deck of the lifeboat.

"I'm Commander Heather Slater, Captain of the *USS Paul Ignatius*."

"Commander, I'm Lars Solberg, Captain of the *Atlantica*. This is Admiral John Reynolds, Retired, of the Royal Navy, formerly one of the passengers on my ship who is now acting in a consultative capacity, and this is Jack Cohen, who is my…" Solberg glanced at the quiet man. "Acting head of security."

"Pleased to meet you all," Slater said, shaking the other two men's hands before gesturing at another serious-looking man standing just outside the hatch. "And this is Petty Officer Miller. He's here to keep me out of trouble. May I?" Slater gestured at one of the uncomfortable-looking plastic seats.

"Of course." Solberg took the seat opposite her.

"I imagine you have a lot of questions. Unfortunately, so do we. It's just we've had somewhat longer to come to terms with our situation," Slater spoke in a calm, measured voice.

"I suspect, Commander, the best place to start would be at the beginning." Reynolds leaned forward.

"Absolutely. On July 12, 2024 we were ten days into an anti-drug deployment, patrolling the Caribbean. It was a singularly uneventful operation up until that point. As of that evening however, we lost all contact with our home base, Mayport, and any kind of support systems or services."

"Humor me. What form did that take?" Solberg asked.

"We lost all sat coms, radio, even our compass was ass-backwards. I presume those symptoms are what you are facing?"

"Something like that." Solberg nodded. "Please continue."

"We spent the next five days trying to resume communications and attempting to find some kind of recognizable landmass — to no avail. What we did find were several boats that were in a similar predicament to us. The big difference was that although they all reported last being in contact with the shore on the same date — those that still had living crews that is — some of them had been lost for a substantial amount of time, some a lot longer than we had. And some of those, Captain, were distinctly hostile. They have effectively set themselves up as pirates, preying on ships as they arrive."

"You say arrive?" Reynolds cocked his head to one side. "An interesting word to use."

"There's no other word to use." Slater turned her piercing blue eyes on Reynolds. "Clearly, we are not where we should be. That implies we have somehow moved. This region, wherever it is, is where the ships and boats are arriving."

"Commander Slater," Solberg said. "I have been sailing in the Caribbean for the best part of two decades, and a decade before that in other places around the world. I'm not adverse to the odd ghostly sea dog story. But if you mention that we've slipped through the Bermuda Triangle, I am not going to be a happy man."

Slater gave a snort. "Captain, I can assure you I'm

not inclined to give credence to those stories, either. The problem, however, is the incontrovertible evidence that we have moved. We are not where we are supposed to be. We have played with every theory we can, and still come out with nothing conclusive."

"I don't think I'm breaching the Official Secrets Act here," Reynolds said. "But even the British military, which doesn't even have a hundredth of the infrastructure of the U.S., would still not lose track of a warship short of its complete and quick destruction. That is something which has clearly not happened to the *USS Paul Ignatius*. Even setting aside the fact that we have lost track of home, how can home have lost track of us?"

"That's the million-dollar question, Admiral," Slater said wearily. "With nearly three hundred warships, several thousand aircraft, and hundreds more ancillary vessels, not to mention what resources the rest of NATO and our other allies would undoubtedly bring to bear, we should have been found by now if we'd simply been lost."

"And, assuming the time issue you mentioned is correct, then something slightly stranger than navigational difficulties is occurring here. What are your theories, Commander?"

"You mean theories that don't involve the Bermuda Triangle, alien abduction, or us all being dead and in mariners' heaven?" Slater's mouth gave the slightest twitch of a grin. "None that hold water."

"You've been here for two years and you have no ideas at all?" Solberg asked incredulously.

"As I say, no. Our operations in this region have been seriously limited by fuel and supplies."

"Speaking of which. I find it a little hard to believe you have kept a functioning warship going for that length of time without provisions," Reynolds said.

"Yes, about that. We were ten days into our patrol when we arrived here. My ship, at a push, can manage an endurance of forty days, tops. We are now nearly two years beyond that." Slater glanced at her petty officer as Reynolds calmly regarded her. The old admiral had an inkling of what was coming. "As we say, there have, periodically been other ships and boats arriving. We are, of course, offering our protection, but that protection comes with a price. A tax, if you will."

"A tax?" Solberg said in a low, dangerous voice.

"My pilot here has used a significant amount of fuel and ammunition to protect the *Atlantica*. Those are resources we can't replace."

"What are you asking, Commander?" Solberg's voice was like ice.

"Simple. Running a ship like *Ignatius* takes supplies. If you want our protection from the pirates, it has to be paid for."

"You're the Navy," Solberg's voice raised in volume. "You have an obligation to render aid."

"Captain Solberg," Slater said in a calm tone, her voice enunciating every syllable. "The Navy is a vast bureaucratic organization which exists in order to transform the resources of a nation into an ocean-going fleet. Those resources, we are no longer in receipt of. My ship can offer you protection, something you sorely need in this region. In return, we need supplies—fuel and food. If you don't want protection, then I can't afford to keep you."

Solberg's face was a furious red. Reynolds held up

a placating hand. "Commander, I'm sure you appreciate that we've had a lot to digest over the last few days. If we may, we should retire to the *Atlantica* and discuss what we have learned so far, and your offer, of course."

"Take your time," Slater nodded as she stood. "Unfortunately, there are no free rides anymore, though. I cannot afford one more bullet in defense of you. I have an obligation to those that I have already taken under my protection, after all."

Chapter 16 – Day 4

"What's your opinion of them, Jack?" Reynolds asked.

They were in the conference room, along with the rest of the *Atlantica's* senior crew, having left Commander Slater to return to her ship. Solberg had filled the others in on the results of the meeting.

"Their uniforms are standard Navy working rig, so that's legit, and the RIB they came in on looked a spitting image of what's in the Navy inventory."

"Quite," Reynolds agreed. "Pity we don't have the internet. We could probably google that captain's name."

"The ship caches websites that people have looked at," Kendricks said. "We might still be able to search for her. If anyone's looked at a website containing her, it'll still be in there."

Leaning over the conference table, Kendricks activated it, turning it into a giant touchscreen display. He canceled away from an alert that showed the internet link was offline. A touchscreen keyboard appeared and he typed in "Commander Heather Slater".

After a moment, an article appeared showing an image of Commander Slater along with an interview in the *Navy Times* entitled, "Women in command".

They scanned through the piece, a short article which seemed written to provide inspiration for young female officers seeking their own captaincy.

"So she is the real deal," Solberg said, sounding disappointed.

"It certainly adds credence to her story." Reynolds nodded.

"Still, my opinion is that woman is no better than those pirates," Solberg was still angry from the meeting. "Demanding fuel and supplies which, if she is telling the truth, we will sorely need."

"However she does have a point," Reynolds said in a placating manner. "She has a ship to run, one which can offer us protection from a faction that has already proven themselves to be highly hostile. I would say throwing a little fuel and food her way wouldn't be the end of the world."

"She's lucky we don't keep her helicopter just for making the demand," Solberg hissed. After a moment he calmed down. "Very well, we have a bowser of aviation fuel. The helicopter can top off from that. Liam, I want a full audit of our fuel and provisions before we even start considering giving anything else away, though."

"Aye aye, sir."

"Which brings me to another point. Carrie," he addressed the normally bombastic Passenger Services Director, who thus far had been silent in the meeting. "We have to consider that we need to break our situation to the passengers."

"Captain," Carrie Matthews' voice was strained. "I'm having trouble processing all this myself. The passengers, and not to mention the crew, will likely have an even harder time."

"I appreciate that, however this is the situation we appear to have found ourselves in. They need to be told their holiday is off."

"In that case," Matthews said. "I think it would be best coming from a personal address, Captain. We could rig out the promenade in street-party mode and you can make the announcement."

"I think it'll be better through the ship's PA system," Solberg frowned. "They will lynch me if I tell them in person."

"Not if we put you up on the span," Matthews replied, referring to the walkway that stretched over the promenade. Her voice was becoming less strained as she focused on the task at hand. Her position was roughly equal in rank to Kendricks's, but she was there to run all of the non-technical needs of the ship—everything from the hotel service to the many bars and restaurants.

"You may need to consider rationing as well," Reynolds said. "I mean, I'm sure the ship's larders are relatively full right now, but if we have to stay here for more than a few weeks…"

"We are provisioned for around two weeks at normal consumption usage," Carrie said, her mind clearly already whirling. "If we get really tight on that usage, we can probably double that out to a month."

"Start putting that in place," Solberg said. "Get it ready to go after I make the announcement."

"Yes, Captain."

"Water shouldn't be an issue; the distillation plants can keep us drinking and showering until doomsday. Neither is auxiliary power with our solar cells," Kendricks said. "But there are items we cannot replenish. Worn parts for one thing. Our 3D printers can help with some things, but the real complex stuff..."

"Liam, I do not intend to be here one day longer than we have to be. I am still hoping this turns out to be some god-awful joke."

"You and me both, sir."

"But Carrie," Solberg said. "A thought occurs. Let's stop using the paper napkins. Just in case."

Her nose wrinkled in disgust at the prospect of what he was suggesting.

***

The battle-scarred *Liliana* swept toward the rocky island, her wake spreading out on either side of her in a white frothing "V" shape. The watch boats gave a brief radio challenge before letting her pass unhindered. As she circled around the cliffs, the setting sun began to give the world a red tinge.

Slowly, it emerged into view. A vast container ship, beached and broken against the rocky flank of the island. Spilled out next to the ship were dozens of multi-colored shipping containers. Remaining on board were nearly nineteen thousand more, piled high on the angled deck.

Urbano Bautista was always impressed on seeing his adopted home. Some of the containers had been re-purposed and were now homes for families, giving the surface layers of the container ship the appearance of a barrio from his youth. Other containers still served their original purpose and contained a wealth of goods.

Even now, years after making the find, they had

only scratched the surface of the massive ship. Crews were actually mining the vessel, chipping their way deeper and deeper into her bowels, never knowing whether they would find something useful or simply a shipping container holding nothing but junk. As the years had gone by, they had discovered everything from hauls of factory equipment to entire arsenals of weapons and ammunition.

They had been quite a find. It seemed someone who had owned the vessel originally, before its arrival that was, had a little sideline in smuggling and gun running. They had found enough hardware to equip a small army.

Right now, the container ship wasn't the *Liliana's* destination. As she surged past the hulk, another equally large ship revealed itself, nestled behind the island. The true center of their fledgling community — the mammoth super-tanker, *Titan*.

***

"Urbano, I trust that the damage to your ship is not as bad as it appears." The man looked at Bautista, not with disapproval, but a sense of resignation that the former drug runner had finally bitten off more than he could chew.

Bautista sat himself down on the threadbare, uncomfortable seat in front of Eric Vaughan. They were in his cramped office aboard the *Titan*. The interior was all exposed sweating metal and pipes; not even the dubious modern conveniences of the *Liliana* were present on this ship.

"Eric, before you say anything. We found something... something good."

Leaning back, Vaughan looked at Bautista for a long moment. That he was a dangerous man was beyond debate. But what was also beyond debate was that he was highly intelligent. It was a sad reflection of his upbringing, Vaughan thought. Bautista could have been become a scientist, an artist, a politician, or a military leader. Instead, he had been born into a drug cartel and his destiny was chosen for him. Still, the fact that he had chosen an alliance with, and eventual command by Vaughan rather than merely dumping him overboard, suggested his innate cunning had won through. Bautista needed Vaughan to run the administration of the community, Vaughan needed Bautista to hunt and keep the other, rougher members in check.

"So enlighten me."

"A cruise ship, a huge one, is here."

"Go on," Vaughan leaned forward, the scarring to the *Liliana* put aside, for the moment, with this news.

"Karl was manning one of the watch boats in the zone. He got picked up by the ship, the *Atlantica*."

"The *Atlantica*," Vaughan cocked his head, remembering the name from years before. "The Crystal Ocean Lines ship? The new one?"

"That sounds about right. She's huge, and stocked full of food, fuel, and supplies. She's got to be the most significant arrival in the zone for years."

"And you tried to take her?" Vaughan asked.

"Yeah, she was cruising toward *Ignatius's* territory. I figured that it was worth the chance to try and get her before she got too near."

"And I take it you were unsuccessful." It wasn't a question.

"We managed to get on board, but their security

was good. They fought us off. I lost twelve people. ten on the ship and two went over the side."

"Jesus, Urbano!" Vaughan exclaimed. "Twelve?"

"It gets worse. The *Ignatius* probably had her own watch boats out and they saw the same thing we did. A floating pleasure palace, stocked to the gills. They wanted her bad enough to send up one of their helicopters. I lost six more to that fucking thing. At that point I backed off."

"Okay, you made your play and lost. Shit happens. You get all the bodies back?"

"No." A flash of pain crossed Bautista's face. "Some we had to leave on board the *Atlantica*."

Vaughan nodded. "We'll have to tell their families."

"Eric," Bautista leaned forward. "That ship can set us up for months… years, even."

"Yes, I agree. But chances are right now she's deep in *Ignatius's* territory."

"The only thing that's stopped the *Ignatius* from wiping us all out is that she didn't have the fuel to come after us," Bautista said pointedly. "She now has a cruise ship full of it."

"Slater won't waste her time, or missiles to do that," Vaughan said, but not with the assured tone he was hoping for.

"Maybe, but all of a sudden she's a threat to us here. Look, Eric, there are two parts to this. One is we need the supplies on that ship. I'm sick of eating fish. And two, we need to end that fucking woman's grip on her territory before she comes after us."

"Urbano, even if we could take on the *Ignatius*, we'd lose so many people doing it that any gains would be completely offset."

"Not necessarily," Urbano gave a grim smile for the first time since coming into the cabin.

"You have a plan?"

"No, but I have a man on the inside, Eric. And that's the start of a plan."

Chapter 17 – Day 4

"We've got to tell her," Jack said to Reynolds as they walked along the corridor. "If she finds out when everyone else does, she'll be pissed."

"I know my daughter," Reynolds said. His voice was as calm as ever, but the faint undertone of irritability was present just below the surface. "I've spent my whole life protecting her from the truth of how terrible this world can be."

"Yes, sir. But you can't protect her from this… she's going to find out anyway." Jack took hold of the former admiral's arm. The two men stopped and Reynolds looked pointedly at Jack's hand. Remembering himself, Jack let go and pulled his hand back.

"Sergeant Cohen," Reynolds said sternly. "I may no longer be in the Royal Navy, but you will afford me the courtesy of a lifetime's service in a NATO country, if you please."

"Apologies, sir," Jack replied, long years in the military making him draw automatically to attention at the rebuke.

"You know," Reynolds sighed, his features softening. "When my wife, Laurie's mother, died, I told my daughter that it was quick and painless. I told her that her last words were how much she loved her daughter. Do you know the reality?"

"No, sir."

"She was in a car crash and horribly injured," Reynolds said in a matter-of-fact way. "The police had called me and my driver had got me to the hospital at the same time the ambulance brought Helena in screaming. She died in the A&E in agony. They didn't even have chance to get morphine into her."

"Jesus," Jack said. "I'm so sorry."

"Laurie will never know that and if you tell her, I will kill you with my bare hands, I don't care how good you are." Reynolds looked at Jack pointedly.

"Sir, I swear, I'll never say."

"But…" Reynolds exhaled, coming to a decision. "You have a point. Whatever shitty mess we're in, we're already up to our knees in it."

"That we are," Jack replied. Then his face twitched in a small, rare smile. "Even's even. Do you want to know my secret?"

"Go on."

"I can remove one of my legs and clean all the shit off," Jack replied as he bent down and slid his trouser leg up, revealing the prosthetic beneath.

Jack stood upright again, the two men looked at each other for a long somber moment. Simultaneously, they both cracked grins before erupting into guffawing laughter.

"What a bloody pair we are, to find ourselves lost in some bizarre *Twilight Zone* nightmare," Reynolds said, finally able to speak. "Come on, tell me the story while we go up to my rooms and let high command know we're in trouble."

***

"So that Captain Solberg arsehole has got us lost?" Laurie said, an incredulous look on her face.

The three of them were seated in the lounge of the Reynolds's suite. The older man next to her, holding her hand earnestly, while Jack sat across from them on the opposite sofa.

"You know I don't like you using that kind of language," John Reynolds admonished half-heartedly.

"Daddy, we're on a ship, completely lost. We've come under pirate attack and you're worried about a thirty-year-old woman's language?"

"Your point is taken." Reynolds leaned back.

"So what now?" Laurie said, looking between the admiral and Jack.

"We're going to throw our lot in with the Navy ship. They can protect us from any more attacks until we figure out how to get out of this mess," Jack said.

"And you say they've been here for two years?" Laurie said. "How the hell can that be?"

"There's a lot we don't know," the older man replied. "You're the science teacher. Maybe you could help figure that out."

"Don't patronize me," Laurie said, standing and walking to the window. She gazed at the sun setting next to the island. "A sixth form teacher isn't going to be able to figure this out."

"Maybe, maybe not. But we don't know how long we're going to be here and you'll have to keep yourself occupied somehow," Jack cut in.

"And how are you going to keep yourself occupied?" She turned to look at Jack.

"Apparently, I'm the new head of security. According to Captain Solberg, anyway."

On cue, the LED television switched itself on and Solberg's face appeared on it.

"To all passengers. I will be making an announcement in an hour. I request you all to congregate on the ship's promenade," Solberg stated solemnly, looked straight out of the screen. "Captain Solberg, out."

"Well, looks like he's decided he's going to tell everyone." Reynolds stood up and straightened the shirt and tie he was wearing. "I suggest we go get some good seats for this and see how that... that arsehole breaks the news."

"Yeah," Jack said. "And I better go assume my new role and make sure no one decides to throw him overboard."

***

The cavernous promenade, running nearly the full length of the ship, was filled to capacity. Over four thousand people clustered into the two hundred and fifty-meter-long space, having been summoned there for the important announcement from the captain. The sounds of conversation and revelry washed over the crowd, despite the recent attack.

Solberg stood out of view at one end of the walkway spanning the promenade and clenched his fists, trying to abate his nerves. He was used to speaking publicly, but never in front of this many people, and never with this kind of news.

Slipping off his glasses, he folded them carefully and slipped them into his pocket. Taking a deep breath, he nodded at Matthews, who handed him a wireless microphone.

Walking forward, Solberg reached the center of the span. The bridge was located halfway along the promenade, and he slowly did a full turn, taking in the masses of people. Slowly they began to notice him and quiet began to fall.

"Ladies and gentlemen, I have called this gathering for extraordinary reasons. As you are all aware, the last few days have been eventful for this ship," Solberg understated matters. "We have recently learned that events are even stranger than we originally thought."

Solberg looked at the passengers. The quiet had turned to complete silence, with every person hanging on to his words. Carrie Matthews' written notes were forgotten in his pocket. How could anyone explain that the whole world had simply disappeared?

"Following the terrorist attack, we set course to return to Fort Lauderdale. On arrival to where it should have been, there was nothing. No sign of the Florida coast, and so we continued sailing due west..." Solberg faltered. Rallying himself, he began speaking again. "There was still no sign. Ladies and gentlemen, as far as we can tell, America has simply disappeared."

A murmuring started in the crowd, a confused buzz emanating from the promenade.

"We have had no contact with anyone from the mainland in days, and no signal from any satellite for our navigation or communication systems."

The murmur became louder. There were no distinct voices, the crowd had become an amorphous single entity, speaking its confusion and fear. Holding his hand out in a plea for quiet, Solberg continued, "We have now made contact with a United States Navy vessel, the *USS Paul Ignatius*, who has confirmed they are in the same situation along with several other boats and ships they have encountered. It is our belief that the terrorist attack was from others who have found themselves here as well."

The crowd had dropped back into silence, staring at him. Solberg turned to face the other way, realizing he'd had his back to half the passengers throughout his announcement.

"Rest assured, with the help of the U.S. Navy, we are protected from further attacks and we will have the support we need to find our way back home. For the time being, we will be remaining by this island until we can establish," *better than saying figure the hell out,* Solberg thought, "what is going on. You will continue to have full use of this ship's magnificent facilities. The only difference you will see is that I have asked the ship's catering crew to limit the menu options somewhat in the ship's restaurants. I promise you, this isn't because we are short of food, it is merely so that we can factor in a small reserve for if this situation continues. I am sure that adequate compensation for any hardship incurred will be claimable upon our return to port. "

The murmuring restarted. Solberg winced inwardly. No matter how he had dressed it up, he was talking about rationing.

"Ladies and gentlemen." This time, Solberg didn't

wait for quiet to resume. He just wanted to get the hell away from the passengers, back to the safety of the bridge. "I promise you, we will return home soon. You just need to have a little patience."

With that, Solberg walked back to Matthews. She had a furious look on her face, her carefully written speech totally unused. What she had worked out had been painstakingly considered to minimize any suggestion that they were so badly lost.

"Captain, what the hell was that?" she hissed.

"You try standing in front of thousands of people and telling them America has disappeared," Solberg said, pushing the microphone into her hands. "I'm going back to the bridge. Put on some music, Carrie. Do your job and keep them entertained while we sort this mess out."

Red-faced, Matthews turned away as Solberg walked over to Jack. "And you, it's about time you find out where that kid has disappeared to."

"The kid?" Jack asked with forced civility.

"Grissom. He's been missing for two days. Now is not the time to be losing crew. You're now the head of security—find him."

"Yes sir." Jack said confusedly.

"As for the rest of you, we need to figure out just what we're going to hand over to that Slater woman for her 'protection'." Solberg held his two forefingers up, mimicking speech marks.

***

Well, they ain't happy at all, Grayson thought as he stood in the middle of the crowd, sipping from a beer bottle. The reaction of the crowd ranged from near hysteria to terrified to, well as near as Grayson could figure, vague disinterest.

"Do you think its terrorism? Maybe they've nuked America, and that's why it's disappeared?" one old lady said in tears.

"I've got to contact my kids!" a man said, frantically trying in vain to get a call through on his mobile phone.

"I can't think of a better place to be stuck," a young woman shrugged resignedly, taking a sip of her wine glass.

"My god, we're lost," an elderly man said.

Yup, you most definitely are, and welcome to the club. Grayson remembered his first few days, weeks, and even months in this place. How he went from scared to depressed, to resigned. Finally, he had been given a purpose by those who had found him, bobbing in a life jacket after... after that day. To find new targets for the increasingly desperate pirates he had fallen in with. And then, of course, there was Kristen...

Not for the first time, he thought his situation was a hell of a lot better on board this ship. If it were only himself he had to worry about, he would have probably just stuck with the *Atlantica* and kept up the guise that he had been found adrift rather than planted in the arrival zone as a scout. Unfortunately, he had his wife and child back on *Titan*, and that changed things for him — a lot.

Making his way through the simmering crowd, he exited the promenade and threaded through the corridors until he reached the muster deck near where he had murdered Grissom. Glancing around, ensuring he was alone, he pulled the CB radio out of his pocket.

"Rain," Grayson gave the code word to show it was him speaking. A security measure he had instituted when he had begun scouting for Vaughan and Bautista.

"Desert," the correct response came after a moment.

"We're staying with the *Ignatius*," Grayson said.

"Good," the reply was prompt. "I have a new set of instructions for you. They come from the man himself."

Chapter 18 – Day 5

"I must say, I'm glad you decided to stay." Commander Slater gazed at them from her seat at the conference table.

"For the moment, it seems like the sensible option until we can properly evaluate our situation," Solberg replied.

"While you decide to remain with us, the *Ignatius* will offer you our protection, of course."

"For a price," Solberg said, looking her straight in her eyes.

"For a price," Slater replied with the slightest of smiles. "Captain Solberg, I can tell what you are thinking. The *Ignatius* has turned into a mercenary vessel, offering her services out to whoever can pay. The situation is more complex than that."

"Enlighten us," Solberg rested his elbows on the table, steepling his fingers.

"It's as I was saying before. In an ideal world, the military is paid for out of U.S. tax dollars," she said calmly. "It is not a free commodity; it is merely free at point of use. All told, defense spending accounts for around sixteen cents in every dollar you give the federal tax man."

"Thank you for the economics lesson," Solberg said testily. "Although I must say, I consider this the point of use."

"My point, Captain," Slater said, ignoring his barbed comment, "is that if you want defense, it needs to be paid for. This isn't so my crew and I can live like kings and queens, I assure you. It's so I can keep my ship running."

"So what do you want?" Reynolds cut in from his position next to Solberg.

"Fuel is my main concern. Without fuel I can't even run my generators, let alone sail my ship. Food is also an issue. Potable water is something we're always on the edge of running out of. I have a crew of three hundred twenty officers and crew, and another two hundred persons who have fallen under our protection prior to your arrival."

"How are you feeding them now?" Reynolds asked.

"We have some farming facilities set up on Nest Island. We supplement that with fishing the local area using a pair of trawlers who have joined with us."

"That island is hardly huge," Reynolds said. "I'm no farmer, but it must struggle to support you."

"Yes it does, Admiral. Like with our water reclamation and distillation facilities, we're constantly on the edge."

Reynolds leaned back, a frown on his face. "Commander, we're bringing to the island the better part of six thousand people. Now, I'm hoping and praying that whatever situation we're in will resolve itself relatively quickly and we can all go home, but if it goes on for any amount of time and we exhaust

Atlantica's stocks…"

"Then we'll starve," Slater said simply.

"That is hardly worth giving up our fuel for. A slow lingering death," Solberg spoke up. "We'd be better off just taking our chances and sailing on."

"You are the most significant vessel that has arrived in this area," Slater said. "With your resources and our capabilities, we will have many more options than we have now."

"It strikes me that you need us more than we need you." Solberg grinned.

"Captain, without us those pirates will follow you to hell and back to get your vessel. You may have fought off an opportunistic assault on your ship by one of their scouts, but you will not survive against a concerted and planned attack."

"Okay," Reynolds said, holding his hands up. "So let's be clear. We need you for defense, you need us for provision. The question is — and let's assume we are stuck here — what do we do with our… alliance?"

"Our objectives should be to establish where we are, why we are out of contact, and get our asses home," Slater said. "Failing that, we will need to find a large enough landmass to sustain us indefinitely until we can service those objectives."

"Let's concentrate on the assumption we'll get home," Solberg replied.

"We can't just ignore the possibility that may be impossible. Clearly something has happened to the rest of the world," Reynolds rubbed his chin in concentration.

"I'm not quite willing to write it off yet," Solberg snapped. "Let us consider a tentative alliance, for the time being."

"That would be a prudent choice, Captain Solberg." Slater nodded.

"As a gift, we have a small bowser of aviation fuel. You have helicopters and we don't. You may as well have that as a… thank you, for the support."

"Very magnanimous, Captain."

"As a second gift, *Atlantica* has the ability to generate a small amount of power through her solar cells. It isn't much, however it will take the load off your generators and save fuel on just keeping your systems running. We can run auxiliary power lines to *Ignatius*."

"That would help immensely, Captain. Thank you."

"Thirdly, if we are going to ally ourselves with you, we better get to know you, your crew, and the island. May I suggest you host a party? We will, of course, bring a few bottles."

"My crew has had an enforced state of sobriety for the last two years," Slater said with a smile. "A party would help with morale."

"Don't get me wrong, Commander. I'm not willing to give up any fuel just yet. But one small step at a time, and we've got more booze than we know what to do with and we can certainly bring food, as well."

"Captain, shouldn't we be rationing?" Kendricks said in a concerned tone.

"Actually, the captain is correct regarding the food," Matthews responded for Solberg from across the table. "You'd be horrified if you knew just how much food we trash at the end of a cruise as it's gone off halfway through. I think we could put together a reasonable spread without impacting on our food supply. There's a lot of stuff we'd have to toss in the next day or so anyway."

"Absolutely. It will be an efficient use of food stocks and hopefully build morale. Something I think is sorely needed right now," Reynolds agreed.

Chapter 19 – Day 6

"So you have no idea where this officer is?" Jack asked Kendricks. They were perched on stools at one of the smaller bars on the ship, below decks next to the casino. Since the announcement, the air on the ship was subdued, even more so than when the *Liliana* had attacked them. People were worried; worried for themselves, worried for their homes, and worried for their loved ones.

"Nope," Kendricks took a swig on his bottle, his left arm still wrapped in a sling. "Last we saw him was the night before the attack. We had sent him to try and use the stars to navigate by, but he never came back to the bridge."

"And you never checked in with him at the time?"

"It's not great management, Jack, but it was late and we had lots on," Kendricks said quietly.

"Okay," Jack nodded before frowning. "I'm not a cop. I don't have a clue where to start."

"The only ex-cops we had on the crew were in the security team. They're... gone now. And we don't exactly want to start telling any who might be passengers that we have disappearing crew members."

"Yeah, I get that. There are more than enough reasons for the passengers to panic without adding more." A thought occurred to Jack and he pointed at Kendricks's smartphone, which was set on the bar. "Don't you all have these phones like the one you gave me?"

"We do, and so did Walt Grissom. It's been going straight to voicemail for days."

Jack drummed his fingers on the edge of the bar, racking his brain where to start the ball rolling to find someone on a ship with as much floor space as a respectable town. "Can you track them? I mean, I know my iPhone has a mode where if it gets lost or stolen it can be traced."

"No, we don't have that ability. It was the first thing I wondered and I ran it past IT. Apparently for that track to work, it need to triangulate off a number of mobile phone towers. We only have one on the ship which then feeds through the communications array and then back to the mainland. That's all we needed."

"Maybe he just decided to end it all... maybe go overboard for some reason?"

"He was a happy guy," Kendricks said. "I mean he was pissed off that we were lost, but at that point we didn't know how far up shit creek we actually were."

"Fair enough." Jack looked up, and gestured with his beer bottle toward the ceiling. "There's CCTV all around this ship. Has anyone done a playback yet?"

"No, we haven't had chance what with the attack. The security staff ran the CCTV and there's not exactly many of them left."

"You know, about that..." Jack said, as he flicked

his eyes to the few other patrons in the bar. "If we are going to be stuck here for any time, we're going to have to start giving people jobs. It can't hurt to regenerate our security force using passengers. Others are bound to have military experience."

"Regenerate? You mean recruit some new ones?"

"Yeah."

"See, you are cut out for this job," Kendricks said, slapping Jack on the back. "Let me run it past the captain. I think for the moment he's still hoping that he'll wake up tomorrow morning, and this will all have been a bad dream. He wants to maintain normality for the passengers as long as possible."

"Solberg is a dick," Jack said.

"Amen to that, but he is my master and commander." Kendricks winced.

"That he is. Anyway, what time did you last see Grissom?"

***

The dark CCTV suite flickered with the lights from the dozens of screens showing images from all over the *Atlantica*. It was supposed to be staffed 24/7 by a security officer, but now there were barely enough officers to split up the tension-fueled barroom brawls that were erupting with increasing tendency since the captain's announcement, and so it was unmonitored.

Frowning, Jack lowered himself into a seat in front of the main console, which like everything else on the ship had a streamlined touchscreen interface.

Pressing "playback", the large screen in the center switched away from a live feed of the swimming pool area and a menu system appeared.

After a few moments of playing around with the options, Jack brought up the view of the entrance of the bridge. Typing in the date and time he wanted, the playback from four days ago appeared.

He watched as a young officer, obvious in his white shirt, black trousers, and epaulettes exited the bridge and walked out of view down the corridor.

It took Jack an hour of trial and error to track Grissom down to deck six. The camera coverage wasn't great—mostly the cameras were focused on the bars but, by process of elimination, he figured there was only one way the officer could have gone, out onto the muster decks. But it was there he found the most frustrating thing yet. The only camera in that area was pointed squarely at what was obviously the orange hull of a mega lifeboat.

The only thing he was sure of was that Grissom had gone out onto the muster deck, but never seemed to have come back in.

Chapter 20 – Day 6

The shouts and cries of the crew members of both *Atlantica* and *Ignatius* echoed over the sea as the much-smaller warship drew close into the vast bulk of the cruise ship. Power lines were run between the two vessels from open cargo hatches, and before long, the two ships were mated together, the smaller vessel hungrily suckling at *Atlantica's* power.

***

Anyone who had wanted to was allowed to come on the "complimentary excursion" to Nest Island. Except, rather than *Atlantica* being serviced by tender ferries, they had to use their own lifeboats. All in all, less than a quarter of the passengers wanted to leave the ship.

"It is beautiful," Laurie said as she walked arm-in-arm with her father up the rickety wooden pier that extended out from the golden sand beach.

"That it is," Reynolds said, looking over at the huts nestled into the tree line. Small boats of every description called this place home. Some were clearly life rafts from larger vessels. A couple appeared to be larger fishing trawlers, and everything in between.

"Welcome to Nest Island," a man said, dressed in a white Navy dress uniform with the three stripes of a lieutenant commander on his epaulettes along with a star denoting he was an officer of the line. "My name's Perry Donovan, executive officer of the Iggy... that's the *USS Paul Ignatius.* If you would come with me, I'll show you to the others."

"Thank you, Commander." Reynolds nodded at the man. Along with the rest of the group, they followed him toward where people were congregating around a barbeque pit.

***

Jack had visited the muster deck after viewing the CCTV, but he couldn't see anything in the low LED lighting.

He'd had to wait until the lifeboats had all been deployed. The whole environment had been comprehensively trodden over by the thousand or so people who had decided they wanted to visit the island but still, Jack wanted to get a feel for Grissom's last traceable movements. *Besides, it's not as if I'm going to go on shore, just in case the Ignatius's crew aren't quite as trustworthy as they're making out,* Jack thought.

He walked along the muster deck, running his hand along the railing, imagining where the missing officer had gone. The end of the muster deck followed around to the aft of the ship. If he'd wanted to see the stars, with minimal light pollution, there would be the obvious choice.

Resting his elbows on the railing, he looked over the side, gazing at the sea. He liked the sound of the water lapping against the hull of the ship. It masked the tinnitus which had afflicted him since the RPG had taken his leg, giving relief from the buzzing he heard constantly.

Sighing, not for the first time, he wondered how that noise hadn't driven him mad. It was constant, but at least it was fading. Or he was getting used to it. Either way, he was finding he wasn't noticing it nearly as much as the first few insomnia-blighted weeks after Syria. But then, when he had been allowed to sleep, the dreams awaited him...

Shaking his head, casting aside his maudlin thoughts, he looked down. He could see some dark specks on the clean white trim the railing stanchions extended up from. It was in stark contrast, since everything on the ship was so immaculate. Using the railing to compensate for his leg, he lowered himself into a kneeling position and looked closely at it. It was brown, the color of dried blood. From his position, he could see that one of the railing crossbeams was slightly dented as well, and there were more specks of blood on that as well.

What the hell do I do with this? Jack thought. During his long convalescence at the Walter Reed Medical Center, he'd gone through more Blu-ray boxsets than he cared to remember, many of them police procedural thrillers. He was vaguely aware that they probably had as much to do with real-life police investigations as the average action series had with military operations, but still, it was a start.

So, we have a missing man, and in his last known place I've found some blood. Jack stepped back, and with the phone he had been given by Kendricks, started to take pictures of the area, getting the best shots of the blood splatter as he could. He doubted Dr. Emodi had the capability to do any kind of forensic analysis on the blood, but hopefully when they figured out where the hell they were and how to get home, someone would manage it. *Yeah, let's get a sample of it.* Opening the phone's directory, he scrolled to the "medical center" number and gave it a call.

RALPH KERN

Chapter 21 – Day 6

The huge bonfire on the beach had reached full intensity by the time the sun had set. Out to sea, *Atlantica* was lit up in all of her glory, blazing as brightly as the fire. Alongside her, the much smaller *Paul Ignatius's* subtler lighting was on display, too.

Spread along the beach were the thousand people who had elected to come to the island. They were subdued, but slowly coming out of their shells as the alcohol took effect. For the residents of the island, the majority of whom had come from the *Ignatius,* along with two hundred more from various ships and boats that had stumbled on the island, the mood was more of a celebration.

"So, tell me, Commander..." Reynolds had retreated from the mass of people, leaving his daughter to work the crowd in that self-assured manner of hers. On the periphery, he had found Slater gazing over the party, a satisfied smile on her face. "And be honest. Would you have really left us to fend for ourselves?"

Slater's smile turned into a grin. "Let's just say, I was a damn fine poker player in my time, Admiral."

"Indeed." Reynolds gave a low chuckle. "Kudos,

Heather. Everyone got what they needed in the end, even if it took some rather impressive bluffing."

"Our little secret, Admiral," Slater said with a wink, "I do have a reputation to maintain, after all."

Reynolds gazed over the crowd for a long moment, enjoying the companionable silence before asking what he knew he must. "You've had two years here to process this... this situation. Do you think there is a way home?"

The smile dropped from Slater's face, and she turned to look fully at the former admiral. "It's paradise here on this island. There are over five hundred people, and this place can feed them all... at a push. We have set up farms. They're probably not the most efficient they can be, in fact I'm sure we can push some more efficiency out of them, but..." her voice trailed off.

"But, not another six thousand people's worth," Reynolds finished.

"No," Commander Slater sighed. "Not even close. What you have on your ship is it. There is no more food. This has to be the last act of gluttony. After this, everyone's belts need to be tightened."

"And even then, we are all going to starve."

"We are all going to starve," Slater repeated. "So in answer to your question, do I think there is a way home? Yes, there has to be."

"Heather. I've worked with the U.S. Military enough to know you people don't give up easily. Do you have a plan?"

"Only one that Solberg wouldn't like," she responded. "*Ignatius* fills her tanks and we see how far we can get, leaving enough fuel to return. We have a range of 4400 nautical miles, so we can potentially get 2200 miles before we have to come back. We can go looking for home, or a larger land mass at least."

"Home," Reynolds rolled the word around his mouth. "Between you and me, it doesn't exist anymore. Does it?"

"I don't know," Slater gave a sad smile. "How can we be away from the satellites and coms buoys? Why are the ships all from the same date, but have arrived here at different times? You know, when the true weirdness started to present itself and we began to realize we were stuck here, four of my men committed suicide. They just gave up, despite your fine words about us not doing so."

"But you're not going to?"

"I have a ten-year-old daughter and husband at home, Admiral." Slater turned to look at him. The steel in her eye showing why she had been selected to command a warship. "No, I am not going to give up. I want to see my Millie again, and I'll do anything to make that happen."

"Then we had better come up with a solution. One that will appease Solberg."

"Yes," Slater nodded. "Come aboard the *Ignatius* tomorrow. I will show you everything we have."

Chapter 22 – Day 7

"Welcome aboard." The executive officer, Lieutenant Commander Perry Donovan, seemed chipper, only his blood-shot eyes giving away that he had clearly indulged the previous night.

"Thank you," Reynolds nodded at him, standing to one side and letting Solberg, Kendricks, and his daughter pass from the gangplank onto the deck of the *Ignatius*.

"Captain Slater will see you down in the CIC. I'm afraid she made no mention of your daughter being cleared to come aboard?" Donovan said.

"If you would provide my compliments to Captain Slater and tell her I request Laurie accompanies us," Reynolds said, automatically adopting the custom of referring to Slater on her own ship as Captain.

"I'm sure there won't be a problem." Donovan shrugged. "If you'll follow me?"

The executive officer led the way from the gangplank toward the boxy grey superstructure of the ship.

Reynolds cast his eye over the vessel as they followed Donovan. His practiced eye could see her design was dated, yet the ship generally didn't have the appearance of the decades of service which was the norm for many a warship.

"You'll have to forgive me, I haven't been keeping up with the hulls in your inventory as much as I used to when I was a serving officer. The *Ignatius* is in remarkably good shape."

"Yes, sir, she is," Donovan beamed. "She's one of the newer Flight IIA *Arleigh Burkes*. Her shakedown cruise was in 2019. In fact, she's only been out of port operationally three times. Since then, she hasn't exactly done a lot of miles."

"It seems like Captain Slater runs a tight ship," Reynolds nodded appreciatively.

"Yes she does," Donovan said. "Although, other than maintenance, there isn't a hell of a lot for the crew to do. If you'll pardon my French."

Reaching the entrance to the superstructure, Donovan un-dogged and pulled open the bulkhead hatch, then led them into the darkened interior.

"As you probably know, sir, the *Arleigh Burkes* are the Navy's jack-of-all-trades ships. The original design may be over thirty years old, but it has been continually improved. Some of those improvements have been evolutionary, and some revolutionary," Donovan said with pride as he pulled open another hatch stenciled with the letters CIC. "This is one of the revolutionary changes. Needless to say, not many non U.S. Navy folk see in here."

"Well, what can I say?" Reynolds exclaimed as the Command Information Center was revealed before him. It looked more the bridge of a science fiction starship than the primitive seeming vessels of Reynold's service. The Plexiglas plotting boards and cathode ray tubes were nowhere to be seen. Instead, a huge LED screen took up the whole of one wall of the dark room, showing a map of Nest Island and all the ships around it. Banks of consoles faced the screen, each with intricate displays of their own. His practiced eye quickly discerned what each one's function was. Weapons stations, command and control interfaces, and communications consoles.

"Welcome aboard, gentlemen... and lady?" Captain Slater said, turning from the screen which she had been regarding, hands clasped behind her back.

"Captain, meet my daughter, Laurie," Reynolds said.

Nodding, Slater responded, "I'm pleased to meet you."

"She's a fantastic ship," Laurie said with genuine enthusiasm. "My father has showed me around some of our navy's vessels and this blows it away."

Reynolds cleared his throat. "Only because I was never able to take you aboard the *Daring*, my dear."

"Don't be jealous, Daddy." Laurie smiled teasingly.

"Well, from our wargames, I would say one of your Type-45s would give us a run for our money," Slater said diplomatically, giving a wink to Laurie, her normally icy demeanor rapidly thawing to the younger woman. She turned and gestured, her wave encompassing the room. "This is the *USS Paul Ignatius*'s brain, where two billion dollars' worth of warship is fought from. She is a Flight IIA *Arleigh Burke*, what we call a technology insertion ship. This means she is equipped with much of the equipment that is going to be fitted to the newer Flight III

Arleigh Burkes. One of those innovations is a true twenty-first century CIC, along with a weapons and sensor suite which is unparalleled. There may be better ships out there for specific roles; air defense, for example, like the HMS *Daring*, but we can do just about everything, and do it well."

Kendricks was visibly fascinated by every facet of the room. He tentatively approached one of the consoles.

"Kindly don't touch anything on there, if you please, Mister Kendricks. I'd rather you didn't volley fire all of my missiles into the *Atlantica.*"

"Yes, that wouldn't be ideal," Solberg said from where he stood looking around the room. "So are we going to discuss our situation?"

"Of course. Perry, bring up the working board," Slater said.

Donovan nodded, taking a seat in front of a console and began tapping at it. The large screen on the wall scrolled out of its close-in view of the island and the swarm of craft around it. The island was quickly reduced to a small green blob in the middle of the blue screen. Along the bottom and right-hand side, red hatching appeared.

"The red, as far as the information we have gathered, denotes the sphere of influence of the pirates you encountered." Slater walked over to stand by the screen and pointed to the hatched area. "We don't have an indication on numbers or types of craft, however it is clear they are using repurposed civilian vessels."

From around the island, a green hatched circle emanated. "This is our sphere of influence. Roughly denoted by the reach of my radar systems, around seventy-five nautical miles or so. Anything within that area, I can see. Unfortunately, my surface-to-surface weaponry is limited to a Mark 45 five-inch cannon or Tomahawk cruise missiles. I'm somewhat reluctant to use my Tomahawks on the pirate's rather frail surface ships. Metaphors about sledgehammers and nuts would be apt in those circumstances. We still have an interdiction zone of 13 nautical miles just with the cannon, though."

To illustrate her point, another circle, this time in orange appeared on the screen, showing the range of the *Ignatius's* cannon.

"I had to make an example of a pirate ship a year ago. Since then, they often dip into our sensor range, but never within range of my Mk-45."

"You have no Harpoons?" Reynolds asked, rubbing his chin as he contemplated the image.

"No, the majority of my VLS cells are full of anti-air weapons, although I do have some ASROCs," Slater said. "But, to be fair, I would be reluctant to blow them on the rather frail surface ships as well."

"You're speaking gobbledygook," Laurie said. "Can someone translate for us non-navy types?"

"My apologies," Reynolds smiled at his daughter. "Captain, it would be valuable to get the insights of all of us here. It is clear that we are facing an extraordinary situation, and one in which a civilian perspective may be invaluable."

"Of course," Slater nodded. "The *Ignatius* is built around what we call the Mark 41 VLS, or Vertical Launch System. It consists of ninety-six cells, set in two banks, and are full of various types of missiles. In my inventory, I have a mix of anti-air missiles, such as RIM 66Ms and RIM 174As, surface attack

Tomahawks, some anti-submarine rockets, RUM 139 ASROCs, as well as ballistic missile defense weaponry, RIM 161 and RIM 162s. Along with all that, I have a five-inch Mark 45 gun, a couple of bushmaster cannons, and what's called a Phalanx CIWS, or Close-in Weapons System. Needless to say, Captain Solberg, those taxes we spoke about are paying for quite a lot of hardware."

Kendricks looked at the panel he had been about to fiddle with, with a newfound respect. "That's a lot of kit."

"Yes, it is," Slater agreed, her hands still clasped behind her back.

"Okay, we know that land isn't where we thought it was. What steps have you taken to try and find it?" Reynolds asked.

"Perry, please scroll out as far as we've got." The large screen pulled out even further, the island shrinking away. "This is as far as we've managed to reconnoiter. Eighteen months ago, a crew took a sailboat a sixty miles pre-event north-west with some forward operating equipment we had. We then fired one of our unarmed Tomahawks from here. It reached one hundred and twenty miles beyond our scout boat…"

"And?" Solberg asked.

"Nothing."

"And how the hell could that be? America was there, Florida was there. That should easily have been over the peninsula. Now it has just disappeared?" Kendricks squinted at the screen.

Slater could only give a shrug. "My Tomahawks have a much longer range, but without support infrastructure, one hundred and twenty miles is the best we could manage and still get a video feed from the camera mounted on it."

"My god. It's all gone?" Laurie's face was white. "Wait, what did you mean by pre-event west? What event?"

"We don't know what the event was. All we know is the date it happened. July 12, 2024," Slater said. "After that date, we lost all contact. We also have had some anomalies in our navigation system; including north and south swapping."

"Swapping? What? As in north became south and south, north?" Laurie asked.

"Yes, we've had to reconfigure a lot of our equipment to compensate."

"We saw that as well," Solberg said.

"So a polar shift?" Laurie said thoughtfully, this detail new to her.

"I suppose you could call it that," Slater said.

"And your systems presumably wouldn't automatically compensate for that?" Laurie pressed.

"I doubt it. I certainly haven't seen it covered in my idiot's guide to the nav systems on this scow," Slater said.

Reynolds recognized the look on his daughter's face. She was working something through in her head. "Laurie, talk us through your thoughts."

"Look, I read a lot of those popular science magazines—*Focus*, *Scientific American*, stuff like that. May I?" Without waiting for a response, Laurie walked to a white board situated on the wall which was covered with what appeared to be a work roster. Grabbing the wiper, she quickly rubbed the board clean and drew a circle. "This is the Earth. That's north and that's south," she drew notches on the top and bottom and then drew a smaller circle within. "The Earth is essentially a huge dynamo, the core spinning independently of the crust we live on. Every few million years, that core can precess, or change orientation. Normally that would cause just a slight shift, a wobble if that, but a large enough precession would cause the poles to quite literally swap. North becomes south and vice versa."

"That certainly would play hell with just about every piece navigation technology we have," Kendricks nodded.

"Exactly," Laurie said. "Bear in mind, my interest is this is only casual, so I only know what I've read. But surely that would cause a lot of the satellites to malfunction."

"It would," Slater nodded.

"Far be it for me to say," Solberg said. "That can account for a temporary loss of contact with the mainland. It doesn't account for the time oddities we are facing. You being here for two years, for example."

"No... no it does not." Slater said. The initial excitement of getting some kind of explanation visibly washing out of her. "Nor the fact we have been out of contact so long. But it could explain why we are having trouble finding the mainland. Navigation 101 is that true north and magnetic north are two different things. We could have fired that Tomahawk in a completely random direction."

"But that still doesn't account for the simple navigation that we used to head west," Solberg said. "We simply put the rising sun to our stern as soon as we realized there was a problem. We should have still hit the mainland."

"So what about these time oddities or anomalies?" Laurie asked.

"Now that is what is concerning me the most," Slater said candidly. "Perry, overlay the arrival's map please."

"Aye aye, ma'am." Donovan once again tapped the console and on the screen and a series of simple-shaped boat icons began popping into existence on it, spread between Nest Island and deep into the pirates' domain. Each had a number attached to them.

"From what we can see, although every ship claimed to arrive on the same day, July 12th. The ones to the pre-west arrived first, and then the arrivals propagated to the pre-event east," Slater gestured with her hand from left to right. "There have been twenty-seven arrivals which we know of, ranging from the odd dingy to ferries. It may be egotistical, but as the *Ignatius* is the most significant asset, we consider ourselves the datum, hence why there are a few negative numbers. Take for example this boat," Slater gestured at an icon denoted by a -342. "This one appeared nearly a year before we arrived. We are zero, the latest ship to arrive is the Atlantica at 742 days. Would you be so good as to tell Perry where you arrived?"

Kendricks looked at Solberg who nodded. Pulling out his phone, Kendricks tapped away at the touch screen for a few moments, pulling up the inertial navigation log.

"Bearing in mind what we spoke about with the screwed-up navigation, by our best estimates we would have arrived around three hundred miles pre-event east-north-east," he walked to the map and indicated deep in the right side of the red zone. "About here."

Perry tapped at the console and a boat icon appeared entitled *Atlantica* and the numbers 742 appeared.

Laurie squinted at the screen. "So as the ships have arrived, time is moving on yes?"

"Yes," Slater nodded.

"And the last ship to appear before us was that one?" Laurie pointed at one to the pre-event west of Atlantica, separated by a stretch of around forty miles that was emblazoned with 715.

"Yes. She was a fishing boat," Slater's spoke in a clipped tone. "She decided to press on west to find the mainland. She never returned."

Turning back to the board, once again Laurie wiped it clean. Glancing between the screen and the board, she plotted the ships and boats denoted on the screen onto the board. Once she had finished, she stepped back and looked at it for a moment.

"Look they follow a pattern," Laurie said after a long moment of silence, her head cocked to one side. "Roughly speaking, as we get further west, I mean pre-event west, they are arriving later right?"

"Right," Slater agreed.

Under the plot, Laurie drew a graph. From the east to the west the graph followed a near smooth diagonal. Until it reached the ship that came through before *Atlantica*, then the line was almost horizontal with only the slightest of upturns until it reached the cruise ship.

"Look, the curve propagating across changes dramatically with us. Why?"

All in the room squinted at the graph. The

difference in the graph was stark. It was like the top of a mountain had been lopped off.

"Unless…" Laurie said, once again she stepped closer to the white board and scrubbed it clean. She began plotting the ship arrival points, only this time over a much larger scale, leaving plenty of room to the bottom and right side of the board.

"What are you thinking?" her father asked.

"Shhh," Laurie said as she finished plotting the points. Taking another color pen, she began circumscribing circles around a center point between *Atlantica* and the other arrivals. After a few moments, a series of concentric circles were visible.

"Until we came, you had just a set linear data set, yes?" Laurie said finally.

"Yes, it was simple, the further pre-event east the later they were arriving," Slater said, exchanging looks with Donovan.

"But we're an anomaly. *Atlantica* doesn't fit in with that data set as a simple west to east progression. We only make sense if you consider there is a locus, and ships are arriving out from that locus. The closer you get to the center of the locus, the later they arrive, yes?"

"Sonovabitch!" Slater exclaimed. Seeing what Laurie talking about. "So there is something in the center of that locus which will come through last?"

"Exactly. Something there," Laurie tapped the whiteboard in the middle of the circles, "is at the center of where all the ships are arriving. That would also account for why the pirates seem to have been here for a similar amount of time or longer, they came through on the other side of this locus. Like *Atlantica*, they probably worked their way through on different radii out from the center."

"And that thing is the cause of us being here?"

"Now that's something that I can't answer, it's certainly one assumption, equally something on the edge could be the cause," Laurie shrugged. "I suspected you have explored that possibility?"

"Well," Slater replied thoughtfully. "Not really. We have no idea where this hypothetical edge is."

"Okay," Laurie gestured at the board. "Still, we have a lead and at least we know where it is, and when it will arrive."

"And when will it arrive?" Reynolds cut in.

"Well, this is just rough work, I'll need to do this properly... but give or take a few days, in three weeks."

"Twenty-one days," Reynolds nodded. "That's my girl. I knew it was a good idea to bring you."

"We might have an answer for all this?" Slater whispered, and the calm, measured tone was gone. Instead a sheer sense of longing washed out of her.

"'We might," Reynolds smiled at her.

"But there are still a couple of problems, as much as I hate to steal your thunder," Solberg said.

"And what's that?" Slater said.

"By your own admission we will all be on the cusp of starving by then. At our best conservation of food, we will barely last that long," Solberg said bitterly.

"But we might get rescued then," Donovan said quietly.

"Captain Solberg is right. We will be down to our last few morsels by the time this... this locus arrives. And who's to say that whoever or whatever is at this locus can help us get home?" Reynolds said. "We still have to consider that we may need to find a longer term solution."

"We've tried," Slater said quietly. "God we've tried. The only thing we've found is this tiny island."

"What we need is better reconnaissance," Reynolds said. "At the very least it will give us something to do while we're waiting for that locus thingy to arrive. And, of course, we have an obligation to discover as much about this phenomenon as we can, even should returning home be possible."

"So what do you suggest?" Slater asked.

"You mentioned you have BMD capability?"

"Yes," Slater said in a confused tone. "I'm equipped with a set of RIM 161s and RIM 162s."

"So, can we use them?"

"I don't see how. They're designed for shooting down ballistic missiles."

"But they have cameras on them?" Reynolds pressed.

"If you mean by 'cameras' IR sensors. Yes, they do. Quite sophisticated ones, as it happens," Slater said, her voice becoming firmer again as she spoke business.

"Can they differentiate between land and sea?"

"I see where you're going with this now. You think you can use one to map the area. No, they're designed to pick up the heat signature of a ballistic missile. They would be quite useless at differentiating between land and sea," Slater said.

"Can we not just mount one?" Kendricks asked the obvious question. "A camera, I mean."

"Mister Kendricks, Each RIM 161C SM-3 is twelve million dollars' worth of carefully engineered rocket whose sole purpose is to shoot down satellites and ballistic missiles. Simply strapping a digital camera on the front will not work at best, and mess with the aerodynamics so badly it'll tear itself apart at worst."

"Ma'am?" Donovan said.

"Yes, Perry?"

"It may be possible to modify a RIM 161, just not with the workshop we have on board the *Ignatius*..."

"But we have probably far more extensive capabilities on *Atlantica*. We have substantial workshops, 3D printers, and trained technicians to use them," Kendricks finished for him. "I mean, I don't know what's involved, that will be where you guys come in."

"Perry, I know in a previous life you worked on the Aegis implementation program. Put together a proposal. If it looks workable—and only if—I will give you a RIM 161 to modify.

"Aye aye, ma'am."

Chapter 23 – Day 8

"So, you found the last place he was, and some specks of blood," Kendricks leaned back in his chair, hugging his injured, slung arm across his body in obvious discomfort. Kendricks's office was a small cubbyhole, kept in his preferred minimalist style. "But nothing as conclusive such as a body?"

After the initial discussions with Donovan, they had all headed back to the *Atlantica* and began to get the ball rolling for the modification of the Rim 161. Kendricks had a lot to square away, from getting a summary of what workable materials they had in the inventory to giving Donovan a copy of the 3D printer tolerances and specifications. Once again, the missing officer, Grissom, had been pushed to the back of Kendricks's mind.

"That's about the extent of it," Jack said. "By the way, get your money back from whatever security consultant placed your cameras. The idiot put one right behind a lifeboat."

"What can I say? It's what you get when you give the work to the lowest bidder," Kendricks said, taking a sip of his tepid coffee and grimacing.

"Is there any possibility one of the pirates got by

you? During the initial attack, I mean."

"You saw it down there, Jack. It was bedlam.

Hand on heart? No, I couldn't say, but I did have a look at the CCTV there after. From what I can see, no. It doesn't look like any managed to break out."

"Yeah, that tallies with what I saw as well," Jack sighed. "Which leads to three conclusions — one, Grissom's still on-board somewhere, enjoying himself, but not reporting for duty. Two, he had a nasty accident and somehow slipped, fell, hit his head, and went overboard. Or three, someone did it to him."

"Great, so to add to our list of woes we may have a goddamn murderer on board," Kendricks said. "You know, just when I thought this cruise couldn't get any worse. Jack, I'm going to need you to handle this. We have another project on the go at the moment and it's taking up a lot of head-space."

"Go on," Jack prompted.

"We're going to try modifying one of the *Ignatius's* missiles. We're going to see if we can launch it high enough to map the entire region."

"That sounds like it's a positive step."

"It is, but we're going to need to convince Captain Slater we can have it first, and that's going to keep me busy."

"Very well." Jack nodded. "Leave the investigation to me."

"Thanks, Jack. Look, Walt was a good kid. Carte Blanche. If someone hurt..." Kendricks squeezed his eyes closed for a moment. "If someone killed

Walt then find who did it. Just do it quietly. Last thing we need is the fact there may be a murderer on board to panic people any more. With a little luck, he's actually just hidden below decks with a house mouse."

"House mouse?" Jack asked.

"You don't want to know. Let's just say, most bachelor officers tend to have one. Just find him, Jack."

"Roger that," Jack said as he stood up. "We also still need to look at recruiting. There has got to be some ex-military and police on board. They can help with security in case we have any more run-ins with those pirates."

"Fingers crossed, that won't be a problem for much longer. I know Lars has been reluctant to go that far. It'll feel like we're up shit creek without a paddle if we have to start finding jobs for the passengers."

"Yeah, but we need to get them in place and trained now, not when we need them."

"Okay, okay." Kendricks held his hands up in mock supplication. "I'll have another word with him."

***

"So, what do you think?" Kendricks asked.

Solberg frowned and with a creak of leather, leaned back in his chair. "Just so we're on the same page here, let me reiterate. You want to recruit from among the passengers for security and to assist Nest Island with farming duties?"

Kendricks glanced at Carrie, who he had invited to the meeting so she could share her opinion. "That's right."

"Not to sound too... ghetto, but that sucker ain't

gonna fly with the passengers," Carrie said after a pause. "As far as they're concerned, it has only been a week. They may understand with their heads we're in trouble, but not with their hearts, not yet. After all, had we kept to our itinerary, we would only just be coming to the end of the cruise."

Solberg steepled his fingers and looked at his two senior staff members intently. Kendricks waited for him to say something, to wade in on one side or the other.

"Captain," Kendricks said, after the pause went on to the point of awkwardness. "This is one of those situations where we have to be decisive. If we wait until we need the security or the food, it'll be too late."

"I take your point," Carrie rebutted. "However, the morale of the passengers is also an issue. At the moment, I have my staff working hard to keep them happy and occupied. But if we start admitting to them we need their help, we may cause a panic."

"Carrie, what is the food situation?" Solberg held his hand up to forestall Kendricks's response.

"My chefs have worked out a more efficient menu. We'll use the perishable items first, then phase in the longer-lasting stuff. At the revised rate of consumption, we're looking at around three weeks before we start to see a major drop in menu quality."

"And after that?

"Then we have another two to three weeks of steadily decreasing and limited quality."

"And then?" Solberg pressed.

"And then nothing. The holds and larder will be empty."

"So six weeks and then we're done." Solberg

frowned—a facial expression he had been wearing most of the time recently. "At least that's longer than our initial estimates."

"We have to get started thinking about what happens after that, Lars," Kendricks said.

"A lot can happen in six weeks," Carrie replied. "We'll be in a worse state if we have passengers rampaging through the ship."

"You're both right," Solberg spoke slowly. "We need to at least consider that worst-case scenario, that this locus doesn't pan out, but let's keep it relatively low-key. No grand advertisements. Just put up a couple of stalls, make it look like it'll be a fun experience rather than actual work. We can't afford to wait on this, but neither can we afford to upset the passengers even more. I, for one, don't want to be keelhauled by a hoard of loyalty card waving customers. Will that satisfy both of you?"

"Not really," Carrie said.

"Nope." Kendricks shook his head.

"Tough, that's as good as you're both going to get from me," Solberg said.

Chapter 24 – Day 9

I can't believe we've got to this. Solberg thought. *A job fair on my promenade.*

Despite his tacit approval, Solberg didn't like the fact they were advertising jobs. Not one bit. It showed just how desperate their situation had become.

Once again, he stood on the walkway spanning the promenade. Below, crewmembers sat behind tables with large, hastily printed posters showed such titles such as "Farming", "Security", and "Fishing".

There weren't many incentives which Carrie had come up with to offer the small queues of people who were lined up at the desks. Free massages in the spa was about the best they could manage, and the promise of recompense when they got home.

Still, it meant at least a few of the passengers were starting to do something more productive than lounging around on the deck working on their tans and eating.

***

Either reality is setting in for them, or they're running out of shows to put on to keep these spoiled assholes amused, Grayson thought as he walked down the promenade, passing the few people waiting to ask about getting a job.

He'd carefully considered the idea of joining the security team. That would presumably give him access to firearms at some point, and that would give him a few options. But that would also limit his movements around the ship, and while he was fairly confident his cover would hold, if someone decided to really press him, he would struggle to answer questions about his time before he was rescued.

Maybe the farming crew, though? That would give him access to the island more readily, plus there would presumably be less vetting.

"Karl," he heard a familiar voice call out.

"Hello, Mister Kendricks. How are you?" Grayson came to a halt and looked over at the staff captain, his arm still in its sling. "What the hell happened to your shoulder?"

"This?" Kendricks patted his arm. "Courtesy of our pirate friends."

"Yeah, about that," Grayson said, carefully moderating his voice. "Thanks again, I truly dread to think what would have happened if they had found me first."

"Well," Kendricks gestured widely with his good arm, encompassing the job fair. "This might be your chance to make good. Can we interest you in a job?"

"I was just thinking," Grayson ad-libbed, "that I should give something back. After all, you've been keeping me in booze and food. Maybe I could help out on one of the farming crews?"

"Not fishing?" Kendricks grinned.

"That got me into this mess to start with," Grayson replied. "No, I think terra firma is where I want to be."

"Well, go see Mandy over at that desk," Kendricks pointed at a rather unpopular-looking table with just a couple of people standing around it. "And sign on the dotted line."

"You can be damn sure I'll be cashing in on those massages the captain promised," Grayson said with a wink as he walked over.

***

Jack walked up Route 66-B, past the security station, into a section of the ship he'd not visited before. The walls became less sterile seeming, safety notices and official signs giving way to music posters and photos stuck to the walls.

The crew had made attempts to personalize their little part of the ship, but the fact remained that other than the senior staff, nearly two thousand crewmembers lived in a cramped space. It was crowded, busy, and noisy.

Finding the cross-corridor he wanted, he turned onto it and tapped on the cabin door he had been looking for.

"Who is it?" A voice called from inside.

"My name is Jack, from… from security. I just need to speak to you."

The hatch opened a crack and a young girl's face appeared. "Yeah?"

"Hi, are you Jenna?"

"Yeah," the girl repeated. She looked Jack up and

down, seeming to assess him. "What can I do for you?"

"May I come in?"

"No," she said pointedly. "It's a mess."

Jack glanced through the crack above her head. It was a disaster in there—clothes were strewn all over the place and magazines filled every flat space. That's what happened when two people had to live in a space barely bigger than the back of a transit van. Depending on the occupants, it would only go one of two ways; become a pigsty or be obsessively and compulsively tidy. The occupants of this cabin had opted for the former.

"Fair enough," Jack shrugged. "I'm looking for Walt Grissom. I'd been asking about, and someone told me you were… friends."

"We are, or were," Jenna said before blowing a bubble of chewing gum, letting it snap. "Then he stopped visiting about a week ago. Now he doesn't answer his phone."

"Any idea where he is?"

"Nope," Jenna said angrily. "If you see him, tell him not to visit again. I'm not some bimbo he can just use and discard. I have a degree, you know."

Holding his hands up to ward off Jenna's anger, Jack responded. "Listen, Jenna. We're a little worried about him. He hasn't turned up for work in a few days."

"Really?" Jenna's fury abated slightly. "He was always such a… square. He wouldn't even get drunk if he was on watch the following day."

"So I understand," Jack nodded. "Listen, if you hear from him, or anyone sees him around, let me or one of the security staff know."

"Yeah, will do."

Chapter 25 – Day 9

"The word is out," Urbano Bautista said to Vaughan. They were standing on the bridge of the *Titan*, high up on the T-shaped superstructure looking out at the huge beached container vessel lying against the island. "It won't exactly be an armada, but it'll be a hell of a lot of ships."

Vaughan nodded. He was nervous about the proposition of attacking a heavily armed warship. They had it good here. So far they had gotten everything they needed, and Vaughan was content with his lot; after all, he had his own empire. It wasn't like he was lacking in anything, although some of the lesser crew didn't have things comfortable by any stretch of the imagination. But if they could take the *Atlantica* and eliminate the threat of the *Ignatius*? Then he, Vaughan, would have undisputed dominance in the region.

"A lot is going to ride on Karl being able to do something about the *Ignatius*, otherwise we are just going to give them a lot of targets to shoot at. It'll be the most one-sided battle in history," Vaughan sighed.

"He will come through; I have no doubt about

that. He is a man of unique skills," Bautista said. "We are helped by the fact we have a bit of inside knowledge around that class of destroyer from one of the boys who works in the engine room on the *Spencer*. He was in the Navy and served on that class."

"Good, I'm sure you're handling the details. When are you leaving?"

"Tomorrow," Bautista said. "The *Liliana* is still the fastest ship we have, even with all the holes that fucking helicopter put in it. I'll be back in a few days. By then, the fleet should be assembled."

"And we'll have to give the go... or no go," Vaughan nodded.

"If Karl manages to do the job we've got lined up for him," Bautista replied. "Then we will be able to sail right up to the *Ignatius*. We might even be able to take her."

Vaughan turned and slapped Bautista on the back. "I like your thinking, but let's not run before we walk eh? The priority is the *Atlantica*. If we get the *Ignatius* too... that's just a bonus."

"Very well," Bautista said, before continuing in a quieter tone. "We haven't discussed what happens to the passengers and crew. There have got to be thousands on board."

"I know, Urbano," Vaughan said quietly. "But we're living in a new world now. We may have to make some brutal choices."

"Ha," Bautista scoffed. "You know, the Urbano Bautista of ten years ago wouldn't have given a flying fuck what happened to them. But I'm a different man now, we all are. For all we know, we are the last people on the planet. Us and the few boats that magically appear, that is."

"Second thoughts, Urbano?"

"No, Eric." Bautista turned toward Vaughan. "I'll do what needs to be done. But I'm not going to smile while doing it."

"Neither am I, Urbano, neither am I."

Nodding, Bautista walked from the bridge, heading toward the stairwell. "I'll see you in a few days."

Vaughan turned back to the railing and ran his hand lightly over the metal.

Who would have thought? Vaughan thought. *Urbano Bautista showing a conscience?*

Chapter 26 – Day 9

"How's your new job going?" Laurie asked.

Jack and Laurie were walking down the promenade, past the thin crowd of people still surrounding the job tables. She had slipped her arm through his, subtly taking a little of his weight, easing the burden on his now very sore leg that had taken a lot of chaffing in the last few days. He liked that; the touch of a woman who simply wanted to help him. It was a far cry from the Jack of even a week ago. He would have viewed it as a mortal insult for someone to have even made the attempt.

"Busy," Jack replied. "I have a missing crew member to find, not to mention setting up something resembling a training program for the new folk. Not that we have many volunteers."

"I'm sure you can handle it. You've handled everything else so far." Laurie smiled.

"Yeah, I guess."

"And how's the leg holding up?" Laurie asked.

Jack stiffened. Quietly taking comfort in her subtle assistance was one thing, speaking directly about it was another. Slowly he relaxed, the casual way she mentioned it burning through his defensiveness.

"It's okay. It still hurts sometimes, but it's okay." Jack said slowly.

"Maybe Dr. Emodi can help with that?"

"No, I don't mean the…" Jack trailed off, before

speaking more strongly again. Articulating himself clearly was something he had gotten out of practice with in his self-imposed social isolation. "I don't mean the… stump. I mean my leg itself. I can feel it hurting, even though it's gone. It burns sometimes. Sometimes it itches, too. You know how frustrating it is when you feel the need to scratch something but you can't reach it?"

"I can imagine." Laurie nodded. "I think I've read about that. Phantom limb pain."

"Yeah, apparently it's caused by junk inputs from the central nervous system. I filled three notebooks with the crap the doctors spouted about it, and didn't take one bit in."

The two approached the gaudy café, Art Deco, and Jack saw the place was only half full. "Would you like a coffee?"

"I thought you'd never ask," Laurie said as they changed course and started to head into the coffee shop.

As they reached the threshold, the phone in Jack's pocket began to ring. Giving an apologetic glance at Laurie, Jack answered, "Cohen."

"Jack, there's a disturbance in Beachcombers, meet me there," Solberg said without preamble.

"Okay, five minutes." Jack disentangled his arm from Laurie's.

"Duty calls?" Laurie asked.

"Yeah, sorry about this."

"No worries, rain check. Go get 'em, Sheriff."

***

"Kendricks should be handling this, instead he's

off playing with gadgets and gizmos," Solberg grumbled as he met Jack and together they walked along into the entry atrium of the buffet hall.

"I'm surprised this warrants a senior officer's attention, Captain," Jack said.

"Damn premium customers. Apparently Carrie can't sweet talk him herself."

The sound of angry shouting was heard outside of Beachcombers as the doors swept open and the two men entered.

" —ridiculous! Do you know how much I've paid for this fucking holiday? Not only does your incompetent crew get us lost, you have us eating this swill!"

The voice was familiar to Jack. He racked his brain, thinking back through the many people he had met over the past week. Circling around the buffet table, he saw a red-faced Brett Jenson standing before him, his embarrassed wife next to him and a bemused crowd watching Carrie Matthews try to placate the furious man.

"Mister Jenson, as I've tried to ex—"

"Finally," Jenson interrupted, seeing Solberg. "Can you tell your staff that we demand a decent meal?"

Solberg held his hands up. "Calm down, Brett. I've only just arrived. What's going on?"

"This is what's fucking going on." Jenson reached over to the buffet table and picked up a tray of what looked like ham sandwiches. "I mean, seriously? What is this? Lunch?"

"Brett—" Solberg began.

"Mister Jenson. I am not on first name terms with you right now." Jenson dropped the metal tray, letting it clatter to the floor, sandwiches and rolls scattering away from it.

Solberg's face went bright red in fury. He stepped forward. Jack quickly assessed the situation and lay a placatory hand on the captain's shoulder.

"Sir, allow me," Jack said quickly before Solberg could let rip. "Mister Jenson. We need you to calm down so we can talk about this rationally —"

"Oh, I'm completely rational." Jenson turned to Jack, as if noticing him for the first time. "Wait, aren't you James?"

"Jack, my name is Jack."

"Well, Jack, I fail to see what business this is of yours. Captain, we are all," Jenson turned and gestured theatrically at the crowd behind him before facing back toward Solberg, "curious as to why you have us eating this swill when we paid a lot of money for decent cuisine."

The crowd didn't look particularly curious about the food on offer; they were far more interested in the show before them.

"As of a week ago, I have been asked to assist this ship with its security functions," Jack interposed himself between the captain and man before him. "And your shit attitude is a material threat to that security. Now you need to calm down, or I'll put you in the brig until you do."

"Jack? Go make yourself busy." Jenson lifted his hand in front of Jack's face and made a shooing motion.

That was as far as he got. Jack caught the hand and twisted it around, forcing Jenson to turn away from him. Jack kept the hand in his own, locking it in what would be a painful gooseneck hold up in the small of Jenson's back.

"Right, to the brig," Jack said loudly in the voice he used to reserve for dealing with any of his dilatory or obstructive former troops.

Pulling Jenson around, Jack shoved the struggling, spitting man toward the door, only hobbling slightly on his leg. Every time Jenson tried to struggle out of the hold, Jack applied a little pressure onto his wrist, which he knew would translate into agony for him.

A round of applause erupted from the onlookers.

Unseen by the crowd, the slightest twitch of a smile crossed Jack's face. He'd wanted to put this pompous prick in his place the first time he'd met him, and it seemed he wasn't the only one.

***

"This is the Light Exo Atmospheric Projectile, or LEAP for short, which is mounted on the RIM 161C—Standard Missile 3," Donovan manipulated the touchscreen interface of the conference room table.

Visible on it was a small cylinder, which had the appearance of a tiny jet engine. Donovan gestured at it proudly. Kendricks wasn't overly impressed — it hardly looked like a super-advanced weapon. From the look on Donovan's face, he didn't think it was wise to say as much, though.

"At the front, we have an IR sensor head," Donovan gestured at the components as he spoke. "The job of that is to acquire a target, whether that be a satellite or a ballistic missile. What it isn't, though, is a camera on the visual spectrum; it only picks up infrared and displays the results in two colors.

Behind that, is what we call the bus. That contains the maneuvering capability, batteries, and communication equipment that keeps it in contact with the launching ship."

"Okay," Kendricks said. "And what about explosives? I mean, I wouldn't be too keen on working on a bomb in our workshops."

"It's a pure kinetic kill weapon. At the speed it impacts a target, it unleashes the same amount of energy as thirty-two kilograms of TNT," Donovan said. "It doesn't need explosives, so don't worry about that. The propellant on board, hydrazine, can be toxic, but I don't propose we mess around with that side of things too much."

"Okay... that's good to hear," Kendricks said, slightly mollified.

"This is a standard launch profile. Please forgive the music, this is lifted straight from the promotional material that Raytheon/Mitsubishi, the makers of this little baby, provided.

Donovan tapped play on the touchscreen of the table monitor. On cue, dramatic music began bellowing through the speakers.

"In a changing uncertain world," a serious sounding voice growled. "Ballistic missile defense is key to America's sec —"

"Sorry, I forgot about the blurb," Donovan said, killing the sound but leaving the video running. "Right then. In a nutshell, how the Aegis BMD system works is as follows."

The video showed a massively-out-of-scale ship, of the same class as the *Ignatius*, sailing on a computer-generated sea. Around the visible curve of the world, a graphic of a missile erupted into view, leaving a dashed trail behind it as it arced over the horizon.

"Normally we would have support from various other battlefield sources, satellites, seismographs and what-not, telling us a missile had been launched and was incoming, but we can detect them ourselves too. Here we have detected the launch and the Aegis system decides whether we have a chance of a successful intercept."

The ship radiated a series of concentric circles, and when one touched the missile, the circle bounced back.

"Right, this shows we've detected the missile and the system says, "Yes, we can intercept." The VLS will then prep a RIM 161 and begin tracking the target to the optimal time for a launch. When that has been achieved..."

From the graphic of the ship, a small missile launched, arcing toward the much-larger incoming ballistic weapon.

"All throughout, the missile will keep talking to the ship, receiving course corrections as it burns through its stages." On the graphic, spent stages of the missile fell away as the remainder continued on and up. "Finally, the LEAP will be deployed and impact the incoming ICBM, satellite, or whatever."

The image showed the final stage of the missile fall away, leaving a tiny cylinder, the LEAP. It slammed into the missile, and they both disappeared in a bright flash, leaving nothing but a dissipating cloud of pixels. Donovan stopped the video.

"That's pretty impressive." Kendricks looked at the computer schematic of the LEAP with a newfound respect. "How high can one of those hit something?"

"Max ceiling is 1500 kilometers," Donovan said proudly. "Although we would need extra battle-space support to hit something that high."

"You're shitting me?" Kendricks noted the small frown twitch across Donovan's face. Clearly he didn't like bad language. "Sorry, 1500 kilometers. That's real Star Wars stuff."

"Yes, it is," Donovan said. "Quite literally. It's actually one of the few developments from Reagan's original strategic defensive initiative that is currently in operational use. The SDI program was referred to as 'Star Wars' in the media, although that was never its official name, of course."

"So how do we turn this thing into a satellite?"

"Well, it'll never be a satellite," Donovan said. "The missile doesn't have the capability to put the LEAP into orbit. It pretty much goes straight up then, if it hasn't hit something, will fall back down and either burn up on reentry through the atmosphere, or simply splash down somewhere."

"Okay then, let me rephrase. How can we turn it into a mapping device?"

"Our problems are threefold," Donovan said. "First we need to replace the IR sensor head with a decent camera. Two, we need to reprogram the projectile to be able to do what we want it to do, which is basically, when it deploys, turn to face the Earth. Finally, we have to transmit the images through the bus and back to us."

"All that seems easy enough."

"It's not quite that easy. For starters, the camera has to be able to operate in space. Then there are literally thousands of lines of coding that dictate the

LEAP's flight profile. Lastly, the datalink has a very low bandwidth—it'll take seconds to transmit each individual picture. It's essentially just designed to send coordinates in the form of raw numbers. Images are something else and consist of far bigger data packets."

"Right... and are any of them insurmountable problems?" Kendricks asked.

Grinning, Donovan said. "Well, that's what we are going to hash out. The camera replacement especially isn't something we could even attempt with the equipment we have on the *Ignatius*, but with your far more extensive facilities... we might just make this work."

Chapter 27 – Day 10

"Welcome to Nest Island, ladies and gentlemen," the middle-aged farmer drawled slowly, tipping his sunhat at them as he spoke. "It is a pleasure for you to be here with us, providing some more willing hands."

Grayson, along with the six other men and women who had agreed to help with the farming duties, looked around dubiously. The field in front of them promised nothing but backache-inducing toil in the burning hot midday sun. The field was hardly extensive, but the earth looked hard and infested with all kinds of weeds.

"May I be suggestin' a hat for tomorrow for those who don't have one today? For now though, I'll just be a inductin' y'all," the man said, his name already forgotten to Grayson in the glum realization that this was actually going to be hard work. "What we have on this here island, is a cross-section of all the fruits and vegetables that we managed to get seed stock from, between all our boats. I'm... ah, hoping your big-ass cruise ship can provide some different sustenance to grow, as I for one am getting sick and tired of the boring shit we've managed to cultivate so far."

They were in one of several fields which stretched across most of the relatively flat land

on the island, around two and a half square miles in total. The central island peak dominated the skyline and some curious looking trees were dotted around the edges of the field.

The man standing next to Grayson had an even glummer look on his face than the others.

"Hey, it's not that bad," Grayson whispered at him.

"Oh yes it is," the man murmured. "Back home, I'm a farmer. There's nowhere near enough arable land here to support everyone from the *Atlantica*."

"Well, hopefully we're not going to be here that long. We just have to fend hunger off a little."

"Yeah, right," the man said distractedly. "You know, a person needs roughly an acre of farmland per year to live off."

"Okay… but the fishing is going to help, surely?"

"It better, or we're just going to be trying to fill up a bucket with no bottom." The man squinted at the edge of the field. "And just what the hell is it with those trees? I've never seen anything like them."

Grayson glanced at them. Sure enough, they were of a type that was common on the scattered islands of the region, but would have been new to the man. They were similar to palm trees, except the leaves were thicker, much thicker, like slabs of green flesh rather than the thin leaves of back home. And every leaf was orientated so the flat edge was facing the sun. Glancing at the other trees, Grayson saw the same thing. He knew that the flat edge would track the direction of the sun throughout the day like actuated solar cells. It was a curiosity of the region. Grayson certainly couldn't recall ever having seen a tree like it before he arrived here.

"I don't know, they just look like palm trees to me," Grayson lied.

"Yeah. Okay," the man scowled distractedly.

Chapter 28 – Day 11

"And this is what you've come up with to slap on the top of one of my missiles?" Slater squinted at the piece of paper. It certainly wasn't an exact blueprint, but it did show the general concept of what Donovan and Kendricks had managed to put together. "It frankly looks like shit."

"Ma'am!" Donovan admonished through gritted teeth.

Reynolds gave a snort of suppressed laughter from where he stood, leaning against the bulkhead of the captain's small grey cabin, which doubled as her office.

Kendricks grimaced as he looked around. There wasn't anything approaching the privacy of the *Atlantica*. If Slater wanted to talk to people alone, it was in her neatly ordered personal space next to her single bunk. Running alongside the bunk was a recessed shelf. It was full of thick folders, books and texts, everything from the rather imaginatively titled *"Captain's Manual"* to *"Sun Tzu's – The Art of War"*. Nestled at one end, closest to Slater's pillow, was a small picture frame. The enclosed photograph showed a handsome middle-aged man with his arms around a beaming Heather Slater, who in turn had her arms around a young girl. To Kendricks, the normality of the captain in that picture was in total contrast to the hard woman before him.

"Apologies, Perry," Slater said absently as she picked up the A3 sheet and turned it around in her hands. "Okay, walk me through it."

Plucking the paper out of Slater's hands, Donovan flattened it on the desk. On it was a drawing of the LEAP's sensor module, a small cylinder that would fit inside the slightly larger cylinder that was the projectile itself.

"We're going to take out the IR sensor completely and replace it with this camera," Donovan held up the expensive-looking, but still very normal digital camera in his hand. "Of course, we'll be taking it out of the casing, basically leaving just the working parts. They should be small enough to fit inside the LEAP. The hard bit is that we need to harden the camera to both the stresses of launch, and the varied thermal conditions it will be subjected to..."

"Which is where *Atlantica's* 3D printers and workshops come in," Kendricks smoothly took over. "We'll produce a module that the camera will fit into, which we can then plug and play into the slot where the IR sensor had been."

"Okay," Slater said dubiously. "You are aware this damn... this thing is going into space?"

Ignoring his captain's curse, Donovan said, "Yes, the module we come up with will be airtight and well insulated. The functionality shouldn't be affected by the vacuum, at least for the time period it'll have to be operational. To cope with the quintessential stresses of launch, we've come up with this novel solution..."

On cue, Kendricks pulled a can of tire-inflator foam out of his pocket. They'd found it in the puncture repair kit for the forklift trucks down in

Atlantica's holds. "We will fill the module spaces with this stuff. That will be enough to protect the camera itself, and will also help with insulating the electronics."

"And how are you going to interface that camera to the LEAP itself so we can actually get some pictures back?" Slater asked, impressed at their ingenuity despite herself.

"By trusty USB, of course," Donovan smiled. "The control board on the LEAP is pretty much off the shelf. Thanks to it being designed by the lowest bidder, the cabling has standard connectors - it's just they're a vacuum hardened version. We can just plug it in. We'll then work with..."

"Tricia Farelly," Kendricks helped him out.

"Tricia, *Atlantica's* head of IT, to reprogram the LEAP to be able to process the pictures and it will send them back along the datalink. She'll also help out with reprogramming the LEAP's flight profile. Basically, when it deploys, it'll turn the camera lens to face straight back down toward Earth and start sending us pictures."

"Gentlemen," Slater exchanged a quick glance at Reynolds who was smiling in the corner. "I have to tell you, I'm still nervous about letting you mess with one of my RIM 161s. When we get home, you can be sure as hell the Pentagon will be asking some rather pointed questions as to why I fired one off."

"Heather," Reynolds said. "You've waited here at this island for two years and not been rescued. If one of my commanding officers had shown this kind of initiative in such a circumstance, I'd be more inclined to give them a medal than a reprimand."

"I think you may be underestimating the bean-counting nature of the Pentagon," Slater smiled despite herself. "But okay. Get the ball rolling. Test the replacement module. I don't know how — set it on fire, put it in a freezer, and then throw it at a wall. If it survives all that, then I might be willing to say yes."

"Yes, ma'am." Donovan's expression was one of pride for his expected new baby. "Oh, about that testing?"

"What?" Slater asked slowly.

"I'm going to need another missile for that. Just something small," Donovan beamed brightly.

"Perry, if I say yes, will you let me swear every now and again without looking at me disapprovingly?"

"Yes, ma'am."

"Then just do it."

***

The *Liliana* was motionless on the open sea, seventy-five miles north of Nest Island, having circumscribed a long arc around it.

"Are you sure you want to go yourself, Urbano?" the *Liliana's* first mate, Davey Grainger, asked.

"Yup," Bautista said as he placed jerry cans of fuel into the gently rocking inflatable boat, enough to get him to Nest Island and back again. Finally, he grabbed the rucksack that he was going to deliver to Grayson and gently stowed it under the plastic seat.

"Let's hope all those days on a floating palace haven't made him go soft." Grainger said with a grin.

"I somehow doubt it," Bautista said as he climbed into the boat and pushed himself away from the side of the hull. "If I'm not back in three days, head home and tell Vaughan not to come."

"No problems."

Bautista gave a nod and started the engine. He swept the boat around in a long arc and raced away from the *Liliana*.

Chapter 29 – Day 12

Letting the rake drop to the ground, Grayson placed his hands in the small of his back and felt his shoulders pop.

"I'm going to take my thirty minutes," he called over to the foreman, who merely grunted in response as he broke a patch of sun-hardened ground with a pick. The weathered old man seemed to have resigned himself to the fact that the soft folk from *Atlantica* had to be eased into hard labor gently.

Grabbing his rucksack from the edge of the field, he slung it over his shoulder and began walking toward the shade of a copse of the weird-looking palm trees, well away from the field.

Entering the shadows, Grayson glanced around, checking to see if anyone was within earshot. No one was.

Reaching into his rucksack, he pulled out his CB radio and turned the dial on the top, switching it on, and was greeted by a crackle of static.

"Rain," Grayson wasn't expecting a response. The watch boats were well away from Nest Island to prevent detection by the *Ignatius*, which made it even more surprising when he heard the countersign.

"Desert," Bautista's familiar accented voice responded.

Hunkering down behind a tree, Grayson hissed into the radio, "Urbano, what the hell am I still doing here? Get me extracted."

"Karl, we will get you away as soon as we can, but for now I have a job for you. I need you to meet me at the northern tip of the island, where there's a small peninsula. 11 pm tonight. Out."

"Shit!" Grayson scowled at the radio, before switching it off and slipping it back into his rucksack.

He glanced back at the work party. Giving a shrug, he stretched out his feet, leaning against the trunk of the tree.

If I'm not getting out of here, I may as well take my full thirty minutes.

***

The industrial-scale 3D printers were set in a room deep in the hull of *Atlantica*. They ranged in size from a microwave to a chest freezer, and were there to produce everything from replacement engine components to the sometimes-bizarre item requests the stewards received from passengers. It was one of the many innovations Crystal Ocean Lines had equipped *Atlantica* with in order to make the ship that much more efficient.

The problem was, what they wanted wasn't in the ship's design catalogue, which was why Tricia Farelly had spent the afternoon on the computer-aided design - CAD - console, following Donovan's specifications — effectively designing the camera module from scratch. But finally, she was ready.

"Right, we're building this thing from ceramic. It's not going to be exactly space-age stuff, but it will do the job," Farelly said, then finished quietly, "I hope."

"Okay, shall we... get started then?" Donovan croaked. The air in the room was incredibly dry. They had placed several dehumidifier units in it, sucking every piece of moisture out of the air they could. It had occurred to Donovan that they would need to prevent condensation from forming on the lens cover when it was in the cold of space, and that meant working in as arid an environment as possible.

Standing up from her stool, Farelly left the room and came back a minute later with a small grey plastic-covered block. Tearing off the wrapping, Farelly placed it in the 3D printer that was about the size of the microwave, closed the door, walked over to the CAD console, and pressed a button.

The 3D printer began whining, cutting, and hissing. Donovan looked dubiously at the vibrating machine. After a few minutes it pinged, signaling it had finished working the raw material.

"That's it? Donovan asked with incredulity.

"That's it." Farelly said as she opened the door with her gloved hands and pulled out the tiny cylinder within. It was thirty centimeters long and ten wide. "Right, let's start fitting the camera components and we can begin testing."

Looking between the printer, the component in Farelly's hands, and a smirking Kendricks, Donovan finally gave a shrug. "Okay then... I guess."

***

The farming team was staying in a small hut on the beach. If it wasn't for all the rigors of a hard day's work, it would have been idyllic. Instead most of the workers were now snoozing, having just had a large supper, a perk of the job.

Once again taking his leave, Grayson began walking. The sun had set on the horizon, and without the benefit of lighting, there was only the full moon to illuminate the island.

Crossing the fields, he skirted around the base of the foliage-covered peak. After an hour of walking, he reached the northern coast, the complete opposite of where *Atlantica* and *Ignatius* were mated together.

Grayson saw the spit of land where he was meeting Bautista. He started walking down it and as the ground became rougher, began clambering over the rocks and shale. Grayson reached the end. Looking over the edge, he saw a small rubber motorboat bobbing in the water.

"Don't move a muscle." Grayson felt something hard jabbing into his back.

"Urbano, it's me," Grayson said as he raised his hands.

"Karl, good to see you." Bautista moved the gun away from Grayson. The two men were little more than silhouettes in the low light of the moon.

"Please say you've come to take me home, Urbano. These assholes have me farming now."

"Not quite yet." The other man's wry smile at the thought of Grayson working in a field was fortunately invisible. "We need that ship, and you are going to help us take it."

"Last time didn't go so well for you."

"No, no it didn't," Bautista replied. "But this time

it's going to be different."

Grayson listened to Bautista's plan, first in incredulity, then disbelief, and finally with a sense of acceptance. If Grayson wanted to protect and provide for his family, the risks he would have to take would go up. Exponentially.

Chapter 30 – Day 13

"So, will it work or won't it?" Slater asked, turning the small module in her hands, looking at it from every angle. It looked clean and well manufactured; in fact, slightly more impressive than the component it was designed to replace. It was a white foot-long cylinder with a clear screw-on lid. Within she could see the lens of the camera. From the opposite end a cable emerged, waiting to be connected to the LEAP.

"We've tested a duplicate as much as we can," Donovan said. "So far it's survived everything we've thrown at it, including a dry test on a duplicate using a RIM-162. But we still have to add the huge caveat that it's just a jury-rigged device we are putting in a spacecraft."

"Will it work or won't it?" Slater repeated as she placed the module down on the desk and looked Donovan straight in the eyes.

"Yes, ma'am. It will work."

Slater turned to Kendricks who nodded, and then to Reynolds.

"It's the best shot at finding land, Heather. Do it," Reynolds said.

Slater took a long moment to make her final

decision. She was the custodian of the *Ignatius* and her inventory. Captains had always had to account for what they used and why, sometimes in painstaking detail. The Pentagon wouldn't take kindly to her blowing an eleven-million-dollar missile for no reason. The launch of a RIM 161 could be career ending for her at best, possibly criminal in negligence at worst in anything other than the most extreme of circumstances. But she was also the steward of her crew and now the guardian of thousands of people. Why have all this capability and not use it?

"Very well, begin the modifications to the missile. We'll launch on the first cloud-free day we have after that."

"Thank you, ma'am."

"Well, now you've sold me on the idea, there's no point in waiting around," Slater said with a resigned sigh.

***

The vertical launch system was two banks of cells containing *Ignatius's* weapons mix. Due to its powerful first-stage booster, the RIM 161s were situated in the front cells, as far away from the superstructure of the ship itself as the missile could be.

With a whine, the heavily armored hatch of the cell containing the missile they had chosen to modify flipped open, revealing the tip of a white cone in the dark hole.

Giving orders over his radio, Donovan had the missile raised out of the cell, exposing the head of the missile fully.

"Easy fellows," Donovan said redundantly to the two technicians who approached the nose cone with electric screwdrivers. They rolled their eyes and knelt down next to it, laying a manual down by their knees already turned to the disassembly procedure.

"This is getting real now," Kendricks said as he watched them working carefully on the huge missile. One after another, the screws were removed and placed in careful order on a plastic sheet.

"Yeah, don't I know it? If this messes up, it will be the definition of a career-limiting move," Donovan said nervously.

"Let's just hope you have a career to limit." Kendricks grinned.

Within thirty minutes, the cone housing was being winched off the missile, exposing the Light Exo Atmospheric Projectile within. It was disconcertingly small. Barely forty centimeters across and a meter long. If anyone had the will and means to launch a ballistic missile at America, that tiny object might be all that could prevent the death of thousands, if not millions of people.

And now it was going to be used to save them.

After another hour of working around the LEAP, the technicians finally had it dismounted and loaded onto a dolly, ready to be taken inside the *Ignatius* for its modifications.

Chapter 31 – Day 13

"It's not exactly an arsenal if those pirates come for us again, but we have enough to equip a decent-sized team." Jack gestured with a sweep of his hand over the table. On it was an assortment of weapons, including those they had seized from the pirates. "The *Ignatius* has her own armory, but unfortunately she had no Marine detachment embarked at the time of her... arrival."

The captain was inspecting the security room and by extension, Jack.

"Very well," Solberg said as he reached for a handgun and hefted its weight before sighting along it one-handed. Jack placed his hand over the top, forcing the barrel down toward the deck.

"My next job." Jack gently prised the gun out of Solberg's hand and placed it back on the table. "Is going to be ascertaining areas of vulnerability and drilling the regenerated security teams in counter-boarding tactics."

"How many volunteers have you got?"

"Between the remainder of the ship's own security complement, and a few volunteers who are military or police, twenty all told. They will be divided up into two teams, squads if you will—"

"Are they any good?" Solberg interrupted him.

"None of them signed up intending to face a concerted enemy on their vacation, Captain," Jack said pointedly. "They're as good as we can expect from this situation."

"And what about the *Ignatius*, can we have some of their weapons and soldiers?"

"I doubt it. As I said, they had no Marines on board. Ship security and boarding operations were a secondary duty for the crewmembers they do have. In other words, they have their own shit to get on with."

"So be it," Solberg said wearily. "I must tell you, I don't like the thought of having people wandering around with guns on board."

"I get that, Captain. But if a situation develops fast, the security teams would have to come down here, kit up, then deploy to their positions. It would take too long."

"The passengers are nervous enough as it is," Solberg frowned, pondering for a moment. "No, no weapons on show."

Giving an exasperated sigh, Jack mulled it over. "How about a compromise?"

"Young man, I'm the captain of this ship, I'm not overly given to compromising." The irritability on Solberg's face was fully evident.

Asshole, Jack thought, and not for the first time. "What I mean, Captain, is the security teams will be equipped with side arms. They will be relatively easy to conceal. For the other weapons, the shotguns and these rifles we recovered, we can stow them in caches just off the promenade. That will make them easily accessible."

"That seems a little more reasonable," Solberg nodded sagely. "Very well, identify suitable storage facilities. They are to be under lock and key. Only the leaders of the security teams and senior officers are to have access. Fingers crossed Kendricks's little project will mean this situation doesn't last much longer, anyway."

"How's that going?" Jack asked.

"Damned if I know, but I had a look down at *Ignatius* from the deck a few hours ago and they were dicking around with one of their missiles." Solberg shrugged. The captain started to turn, before pausing and looking back. "Oh, have you found Grissom yet?"

"No, Captain. The leads have dried up."

Solberg shook his head in frustration. "Just keep trying. It's been well over a week now. I'm beginning to doubt he's made a gin palace for himself down in the bilge."

"Yeah, Captain. I very much doubt that, too."

Chapter 32 – Day 13

With a subdued grunt, Grayson managed to gain purchase on the edge of one of the two deck overflow pipes, which were low on the stern behind *Ignatius's* flight deck.

Caging covered the hole, preventing anyone from crawling up inside, as was designed, but his fingers could just work their way into the mesh. Slowly, silently, he hauled himself up.

Frowning, Grayson looked up. Above were three pipes mounted horizontally, one above the other. It looked to be a hell of a security risk for the ship, but it did provide him with a fair facsimile of a ladder to make the rest of the way up to the deck.

Finally gripping the edge of the deck he slowly pulled himself up until just his head was over the side. Glancing left and right, he looked for the sentries he knew must be patrolling the area. He couldn't spot them, and that worried him.

It was the dark before dawn, and the majority of the lights were subdued. *Ignatius* may have been getting power from the *Atlantica* now, but that didn't mean she could waste it. In the middle of the gently swaying flight deck sat the Seahawk helicopter, powered down and vulnerable.

Grayson squinted at it, wondering if he should somehow sabotage the helicopter which had been such a bane to them. But could he do so silently and still complete his mission? No. He needed to stay on task.

Hauling over onto the deck, Grayson ran silently on bare feet, shrugging his rucksack off his back as he did so, and ducked under the helicopter fuselage, lying flat beneath.

He went stock still as he finally realized where the sentry was, He could see four legs of a chair and two of person just on the other side of the helicopter fuselage. Grayson cocked his head, and he could just hear the sound of heavy breathing over the sound of the sea.

Pulling a small hand towel out his rucksack, he silently dried himself, keeping one eye on the legs, watching for any movement. He doubted his wet footprints would be visible on the low lighting of the flight deck but when he had to go inside, it would be a different matter.

Sliding himself back out from under the helicopter, Grayson glanced up. The hull of *Atlantica* rose in a sheer white and blue cliff face to the starboard of the *Ignatius*. It would be awkward for anyone to look down on his position, and he hoped most would be inside, tucked up in their cabins anyway. No, he was not too concerned about people on board the *Atlantica*, but he was concerned about the *Ignatius's* night watch, even if it did look like they were using the opportunity to catch up on sleep.

There were two hanger bay doors forward of the flight deck and both were open, subdued lighting shining out of the cramped, pipe and conduit-strewn space. Grayson knew they were a dead-end; the only access out of the hangers was by the huge roller shutter doors.

So, that's why we've only seen one helicopter. Another Seahawk, with rotor blades folded back so it could fit within, nestled in the starboard hanger. The helicopter's fuselage access panels were open and it looked to be in a state of partial disassembly. *They must be cannibalizing one of the Seahawks to keep the other flying.*

Darting a look back to where he knew the guard was snoozing, Grayson made his way to one side of the hanger door where there was a hatch leading into the interior of the ship. Looking through the tiny porthole, he could see the access corridor beyond was clear and, with one more look back at the sleeping guard, he quietly un-dogged the hatch and slipped inside.

Grayson padded down the corridor, every sense stretching out to detect any crew, but other than the hum of electronics, the ship was silent. He slipped through another bulkhead door and found himself in a corridor with messes off either side.

A hatch opened and a figure stepped out of one of the messes and looked though bleary eyes at Grayson. Grayson stopped dead in his tracks, tensing. The man muttered something inaudible and rubbed his eyes.

"Me first," the crewmember repeated.

The man sleepily crossed the corridor, opened up a hatch with "head" stencilled on it, and entered.

Grayson let out a long exhalation, the adrenaline coursing through his body reaching new heights and almost pushing him into fight or flight mode. Shaking his head, he set off again, walking past the head.

Finally, he reached the hatch and exited into the night. He found himself behind the towering bridge superstructure upon which radar domes, and communications masts speared high into the sky.

This bit would be a little easier. He had a nice convenient ladder to climb, and was in an area of the ship that even with the bustle of regular daytime business would be deserted.

Climbing to the top of the superstructure, he found himself at the base of the cluster of antennas and radar at the top, the eyes and ears of the deadly warship.

Once again, he reached into his rucksack and pulled out a small package and unwrapped it. Glancing around, he found a dark, secluded area to place it, and wedged it as far out of sight as he could.

Giving a grimly satisfied nod, he climbed back down the ladder and headed toward the side of the ship. *There's no way I'm going back through there.* Grayson thought as he climbed over the railing and let himself drop into the black sea below.

Chapter 33 – Day 14

"It's a fine day, Captain." Slater smiled at her counterpart from the *Atlantica*.

"Yes it is," Solberg said, glancing up at the clear blue skies, not a single cloud evident above them.

The RIM 161 was ready, and today was the day they would finally get some answers. Or that was the plan, at least.

"Ladies and gentlemen, if you'd be so kind as to join me in the CIC." Slater waved her hand toward the hatch leading into the superstructure.

"May I stay on deck?" Laurie asked. "I would love to see the missile launch."

"Unfortunately not. The reason we have moved so far clear of the *Atlantica* is because of the engine wash of the missile. There would be nothing left but ash if we put you anywhere where you would actually be able to watch from, and the bridge is going to have the blinds down," Slater replied. "If you wanted to watch the actual launch, *Atlantica* or the island were the places to do it, I'm afraid."

Slater opened the hatch and led Solberg, Kendricks, Reynolds and his disappointed daughter within, and down to the now-bustling CIC. The screens were covered with schematics of Earth and CCTV images of the launch cells.

"Perry," Slater walked to her executive officer's seat. "Are we good to go?"

"Yes, ma'am," Donovan said as he looked at his console. The screen was filled with complicated diagrams and indecipherable-looking acronyms. "All systems are checking out."

"And, Mack, are you ready to cast your keen eyes over the images?"

"Yes, ma'am. Ready and eager." Mack grinned.

"Good stuff. Let's be about it then shall we?" Slater replied.

With a grin, Donovan tapped his console. On one of the screens a graphical representation of the fore launch cells appeared and one of them began blinking red.

"On your go, Perry."

"Aye ma'am. I'm ready. We'll be launching in 10, 9, 8..."

***

Along with as many of the passengers and crew who could fit on *Atlantica's* deck, Jack watched the distant *Ignatius*, which appeared as little more than a toy.

Leaning forward onto the railings, he checked his watch. *Any time now.*

***

"Guys, if you want to watch, now is the time to do it," The foreman called.

Turning, Grayson leaned on his hoe and looked down the incline of the field to the beach and sea beyond.

From the distant warship, a piercingly bright flash of light appeared, followed by a rumble like distant thunder. The whole ship became occluded by a cloud of smoke.

If Grayson hadn't known better, he would have been surprised that the ship was still there when the cloud cleared, such was the apparent fury of the launch.

Frowning, Grayson's thoughts turned to the package he had deposited.

***

At first, a geyser of fire erupted from the vents on the side of the launch cell with a ferocity that seemed like it would destroy the *Ignatius*. It appeared a volcano was erupting through the bow of the ship. A second later, the white missile itself raced out.

There was none of the gentle, majestic rise of a space shuttle launch. The RIM 161 was designed to launch without consideration to human comforts; its job to get into space as quickly as possible.

On a column of fire and with a deafening roar, the missile streaked skywards. The bulky Mark 72 booster on the base of the weapon burned hard to fight against the gravitational shackles of the Earth.

Within sixty seconds, the booster burned out. The explosive bolts attaching the booster to the missile detonated and it was jettisoned. Already high above the surface, the booster began falling back toward the sea.

***

"We have stage one separation, ma'am," Donovan called excitedly. "The Mark 72 has been released cleanly. Stage two ignition is... looking good. Altitude twelve km, down range two km. She's going pretty much straight up like she should."

***

The cloud of smoke slowly cleared, revealing the unharmed *Ignatius*. Grayson gave a sigh of relief. The launch didn't look like it had caused any... unforeseen events.

Holding his hand up to block the blazing sun, Grayson looked up at the slowly dissipating column of smoke stretching straight up into the sky.

***

The stage two rocket was firing just as savagely as the stage one had, but now, without the weight of the heavy booster, the missile could actually control herself properly.

The flight control computer checked and rechecked the path that had been programmed in for her, fighting to keep to it, even as the atmosphere started to thin out and the control surfaces at the base of the missile had less air to bite into.

***

"Time elapsed three minutes, altitude is now

thirty km, down range six km, and we are at Mach 1.6. Beautiful!" Donovan cried out. "We have good chamber pressure in the one oh four. Temperature is looking good. Everything is on the button."

***

Mark 104 duel-thrust booster took the small missile higher, the curvature of the Earth becoming more and more pronounced as the missile rose. The deafening roar of the engine had stopped far below. Now the missile was racing upwards soundlessly as the air thinned. It wasn't in space yet, but it was a good portion of the way there.

The missile streaked ever higher, spearing through the mesosphere and then thermosphere.

Finally, it reached space.

***

"Stage two separation... Now!" Donovan cried out as he checked his console. "Altitude ninety km, down range fifteen km. We are at Mach 7.1."

***

The cylinder of the Mark 101 engine seemed to drift away from the rear of the missile, falling below slightly before being incinerated by the much smaller third-stage rocket engine erupting into life. The now far-lighter missile head streaked upward at an even more furious rate of acceleration, unencumbered by the rest of the rocket.

***

"Altitude five hundred km, ma'am. We're leaving the International Space Station far behind now. Down range fifty km and we are at Mach 12.8. Ts and Ps are still good. Standby." An urgent beeping came from Donovan's console. He frowned, quickly tapping away at his keyboard. "Looks like the guidance system is interrogating the *Ignatius* about why it isn't receiving information on a target and it's counting down for a self-destruct."

A single bead of sweat trickled down Donovan's cheek as he frantically worked at his console. After a moment he gave a sigh of relief as the beeping stopped. "Self-destruct canceled." Donovan glanced briefly at Slater. "Apologies, Ma'am. Must have missed a fail-safe. We're looking good now."

***

The engine throttled down and the flame torch flickered to nothing. With the release of more explosive bolts, the final stage was left to begin its long fall to the surface seven hundred km below. The pointed nose cone popped off and tumbled away, releasing the tiny LEAP. The monopropellant thrusters began firing on the LEAP, lances of white-hot flame burning to keep the projectile on course.

***

"The LEAP has been released, ma'am. It will begin its rotation shortly. It'll continue straight up ballistically until we reach around nine hundred km, then it will begin coming down. We didn't program for higher than that as we may lose the data-link without battle-space support."

***

The small drum that was the LEAP continued to fire its thrusters in short, violent spurts, turning the seeker head back toward the Earth.

Even from more than twice the altitude which the ISS orbited, the Earth was huge, filling the sky. The vast ball of green, blues, yellows, and whites drifted in front of the camera as the LEAP rotated.

As if designed for the purpose from scratch, the camera started taking its pictures and squeezed the images down the datalink to the ship far below.

***

"Datalink is holding... we're getting the first image come through," Donovan shouted.

On one of the large screens, a picture began to appear, thin line by thin line, like an image being downloaded on an exceptionally slow internet connection.

"Well done, you two, well done," Slater murmured as the image loaded itself onto the screen with painstaking slowness.

"We are now at nine hundred km, and beginning to fall back. Datalink is weakening but holding as we expected. Just a waiting game now, ma'am.

The image filtered down slowly but surely, then another, then another.

Mack looked at the display closely. Her eyes were practiced at picking at small and subtle details from far above, a skill that she had cultivated in her long years as a pilot... a skill which she didn't now need. What was before her on the screen was so obvious. And so terrifying.

"Oh shit," Mack whispered.

Chapter 34 – Day 14

"That's a lot of ships," Davey said. "I've never seen them all together at once."

"That's everything we have," Bautista replied. The two men were on the bridge of the *Liliana*, surveying the ragtag fleet which had assembled around the *Titan*.

There was a mix of everything from the graceful lines of island hopper ferries to dirty, workman-like fishing trawlers, and every kind of craft between. Twenty in total.

"If *Ignatius* can still fight, we're going to lose them all," Davey murmured. "That helicopter's going to be bad enough, but that warship will rip us all apart."

"Karl's last message said he'd managed it," Bautista said with more confidence than he felt. "We'll be fine."

The *Liliana* sailed in closer to the *Titan*, the flagship of what was now an armada.

***

"This can't be," Solberg said in disbelief as he stared at the CIC master screen. "What the hell has happened?"

The best image they had was on the display. Much of it was obscured by roiling masses of white cloud, but enough was uncovered to show the major landmasses.

A large section of the North and South American eastern coasts were visible and recognizable, yet they were folded in toward each other as if they were a mouth closing on Nest Island's location. Both continents were much farther west than they should have been.

Most features on the mainland had changed. The peninsula of Florida was half of its original size, only a stumpy central spine visible. The coastlines were all different as well, with strange new bays and protrusions of land. It was only the overall shape which was roughly the same.

"Nothing could have done this." Slater looked intently at the display, her voice tight but controlled. "There are no weapons in the inventory which could come close."

"Well, something did," Solberg whispered.

"Could that polar shift have anything to do with this?" Slater glanced at Laurie.

Laurie swallowed before shaking her head. "No, that would just effect the orientation of the poles, I can't see how it would have done anything physical to the... to the geography."

"Something is starting to make sense, though," Kendricks said slowly, forming the words carefully as his mind processed what he was seeing.

"Pray tell," Solberg didn't even look at him, just carried on focusing on the display.

"Continental drift. Every continent moves slowly,

right?"

"Yes," Laurie said. She moved over to stand before the screen, regarding it carefully. "But that's a slow movement. Tiny. I think it's something like a few centimeters a year."

"Yeah, but think about it. We're getting all kinds of temporal weirdness here. We have ships in this region that have appeared years before others. What if we've somehow gone backward or forward in time. That would explain," Kendricks paused then gestured at the screen. "This."

"That is ridiculous," Solberg said, without his usual fire. "How the hell would that happen? You're talking like we've dropped down some kind of... some kind of time hole."

Those in the room could only shrug.

***

The ships and boats of the fleet had clustered around the huge flagship, *Titan*. As one, they came about and began to sail in the direction of the fiery setting sun.

Chapter 35 – Day 15

"Passengers and crew," Solberg swallowed, his voice catching. He lowered the microphone to his waist and cleared his throat, looking over the collected mass of people gathered in the promenade. *How am I to tell them, when not even I understand?* Bringing the microphone to his lips again, he started speaking again, "Passengers and crew. Yesterday, as you saw, the *USS Paul Ignatius* launched one of its missiles with the express purpose of using it to map the area. We have the results of that now."

There was silence across the promenade. Thousands of people just looking at Lars Solberg. He slowly turned around on the span, to address the people behind him.

"We have spent the time since trying to process what we have seen, to understand it. What the missile showed was that..." Solberg paused again. "It shows that the world is not as we know it."

A murmur washed over the crowd. Everyone looked at him intently.

"The world has changed. The continents have moved, that is why we were lost."

"How?" a voice shouted out of the crowd. A single spokesman for the thousands clustered down in the promenade.

"We don't know," Solberg could only hold up his hands at the torrent of noise that responded to him. The anger and fear was palpable.

Slowly, over long minutes while Solberg held his arms up, trying to placate them, the noise subsided, with one last cry of, "And what about our families?" ringing out.

"We don't know," Solberg repeated. "But what we do know is that we are safe on board the *Atlantica*. We have the protection of the United States Navy and we will do our utmost to get you all home. And I do promise you that, that we will get you home."

Solberg lowered the microphone again, more aware than ever the promise he had just made, he might not be able to keep.

***

"We need an objective; a light at the end of the tunnel, whatever you want to call it," Reynolds said. He was seated at the head of the table in the conference room. It had been a subtle shift of power, the two senior captains deferring to the older man's presence.

"And what do you propose?" Slater asked, tapping her pen lightly on the table edge.

"There are two obvious ones," Reynolds said. With a groan, he stood and went to the screen, displaying the map of the now-strange world. He pointed at the distant coast of America, what would have been the Eastern Seaboard before the jaws of the two continents had started to close. "Somewhere along here are three major cities—New York, Philadelphia, and Washington—or where they should roughly be, anyway. With the clear and obvious... flooding that has occurred upon the Floridian peninsula, they would be the best bet for some kind of survivors of this catastrophe. They are certainly the closest major cities to our current location."

"If we go by Liam's hypothesis though, those cities might not even be there anymore, or not exist yet," Slater said quietly. "Whichever way we are looking at, they won't be there."

"Maybe, but then it is certainly something we need to discover, and sooner rather than later."

"You said two obvious objectives?" Kendricks asked.

"Yes, the second one is that in a couple of weeks this locus, whatever that may be, will appear. That may be our only chance of establishing just what has happened."

Slater regarded the map with her cool blue eyes. After a moment she began speaking, "We are extremely limited by our current fuel loads. While *Atlantica* can make the journey to the Eastern Seaboard, or the Southeastern Seaboard as it now is and back, unless she is willing to offload a substantial portion of fuel to the *Ignatius*, we cannot. Bottom line though, if we go in convoy, once we make for the States, we are going to be stuck there."

"Exactly," Reynolds nodded. "That is why that, although the temptation is to make straight for the mainland, we need to resist it. The most efficient use of our supplies would be to remain here until we can investigate this locus and then, if need be, we can push on to the U.S."

"But we do have another concern." Solberg had

been subdued, depressed even since the first pictures from the LEAP had come in, his usual cutting nature diminished. "Food. We are using it up at a far faster rate than we can replenish. Even with those work parties we sent. We aren't going to get anything close to a substantial crop for weeks."

Reynolds leaned back and looked across the table. The most critical issue was feeding the thousands aboard the *Atlantica* and the hundreds on Nest Island, and there was no easy solution. There was a supply and demand problem that simply couldn't be closed.

"The two fishing trawlers we have are working overtime," Slater said. "They are the only way of even beginning to stem that particular tide. But yes, we're going to have to hope that either this locus is able to return us, or when we reach the coast we can find food, no matter what condition the country is in."

"And what condition is the country going to be in?" Solberg waved his hand at the map display on the conference table. "Even if everyone came through this event with us, then the damage to the infrastructure will be immense."

"A good point," Reynolds agreed. "There is the very real possibility that even with our current logistical problems, we might face the prospect of being in far better shape than anyone on the coast."

"My first instinct," Slater said slowly, "is that we have to consider what relief we may be able to offer. But then the practical side of me says—"

"That we have no relief to offer," Reynolds interrupted. "Heather, the thought we may not be able to help anyone is painful to you. I know this, because that is my feeling too. But what is the cardinal rule of first aid?"

"Don't become a casualty yourself," Slater said quietly.

"Exactly. If there are survivors, we should—no must—help them. But we have to do it in the most effective way. We will assess when we get there and render aid in a controlled manner."

"If we are able to," Solberg said pointedly. "We are going to have no food to offer."

"If we are able to," Reynolds repeated.

Chapter 36 – Day 15

"One, two, three, four…" Jack counted the small plastic boxes on the security room table, each containing one hundred rounds of 9mm Parabellum ammunition, tapping them with his pen nib as if to confirm their existence.

Satisfying himself, he put a tick on his clipboard which contained a list of what he was taking to the island. There wasn't nearly enough ammunition to do a full range day, but he wanted his security recruits at least to be refreshed on firing an actual weapon. He was willing to let them use a few rounds for training.

Walking over to the armory itself, Jack unlocked the door with the two keys he now had possession of and began counting out the handguns.

"Hey," he heard from behind him.

Turning, he gave a smile as he saw Laurie stood in the doorway of the office. "You're not supposed to be allowed in here."

"I used my feminine wiles." She returned his smile as she came in to the room.

"I really need to have a word with security if just a pretty face is getting you past them," he said in a joking manner. *And I actually do as well. This is just the kind of thing that needs to stop. Still, it's good to see her.* Jack gestured at one of the chairs. "Take a seat."

Sitting down, Laurie glanced over the table full of ammunition boxes and cleaning kits. "So you're going to be training these guys commando-style?"

"I wish. But no. They all have firearms experience. I just need to get them shooting again, and make sure there's no 'Walter Mitty' types who have been exaggerating about their experience."

"Yeah, I imagine there might be more than one of them." She picked up one of the ammunition boxes and gave it an experimental rattle, hearing the noise from within.

"Any more news?"

"No," Laurie sighed, placing the box down. "Not yet. People are scared but there are just no answers to give them. We'll make for the locus, and if whatever is there can help us, then hopefully we are going home, otherwise…" She trailed off, giving a helpless shrug.

Turning back to what he was doing, Jack opened one of the black foam-lined plastic cases, and began clearing the handguns in a deft, confident manner and placed them carefully within.

He heard a sniff from behind and looked back, and saw Laurie cupping her face, her shoulders rocking. Pausing, he didn't know what to do. Her behavior was a stark contrast to her sunny demeanor of a few seconds ago.

Hesitantly, he approached, then stood over her and lay a hand on her shoulder. She leaned into him, her cheek buried in his stomach as she began sobbing.

He began stroking her hair, making cooing noises. "It's okay. We'll be okay."

Pulling back, she looked at him, her eyes red. "It won't be. You haven't seen it. Everything's changed. Everything! And we're trapped and we're not going home. There's bloody pirates trying to take over the ship given half a chance, and assuming we survive them, we're either going to slowly starve to death or end up drifting without fuel. How can we be okay?"

Awkwardly bending his prosthetic leg with his hand, Jack knelt next to Laurie so he was looking her in the eyes. "It will be. We've got a warship to protect us and we have a destination. Let's not write ourselves off before we've exhausted those options."

"How can you be so bloody calm all the time?" she snapped.

"You just need to break big problems down to little problems, then kick their asses." Jack replied, taking her hands in his. "Take my... problem from a few months ago. I lose a leg? That's a big problem. I need to figure out how to walk again? That's another big problem... but if I can overcome that, then I overcome the problem of having only one leg. And how do you walk?"

"By taking steps."

"By taking steps," Jack nodded. "Pretty small, uncertain steps at first, but gradually getting bigger. Eventually, after a while, you get to be able to run again. Then all of a sudden, the lack of a leg isn't so big a problem anymore."

Laurie looked at him for a moment before giving a sniff. "And what's the next problem to overcome on that front, Jack?"

Jack looked down. "I don't know. I don't think

there are any more stages. I can run, can't I?"

"I think there is. I think you need to accept what everyone else here already does."

"What's that?"

"Accept that you are just as much of a man now as you were before. That someone can still want you."

Jack was quiet for a long moment before starting to speak slowly. "I was engaged to someone. Before I went to The Vortex, to Syria, I mean. She came to see me while I was in the hospital. Told me she was leaving me, that she had met someone else while I was away." Jack swallowed. The shrink had tried to tease this out of him, but he hadn't wanted to say anything. He hadn't told anyone, in fact. "She kept looking at the bed sheet. She could see it was flat where it shouldn't have been. She kept saying it was nothing to do with my injury, that she would have left me anyway, but she kept looking. Then she left and I never saw her again."

With a grunt, he stood up. "I always wondered whether it was an excuse, or if it was real that she'd met someone. And if it was real and if I was... whole, could I have won her back?"

"Jack, that's awful." The tear that rolled down her face was no longer because of her fear, it was because of her sadness for him.

Shrugging, Jack turned to the table, pretending to busy himself there, but in reality doing nothing more than shuffling a few of the ammunition boxes around.

"We're not all like that," Laurie said.

"Maybe." Jack piled the boxes, one on top of another, the movement serving no purpose beyond giving his hands something to do. "Maybe I just need time to realize that."

"Boss?" a voice called from the hatch. One of the few surviving original security officers, Josef, stood in the entry, breaking the moment. "I just came down to see if you need a hand?"

Jack glanced at the woman before him. She gave a nod and said, "That's fine. I just have to... I just have to go and do something."

She stood and kept her face angled away from the young security guard as she hustled out of the room.

Josef watched her leave, an appreciative look on his face. When she was safely out of earshot, he broke out in a grin. "I wasn't interrupting anything, was I?"

***

"You got everything? Good, then let's get aboard the *Atlantica* and start cashing in on some of our hard-earned privileges." The foreman said with a whoop.

Grayson was a fit man, but even his back had started to constantly ache under the long days of working the fields. The good news was now there were a hell of a lot more volunteers starting to come over since the announcement by Captain Solberg, the news of which had filtered its way to the island.

The work party was waiting at the end of the pier, watching the mega lifeboat make its way through the early morning mist. Slowly the large boat chugged its way in, finally nestling against the rickety creaking wood. The calls of the shore hands and the crew echoed back and forth as the boat was secured.

Grayson watched, his hands pressing into the

small of his back as dozens of people disembarked. The days of the mega lifeboats taking a fraction of what they could carry were well and truly over. Now they only moved when they were nearing capacity so as to be as efficient as possible.

He saw some of the people he'd previously identified as security officers. Some of them were carrying black plastic cases, some even had mannequins from the promenade shops awkwardly lofted over their shoulders.

Range day, huh? Well, everyone needs ensure they keep their skills and drills up to scratch. Once the crowd of people had moved down the pier, Grayson and his new friends climbed aboard the mega lifeboat.

And if most of the security is on the island, then who's protecting the Atlantica?

Chapter 37 – Day 16

"Step to the firing line!" Jack shouted. The earplugs that he had taken from the *Atlantica's* engine room muffled most of the sound, leaving only the loudest noises and the ringing of his own tinnitus.

As one, the five security recruits trudged forward across the dry dirt and rock, careful to keep their handguns pointed down the makeshift range toward the mannequins and turquoise blue sea beyond.

"Make ready!"

As one, the recruits drew the slides on the top of their handguns back and released them.

"To your target in front… go on!" There was a brief hesitation, as if they were all nervous to be the first one to shoot. After a long moment, the first shot rang out, followed by a ripple of fire from the others.

Down the range the mannequins disintegrated under the fire. The 9mm rounds smashed into the figures, causing plastic limbs to fly off in every direction. More than one of the figures toppled over.

Maybe the mannequins weren't such a good idea, Jack thought. *But better than empty beer bottles.*

After the last shot, Jack waited a few seconds in case someone was taking their sweet time, before shouting, "Stop… unload and show clear!"

With varying degrees of speed, each of the shooters released their magazines and performed the clearance drill before presenting the gun's empty chambers, muzzles still pointed downrange.

Jack quickly walked past them, repeating "clear," as he checked each weapon.

"Okay, ladies and gents, place the weapons down and step over here for a debriefing." The five shooters came and stood around him in a semi-circle. "Okay, how do you think that went?"

They began to discuss each of their performances. They didn't have proper targets, but at least they could see that the targets were being hit.

"Okay, now more importantly, why the delay before the first of you fired?" Jack cut in after letting them talk for a while.

***

"How are they doing?" Laurie asked from where she was seated on the edge of the pier, her legs dangling down.

Jack lowered himself down next to her. "They're okay. Some a bit rusty, but no complete idiots, at least."

"That's good, so your crack commandos are well on the way to being formed. Are they all going to get tattoos that match yours?" Laurie pointed at the one on Jack's right arm.

"Ha." Jack glanced down and slipped up the sleeve of his t-shirt, revealing the crest of the Marine Force Reconnaissance Unit, a pair of wings with a scuba diver etched onto them and a parachute behind. "Yeah, maybe after a little more training."

The day had been long, and Jack was tired from having to concentrate for hours. Every movement was checked, every piece of advice he could think of offered. They didn't have the ammunition to do this many more times, but at least they'd had some live-fire training.

Atlantica and *Ignatius*, along with the few other vessels surrounding them, looked like something out of a brochure as they nestled in the bay. The water was so clear and blue, the sky contained only the faintest wisps of cloud.

It seemed like paradise.

***

Grayson rubbed his tired eyes. He was getting sick of waiting for one of the senior officers to wander past, but at some point, one was sure to. He'd been seated outside of Art Deco at one of the tables for the last three hours, the bustle of the promenade all around him. *Life truly goes on,* Grayson thought. *Even when everything else seems to come crashing down.*

He'd long-since resigned himself since his own arrival that something was very wrong with the rest of the world. The rumors he'd been hearing from the other passengers, as curious and weird as they were, hadn't quite settled into full-scale alarm for him, but still, it was news to him and his brain had been whirling. What the hell did it truly mean that the rest of the world was gone? Surely it couldn't have anything to do with his original reason for being in the Caribbean?

Grayson saw Liam Kendricks walk past Art Deco, breaking his thought process.

"Hey, Staff Captain," Grayson called out.

Kendricks gave a little start and turned to look at him. Grayson noticed his arm was finally out of its sling, but the man was still holding it stiffly and giving the occasional wince.

"Buy you a coffee?" Grayson gestured with his cup. A look crossed Kendricks's face like that of deer trapped in headlights. His eyes darted left and right, seeking an escape route, as Grayson pressed on, "I insist."

"I'm a bit busy right now, Karl. Maybe later."

Standing, Grayson walked out of Art Deco and joined Kendricks on the promenade. He would try a different tack. "Staff Captain, look, I've tried to make myself useful around here. I've already joined one of your work crews. I'm not saying you owe me... God no, you saved my as after all, but we were hearing some pretty strange rumors flying around from when I was on the island shoveling shit. Something about the world being totally different?"

Kendricks gave him a considering look. "Okay, Karl. Yes, things have gotten awful strange. Truth be told, we don't know what to make of it."

Kendricks quickly and succinctly filled Grayson in on what they had found from the launch of the LEAP.

Grayson gave a low whistle. "Okay. Well, where does that leave us?"

"We have to go somewhere. This locus is as good a place as any."

"Yeah," Grayson's mind whirled. Finally, solid new information. After years of being trapped here, something new, something tangible. The question is, would that stop what was coming?

***

Eighty miles from the island, the fleet heaved to. Twenty ships were finishing fitting machine guns onto them. They ranged from relatively modern M240s through FN MAGs to the many ancient PKP Pechenegs they had found stashed in the container ship.

The pirates had even modified a couple of the ships with jury-rigged trebuchets on them, each one ready to launch canisters of fuel that would become improvised explosive devices

One ship even a primitive cannon stretching along its length. Barely tested, probably barely functional, yet nevertheless another testament to the ingenuity of the crew of the fleet.

But now, they were ready and waiting for the sign that they could attack. That the one ship that would be able to fight off all that ingenuity and effort was no longer a threat.

Chapter 38 – Day 16

"I think you should call a halt to the attack," Grayson's crackly voice came from the radio.

Vaughan exchanged a frown with Bautista before lifting the radio mic to his lips. "Karl, this operation has already cost us a lot of fuel. If we turn around now, there's a damn good chance I'd face a mutiny."

"Yes, but they have found something, something that could get us home," Grayson pressed.

"Karl, nothing will get us home. We've been here for years… we've looked and we've looked. Get that thought out of your head."

Vaughan and Bautista were in the cramped radio room of the *Titan*, the analog equipment and dials looked old and dated. They matched the tiredness of the flecked paint and worn nature of the furnishings.

"But—"

"But nothing. You're telling me everyone on that island is up and leaving for this locus? Well, they can out run everything but our fastest ships if they go. Our one chance, our only chance, to take *Atlantica*, and if we're damn lucky *Ignatius*, not to mention those trawlers, is now. With the element of surprise."

"We have to consider that—" Bautista started to

say.

"Don't you start. Stand by for our signal,"
Vaughan snapped.

"Listen, Vaughan—"

"No you listen, Karl," Vaughan snapped, the base
of his fist thudding onto the laminate worktop the
radio set was upon. His calm tone had melted away
to reveal a simmering anger beneath. "Everything we
are doing is for our families, just you remember
that."

The speaker was silent for a long moment. Finally,
a dangerously calm voice came from it, "Are you
threatening my family?"

Bautista shook his head slightly and said quietly
to Vaughan, "You don't want to go down that route.
He's a very dangerous man. You do not want him as
an enemy."

Vaughan clenched his teeth, forcing the anger
back down within before keying the mic. "No, Karl.
I'm merely pointing out what's at stake. If they
decide to up and sail off toward this... locus or
whatever the hell it is, without us, then we might
never track them down again."

The silence drew out for long moments. Finally
Karl responded, "Very well. Tomorrow morning.
1100 hours.

***

Karl lowered the CB radio, grinding his teeth. He
quickly stuffed the radio in his pocket and gripped
the muster deck railing so hard his knuckles turned
white.

That prick thinks he can threaten me and mine? Cold

fury washed through him. He knew about Eric Vaughan's history, the executive who had finally carved a real empire out, not just a business one. He wasn't even convinced Vaughan would go home if he was given a chance. The fact was, here he was the most important person in the community.

Sure he needed his muscle, Bautista, to keep order and to handle the physical side that Vaughan so sorely lacked. And he needed people like Grayson, with the cunning and skills to operate as scouts and saboteurs. And of those scouts? Grayson was the best, given his... interesting background.

Grayson turned from the railing, taking a deep breath and forcing the anger down.

If Vaughan wants to go down that road... well, we'll just see who comes out on top.

Chapter 39 – Day 17

The explosion tore through *Ignatius's* superstructure, ripping a brutal wound in the tower. The radar domes disintegrated in a shower of debris, blinding the deadly warship while the masts and tower itself groaned and creaked. For one long moment, it seemed as if the whole array would topple and fall into the sea. Somehow it remained upright, coming to rest at an angle.

Coughing, Perry Donovan stood up from where he had fallen to the deck of the bridge. His ears were ringing from the explosion going off so close to where he was.

"Rep—" Donovan gave another hacking cough before trying again. "Report!"

Slowly, the other bridge crew shook off the effects of the vicious explosion, and returned to their stations. Some of the consoles were damaged, others had no feeds from outside, but mainly what Donovan wanted to know was, was the damn ship sinking?

"No indications or reports we're taking on water, sir," one young petty officer called out. "It was definitely above the waterline. Seemed like it was on top of us."

"Get damage control parties assembled and coordinated." Donovan wiped blood out of his eyes and glanced upward. He didn't know where it had come from and right now, he didn't have the time to even figure out if it was his or not.

"Sir, most of my feeds are down." The petty officer slapped his console in frustration. "I suggest we shift damage control down to the CIC."

Donovan glanced around the bridge, the screens flickering and the many of the windows smashed. The deck was covered in shards of glass and his bridge officers were nursing cuts and bruises.

"Do it," Donovan said. "And inform the Captain she's better off running the show from down there."

***

Grayson had dropped the small mining remote detonator into the sea as soon as he had pressed the button on the top. Even he had been shocked by the size of the explosion; whatever was in the bomb he'd planted on the radar array of the *Ignatius* had been pretty damn potent.

Now he was amid a throng of people who had ran to the railing surrounding the top deck looking over the damaged warship below. Close to the *Ignatius's* superstructure, part of *Atlantica's* railing had been buckled by the blast. People were injured and the sounds of crying and moaning came from them. The unfortunate people had been too close to the explosion.

Grayson felt a twinge of conscience. He quickly forced it back down. He was doing this for his family. Still, he didn't want to cause more misery than he had to.

Smoothly segueing from instigator to helper, he knelt down next to one moaning old man who was clutching his bleeding face and began checking him over.

"It's okay, it's okay, we'll get you down to the infirmary. I just need you to stay calm…"

***

"Stop!"

The people on the firing points immediately applied the safety catches on their weapons and looked around questioningly. Jack noted, even while distracted, that the security staff all kept their weapons pointed down the range. As they should.

Jack pulled his earplugs out and looked around. The noise he had heard sounded wrong, a bang that was far deeper and more echoing in tone than a gunshot.

He couldn't immediately see what was the source, but something just wasn't right.

***

"The SPS-67 is down," a CIC technician called.

"Noted," Slater said as she switched her console over to display her ship's status. The room had erupted with activity since the explosion. Many of the screens and consoles in the CIC were flickering or down completely, the feeds damaged or destroyed. People checked and rechecked their equipment, pulling together damage reports and figuring out just what the hell had happened.

"Same with the SPS-73, we've got a judder in the AN/SPY... no it's gone offline, too. We've lost all surface search ability."

"Noted." *Shit, we are completely blind. This wasn't an accident, this was a deliberate surgical strike,* Slater thought grimly.

"Captain, I have *Atlantica* on the radio. She's asking if we require assistance."

"Negative. Tell them we're watertight, we're assessing damage now. My compliments to Captain Solberg, but we need to square our shit away before we have a crowd of people on board."

Flicking the intercom to the bridge, she called up to Donovan, "Perry, secure the ship. I want us away from *Atlantica*. This was a surgical attack on our radar systems. Until we grip whatever the hell is going on, I want some space between us and anyone else."

"Aye, ma'am. Securing to move now."

***

A dozen speedboats, each containing five men, were the first wave. They hit the beach at full speed and slid up the golden sand with a hiss. They had beached themselves on the opposite side of the island from where *Ignatius* and *Atlantica* were, using the island itself as cover. The men and women on board jumped out, their weapons ready and began sprinting up the incline of the beach toward the tree line.

Behind them were the heavier boats containing even more people. And behind them, the ships which would circumnavigate the island and launch the attack proper.

***

"I*gnatius* is casting off and requesting we secure ourselves." Kendricks watched the CCTV camera image of the wounded destroyer. The smoke was rapidly clearing as a last flickering flame was unable to take proper hold on the warship's armored structure.

"By all means, let's give them a little room," Solberg nodded. "And get our security team ready. It looks like we could have big problems coming our way."

"Sir, the majority are on the island on a training exercise."

"What the hell is the use of a ship security team if they're not on the ship?" Solberg barked incredulously. Shaking his head in disgust, he

keyed the intercom. "Whoever's left in security, get ready. And someone get that LRAD up on deck."

***

A thin column of black smoke was visible to Jack back in the direction of the ships.

"Guys, secure your weapons, we're heading back. Now."

It was then that the first of the popping sound of gunshots came from the direction of the fields.

Chapter 40 – Day 17

"General Quarters. All hands to general quarters," Slater's measured voice rang out over the 1MC.

Mack pulled on her olive green flight suit and grabbed her helmet out of her locker before running for the flight deck on the stern of the *Ignatius.*

"Come on, people, let's go," she shouted to her crew who were following on behind.

Climbing into the cockpit of her Seahawk, she tugged on her gloves, began flicking switches, going through the process of bringing her helicopter to life. Her copilot dropped into his seat next to her. Quickly they worked through the pre-flight checklist, stopping just before engine start-up.

Fuel still had to be saved.

"*Ignatius*, Sierra Hotel 1-1. We are holding at engine start-up. Let's get loaded up with a couple of AGM-114s while we're waiting to see what's what. I don't want to be caught short this time," Mack called out.

The armorers quickly responded, drawing two of the missiles out of the blast lockers. They were loaded onto dollies and wheeled over to the helicopter.

***

"Come on folks, get loaded up. Those that have handled rifles before, take one." Jack picked up one of the M16A4s. He loaded a magazine into it before pulling back on the charging handle and releasing it. The handle slammed forward, making the weapon ready.

A couple of the others did the same while the rest quickly started pushing bullets into the handgun magazines. The security team nervously started every time the sound of a gunshot echoed over the island while exchanging tense looks with one another.

Jack pulled his phone out of his pocket. It showed no reception. They were too far away from the *Atlantica* for her masts to service it. *Goddamnit! Okay, don't show panic, give clear decisive orders.* "Listen up, folks. Somethings obviously happening back at the ranch. Here's what we're going to do—objective one, we head back toward the coast and get some kind of communication going with *Atlantica* or *Ignatius*. Objective two, we find out what the hell is going on."

Jack waited while the others got themselves ready, loading up their weapons.

"Objective three… we'll figure out when we get there. Let's move out."

Okay, maybe objective three could have been clearer, Jack thought as he began jogging back in the direction of the *Atlantica*.

***

"Ma'am, we are getting sporadic reports of gunfire from the island." The technician was holding the earphone tightly to his head to better discern the crackly voices coming over the much-diminished radio network.

"Very well, the game's definitely afoot." Slater nodded, and pressing the intercom key she called to Donovan on the shattered bridge. "Perry, advance to steerageway. I want us able to maneuver."

"Aye aye, Captain."

The four General Electric LM2500-30 gas turbines hidden deep within the bowels of the ship began to roar, powering the two five-meter screws on the rear of the ship. The warship pulled off, leaving a frothing white wake behind her.

***

"The first wave has secured the beach. The second wave will make land in a few minutes," Bautista released the microphone key and looked at the steadily growing peak lying in the center of Nest Island.

"Let's start circling the island. I want at the *Atlantica* before she even thinks of moving off."

The *Liliana* and the other faster ships of the fleet leapt forward to full speed and, in a coordinated move, began to hug as close to the coast as they dared.

***

"Captain, we have returns on the radar! They're circling around the eastern side of the island."

Solberg looked at Kelly Maine, freezing for a long moment. *We're actually under attack! We are not a fucking warship, what the hell are we supposed to do?*

"Captain, do you want me to update *Ignatius*?" Maine prompted in a sharp tone, cutting through Solberg's indecision.

"Yes, yes. Please do." Solberg said finally.

Maine quickly and concisely summarized what they were seeing. A collection of radar returns circling the island, their destination obvious. They were coming right at them.

"Thank you. *Atlantica*," Slater's voice crackled, half the words dropping out. "You are... to have to be ... eyes until we... repairs."

Solberg looked through the bridge windows at the warship pulling away. The blackened and warped masts and tower would obviously not be repaired anytime soon.

***

The Seahawk lifted off the helipad, now loaded with a pair of deadly Hellfire missiles. With *Ignatius's* weapon systems so reliant on the brutally damaged radar systems, Mack and her crew would be the principle defenders.

"Geraldine is locked and loaded," Hank called out.

The large grey helicopter dipped its nose toward the sea and raced forward.

"Mack... *Ig*," Slater spoke, her voice nearly occluded with static. "Take a look at the... and for us... I want to see... going on. Then... you... recon those bogeys... around to the east... of the island."

Mack blinked, interpreting the orders of her commanding officer.

"Roger that, *Ignatius* Actual. Beginning recon mission. Confirm *Ignatius* is receiving the datalink from our LAMPS."

"Neg…" came the broken reply.

Mack gave a scowl. With the datalink down, *Ignatius* couldn't feed off of the Seahawk's sensors. The ship was blind and deaf until they could affect repairs.

The Seahawk accelerated toward the island, rapidly crossing from the rolling blue sea, across the band of golden sand and over the lush green vegetation clad central peak.

Mack craned her head as they swung around the mountainous terrain at the center of the island. There was a small collection of boats nestled onto the shore and more coming in.

"This isn't an attack, it's a goddamn invasion," Mack's copilot, Mike Phillips, growled.

"Yeah, roger that, and update the *Iggy*," Mack said distractedly as she banked over toward the east. "Let's go take a look at those returns."

"Mack, look." The copilot pointed. "The horizon."

She glanced in the direction her copilot was indicating. A large dark ship was visible. At this distance it was little more than black shape yet the fact it was even visible from this distance a testament to its sheer size. It was miles away.

"*Ignatius*, Sierra Hotel 1-1. We have a large ship of some description. Want us to go take a look?"

"Negative… near targets… first… You… go… hunting… after." Static washed through the radio, then the voice repeated. "Negative—"

"Roger that, I received your first, *Ignatius*."

The helicopter swept toward the targets speeding around the coastline, heading toward the *Atlantica* and *Ignatius*.

"Looks like our old friend from the attack a couple of weeks ago," Hank called from the back. "She's got some buddies with her too. Shit! We have incoming."

From the collection of seven ships came a deluge of fire, far more concentrated than the last time the Seahawk had been attacked. This time their opponents were ready for them, and had the firepower to keep their attacker at bay.

"Evading." Mack snapped the Seahawk around, descending sharply and making for the safety of the mountain.

"We have seven fast-moving vessels. Repurposed ferries mostly. They are heavily armed," Mack called out.

"Roger… engage… will. Weapons free."

Mack gave a wolfish grin. "It's on, boys."

***

Jack watched the helicopter thunder overhead, desperately evading the streamers of tracer fire reaching for it. From the open side door, the helicopter answered with a torrent of fire from her minigun. He couldn't see what the Seahawk was shooting at, but it was giving them hell.

"Come on. Let's move, people."

Jack turned and began marching as quickly as he could, not even bothering to go to the effort of hiding his limp. It was all about getting back to the jetty as quickly as he could now. The scrubby paths they followed had been lightly beaten down by the passage of people over the last couple of years, but they were not paved roads by any stretch of the imagination.

The other security officers followed him, fear and uncertainty in their eyes. They were going to go into combat a lot sooner than they had ever imagined.

Within minutes they had reached the more populated area of the island. Dozens of people were milling around in panic.

"Make for the jetty, everyone. We need to get you back to the *Atlantica*," Jack roared out. The milling continued, no one listening to him. Giving a weary sigh, Jack pointed his rifle in the air and let off a shot.

"Back to the lifeboat, move, move, MOVE!"

Finally, the general direction of the milling started to head toward the pier. There were far too many people to fit on the one lifeboat, mega or not, Jack realized grimly.

"Ladies and gentlemen, we need to set up a perimeter," Jack called out to his security team. Using a handy stick he'd found lying on the ground, he quickly scratched out a rough diagram of the jetty area and began gesturing with it as he pointed out where he wanted the security officers to position themselves. "You, you and you, take up position here. You two, over at the hut. You four, stay by the pier, you're my reserve to bolster the line. Until then, keep people moving onto the boat, no matter what. Everyone, keep cool, keep calculated, and check your targets. And most of all, keep them the hell off our beach."

Quickly, the security officers ran to their assigned positions. Jack pulled out his phone and checked the reception. He had a couple of bars and rang in to the bridge of the *Atlantica*.

"Captain, this is Cohen. What's our situation?"

"Our situation, Cohen, is that the island is under attack and someone has already damaged *Ignatius*."

"How the hell has *Ignatius* been hit?" Jack called, glancing at the tree line and fields. He watched the helicopter swing back into view and heard the rumbling growl of its gun firing.

"We don't know, there was an explosion and most of her radar arrays are smashed."

"Is she still combat effective?"

"Damned if I know, but she's moving," Solberg said.

"Okay, Captain. We have a lot of people on the beach. We're going to need another boat to come get them. There's no way they're all going to be able to fit on the one here. We need them safe back on the *Atlantica*."

"I hear you, but we are going to have to see about that once we get the situation under control."

"Captain, there is no guarantees we will get the situation under control. We need them safe now!" Jack barked.

"I said we'll see about it, Cohen! *Atlantica*, out."

"Asshole," Jack muttered, resisting the urge to throw the phone on the ground. Pocketing it instead, he glanced back at the tree line. There was movement in the shadows. Small silhouettes of figures darting amongst the trees.

Running to the side of a hut, Jack planted the butt of his rifle in his shoulder and sighted back

toward the figures. Lining the sights over a distant body, Jack breathed in, then exhaled. He paused before taking his next breath, steadying his aim, and squeezed the trigger.

Chapter 41 – Day 17

The *Ignatius* surged forward to twenty-five knots, thundering toward the seven ships that were circling the island in the opposite direction—both forces on a collision course.

"We are not going to be able to bring the VLS into play, people, so we're going old fashioned on this one. The five-incher, bushmasters, and CIWS are all we have, so I need you aiming straight and true," Slater said calmly. The captain's demeanor was a carefully effected mirage. A gnawing worry had infested her belly, not that she would ever show her crew.

"Ma'am, without radar control, the Mk-45 is going to be pretty hit and miss," the weapons officer called over to her from the console.

"I need you to do your best, George. Give me more hits than misses and I'll be happy. I want the bushmasters locally controlled."

"Aye aye, ma'am."

"Weapons free."

The Mk-45 five-inch cannon situated near the bow of the ship swung up with the whirr of motors, sighting toward the seven ships advancing toward the *Ignatius* at flank speed.

"Shot out!" George cried.

With a deafening boom, the cannon fired. The heavy shot fell between two catamaran ferries. A fountain of white frothy water erupted meters high in the air. With mechanical efficiency, the autoloader in the turret slammed another round into the chamber.

"Adjusting fire," the weapons officer called. "Shot out."

The cannon boomed again.

***

"Get us zigzagging. Now!" Bautista shouted to Davey as the second shot plunged into the water a few meters off the port side of the *Liliana*, causing the whole ferry to rock in response.

The *Liliana* and her escorts, already peppered by bullets from the helicopter, began weaving toward the grey warship ahead of them. Bautista watched as the cannon on the bow of the *Ignatius* flashed again. A second later a whistling noise pierced his ears.

The shot slammed into the bow of the small ferry running alongside the *Liliana*, the explosion as the shell detonated driving its prow deep into the water. The stern flipped over the top, a summersault of thousands of pounds of metal. In seconds, the wrecked carcass of the small ship had rolled and disintegrated before slipping beneath the waves. It was obvious to Bautista that there would be no survivors.

"Boss, we're moving into range," Davey shouted.

"Wait for it," Bautista called back, snapping his

attention back to the warship. "We'll open up on them when we have a chance of hitting something important."

Bautista looked back at the heavily armored ship steaming toward them. Not that there was much of a chance of penetrating her thick hide.

***

"Good work. Now do it again," Slater said.

"Ma'am, they'll be in our M242 firing arc soon, after they pass through their arcs, we'll just have the CIWS until we can come about."

Slater leaned back in her chair, regarding the map that one of her technicians was quickly updating on his console. With the radar down, he was having to update as fast as he could, the semi old-fashioned way, with a stylus on a touchscreen.

"By the time we do come around," Slater leaned forward, "I want us mopping up nothing but floating Swiss cheese. You hear me?"

"Aye, ma'am."

"Good. Now give 'em a broadside!"

***

The pirate fleet and *Ignatius* drew closer. The fast ferries began to spread out, three on each side, striving to pass close by the warship. The Seahawk that had been harassing them with minigun fire swept away. The ships were going to pass so close there was the very real danger of friendly fire.

The Mk-45 cannon traversed to the port side, attempting to follow a fast-moving craft before stopping movement as it reached the limit of its firing arc.

With a repetitive thud, the bushmaster 25mm cannons, one situated on each side of the *Ignatius,* opened fire. This time, the ferries answered with their own weapons.

***

"Now!" Bautista shouted.

Along the flank of the ferry, windows dropped and guns poked out. A volley of fire began pinging off the *Ignatius's* thick hide. More crew began throwing their explosives. Some were basic Molotov cocktails, a few were the same mining demolition charges they had used to so sorely wound the *Ignatius.*

Many of the projectiles bounced off the hull. The Molotov cocktails smashed, spreading fire over the grey ship. It achieved little more than to give the vessel a fearsome burning visage. Some of the bombs arced onto the deck, exploding and putting dents in the armor. One, more by luck than judgement, skittered to the base of the Mk-45 cannon turret before exploding. A brutal dent was smashed into the thick armor of the turret near the base.

The noise was deafening to the pirates, yet still they persisted as the ferries tore past the *Ignatius.*

The *Ignatius* answered with the roar of her bushmaster cannons. The heavy rounds from them ripped into the flanks of the ferries. Each 25mm shot that landed smashed huge holes in the delicate ferries. The onslaught was brutal. One of the small ships was shattered into little more than a floating hulk, her superstructure nothing but twisted metal. Another fell behind, something vital damaged in her engines or controls. Still, the crew on the deck fired toward the *Ignatius*. Without mercy, the orbiting Seahawk pounced, riddling the crippled ship with gunfire.

***

Bautista picked himself off the deck and shook his head clear from the ringing of the explosions and gunfire. *Liliana's* bridge was shattered, her consoles smoking with fried electrics and not a single intact window. He realized the *Liliana* was slowing.

"Davey, full speed," Bautista coughed out, blinking the blood and smoke out of his stinging eyes. Not hearing a response, he looked around. Davey's corpse was slumped in the chair, a gory hole in his chest. One of Davey's hands was on the throttle lever. As he'd died, the weight of his body had pulled it back.

Bautista staggered to the helm and pulled the dead man's bloody hand off the lever and rammed the throttle forward to the stops. He needed to get his ship out of the firing arc of the horrific bushmaster cannons.

With a sickening feeling, he knew that this wasn't the last trick the *Ignatius* had up her sleeve. The four remaining ferries tore on, desperate to escape the savage weapons.

***

"Shit, the Mk-45 has taken a hit. Can't tell the

damage but I've lost the lateral traverse on it."

"Understood." Slater nodded. She watched as the frantically updated manual plot showed the enemy vessels surging past the *Ignatius*, the bushmasters roaring fire at them.

"They've cleared the bushmasters, ma'am. Looks like Sierra Hotel 1-1 has taken another one down and the rest are smashed up pretty bad."

"Keep the map updated," Slater said. Grabbing her mic, she addressed the bridge, "Perry, slow us down to steerageway, I want them in the arc of the CIWS for as long as possible."

The weapon systems operator hunkered over the LCD screen with a wolfish grin on his face, the image from the camera on the CIWS mount reflecting in his face.

***

Bautista glanced back, seeing the turret of the minigun mounted on the rear of *Ignatius* swing around.

"Everyone down!" he roared at the few survivors on the bridge and flung himself back to the deck.

The Phalanx Close-in Weapon System wasn't designed for anti-ship operation. It was meant to shoot down aircraft and missiles, but it could still do a damn good job of it when called upon. Capable of firing five thousand rounds a minute, it could expend its reserve of two thousand rounds of 20mm ammunition in just over twenty seconds.

One of *Liliana's* escorts simply disintegrated under the near solid beam of armor-piercing tungsten that erupted out of the six barrels. Nothing alive was left on board the ship.

***

"I'm down to forty percent ammunition count, ma'am. This isn't exactly an efficient way of working," The WSO said with a wry grin. "I'm showing an overheat, too. I'll need to cool for a few seconds."

"We're four down, and that's good by anyone's standards. Perry, bring us about. It's time for round two."

"*Ignatius*, this is *Atlantica*. We have more coming around from the western side of the island. They're right on top of us!" Solberg's voice was tense over the radio.

"Goddamn it," Slater breathed. "Those poor bastards we shredded were just the decoys. Mack, get over there and help out *Atlantica*. Now!"

Chapter 42 – Day 17

Jack lined up the iron sights on the distant target and squeezed the trigger. The M16A1 barked in response and the figure ducked out of the way.

"Damnit," Jack muttered.

A flurry of attention in the tree line caught his attention. Squinting down the length of the weapon, he focused on it. "Shit… down!"

The PKP machine gun opened fire, the bullets hissed by Jack as he threw himself around the corner of the hut. Splinters of wood exploded over him as the rounds slashed through the building and he squeezed his eyes shut to protect them.

That machine gun is going to rip us to shreds. Jack leaned out of cover and squeezed the trigger, visible lines of tracers reached for him even as his own fire sought the enemy.

The tree line erupted in a cloud of wood splinters as Mack's Seahawk thundered by, the loud drone of the GAU-17/A minigun firing silencing the PKP.

The Seahawk turned and sped off back toward the beach. Jack gave a silent thanks to the crew as it went to cover the mega lifeboat which chugged its way toward the distant *Atlantica*, full to the brim with evacuees from the island.

Hunkered down by the pier were still over a hundred people who couldn't fit on the first boat out, crying out in fear.

Sweeping the tree line with his sights, Jack saw more movement, indistinct figures darting back and forth. More were coming. Swiveling back behind the hut, Jack pulled his phone out again. "*Atlantica*, we are going to need a ride off this island ASAP. We are in contact with many bandits and looks like our top cover is heading back to you."

"We'll work something out," Solberg's harassed-sounding voice answered.

Jack fought the temptation to throw the phone away from him again and slipped it back into his pocket.

The battle had reached an impasse. The pirates were in the tree line, while the defenders were hunkered down around the small collection of huts near the pier. Whenever one side or the other broke cover, it was answered by the sound of gunfire. With the helicopter in demand, they had no chance of breaking the stalemate.

What's their end game? Jack thought. *We just have to wait until we get a ride. What the hell are they waiting for?*

Sighting back toward the trees, Jack squeezed off another shot at one of the figures who appeared in the wreckage of the tree line.

***

"The Iggy gave 'em some navy. She really kicked their asses," Hank called out over the roar of the rotors.

"Yes she did," Mack agreed.

The three surviving ferries were running at top speed for the southern side of the island where

Atlantica and the few other ships were nestled in the crystalline blue bay. As the Seahawk thundered over the mountain, she saw the new problem presenting itself.

While the warship had occupied the fast-moving ferries, another contingent made up of slower freighters and fishing boats had hugged the cliff edge on the western side of the island and had a clean run at the bay.

"I want to save the Hellfires for that big sonovabitch," Mack called out. "We'll do our best with the GAU."

"Roger that, ma'am." Hank pulled out the empty ammunition canister from the side of the minigun and tossed it into the storage bin and fitted another. "We're on our last ammo drum, then we're gonna be Winchester."

"We can't take it with us when we're dead. Use it or lose it," Mack's tone was laconic. She squinted at an odd structure on the deck of one of the pirate ships. "What the hell is that thing?"

The Seahawk swept lower. Some of the pirate ships were scribing long frothy trails, heading toward *Atlantica.* She was moving too, a churning wash emanating from her stern.

Between the cruise ship and the coast, apparently unnoticed or uncared about, was the bright orange lifeboat, making its slow way home. Two other pirate ships were making for the beach, and on top of one of them was a strange framework, two inverted Vs thrusting into the air.

Squinting at it, Mack saw a flickering flame next to it on the deck, the source of which looked like an oil drum. With a sudden snap, the drum launched upward, scribing an arc toward the beach.

***

The flaming trebuchet-launched drum flew over the beach and smashed into a hut, engulfing it in flames. The two security officers using it for cover were covered in burning oil.

Jack watched in horror as the two died an agonized, screaming death, staggering a few steps forward on fire before mercifully falling to the ground, silent.

"No," Jack breathed. One of those men was Josef, the perpetually smiling young security officer, one of the few who had survived the original attack.

"Surrender." The voice that came over the loud speaker from the trees was firm and authoritative. "You cannot win. Lower your weapons and you will not be harmed."

Jack glanced at the other end of the hut where another security officer was sitting, legs drawn up, weapon discarded next to him. He was staring at the still-burning corpses, his eyes locked on them.

Jack turned and looked back at the now-silent throng of people who were gathered by the rickety jetty, waiting in vain for a boat which seemed it would never come.

And beyond that, the ship with the strange wooden contraption on it; the source of the horrific fireball.

***

"Ma'am, bring us around a touch, I can't get a

bead on it."

Mack looked closely at the light freighter. It had rearmed and was ready to go. The deck crew had worked with well-rehearsed efficiency and reloaded the trebuchet.

"Standby," Mack said. Yawing the helicopter around so the cockpit was pointed at the beach, she saw there was a crowd of people hunkered there, directly in line of the trebuchet.

"Round a little more…"

"Hold your fire, Hank."

"Ma'am?"

"I said hold your damn fire," Mack barked.

***

Jack stepped out into the open, his hands up high, his rifle left leaning on the side of the hut.

"Hold your fire. We surrender."

Two young men approached him with AK-47s — which looked older than they were — trained on him.

"Just don't harm them," Jack said, looking them in the pirate's wide eyes. They were scared, nervous, and that would make them unpredictable. "You have us, okay? Just don't hurt anyone else. Please."

"On your fucking knees!"

Jack awkwardly lowered himself down, reaching slowly down with one arm to move his prosthetic leg.

"Keep your hands up!" one of the pirates screamed. "I said keep them fucking up!"

"I can't," Jack said as calmly as he could, continuing to move his hand down.

One of the pirate charged forward and smashed

the butt of his rifle into Jack's head.

Dizzyingly, the world lurched to the side as he was knocked down. He found himself looking back at the beach. The last thing he saw before blackness took him was Laurie standing from amidst the throng of people, looking at him, fear and concern on her face.

Chapter 43 – Day 17

"Come on, come on," Kendricks murmured as he watched on the CCTV monitor as the mega lifeboat drew alongside the *Atlantica*. Glancing up through the window, he could see the pirate ships converging on them with menacing purpose.

With a metallic screech, the lifeboat slid into the dolly and sailors leapt out of the top hatch and busied themselves securing the craft, deftly threading carabiners into the eyelets on the top of the boat. One of the sailors gave a thumbs up to the crane operator high above.

"They're attached," Kendricks called over to the captain. "We're hauling them up."

"Finally," Solberg said. "Kelly, get us moving, increase to emergency dash speed."

"Captain, we need to wait until they're up," Kendricks said, eyeing the monitor uneasily.

"We move now or those ships will be on top of us."

Atlantica began to surge forward, ponderously gathering speed from steerageway. The slowly rising lifeboat swung back on the crane like a huge pendulum, slamming into the hull. The crane whined as it struggled to haul up the heavy boat. Finally, it reached the stop and the boat was secured to the muster deck.

"They're up!" Kendricks said.

"Excellent," Solberg keyed his console. "Captain Slater, we have many ships converging on us. We need your support, now!"

"On my way," Slater's crackly voice came over the radio.

***

The *Atlantica* thundered forward faster and faster. The two trawlers and smaller boats of the Nest Island community following in her tumultuous wake.

A pirate ship made to intercept the huge vessel. Misjudging, it put itself directly in front of the *Atlantica*. With a loud thud, the prow of the cruise ship smashed into it, barreling the smaller craft out of the way and leaving it listing and yawing away from the impact, water flooding in through the gaping wound in its flank.

Atlantica powered on undaunted, with little more than a dent and damage to its paintwork. She began to turn a wide curve, striving to rendezvous with the still-flaming *Ignatius* which had come about and was arcing away from her pursuit of the surviving diversionary flotilla.

***

"That's a negative, ma'am. I have no control over the Mk-45. I can fire it at the angle it's at, which is about 60 degrees off centerline to the port."

"Understood," Slater nodded. "Perry, move to rendezvous with *Atlantica*, we need to stick to them like glue."

"And the people on the island?"

They had listened in horror to Mack's report of the capture of the hundred plus civilians on the island.

"We have nearly six thousand on that cruise ship," Slater's voice was ice cold. "They have to be our priority."

***

"Captain, my daughter?" Reynolds asked.

"I'm busy right now," Solberg said as he watched the radar screen intently. The pirate ships were following *Atlantica* like a pack of wolves hunting their prey.

"She was on the island. I need to know if she got off."

"Can you be—" Solberg started.

"Admiral, please use my phone and speak to the deck hands," Kendricks handed his smartphone to the older man. "The muster deck is in the contacts list under M."

"Thank you." Reynolds took the phone from him.

***

As the *Atlantica* and the other ships rendezvoused with the *Ignatius*, the pirates hounding them backed off, withdrawing to the coast, seemingly reluctant to face the same savage beating that the decoys had received.

***

"We need to withdraw," Solberg said into the radio.

"Agreed," came the static laden response. "Cannon... disabled... low... ammunition... CIWS. Weapons... left bushmasters... swarm ... protect you and us."

"But what about the people left on the island?" Kendricks struggled to pick out what Slater was saying.

"When... safe... come back..." Slater crackled in response. "But... we stay, you... risk. We need... leave now... another assault."

"That sounds like a plan to me," Solberg nodded. "Kelly, lay in a course away from the island. And for God's sake, keep the *Ignatius* between us and those pirate bastards."

"Captain," Reynolds said from the rear of the room. His face had lost all color. "My daughter. She wasn't on the lifeboat."

The room went silent. Kendricks walked to Reynolds and laid a hand on his square shoulders. "We'll get her back. But we need to make sure every other person we have on board

Atlantica is safe.

Reynolds opened his mouth, a conflicted look on his face. He closed it again and visibly gathered himself, straightening his shoulders. "Yes... yes we do," he said, his voice firm again. "And then we sure as hell need to go back."

"Damn right."

***

As fast as the slowest trawler, the small collection of ships began to pull away from the island. The pirate fleet converged on the island, both sides licking their wounds.

***

"Keep us between *Atlantica* and the island, Perry," Slater said before keying the mic to the helicopter's channel. "Mack, I am going to re-assign you…"

Chapter 44 – Day 17

"Time for payback," Mack growled to her crew. "We're going for the big game. We're going to teach these pirate shits what it means to mess with the Iggy."

"Hoo-fuckin' yah," Hank whooped.

The Seahawk ceased orbiting the *Ignatius* and *Atlantica* and set course directly for the ship that hung on the horizon on the opposite side of the island from the retreating fleet.

"Finally," the copilot said. "We gonna heat them up?"

"With Hellfire, Mike, With Hellfire."

The Seahawk thundered its way toward the vessel. The sheer size of the ship steadily began to resolve itself. It was huge, lumbering. She hung low in the water, complex pipe work all over the top side of her deck.

"*Ignatius*, Sierra Hotel 1-1. I have an oil tanker of some description. It's a big one," Mack said, pressing the radio transmit button on her collective.

"Seaha… nsmiss…. Ken. Say …. Gain… ver."

"Damnit," Mack breathed, the distorted coms had gone from difficult to unintelligible. "If you're receiving us, we are moving to engage. Gentlemen, that thing is one hell of a beast. I want to do a flyby. We need figure out how to send it to the bottom."

Mack looked at the ship as they closed on it. The massive vessel was easily as large as *Atlantica*, at least three hundred and fifty meters long. Emblazoned on the tired paintwork of the hull was broken lettering. *Titan*.

"Okay, Hank, listen up. Pick your target spot carefully on this pass and we'll pump our AGMs into it. If we don't be selective about this, we're going do jack shit to that monster."

"Roger that," he replied with a low whistle. "That sonvabitch is huge."

As the Seahawk swung closer a stream of tracer fire extended from deck of the ship. Mack hauled up on the cyclic and swung the Seahawk around, orbiting the ship.

"Looks like they've bolted something on, amidships. Take a closer look at it, Hank."

The Seahawk swooped around the ship, the WSO's practiced eye examining every inch of it.

"Ma'am, looks like a collection of cylinders and tanks. Definitely looks makeshift."

"Does it look like it'll go bang?" Mack asked, thrusting the cyclic down. The helicopter descended under a stream of fire reaching for the helicopter.

"Holy shit," Hank called out. "I know what it is. They've built a goddamn refinery on top of the ship!"

"Say again?" Mack yawed the helicopter around, cutting around the ship to its stern, behind the T-shaped bridge superstructure.

"They must be processing the oil on that thing,

turning it into fuel. I ain't entirely sure if that would pass quality-control standards, but it explains why the pirates have always been so flush with fuel."

The Seahawk thundered up the side of the vessel, angling away to get out of range of the crew who were still firing rifles at them. The occasional pinging on the helicopter's armor made Mack wince.

"It'll definitely go bang," Hank said. "That'll make a good target. I say, give them one in the refinery then I'd suggest we hit below the waterline amidships. Yeah, one above and one below might well break its back. But that thing is so big our best chance is cooking off the oil."

Oil, Mack thought, her mind whirling. *A refinery.* Something they were desperately short of — *fuel.*

"We're not attacking," Mack said after a moment.

"Say what?" the WSO called from the back in disbelief.

"That thing is the only source of fuel in this godforsaken region. We sink it, it'll only be so long before we're completely out. And when that happens, we're dead."

"But... ma'am?"

I'm taking us home. Secure down."

"Aye aye, ma'am." Hank's voice was disappointed.

Turning again, the Seahawk began racing back toward the *Ignatius.*

***

Vaughan gave a long exhalation of relief and relaxed back into his threadbare chair on the bridge. Whoever the crew was on that helicopter had clearly realized that the *Titan* was a valuable commodity. The question was, what would they do with that information?

Chapter 45 – Day 17

The Seahawk hovered over the fire-blackened flight deck of the *Ignatius* and lowered a guide cable. Two crewmembers hooked the cable to the flight deck winch and slowly the bullet-scarred helicopter was pulled to the deck.

Once safely down, Mack shut down the engines. The Seahawk's rotor blades slowed and finally whirred to a stop. Pulling off her gloves and helmet, Mack wiped her sweat-glistening ebony brow with the back of her hand. She looked at it in surprise. Up until this moment, her hand had been rock steady, now it was shaking uncontrollably as if she was freezing cold. She clenched her fist, stopping the trembling, and glanced at her copilot. "You okay, Mike?"

Her copilot had sweat pouring down his face, and his short blond hair matted. He leaned back in his seat, closed his eyes, and gave a long exhalation. "I need a shower."

"Yes you do." Mack turned in her seat. "Hank?"

The WSO unclipped himself from his harness, and gave a wince before shaking himself like a dog. Spent shell casings skittered from every fold in his flight suit. "I'm going to be finding those in pockets for weeks."

Raising an eyebrow, Mack looked down at the deck of the helicopter and saw brass covering every inch. "You've got some sweeping to do."

***

The CIC was bustling as Slater called out orders. Glancing at the hatch, she saw Mack enter and looked around.

"Is your crew okay?" Slater asked, looking the pilot up and down.

"Yes, ma'am. My bird has a few more holes in it but…" Mack gave a shrug.

"Better than people having holes," Slater said. "I also see you've come back with the same number of missiles as when you took off. Any particular reason?"

"Yes, ma'am. That ship, it's an oil tanker. It was sitting low in the water. It's got to still be carrying a big payload. Not only that, but on top was a structure that looks like it's been welded on. We'll have to play back the nose camera footage, ma'am, but it looks like they've constructed a refinery of some kind on the deck of that ship."

Slater rubbed her cheek and gazed at the pilot. After a pause, she said, "So you made the call not to take it out, despite my orders?"

Mack drew herself to attention, looking earnestly at her captain. "That's correct, ma'am. I thought—"

"You thought?" Slater interrupted. "You thought at some point we could make a play for that tanker. You thought with fuel at such a premium, we couldn't afford to destroy potentially the only source in this region. That's what you thought."

"Yes, ma'am."

"Good call, Lieutenant." Slater smiled and Mack visibly relaxed. "My officers are paid to think."

Mack gave a cocky grin. "The eagle hasn't taken a shit in two years, ma'am."

Slater arched her eyebrow, before inclining her head at the hatch. "Back to your bird and start getting it patched up."

"Aye aye, ma'am." Mack saluted, turned on her heel and hustled out of the CIC.

"Pilots," Slater muttered with affectionate exasperation as the other woman left. Slater turned and raised her voice. "Ladies and Gentlemen, I want a preliminary report on all damage within thirty minutes."

***

"So, we've lost three quarters of our new security team?" Solberg grimaced. "Maybe we should have gotten them red shirts."

"Sir?" Kendricks asked quizzically, the reference lost on him.

"Never mind. And how many passengers?"

"Unknown at the moment. We're looking at around one hundred left behind, but that'll be a mix of Nest Islanders and *Atlantica's* passengers. Carrie's getting a roll call done now, but it looks like a lot."

Kendricks turned and looked back at Reynolds. He was seated in a chair, his back ramrod straight, staring out of the window.

Chapter 46 – Day 18

The corner of his eye caught a movement in one of the upper windows of the school. The bright light of the Syrian sun contrasted with the darkness inside the structure. Jack began bringing his rifle to bear on the window.

"Thunder, Steel. I ha – "

The RPG round lanced out of the building, a trail of smoke behind it. It seemed to travel in slow motion straight toward him, the whoosh noise of the rocket washing ahead of the grenade itself.

Jack began to react, his muscles moving slower than the spear of the RPG round racing toward him, as he attempted to reach the safety of the ground. The lance approached as he felt himself falling to the dirt. Time moved slower and slower. A race between him reaching the sandy dirt and the grenade striking.

Jack woke with a cry, sitting up quickly. A pain lanced through his head as he did, his vision darkening around the edges, and the room spun dizzyingly.

"Shhh, easy." Jack heard Laurie's voice. He felt her grip his shoulders and tried to ease him back down next to her. He waved her off and looked around the room they were in.

"Where the hell are we?"

"We're on board one of their ships," she said. "They brought us here after the battle."

"How long have I been out?" Jack said with a groan, touching his fingertips to the side of his head.

"I don't know... hours, maybe a day, we can't tell. I thought you were in a coma or something, but then..." Laurie gave a nervous attempt at a laugh. "You started snoring. I thought it was best to leave you."

They were in a hold of some sort. White-painted walls glistened with moisture and harsh strip lighting illuminated the room. It was filled with people, the other prisoners, and smelled of sweat and fear.

Jack held his hand against his throbbing temple, feeling the huge welt from the butt of the rifle. Giving another groan, he braced himself and made to stand up. It was then he noticed his prosthetic leg was missing.

"No, where is it?" He patted his empty trouser leg in a desperate hope that somehow his addled brain was mistaking its absence. "No!"

"They took it after they searched you, Jack. I told them to leave it but they wouldn't."

"No, no, no..." Jack said, a look of panic crossing his face. After a second he calmed himself, taking a deep breath, then gritted his teeth and nodded. *Fine, that's the hand I've been dealt.*

The hatch opened with a clang. In the doorway stood a man who looked like he had been through the wars. He had cuts all over his face and a blood-stained bandage covering one of his forearms. He looked around the room, regarding them all, before his eyes settled on Jack.

Jack felt a tug of memory. He looked familiar. After a moment, recognition dawned. He was one of those involved in the first attack on the *Atlantica*.

"Him." He pointed at Jack.

Four men entered the room, brushing past the other prisoners, and reached Jack. Two of them hauled him bodily up by his arms.

"No!" Laurie shouted, standing quickly.

The man at the door cocked his head, watching the interplay, before saying, "Her, too."

Half-supporting Jack, half-dragging him, two men pulled him out of the room. Another man grabbed Laurie firmly by the top of the arm.

Together they walked—or in Jack's case, hopped awkwardly—down the labyrinthine corridors of the ship. Their footsteps and the distant voices of unseen crew echoed metallically, yet their escorts themselves were silent.

Jack noted with a vague satisfaction that the leader, the one from the attack on the *Atlantica*, seemed to be holding himself in some pain, grimacing every few steps.

Eventually they reached another hatch. The leader opened it, revealing a small room with a grey-haired man seated at a table within.

"Please, sit down." The man gestured at the plastic chairs on the opposite side of the table.

Wearily, Jack and Laurie lowered themselves into the seats. The man gestured at the opaque plastic jug and glasses in front of them. "Water?"

"Thank you, no." Laurie responded.

The leader of their escort walked around the table and took up position to the right of the man while the guards remained standing next to the hatch.

"My name is Eric Vaughan. Leader, if there is such a thing, of our small community, and this is Urbano Bautista, my head of operations." He gestured with one open hand at the man next to him. "My reports suggest that you are the most senior person we have captured?"

Jack looked Vaughan back straight in the eyes. "I am Jack Cohen, formally a staff sergeant in the United States Marines. The former part kinda makes my service number irrelevant. My date of birth is October 4, 1990 I will tell you now that while I may not be in the Marines anymore, I will follow the guidance of Article V of the Code of Conduct for the U.S. Military and answer no further questions."

Vaughan leaned back and cast a bemused glance at Bautista, who continued looking stonily at Jack.

"Thank you for that, Jack. May I call you Jack?" Vaughan was greeted with nothing but silence. "I appreciate and respect that you are following a code of conduct, even for a country that no longer seems to exist. And you, my dear, from your accent you are clearly not from the States?"

"Well done," Laurie replied with sarcastic venom. "What I want to know is, why did you attack us?"

"Far be it for me to take the role of a stereotypical interrogator and tell you that I'm the one asking the questions here, but…" Vaughan opened his arms in a gesture of false helplessness. "That is the situation we find ourselves in."

Laurie made to open her mouth, but Jack quickly spoke over her. "No dice, Vaughan. We're not answering anything."

Nodding, Vaughan reached under the table and lifted a long cloth-wrapped object out of a box on the deck.

"Here's a deal sweetener." Vaughan unwrapped the object, revealing Jack's prosthetic leg. "You can have it back for one question."

"Go on, ask then," Laurie said, before Jack could respond.

Vaughan gently pushed the leg to their side of the table.

"No!" Jack said.

"Quiet, Jack. I'm not a bloody soldier. I do what I want," Laurie said. "Now ask."

"What I want to know," Vaughan said, leaning forward, "is just what the locus is."

"How do you know about the locus?" Laurie asked, confusion evident in her voice.

"When you're on this side of the table, you can ask. But for now?" Vaughan smiled, "That isn't the case."

"We don't know."

Vaughan raised an eyebrow, before giving a nod.

Jack felt himself being lifted out of the chair by the rough hands of the men behind him. A rope was wrapped around his wrists and the loose end slung over a strut crossing the ceiling. The rope was hauled taut, dragging him upright.

Bautista moved to the table and took the cloth which had covered the prosthetic leg. He ripped two strips off it and wrapped them with deliberate slowness around his hands.

"Allow me to ask again," Vaughan said with deadly calm. "What is the locus?"

Laurie started to stand and was thrust back down hard into the seat by the guard behind her. "I don't know!"

With savage force, Bautista punched Jack in the stomach. Jack grunted in pain, before erupting in a hacking cough.

"I asked," Vaughan said in a measured tone. "What is the locus?"

Chapter 47 – Day 18

"My fuel is down to ten percent," Slater's cool blue eyes were bloodshot. She, along with the rest of the *Ignatius's* crew, had had a long night repairing what they could. "And ammunition is heavily depleted. Sure, we kicked the asses of what we faced, but the weapon systems I had to fall back on are not exactly the most efficient for anti-shipping operations."

Reynolds pinched his nose in a vain attempt to squeeze out the stress headache lingering in his head. He was sick with worry for his daughter and the effort to focus was affecting the controlled demeanor he normally portrayed.

"And your repairs?" he finally asked.

"We can maybe get the SPS-67 back online in a couple of weeks, if we have the support of *Atlantica's* 3D printers. The 73 and SPY will take a lot longer, but it is possible," Slater said with a shrug. "The damage is heavy. They knew just where to hit us. If I'd had the radar or VLS, *Ignatius* would have cleaned up that rabble without them being able to fire a single shot."

"And I presume *Ignatius* has that support?" Reynolds turned to Solberg.

"Of course," the cruise ship's captain nodded.

"And some fuel?" Reynolds pushed.

Solberg opened his mouth, then closed it again.

"But of course," Kendricks cut in. "After all, I think yesterday proved that we need *Ignatius*. Didn't it, Captain?"

"Yes," Solberg gave Kendricks a pointed look. The subtle power plays were clearly not lost on him — Reynolds chairing the meeting and Kendricks answering for the *Atlantica*. "Yes, of course."

Good, at least I don't have to encourage Kendricks to mutiny before this bloody crisis is resolved, Reynolds thought.

"You reported damage to your Mk-45. Can you get your cannon operable again?" Reynolds asked.

"Yes, fortunately the traverse was just blocked by warped deck armor. The actuator itself isn't damaged. That'll be sorted by the end of the day."

"Good, then we need to get back into the fight," Reynolds nodded.

"It's not that simple," Kendricks said. "The locus will appear in five days or so, and our last radar fix showed a good portion of the pirate fleet moving away from the island. If the prisoners were on board one of those ships, then they're going to take some tracking."

"And we have another matter." Slater leaned back. "The blast damage pattern to my ship suggests it wasn't some kind of projectile that blinded *Ignatius* — it was a placed charge."

"You can tell that already?" Kendricks leaned forward.

"The seat of the explosion shows that it must have been planted. There's simply no way for it to have gotten there otherwise."

"So to add to all our problems, you have a saboteur onboard." Solberg winced. "Why? Why would one of yours do it?"

"Hold on a second." Slater looked Solberg dead in the eye. "Who is to say I'm the one with a traitor? The *Ignatius* was mated to you, drawing power. It's not inconceivable they could have come from the *Atlantica*."

Kendricks looked thoughtful for a moment. "We picked up a survivor prior to meeting you. A Karl Grayson. He's the only one from the *Atlantica* that didn't arrive with the ship."

"You're saying he's a plant?" Solberg said before shrugging. "It's possible."

"Again," Reynolds said. "There's a problem with that, though."

"Exactly, sir." Slater nodded. "We've been scooping up survivors for the last two years. There's around two hundred people that are not part of *Ignatius's* or *Atlantica's* complement, or passengers... or around one hundred and seventy-five now that some have been captured."

"So what do we do? Round up every single one of them?" Solberg asked. "Because that has my vote. Clearly they are a threat."

Slater cocked her head slightly, visibly processing the difficult thought. "That won't go down well. We have all those people to control. Most, if not all of them, are innocent, and we're talking about putting them under lock and key?"

"There could be a way around that," Kendricks looked thoughtful. "Look, we need to find these people somewhere to stay, and we don't have enough staterooms for them. Let's put them in one room, under the pretense of accommodation, and we can keep an eye on them all."

"And we can give them some line that we're in a state of emergency due to the attack. We can restrict their movements." Solberg nodded.

"How about the bingo hall, Captain?" Kendricks said. "It's a big space, we can rig it out with accommodations… you know, camp beds and what-not from the camping excursion tours. In the annex area we can put some luxuries in so they don't feel too hemmed in."

"Sounds good to me," Solberg said. "Make it happen."

"Now we have a plan for that. I'm still concerned about my daughter in the hands of a rabble of blood-thirsty pirates," Reynolds refocused the conversation. The tendons in his neck felt tight, more like rigid bars of steel than sinew, a sign of the tension he was under.

Slater reached across and laid her hand over the top of his. "Admiral, we'll get her back. But the only opportunity we have of saving everyone is to get people to this locus. Once I know *Atlantica's* safe, you can move your flag to *Ignatius*, and then I promise, we'll hunt them to the ends of this messed up Earth to get her back if we need to."

Reynolds looked at the icily competent woman and gave a slight nod.

***

"Bring us alongside and lay out the fuel lines. Let's give *Ignatius* a drink," Solberg said. He wasn't happy at giving up his precious fuel, but now? It was necessary if they wanted the protection *Ignatius* afforded them.

When they had escaped the island, there had been two fishing trawlers, a light freighter, and several pleasure craft along with the cruise ship and destroyer. Now pure prudence took over. With that many craft, with a corresponding amount of engines and fuel burn, it wasn't efficient. They would cast the pleasure craft adrift along with the freighter after they removed everything worth taking. The trawlers would then be towed by the other two ships.

Before long, the supplies had been redistributed, and there was just one more thing to do.

***

"Sir, if you'd please come with me." The steward at Grayson's door was smart, well presented, and polite to a fault.

"Sure, where we going?" Grayson slipped on a shirt. Glancing out of the cabin, he saw a security officer standing next to the steward. He didn't exactly look on high alert. He quickly weighed up and measured what the steward knew, completing a mental threat assessment. He was in the clear.

"The recent situation on the island, sir, has meant that we are having to swap around cabins to house all the refugees. I'm afraid this one will need to be reallocated to a family, and you will be required to come to the main refugee center on deck four."

Grayson glanced around his comfortable, but small stateroom and gave a sigh. "I guess I can't complain? Give me a few minutes to pack."

"That's quite alright, sir." The steward stepped to one side. "I will come and do that shortly."

Grayson looked the steward in the eyes and repeated coldly, "Give me a few minutes." With one smooth movement, he slammed the door shut in his face.

Quickly, Grayson began throwing his small collection of possessions into his rucksack. Reaching between the cushions on the small settee, he retrieved his CB radio and other kit and stuffed it in his bag before looking around, making sure that there was nothing left that was in the slightest bit incriminating.

Nodding to himself in satisfaction, he opened the door, seeing the red-faced, angry steward standing there.

"Right, I'm ready. Lead the way."

Chapter 48 – Day 18

Jack's face was red and swollen, both eyes blackened, and his teeth loosened. Spitting the blood out his mouth, it splattered on the deck.

"I think that's quite enough." Vaughan stood. "I doubt you have anything more to tell us, do you, my dear?"

With raw hatred in her eyes, Laurie stared at Vaughan before giving the slightest shake of her head.

"Good. Urbano, if you would like to take our guests back to their… suite and join me on the bridge." Vaughan swept out of the room.

Bautista released the ropes and gently, in stark contrast to his brutal demeanor of the previous hour, lowered Jack to the deck.

"Why?" Laurie whispered. "Why did you do that?"

"We're dying." Bautista poured a cup of water and knelt next to Jack and offered it to his lips. "Our only chance of survival is preying on others who come through. This is the way the world is now."

Her eyes puffy with tears, she looked at the man. "If we'd worked together, we could have helped each other, been more than the sum of our parts."

Bautista stood. "Maybe, but we couldn't take that risk. We have families here. People we would do anything to protect and provide for. As I said, the world is a different place."

Walking to the table, he took Jack's prosthetic leg, turned, and offered it to him. Giving a cough, Jack paused for a moment before, with a trembling hand, he took it.

"Come, I will return you to your people."

***

"Eric, if the locus offers us a chance to save our people, we have to take it." Bautista thumped the desk to emphasize his point.

"No!" Vaughan shouted. "It's a pipe dream. A fantasy. Nothing can get us home."

"We have to try!"

"Do you really want to face off against the *Ignatius* again, Urbano?" Vaughan said. "Last time, it didn't go too well."

"Fuck you. This was as much your plan as it was mine," Bautista growled.

Vaughan stared at him, the anger burning in his eyes. Slowly it subsided. Giving a sigh, he said, "Urbano, you want to go home. We all do, but that isn't going to happen. Whatever this locus is, it isn't the answer. We have the information from the *Ignatius*, thanks to our new friends downstairs. We need to make for the coast."

"And what if it can get us home, Eric? What if we can stop scrabbling around, preying on the weak just for a little bit of extra time?" Bautista said earnestly.

"What if we can go back to our lives?"

"Urbano, this has always been your life," Vaughan said quietly. "Even if you go home tomorrow, what would change? You would go back to being the two-bit gunrunner and drug trafficker you were before. Here, those skills make you a leader, someone to be respected. At home… you are nothing but a criminal."

"I don't care what you say, you don't really want to go home, do you?" Bautista shook his head in disgust. "You are like me, a no one. No… worse, a barnacle on the ass of humanity. Back home, you sucked the world dry for oil and profit."

"Maybe," Vaughan said introspectively, before finally nodding. "But here? We are made for this world, Urbano. Why give it up?"

"Because we have a responsibility now, Eric. We have a responsibility as the leaders of our community to do the best by our people. And if it gets out, no, *when* it gets out that we didn't at least try, what do you think will happen to us? We will take a long walk off a short plank, if we're lucky. In fact, we'll be lucky to see the week out anyway, considering the amount of people we lost trying to capture that fucking ship. We have precisely nothing to show for it other than an island we can't hold if the *Ignatius* comes back. But what we do have is a sliver of information that will give our people hope."

Vaughan drummed his fingers on the desk. Bautista was right. They needed to show some kind of result, any kind of result for the attack. A hope, even a weak one, might just be enough to save both their necks.

"Your point is self-defeating, Urbano. I can

guarantee the one place where the *Ignatius* will be, and that's at this locus."

"Yes. The obvious and major fucking problem is that if we go there, the *Ignatius* will blow the hell out of us. Again. How do we stop that?" Bautista asked. The undertone of fear lacing his words. The horrific beating even the severely disabled warship had landed on him was more than enough to strike terror in his heart.

"They've demonstrated they know that the *Titan* is too much of a commodity in this region," Vaughan thought out loud in response. "She's still stocked full of oil. They'll want her intact just in case the locus doesn't pan out. The fact that the helicopter backed off when it could have put a damn big hole in the ship tells us that."

"And the other ships?"

"Disposable. Sure, they've shown a reluctance to sink them as they know we have our own non-combatants on board, but we've angered them now and they'll smash them given half the chance. Unless we give them a damn good reason not to."

Bautista looked across at Vaughan, seeing where his thoughts were taking him. "And we have a reason now, don't we?" he said quietly.

"We have over a hundred reasons." Vaughan smiled.

Chapter 49 – Day 18

Grayson was led into the large bingo hall, which now appeared to be little more than a refugee camp. The former opulence of the room was hidden behind a hastily established indoor shantytown of thin white bedsheet-divided cubicles.

It was full of the dispossessed. Those that had no ship, boat, or island anymore. Those who were now staying at the sufferance of *Atlantica's* master and commander.

Slinging his rucksack onto a creaking camp bed, he couldn't help but give a bitter smile. He had seen this before, many times since his own arrival. When *Atlantica* realized they were just more mouths to feed, more people to protect, and more people than their rapidly dwindling resources could cope with, they would, if they were lucky, be cast adrift.

That was just the way of the world now.

He looked into the crowd of quietly murmuring people and he also knew that *Atlantica* knew that someone, maybe more than one person, in the room was a saboteur. A plant. That was the only reason for gathering them all in this one place. And the reason for the guards who were now at the doors.

Unfortunately, one of the innocent people in this room would just have to take the fall for him.

***

"Keep an eye on them. No one is allowed unaccompanied beyond the annex," Kendricks finished briefing two of the remaining hastily recruited security staff on board. "We'll begin the searches later today. You might get a little resistance, so make sure you keep your wits about you, got it?"

"Yeah, no problem," the security officer said. The man was a recent recruit and Kendricks forgave him the lack of reference to his rank.

Turning, Kendricks walked away from the imposing automatic double doors of the bingo hall itself, which would provide the sleeping accommodation for the refugees. He crossed through the annex which would form a makeshift dining and recreation hall, nodding to himself in satisfaction that all was in place.

Kendricks didn't like this one little bit. But the truth was, at the moment someone, or perhaps several people in that hall didn't have the best interests of *Atlantica* at heart and right now, the only thing they could do was start the slow process of searching everyone in the room. Something that would take hours.

***

"Shot out!"

Perry watched through the binoculars as the distant splash signaled where the shell the Mk-45 cannon had boomed out plunged into the water.

"We had a clean fire," Donovan said.

"Accuracy is still shit, though." Slater lowered her own binoculars. Donovan didn't even seem to notice her profanity and simply nodded. The collection of barrels they were using as a target floated unperturbed by the cannon shell that had landed fifty meters away from them.

"I've been thinking about that." Donovan gestured upward, signifying the twisted wreckage atop the bridge superstructure. "We can repair all that, but not nearly soon enough to help us out if we run into trouble between here and the locus."

"Perry, we're all very tired," Slater sighed. It had been a long few days trying to get the ship back to something approaching combat readiness. "You're a very smart man, and I know you have some cunning scheme to help us overcome our current disability. Would you be so good as to cut to the chase?"

Giving a tight smile, Donovan nodded and turned to face his captain. "*Atlantica* has a working radar system. I mean, it's nowhere near up to military specs, but it can certainly help with our range finding. We can draft up a simple program that will take into account our relative positions, compensate and pipe the information through to fire control. It is, in principle, little more than basic trigonometry. The VLS will still be down, but at least we'll have the Mk-45 back up to something approaching combat standard."

"Maybe," Slater nodded. "But the datalinks are still bust. We're still struggling with basic coms."

"Well, they have a mobile phone mast on there," Donovan inclined his head at *Atlantica*, the huge white and blue ship keeping pace next to them. "We just need to appropriate one of their smart phones. Hell, half the crew probably have them shoved in their lockers. We could just use theirs. The information could be sent that way and we feed it into the CIC manually. As long as we remain close to *Atlantica,* that is."

"Good thinking, Perry. Okay, get on it."

"Aye aye, ma'am. Would you be so kind as to arrange someone to cover my watches while I work on that? I'll probably have to link in with Tricia, she has the know-how."

"Perry," Slater said, a rare smile crossing her face as she purred the R in his name. "Are you just coming up with excuses to talk to that good-looking lady on Solberg's crew?"

"Ma'am?" The confused look on Donovan's guileless face was entirely genuine. "She's just their IT expert; she can help with this kind of stuff."

"Right," Slater gave a mocking nod while forcing the smile from her face. The captain gestured with an open hand at the *Atlantica* cruising alongside. "By all means, run it through her and I'll sort out the watch roster."

"Thank you, ma'am."

With a slight bounce to his step, Donovan made his way to the hatch.

Slater shook her head and gave a tired smile as she watched him leave.

Chapter 50 – Day 19

Jack's head was still pounding from the blows that Bautista's fists had landed on it and his body didn't feel much better.

Gargling water in his mouth, he spat the now-pink liquid down a small drain in the deck he was sitting next to. With a grimace, he looked at Laurie's concerned face. "Sorry… gross, I know."

Reaching across to him, Laurie gave his hand a squeeze. "It's okay. I'll make an exception seeing as you've had a damn good pasting."

"A pasting? I think that means something different where I'm from," Jack managed a smile.

"I dread to think." Laurie kept squeezing Jack's hand and looked around the crowded room. "Jack, how are we going to get out of here? I mean all of us, not just you and me."

"At the moment, they want us alive," Jack said introspectively. "And the only reasons I can think of are either as bargaining chips or as a human shield."

As if to confirm their fears, the door to the hold slammed open and the murmuring within the room went silent as a group of armed men walked in.

"Five. Those will do." One of the men gestured at

a family huddling by the door.

"No!" The man, clearly the father of the children, stood up. "Leave them here. Take me, just not them."

"Either come with them, or watch them go." The pirate's tone was cold as his men walked in and roughly grabbed each of the family members by their arms.

"Where are you taking them?" Laurie shouted, standing as she did.

The pirate looked at Laurie before electing to simply ignore her as the family was hustled through the hatch. With a loud clang, it slammed shut.

"I think that's answered that," Jack said.

"Bastards," Laurie spat.

"They are that."

***

What the hell is wrong with me? Bautista thought to himself as he watched the terrified family make their way down the metal steps on the side of the vessel. The bottom of the steps rested on the blackened, scarred roof of the *Liliana* where she nestled against the *Titan's* vast flank.

There was a time, long ago, where his conscience was as vestigial to the former criminal as his appendix. He had killed, trafficked weapons, drugs, and people along the Latin American coast and cared not in the slightest for the misery he had wrought.

Now though, that conscience was worrying at him like a brain tumor. It was like a pervasive ache, threatening to overwhelm him.

He had lost dozens of men and women on two ill-conceived adventures to take the *Atlantica*. Still, every person in their little community was looking to him and Vaughan for leadership. Instead of even considering an alliance with the *Atlantica* and *Ignatius* to survive this strange place they had found themselves in, they were doing their level best to kill each other.

And for what? Was the model the pirates had established years ago working? Preying on the weak, recruiting or killing those they found? Well, it wasn't working any longer. Since *Ignatius* had come here, they were no longer the meanest thing on the seas. There was a beast out there and now they had awoken it.

And that beast was angry, and undoubtedly *Atlantica* would give the monster the sustenance it needed to come after them. Fuel.

They reached the gangplank and the family was hastened across toward the shattered *Liliana*. He stepped on, about to cross to his own vessel.

"Urbano?" Bautista looked back and saw a dark-haired woman standing on the steps. She must have followed them down and just caught up. "Urbano... Karl, where is he? He was supposed to be home. You said he would be after the attack?

"I know, Kristen," Bautista addressed Grayson's wife. "He'll be back soon."

"Don't give me bullshit, how the hell is he going to get back now?"

"We'll find a way, or he will."

"He better, Urbano, or I swear, I'm going to steal a ship and go get him back." Kristen stormed back up the ladder.

And she will as well, Bautista thought. *I'd put money on it.*

Bautista clenched his fists as he watched her disappear back inside the *Titan*. The ache of his knuckles was slight, but a reminder of the torture he had administered on the man below.

But that act, as barbaric as it had been, had given him something that he realized had been lacking in his life — Hope.

Hope he could guide these people out of the region.

Whatever the locus was, it must be able to help them.

If the *Ignatius* didn't get them first.

Chapter 51 – Day 20

"Shot out!"

The shell whistled in a long arc toward the collection of floating barrels. This time, it clipped the edge of the cluster of flotsam, ripping some apart and scattering the others.

"It's not up to military accuracy," Donovan said, regarding the scattering debris though his binoculars.

"What have we got our inaccuracy down to?"

"We've been getting a consistent three-meter margin of error over two nautical miles."

Slater lowered her own binoculars and furrowed her brow. It was nowhere near the pinpoint accuracy *Ignatius* could achieve over those distances. The warship could, if called upon, put a shell through a car window from much higher ranges — with a fully operational targeting suite. Slater gave a sigh, "That'll just have to be good enough for government work."

It wasn't the most efficient way of doing things. *Atlantica* would use its own radar to get a positioning fix for the *Ignatius* and the target, and feed that through to the hastily designed program running on a computer in the warship's CIC which would calculate a firing solution. The weapons officer then had to feed that into the fire control systems for the Mk-45. The math was simple, but the system could only be made so slick considering their current situation.

Atlantica's radar was nowhere near as accurate as the *Ignatius's* wrecked systems, but it was a hell of a lot better than measuring up the old-fashioned way.

"Right, Perry. Next job." Slater slapped Donovan on the back. "Let's see how the fuel top-up is going."

***

"We're finally getting there," Solberg said, his eyes bloodshot from exhaustion.

We're all tired, but he is really showing it, Kendricks thought. The captain's desk was covered in half-drunk mugs of coffee and cans of energy drinks. A stark contrast to the spotless clear surface Solberg normally worked on.

"Captain, we plan to make for the locus tomorrow. Why don't you get some sleep? I can hold the watch."

"Right," Solberg looked at him. "And what then? I find you have taken over completely?"

"What?"

"What *Captain* to you," Solberg hissed. "We need to talk about your growing insubordination. You've given up nearly thirty percent of our remaining fuel stock and didn't even look at me to ask permission."

"Captain, I'm the executive officer on board this ship," Kendricks tone was genuinely confused.

"My job is to manage resources."

"And I am the master of this vessel!" Solberg slammed his fist down on the desk, causing the mugs to jump.

Kendricks looked at Solberg. Was the stimulant-filled clutter of the desk reflective of the captain's mental state?

"Captain. We need *Ignatius* with us. We couldn't just abandon her. The other ships… maybe we don't need them, but if those pirates attack again in numbers before we reach the locus, then we wouldn't stand a chance."

Solberg opened his mouth to reply before visibly calming himself with a deep breath. "Sorry, Liam. I'm just tired."

"I know, Captain. Please, just get some sleep. We need you at your best for when we get to the locus. God only knows what we'll find there."

"You're right." Solberg sighed, closing his bloodshot eyes for a moment before standing from his leather chair. "I'll be in my quarters."

"Good, I'll let you know if anything happens."

"Thank you, Liam," Solberg moved around the desk. "Just please, no more unilateral decisions. We're in a new world now. We need to manage what resources we have. One day, when we get home, you'll be captain of a ship. Then you'll know the responsibility of looking at the… big picture."

"Sure, Captain. Sure."

Kendricks followed his captain out into the corridor and turned into his own, much smaller office. Sitting at the desk, he paused and gave a deep breath. *He's losing it,* Kendricks thought. *In fact, scratch that. It's past tense. The old man's lost it.*

Pursing his lips, Kendricks flipped open his

laptop and brought up the intranet policy page he wanted.

Scrolling through the menu, he found what he was looking for.

Guidance on a captain's unsuitability to command.

Chapter 52 – Day 20

Grayson reached the front of the line and picked up his white paper lunch bag. Glancing inside, he saw the unappetizing fare—some sandwiches, a bag of salt and vinegar potato chips, and a bottle of water.

Nodding his thanks at the server behind the folding table, he slowly made his way back into the main room.

Grayson's attention was drawn to a couple of security staff gesturing a young couple out through one of the other exits. He couldn't hear over the bustle in the room, but one of the security pointed at the couple's bags, and the man grabbed them before following the uniformed officers.

Shit, Grayson thought. *They're running searches.* Remaining outwardly calm, he took a quick mental inventory of what he had on him. The CB radio was accounted for. Kendricks had, after all, allowed him to keep it. Did he have anything else on him that was suspicious?

Yes, he did.

Thinking quickly, he rapidly put together a plan. Spotting someone who would fit into it, he casually sauntered over and sat down on the sofa next to him.

"Hey, have some of this." Grayson handed the man the other triangle of sandwich from the plastic packaging.

The man looked at him, nodded, and took it from Grayson's outstretched hand. "Thanks, man."

"I'm so bored in here," Grayson said between bites of his own. "How long you reckon we're going to be stuck in this room?"

"Damned if I know," the man grumbled between chewing on the ham sandwich.

"I'm Karl." Grayson stuck his hand out.

"Roger." The other man shook it.

The room, as big as it was, already starting to smell of too much humanity packed together. The restlessness of children running around was even beginning to test Grayson's considerable patience.

"What's your story then?" Grayson asked.

The man continued chewing for a moment, gazing at nothing in particular in front of him. "Same as most in here," he finally said. "I was happily bobbing around in my Hunter 50. Next thing I know, I'm stuck in this region."

"Yeah, I get that." Grayson nodded sagely. "I was just doing a little fishing. Knew I should've just stayed at home and watched crappy reruns."

"Well now, my little beauty is probably being used as some pirate's passion pad. Got left behind, didn't it?" Roger bemoaned.

"I sympathize. My Ocean 42 has probably been broken up for firewood."

"It sucks man, it sucks." There was no denying the words of wisdom the man presented.

"Yeah, anyway…" Grayson looked across at the large LCD TV at the other end of the hall. "Looks like we get some cartoons to watch. Think I'm going to go sing along."

"Just not too loud. Please god." The man rolled his eyes.

Flipping a jaunty salute, Grayson stood and walked away from the man. Who was roughly his build and appearance, and seemed to be alone.

***

Grayson withstood the cartoon as long as he could. It was some popular movie from a year or so back... prior to the event. His own kid loved it, only he had to watch it on some crappy little CRT TV in the bowels of some shipwrecked, stinking container ship that made the environment he currently was in seem sparsely populated.

"Excuse me, sir?"

Grayson looked up at the two security officers standing over him. "Hey, what's up?"

"If you would care to come with us," the officer said formally. "We have orders to conduct a search on everyone in the room. You'll be back in a couple of hours."

"Sure, no problem."

***

"And your name please?" The bored-looking crewman spoke without looking up from his tablet.

"Roger, Roger Brew." Brew stood by the table, his duffle bag containing his worldly possessions atop it.

"And you're from Nest Island?"

"That's right."

"Okay, Mr. Brew," The crewman finally laid his

tablet on the table and began tugging on some blue rubber gloves. "We have permission to search everyone's belongings as a security measure. It's nothing to be worried about."

"I'm not entirely happy about this," Brew said pointedly.

"Neither am I, Mr. Brew, but that's the way things are." The crewman glanced at the security officer standing to one side, who merely responded by blowing a bubble with his chewing gum, letting it burst.

The crewman ran a metal detector wand over the duffle bag. It beeped intermittently, but seemingly not in a way that concerned the crewman. He unzipped the top and began pulling the contents out, laying them carefully on the table. They were mostly clothes, a few wash items, and other odds and ends

Once the bag was empty, the crewman began sifting through the items. He patted down the clothes before reaching for a scrunched-up slip of paper.

Flattening it out, he looked at it, turning it in his hands.

The crewman's eyes widened and he waved the security officer over to him, who took one look and drew his gun from its waist holster and pointed it straight in Brew's face.

"Get down on your knees, now!"

***

"Yes, Heather, yes we have a suspect." Kendricks was in the security office. Next to it on Route 66 was the ship's brig. There were four cells, which normally reserved for drunks, the occasional assault or theft which occurred. For the moment, the brig contained just one man, Roger Brew, who was seated in there with flexicuffs on.

"And has he admitted to anything yet?" Slater's voice was still distorted from the damaged coms on *Ignatius*, but it was a lot better than it had been.

"No, he's pulling a pretty convincing confused look right now. You want us to hold him or transfer him over to the *Ignatius*?"

"With my compliments," Slater said. "Would you be so good as to hold him there? We're still putting my ship back together again."

"No problems, Heather."

"I can send Perry across to ask him some questions."

"And damage the U.S. reputation for being harsh interrogators?" Kendricks chuckled.

"It's the twenty-first century, you know. Softy softy touchy feely, and all that jazz." Slater gave a laugh in return before becoming more serious. "How's the admiral holding up?"

"As well as can be expected. The man's worried sick."

"Who can blame him? And Captain Solberg?"

"Stressed. Very stressed." Kendricks said quietly. "I don't want to talk out of turn. He's a good captain... when things are going to plan."

"Things most definitely aren't going to plan at the moment," Slater cut across.

"I know. I'm taking as much of a load off him as I can, but... well, hopefully this locus will pan out."

"For us all," Slater replied. "Okay. You're a good XO, Liam. Your job is to make sure he can make the big decisions, okay?

"I know."

"If he can't, Liam, you know what to do, don't you?"

"It won't come to that."

Chapter 53 – Day 20

I need to get off this ship and get my ass back to the Titan, Grayson thought. *If we get to the locus and are somehow transported back, then Kristen…*

Grayson shook his head. He needed to come up with a plan. The heat was off him for the time being, while that poor unfortunate man was having the thumbscrews applied. Still, he needed to be able to communicate with the *Titan*, and he couldn't do that in this crowded room.

***

"Roger, is it? Yes, Roger." Donovan theatrically tapped his clipboard with his pen. "Off of the *Daffodil*. You've been on Nest Island for just over a year."

Roger Brew nodded, perspiration glistening on his face. "I am. Look, I'll help you in any way I can. I've got nothing to hide."

"That would be most appreciated, Roger." Donovan beamed, his visage marred by the cuts crisscrossing his face. He placed the clipboard down on the table in front of him and opened his hands.

"So, tell me about the explosion on the *Ignatius*."

"I don't know anything about that," Brew whispered. "I wouldn't even know where to start with a bomb."

Kendricks, watching from where he was standing in the corner of the tiny, brightly lit brig office, wasn't feeling it. The man was trembling in fear, and they hadn't exactly exerted any pressure on him.

"So perhaps, Roger, you could explain this?" Donovan said.

On cue, Kendricks walked to the table and placed the clear plastic bag containing a pen-scrawled deck plan on the table.

"What's that?" Brew asked, reaching for it. Donovan picked it up first and held it up.

"This, Roger, is a hand-scribed deck plan of the *Ignatius*. It was found scrunched up in your bag."

"I've never seen that before in my life." Brew's brow was furrowed in confusion.

"Haven't you, Roger?" Donavan's voice became firmer. "I think you better tell us the story again leading up to you happening across Nest Island…"

Chapter 54 – Day 21

"I wish to apologize for your rough treatment," Vaughan said.

Jack and Laurie had been led from the now-deserted hold to the bridge of the *Titan* by a pair of heavily muscled guards. The bridge was far wider than it was long, stretching across much of the "T" of the supertanker's superstructure. Jack could see that in stark contrast to the advanced touchscreens and clean lines of the *Atlantica,* or the far less aesthetic yet still high tech *Ignatius*, the bridge of the *Titan* was old and rugged-seeming. Analog to the other ships' digital.

"Apology accepted," Laurie said.

"Really?" Vaughan raised an eyebrow. "That's very magnanimous of you."

"No, of course not really. Fuck you," Laurie snapped.

Vaughan swiveled in his chair and looked at Jack. "I suspect you have your hands full with this one."

Jack looked back at Vaughan, a stony expression on his battered face. "I'm not really in the mood for small talk with you. Is there any particular reason we're up here?"

Vaughan nodded, stood, and walked to the map table, gesturing at the two to follow.

"We are going to the locus." Vaughan pointed at the hand-drawn map. To the western side was Nest Island, to the east another small landmass with "home" written on it. The locus was halfway between the two. Jack filed the rough location away. If ever they got back to *Atlantica*, he was damn sure he was going to let Captain Slater know, who would undoubtedly reap a furious vengeance on "home".

Not that they're likely to let us return, having seen that, Jack thought.

"There is every chance that the *Ignatius* and *Atlantica* will also be at the locus. As such, we have divided up our... guests between the ships of our fleet to dissuade an attack upon us."

"Mister Vaughan," Jack interrupted him, his tone icy. "I may have been on a hiatus from the Marines for a few months now, but I've seen nothing to make me think the policy of non-negotiation with terrorists — and in Captain Slater's eyes you are a terrorist — has been rescinded. When she comes for you, and she will, she will not let hostages stop her from ripping your little fleet to pieces."

"That may be the case, in theory, Sergeant." Vaughan smiled. "In practice, I do not think she will fire when she knows innocent people are on the decks of our ships. After all it's a different world now. There is no Pentagon to enforce that policy — "

"Pearl Harbor. December 7, 1941," Jack interrupted, "was a major surprise attack on the U.S. military. If you recall, that didn't end too well for the aggressors. If I was her, I'd sink your ships one at a time until you either surrender, or one of your own crew puts a bullet in you and surrenders for you." Jack raised his voice so the other crew on the bridge could hear, "You can avoid a lot of pain and suffering by cutting to the chase."

The crew glanced at each other uncertainly as Vaughan regarded Jack for a long moment, the silence stretching out. Finally, the older man spoke in a chilly tone, "I'm a reasonable man, but I'd stop that kind of talk now or I'll have your other leg hacked off. Am I understood?"

"Perfectly," Jack said. He could feel the raw hatred building for the smug man in front of him. Everything about the fat cat filled him with loathing.

"Good." Vaughan smiled falsely. "As I was saying. Our intention is to go to this locus. There we will see if it is a means home, or at least can help us with the current situation. From what you've told me, it is logical to assume that something will arrive. It is clear to me that whatever that thing is, it is the source of our current predicament. Do you concur?"

Jack and Laurie looked at each other. *Don't tell him shit,* Jack thought furiously to her. Unfortunately, she wasn't telepathic.

"I concur," Laurie said slowly.

"And what is this thing?"

"I've already told you. We don't have a clue," she replied.

"But you have told us it arrives in three days."

"Yes."

"Then shall we go find out?"

***

Bautista scrubbed and scrubbed the deck of the

bridge right under the chair where Davey had been seated when he had been eviscerated by the bushmaster's 25mm round.

No matter how hard he wiped, the brown stain wasn't coming out, yet he continued trying to clean the blood off of the deck.

Finally, he gave up. Rolling from his hands and knees to a sitting position against the bulkhead, he stared across the savagely mauled bridge of his *Liliana*.

Anyone who had known him back in his old life would have been shocked to their core to see the tear trickle down his glass-cut face.

"Urbano? Urbano, are you there?" Vaughan's voice crackled from the radio.

Bautista, gave a sniff and wiped his cheek. He stared at the back of hand, surprised to feel the wetness. He shook his head, clearing it, and stood, grabbing the mic. "Yes, Eric, I'm here."

"Good, make sure your fuel is topped up. We're going to head out to the locus tonight."

Bautista gave another look at the shattered bridge, letting the mic dangle in his hand. He could feel the churning fear in his belly. A fear of going into battle again. A fear of killing and seeing his friends being killed.

Once he had reveled in the fight, loved it. Knew that he was good at it and that his luck always held. Now, he could feel he was losing his nerve. He didn't want any more pain or suffering.

Yet he knew they had one more fight.

And this time their enemy would be ready for them.

Chapter 55 – Day 22

"Heading is set, ma'am." Donovan stood, his hands behind his back. "We're ready to head to the locus."

Slater lowered herself into the watch officer's chair and looked around the bridge. It had been hastily repaired. New windows had been slotted in, but some of the fixes had involved a less than neat solution, and cables ran between the consoles, duct taped to the deck and bulkheads.

"Very well, Perry. Signal *Atlantica* and let's get sailing, shall we?"

***

"Message from the *Ignatius*, Captain," Maine turned in her chair and looked at Solberg. "They are ready to go."

"Good." Solberg drummed his fingers on the armrest of his black leather chair. "It's about time we see whether this locus can get us home."

"Aye aye, Captain."

***

The two ships began to move off, leaving the two fishing trawlers they had towed stationary. The coded military beacons *Ignatius* had left on them would mean they would be able to find

them again if they needed them. For now, they didn't want the added fuel burn towing them would entail.

Ignatius and *Atlantica* began to pick up speed, the smaller, agile destroyer running alongside the vast bulk of the cruise ship like a remora swimming next to a whale.

A hundred nautical miles away, the *Titan* and her escorts were joined by the light freighter containing the family and non-combatants that had been left at the container ship village.

As one, the ships and boats of the pirate fleet turned and began steaming toward their destination.

The two forces on an intersecting path.

The point of meeting—the locus.

Chapter 56 – Day 23

"There's nothing here, dammit." Solberg stood staring out of the windows at the empty blue ocean. He turned and looked at Reynolds. "Nothing."

"Laurie only provided her best estimate of when she thought the locus would arrive. It wasn't an exact time by any stretch of the imagination." Reynold's face was still drawn and pale. The worry for his daughter had prevented him from sleeping for days. The old man was powered by little more than caffeine and determination to get these people safe so he could go back to searching for his daughter. "We don't even know her margin for error."

Solberg began pacing back and forth before the window, shaking his head in frustration. "What if this damn locus is nothing? All we would've succeeded in doing is burning fuel and food when we could have been... could have been doing something."

"Captain, let's just wait," Kendricks said. "We know it's roughly here we have to be, and we know it's roughly now that we have to be here."

"And by the time we get back to the coast?" Solberg said. "We will have that much less food. The people downstairs will be eating each other."

"*Atlantica*, *Ignatius* Actual," Slater's voice

crackled.

"Yes, Heather. We know, there's nothing here," Solberg snapped.

Reynolds and Kendricks glanced at each other at the shortness of the captain's tone.

"That's all we're getting, too. We've discussed this over here, and we feel we wait it out for a couple of days."

"Oh, do you?" Solberg muttered, just below the volume threshold the microphone would pick up before speaking louder. "And we've discussed the food situation. We believe it would be prudent to head toward the coast as per Plan B."

"Oh no, we didn't," Reynolds growled. "Look, Captain. Frankly I want to offload this ship as quickly as possible then head back west to track down the bloody pirates who have my daughter. Trust me, no one has as much incentive for the *Atlantica* to be safe as me. We wait here."

"Last time I checked," Solberg shouted at the top of his voice. "I was captain of this fucking ship."

A shocked silence filled the bridge, the officers and crew either watching the interchange with horrified fascination, or busying themselves in their consoles.

"Captain... Lars," Kendricks walked toward Solberg. "Let's go to your office and discuss this."

"There is nothing to discuss." Solberg's eyes were bloodshot, his face taut, and a vein protruded from his forehead. "We make for the coast."

"Please, not yet," Kendricks said gently.

"No, now."

Kendricks again looked at Reynolds, who gave the slightest of nods. Kendricks returned it, then looked down.

"Captain, under Crystal Ocean's policy 4.12, I am formally relieving you to undergo a medical assessment with Dr. Emodi. This is a temporary relieving of command until that assessment is complete."

"Liam, no one memorizes policy numbers. You've researched this, haven't you?" Solberg hissed. "Planned for it. You've been waiting for the slightest excuse to take over."

"Lars, you don't look well. Please, I'm your friend. Just go get seen by the doctor. You've been carrying the weight of command for over three weeks in the most testing of circumstances. If you just get some rest, you'll be back to the grouchy captain we know and love." Kendricks gave a reassuring smile.

"Don't fucking patronize me." Solberg looked around the room, his attention focusing on Kelly Maine. "They won't accept your command."

"4.12 isn't optional, Captain. Once it's invoked, you must present yourself for assessment. If I'm found to be wrong, I'm sure I'll be suitably punished. But there is no debate. You need to report to Dr. Emodi," Kendricks said quietly.

"No, I do not. As I recall, the policy requires the concurrence of at least one other senior officer," Solberg's voice strained with forced civility. "What say you to all this, Kelly? This, and I choose my words carefully here, mutiny?"

Kendricks looked at Maine, his teeth clenched, willing her to support him.

"As the staff captain said," Maine said slowly at first, her voice becoming firmer. "Things are getting to you, sir. I must concur. The policy is invoked. I now follow Acting Captain Kendricks's orders."

Solberg's mouth opened and closed in incredulity. Without a further word, he stormed to the door and jabbed at the keypad. With a rumble they opened and he swept out.

"It had to be done, son." Reynolds walked to Kendricks and laid a hand on his shoulder. "It had to be done."

"Then why do I feel like a mutineer?" Kendricks whispered.

"Secure it, Captain," Reynolds said. "You have a job to do. Now be about it."

Nodding, Kendricks walked to the command seat and lowered himself into it. "Kelly, reopen the channel to the *Ignatius*."

"Aye aye, sir. Channel open."

"Captain Slater? This is Acting Captain Kendricks. I have assumed command of the *Atlantica*."

There was a pause on the radio before Slater's voice crackled through again, "Understood, Acting Captain. And what is *Atlantica* to do?"

Once again Kendricks looked around the room. The faces of the bridge staff were uncertain, scared at the drama they had just seen unfold in front of them. The world had just changed for them again. He needed to give them an objective. Something to do. Right now, that something was simple.

"We wait."

Chapter 57 – Day 23

"Boss, we'll be in range of *Atlantica's* radar shortly," *Titan's* captain looked at Vaughan across the map table. "She will undoubtedly inform *Ignatius*. And then, we could be in trouble."

Vaughan leaned over the table, pressing down on it so hard his knuckles were white. This was the critical part. Too soon, and they would be engaged in a standoff while the locus appeared, to do... whatever it was going to do. Too late and they might miss it.

"Is there anything strange? Odd? No matter how small," Vaughan finally asked.

The captain glanced around the bridge, before shaking his head. "It seems not."

"Then let's hold position here. While our radar has a longer reach than *Atlantica's*, we have the advantage.

***

We must be there, Grayson thought as he looked out of the portholes along one side of the ship. The sea, which had previously been sweeping by, had come to a halt. *Atlantica* was stationary other than the near imperceptible motion of the ship in the water.

What he didn't know was where his compatriots were. Had they pursued *Atlantica* and *Ignatius*? Or had they retreated to the safety of the island to consolidate their gains?

He had an easy solution to find out. Get out his CB and give a test call. Grayson looked around the room and saw there was scant opportunity. The conditions were so crowded with the bustle of humanity in here, he would be spotted or overheard in a heartbeat.

They hadn't been allowed out for the better part of a week. Grayson wasn't overly given to claustrophobia, but some of the others in here clearly were. Arguments were starting to occur more and more frequently. Not even the prisoners at Guantanamo Bay had been treated like this.

But perhaps there was an opportunity to turn this pressure kettle to his advantage.

Standing from his camp bed, Grayson marched determinedly toward the two security officers standing by the doors, gazing in a bored but watchful way over the room.

"I want to see the captain," Grayson said loudly as he approached.

"Please, sir. Sit down," the security officer said.

"No, listen up. We've all been stuck in here for what? Five days now?" Grayson turned and gestured toward the throng, some of whom were looking up at the sound of Grayson's raised voice. "We need fresh air."

"That's right, we're not animals," a voice called from the crowd.

From behind him, Grayson could feel the mood of the crowd starting to take a darker turn. Stepping closer to the young woman in the security outfit, he said, "Look, these people are going to boil over. Get your captain down here and start allowing people up on deck or something bad is going to happen."

The woman gave a terse nod and reached into her pocket for her phone.

***

"Jesus, how could we forget about them?" Kendricks muttered to himself. "We have nearly two hundred people shoved in there."

He slowly massaged his temples with his fingers, thinking quickly. The people in there needed to have somewhere to stay even though they had a suspect in custody, although Kendricks had his doubts about Brew.

Roger Brew was clearly petrified. After a day of denials, the man was agreeing with whatever they put to him, but then was unable to fill in the specifics.

So far, he had admitted he had blown up the *Ignatius*, but couldn't tell them how he had gotten the explosives nor how he had gotten them on board the destroyer. In other words, he was just saying whatever he thought the questioner wanted to hear.

The bottom line was, Kendricks suspected someone may have used Brew as a patsy, planting the evidence on him.

But even if someone, or several people in the bingo hall were involved, the majority undoubtedly weren't.

And they had been stuffed in a room and

forgotten about.

First big decision, Liam. Let them out, or keep 'em stuffed in there? He leaned back and sighed.

"The refugees?"

Kendricks turned and looked at the drawn face of Reynolds. "Yeah, the refugees. We... I need to decide what to do with them while we're waiting."

Reynolds stepped toward the window and gazed through it. The sun was starting to set and the sky was darkening over the empty sea.

"Not easy, is it?" Reynolds looked at Kendricks, smiling tiredly. "Being in charge, that is."

"Not at all," Kendricks agreed. "We have hundreds of people, most if not all of whom are innocent, stuffed in a room because of a security threat when we already have someone in custody. They're about to riot if they don't get some fresh air. What do I do, let them out?"

Reynolds eased himself into the chair next to Kendricks. "One year, I had a stint lecturing at *HMS Collingwood* for the International Ships Command Course. Captain school, basically," Reynolds spoke slowly. "The subject of one of my lessons was that command never comes easy. Never has and never will."

"Some take to it more naturally than others, though." Kendricks gave a rueful smile.

"Oh, I agree. Some have aptitude." Reynolds shrugged. "Most don't, although to a certain extent, it can be learned. You know, I joined the Royal Navy as a midshipman in 1982. I did my course at Britannia and as part of that we had to do what we called initial fleet time... in other words, serving on a ship. I got lucky, or so I thought. I drew a position on a destroyer, the *HMS Sheffield*, a pretty plum posting. Do you know what happened that year?"

Kendricks shook his head. "Other than the fact I was at school?"

Reynolds gave a brief smile before letting it drop away. "The Falklands War was declared. So there was me, young, dumb and full of cum, as you yanks would say, sailing off to war. It was a tough conflict, one of the few times in recent decades where two sides have fought with anything close to parity. Sure, there's been plenty of wars since, but without devaluing the efforts of the brave sailors and soldiers that fought in them, during the Falklands we didn't have much of a technological edge over the Argies. Hell, we didn't even have any supersonic fighters in the theater. Anyway, *Sheffield* was ordered out to act as a picket to defend the aircraft carriers. The problem is, we got hit and hit hard by an Exocet missile. It was madness in the ship, Liam. The electrical system controlling the emergency vents was hit, so the corridors filled with smoke. The water main was smashed, so we couldn't extinguish the fires. Everywhere were the cries of the dying and the injured.

Reynolds face took a distant look, and he paused, clearly thinking back to that day.

"And there was me, a young midshipman with the responsibility of helping with the evacuation. I didn't have a bloody clue what to do. All the training and procedures went out of the window. I just had to lead. Lead my people out of there. And I did, Liam, I did. I may not have followed the right procedure but I damn well got them out."

"It must have been awful," Kendricks said quietly.

"It was. Twenty brave men lost their lives that day." Reynolds shrugged. "Anyway, a good few years later, in the Gulf War, I had my first combat command. In its own way, it was just as confusing. Hundreds of ships were involved from a dozen nations. I was so worried I had that sick feeling in my stomach. Was I taking my ship to the right place, at the right time, and doing the right thing? Had I confused any of my orders? I realized the feeling I had then was that which I had on the *Sheffield*. What the bloody hell do I do?"

"You come across as so confident," Kendricks said. "Presence, you know?"

"Do you want to know the secret of how I do it?" Without waiting for an affirmative, Reynolds leaned forward and whispered theatrically. "It's all a lie. I bullshit my way through convincingly, and I don't show my worry. Whether that's leading my men out of a burning ship as a midshipman, commanding a Type 23 Frigate in the Gulf as a captain, or telling the Prime Minister just why we need to invest in a bunch of new ships as an admiral. We muddle through, do the best we can, and show those who rely on us that we're cool, calm, and collected."

"Like Captain Slater, you mean?"

"Yes," Reynolds said with a smile. "Although I suspect that woman has had a transfusion of ice water into her blood stream."

"Ha!" Kendricks laughed." "Well, I think we better figure a way to muddle through, hadn't we?"

"That's the spirit."

Kendricks pulled up a deck plan of the *Atlantica*.

Chapter 58 – Day 23

"You know what?" Grayson tossed the packet of cigarettes to the young woman who was trying to bum one off him. She caught it deftly. "Keep them. I think the time below has broken the habit."

"You sure?" she asked, pulling the plastic packaging off and opening the packet with desperate hands.

"Yeah, frankly the wife hates it anyway."

"Thanks." She lit one of them and took a deep drag on it before breathing out a stream of smoke with a look of abject contentment.

"No problem."

Grayson smiled and continued walking around the railing of the ship. It was nice to breathe fresh air. The conditions in the bingo hall had been getting pretty stale. Finally, they had allowed them to come up to the cordoned-off rear section of the top deck.

Not to mention, I'll hopefully find a little space to myself now.

Grayson looked across at the *Ignatius*, feeling a twinge of guilt as he saw the damage he had inflicted on the warship. Her superstructure was blackened and the mast containing the complicated arrangement of radar and sensors was tilted at an angle. Stanchions, hastily welded to the superstructure, supported the mast.

The rest of the ship bore scars, too. The gray paintwork was scorched dark where the fires from the Molotov cocktails had struck, the discoloration covering wide swathes of the decking.

He carried on pacing around the deck, moving out of sight of the security officers presiding over them with a bored watchfulness.

Here, Grayson thought as he reached a relatively secluded area by a children's play area, a mess of paddling pools, slides, and plastic forts. Sitting down, he pulled out his CB and glanced around. Seeing no one in sight, he turned the knob on the top.

"Rain," he hissed, still looking around furtively.

***

"You can help avoid unnecessary bloodshed," Vaughan's voice was earnest, trying to get through to his two prisoners.

Laurie and Jack had been brought to the bridge again. The swelling on Jack's face had started to fade, but the reddening was still a testament to his mistreatment.

"You know, ISIL and al-Qaeda used to do this a lot," Jack snorted contemptuously. "Getting prisoners to record little videos. The world saw them for what they were. Utter bullshit."

"Please don't equate us with those savages,"

Vaughan said. "You will simply record a message saying that we wish for no further violence. If this locus happens to pan out, that is."

"And if they do want to shoot, every ship has hostages on board. Very civilized."

"Mister Vaughan, we're getting a message from Karl." A bridge crewman cupped his hand to the earphone.

Vaughan darted a furious look at the crewman, who was looking intently at his radio set and missed the glare.

"He's asking for extraction again. What should I tell him?"

Laurie's face took on a confused expression. Jack lightly tapped her leg with his foot, catching her attention and shook his head slightly before Vaughan could turn back to them.

"Tell him to wait a moment," Vaughan said through gritted teeth.

The crewman nodded. "Karl, we'll have to get back to you."

"You two will have to excuse us." Vaughan gestured at the guards. "Please return them to their quarters."

***

The heavy metal hatch closed with a slam, and Jack heard the sound of it being locked.

"What was that about?" Laurie asked. The room was spacious with just the two of them in it now, yet it still smelled of stale sweat from the hundred people who had previously been packed in there. The hundred people who were now distributed throughout the fleet as human shields.

"They've had someone on board the whole time," Jack said, his voice a mix of wonder and anger. "That

342

man who was picked up the day after we lost contact with land. His name's Karl, Karl Grayson. Sonovabitch. This whole time he's been working for the pirates."

"Jesus," Laurie breathed. "The attack on *Ignatius*? He was responsible?"

"It's a good bet." Jack lowered himself onto one of the cots. "And Grissom, maybe?"

"That officer who went missing?"

"He disappeared the day after Grayson was picked up. Maybe Grissom found out somehow?"

"We need to tell them, before he does any more harm."

"Yes we do, and damn fast too." Jack looked around the bare metal walls of the hold. Inspiration wasn't striking him.

***

"I've been on board this ship for three weeks, dammit," Grayson whispered.

"We need someone on board until we figure out this locus, Karl. Not much longer now."

Grayson gritted his teeth. There was always something. Some reason Vaughan was keeping him on board. He'd known this in his previous life. Those in charge always pushing for a little more. Hell, he'd been one of those doing the pushing at times.

"Vaughan, just for the record, I'm getting seriously unhappy. Out." Grayson finally snapped, turning the dial angrily, switching the radio off.

Chapter 59 – Day 24

"What the hell is that?" Bautista squinted at the strange cloud that was building ahead of them. It had coalesced into a column, stretching perfectly straight up from the sea high into the sky. Ethereal light flickered from within the dark mass.

Standing up, he walked to the shattered window at the front of the bridge, still unrepaired after the battle of Nest Island.

The scarred skin of his face registered the slightest of breezes. As he watched, he saw a low wave stretching across the horizon race toward the Liliana.

In moments, it swept past the *Liliana*. The ship reacted with the slightest of rocking motions.

Bautista glanced around the smashed, hastily patched together bridge. His crew looked as confused as he felt.

The ferry rocked again, and this time the wave raced from stern to bow, heading back in the direction it had come from, toward the column of cloud. As the ripple shrunk into the column base, a blue shaft of light speared vertically through its center.

Bautista blindly felt for the radio, his eyes locked

on the horizon. Finding the mic, he lifted it to his lips.

"Eric? The locus. I think it's here."

"We see it, Urbano."

Bautista looked again at his bridge crew, the men who had followed him toward the horrific meat grinder guns of the *Ignatius*. People who wanted to go home. Something he had sworn to himself he would do if possible.

"Eric, we're going to go take a look."

"No, hold position. You will give us away to the *Ig*—" Bautista cut the radio.

"Urbano, are we going home?" the young girl, Katerina, who had the helm spoke.

"Yes," Bautista lowered himself into his chair. "Yes, we are. Full speed ahead."

With a roar, the engines of the *Liliana* began pushing the ferry toward the column of cloud in the distance.

***

"What the hell is he doing?" Vaughan shouted. "Get him back on the radio, now!"

"He's not responding," the radio operator called.

Vaughan stood and walked to the grimy window on the front of the bridge. The long length of the supertanker, marred by the bolted-on storage tanks and processing units of the refinery, stretched far in front, pointed straight at the strange column ahead.

"Boss, our position is blown," *Titan's* captain murmured. "We need to go or retreat."

Vaughan closed his eyes. Everyone they had from their small community was aboard the ships of the fleet. Men, women, and children. If they backed off, they would lose every piece if initiative they had. And all because of that bastard Bautista.

Vaughan opened his eyes again.

"Forward," he said decisively.

***

"Report," Slater called as she paced into the CIC. Her hair was wet and down around her shoulders, her dishevelment a rare sight for the crew.

"We have some kind of atmospheric event occurring dead ahead, Captain." Donovan stared intently at his console. "It... doesn't look like anything I've seen before."

"The locus?" She leaned over him, looking at the camera image of the cloud column, an unnatural light coursing up through it.

"Unknown."

"Very well." Slater finished buttoning up her uniform and pulled the mic off the console. She switched to the 1MC. "General quarters. All hands to general quarters."

Hooking the mic back on the side of the console, Slater stared at the column on the main screen. It didn't appear to be moving, more a solid tube of cloud. From the base, where it touched the sea, there came a series of ripples, and then even more strangely, a reverse effect, like the water was being drawn back in. The pulsing effect repeating over and over.

"Get our Seahawk up. Tell them to go take a closer look."

"Aye aye, ma'am."

"And get me *Atlantica*."

Chapter 60 – Day 24

With a lurch, the Seahawk lifted off the pad. Clearing high over the *Ignatius*, Mack yawed the aircraft around, dipped the nose, and raced toward the column.

"I'm getting no sense of abnormal wind or weather conditions," Mack began her commentary and looked up. "I can't tell how high this thing is, but it looks like it goes a fair way up."

Wearily, the Seahawk began circling around the phenomena, keeping its distance. Deep within the cloud, the light began to pulse rhythmically.

"This is pretty X-Files," the copilot murmured. "I damn well knew it was aliens who brought us here."

"Yeah, I'm beginning to believe it," Mack responded.

Steadily, Mack kept the helicopter spiraling upward, climbing around and around the phenomena. Glancing around, in the distance, she saw a collection of dark specks on the horizon.

"Shit. *Ignatius* Actual, the pirates are here."

***

"Liam, I mean Captain, we're picking up radar returns. Many ships," Maine shouted.

"*Ignatius* has been informed," the radio operator called across the bridge. "She's moving to interdict."

Kendricks glanced at Reynolds, the tension which had aged his face seemed to wash out of the old man, replaced by a zen-like calm.

"Admiral, do you want the bridge?" Kendricks asked.

"Not at all, my boy," Reynolds replied with a reassuring smile. "Commanding a single ship at battle is well below my pay grade, at least when I used to serve. But I stand ready to assist with whatever pearls of wisdom I can offer."

"Very well." Kendricks nodded. Strangely, he drew strength from the retired admiral's calm. "Helm, bring us about, and keep *Ignatius* between us and the pirates."

Pulling his phone out, he dialed Farelly. "Tricia, get up here. I'm going to need you on the radar piping through fire control information to the *Ignatius.*"

Placing the phone down on the console in front of him, Kendricks looked around at the bridge crew.

"Ladies and gentlemen, whatever happens, we are charged with protecting the passengers on board this vessel. We will do whatever it takes. And we will succeed. Understood?"

The bridge crew looked at each other uncertainly. Finally, Reynolds said loudly and firmly, "We all understand."

One after another, the officers chorused their agreement.

***

"Charlie, Charlie, Charlie," Kendricks's voice called from the speakers. "Passengers of the *Atlantica*, we have sighted the enemy. Everyone please make their way below decks to the promenade area."

Grayson turned from gazing at the strange column a few miles off *Atlantica's* starboard side. All around him were people running for the deck entrance where their security watchdogs waved them frantically through.

Smiling faintly to himself, Grayson joined the milling throng heading toward the safety of the interior. As he started to be swept along, he saw his opportunity.

He twisted his way into an alcove in which a service door was recessed. Pulling it open, he saw it was an area used to store towels for the sun loungers.

Glancing around the small room, he saw a dirty laundry bin, half full. With a grimace, he climbed inside and covered himself in a mass of damp, chlorine-smelling towels.

***

Solberg slouched in his armchair staring out at the sea through the open sliding door of his stateroom. His dressing gown had fallen open, revealing he was wearing nothing but underwear underneath.

"I say again, Charlie, Charlie, Charlie," Kendricks announced over the PA.

Solberg took a sip on the glass of scotch he had been nursing.

***

"You're coming with us," The guard bellowed from the hatch.

Jack and Laurie released each other's hands. At some point, unconsciously, they had sought that small physical comfort with each other.

Standing up, Jack moved forward. "Where are you taking us?"

"Back to the bridge. Now move it." The guard unclipped the black leather strap on his sidearm holster to emphasize his point.

"Lead the way."

***

The *Ignatius* surged forward, placing herself between her charge and the pirate fleet which was thundering toward them, led by the *Liliana*. To one side of the colliding forces, the column lanced out of the water, high into the air; the three elements forming a triangle on the watery battlefield.

At the base of the column, hidden by the swirling mist, something arrived. Something physical. And with keen interest, it began to watch the unfolding events.

Chapter 61 – Day 24

"Confirm we're getting the fire control feed from *Atlantica*?" Slater crossed her legs and leaned back in her chair, her demeanor one of composed confidence.

Donovan, hunched over the laptop set on his console, nodded. "Aye, ma'am."

"Excellent, let's see if they're willing to talk, shall we? Give me Channel 16, if you please."

"You have the channel," the coms operator called.

"Pirate fleet, this is the *USS Paul Ignatius*," Slater's voice was as composed and confident as her appearance. "Your organization has taken a number of hostages. I want them back. You will disembark them from your vessels onto a lifeboat or other such small craft and withdraw."

The speaker was silent for long moments. Just as Slater was starting to wonder whether anyone was actually monitoring the channel, a voice spoke.

"*Ignatius*. This is *Titan*. I'm afraid we will not be dictated to by you. I'm sure you appreciate that we are more than aware of your superior firepower. Our... guests negate that advantage. Please withdraw from the locus."

"It seems we have a feisty one here," Slater

murmured with a raised eyebrow. Around the CIC, the officers and crew smiled at her dry tone.

"*Titan,* for the avoidance of doubt—I may want those hostages back, but I will not let their presence on your vessels stop me from defending this ship and *Atlantica* with all of the rather formidable weaponry I have at my disposal. You will disembark your hostages and withdraw. I am in no mood to negotiate. Weps, give me a warning shot over the lead ship." Slater didn't break the radio link as she issued the order.

"Shot out."

The Mk 45 boomed. The shell erupted from the barrel in a cloud of smoke at over eight hundred meters a second. It whistled in a parabolic arc up and over before slamming into water close enough to the racing *Liliana* that the ferry was doused in spray.

"Right where I wanted it, ma'am."

"*Titan,* as you can see, since our last encounter we've worked through some of the issues stemming from a little incident that occurred on my ship. I say again, release your hostages and withdraw."

Again, there was a long pause.

"No."

***

Bautista felt a sickening sensation in his stomach as he heard the dreaded whistling herald of an incoming shell.

It splashed into the water next to the ferry, spraying water over the *Liliana's* flank.

Taking a deep breath and calming himself, he shouted at his crew. "It was a warning shot. Keep going. We must reach the locus."

He realized he was gambling everything. Maybe once the *Liliana* reached the base of the cloud column, they would be magically transported home. Maybe they wouldn't, but he believed it, he hoped it. And if he could show it was the way out of this region that had caused nothing but misery, the madness would stop.

"Urbano, *Titan* is still trying to get us to come back."

"Ignore them."

The *Liliana* carried on racing forward, desperately striving toward the locus.

***

"That little shit," Vaughan growled. "We're cutting him off."

"Boss," *Titan's* captain gestured at the entrance where Jack and Laurie stood, watched over by the guards.

"You two," Vaughan stood and gestured angrily toward the radio set. "No more dicking around. Send a message to the *Ignatius*, tell them we have distributed the hostages throughout the fleet. Every ship has at least a couple. If they don't want their deaths on their conscience they are to stand down."

Laurie stepped forward. "Very well, I'll do it. To save lives."

"Good," Vaughan said. "We're on the same wavelength then. Now get to it."

Laurie walked to the radio and the crewman stood, making space for her. She lowered herself slowly to the chair and hesitantly picked the mic up and examined it, finding the push button on the side.

"Captain Slater, Captain Solberg. If you can hear me, they have split the hostages up among the fleet. If you hit any of the ships, you will kill them."

There was a moment's silence, then Reynold's cultured tones were heard, "Your message is received."

Laurie fought every instinct to refer to him as her father. It would just give the pirates more ammunition. She closed her eyes briefly, fighting it. She longed to be told that everything was going to be okay by her dad. Opening them, she glanced at Jack before saying into the mic as clearly as she could. "Karl Grayson is a pirate. He's one of them. He is—"

Vaughan reached across, snatching the mic out of her hand, and gave her a savage backhanded slap, knocking her off the chair.

Jack turned and punched the guard with all of his strength in the mouth. The guard reeled back, momentarily dazed. Jack followed it with a second punch, then a third, and the guard's nose flattened under the blow and he fell to the deck.

Jack fumbled for the guard's sidearm, drawing it out of the holster. He turned, bringing the weapon to bear on the pirate leader.

Vaughan was standing, Laurie before him, with the barrel of a gun jammed into the side of her head.

***

"Karl Grayson is a pirate. He's one of them. He is—"

The radio cut off and Reynolds stared at it for a moment before gently placing it down.

Kendricks gently squeezed the old man's shoulder. "She'll be okay. She's a valuable resource to them. They won't do anything to her. They clearly know the value of having hostages."

"Stupid girl," Reynolds murmured. "Stupid, brave bloody girl."

"Admiral, take a moment please, but I've got to get back to business."

Like the fact Karl Grayson, that ungrateful bastard, has been playing us all along.

Grabbing his phone, he dialed the acting head of security. "Karl Grayson, the man we picked up from that yacht... yeah him. Find him and detain him... yes, now. And be careful, he's dangerous."

Chapter 62 – Day 24

"Permission to engage, *Ignatius*." Mack yawed the helicopter around, keeping out of range of the battered white ferry that had lanced ahead of the main pirate fleet.

"Negative at this time, we have possible hostages on board the enemy vessels. Continue reconnaissance mission."

"Dammit," Mack muttered.

The weather phenomena was on her left, the huge mysterious tower of grey mist dominating the seas. Mack couldn't help glancing at it - then gave a double take. The light was gone. She couldn't decide if it was ominous, or a sign of hope.

***

Someone had briefly come into the towel room, presumably looking to see if anyone was within, and then left.

After a few minutes, Grayson climbed out of the bin, his nose twitching from the musty scent and chlorine, and walked to the hatch. The only illumination in the room was from a single emergency light, just bright enough to be able to navigate the bins and cabinets containing the laundry.

Pressing his ear against the hatch, he listened intently. He couldn't hear a thing through it. Opening it slightly, he glanced out and looked around. The deck was deserted.

Pulling it fully open, he stepped out onto the deck and walked to the rail. Far beyond in the slowly setting sun, the misty tower stood uncaring as the tiny black speck of a helicopter circled it.

Disregarding it for the moment, he pulling out his CB. "Anyone listening in, this is Grayson. I'm still aboard this goddamn ship."

"Karl?" A voice he recognized, Bautista, responded.

"Urbano, where the hell are you?"

"I'm heading for that tower thing. The big cloud."

"You're not far from the *Atlantica*. Can you get me extracted?"

"The *Ignatius* is between us and you, there's no way I'm taking my ship near her."

Shit! Grayson thought. There wasn't a chance in hell he could swim for it.

"You. Freeze!"

Grayson looked around. A team of security officers were streamed through the doors leading inside *Atlantica,* some of them with shotguns on display.

Turning, Grayson sprinted as fast as he could away from them toward the stern of the ship. The sound of a gunshot rang out and he heard the zip and ping as a bullet passed him close by, striking metal.

He reached a set of automatic glass doors which stubbornly refused to open. He was dimly aware it led into a videogame arcade and children's play area.

Grabbing a red fire extinguisher off the wall, he hefted it and slammed the base into the glass as hard as he could. The pane shattered into a million pieces. Grayson ran through, his pursuers not far behind.

Looking left and right as he ran through the arcade, beeps and rings of the video games emanated from all around him, he saw a white service door and crashed through it. Finding himself in a stairwell, he started down.

***

The *Ignatius* had turned to present her broadside to the pirate fleet, her Mk-45 turned to bear on them, along with a bushmaster and the CIWS. Behind her *Atlantica* waited, her engines were primed and ready to go to emergency dash. Save the *Titan*, she was the biggest, most cumbersome vessel, but once she got to full speed, she wouldn't be stopped easily.

From Mack's vantage point, far over the battlefield, she could see at least two dozen frothy white Vs making their way toward the two ships. If they got much closer, they would be able to swarm even *Ignatius's* myriad defenses.

Yet the first ferry was the most curious. It had departed the fleet and was intent on making its way to the locus at full speed, diverting away from the mass of her sister ships.

***

"I suggest you drop the gun." Vaughan screwed his weapon into the side of Laurie's head, causing her to yelp in pain.

Jack had Vaughan's own head neatly in his sights. He was stood in a textbook weaver stance, one foot in front of the other, already controlling his breathing, ready to take the shot.

At this distance, he knew he stood a good chance of hitting him, as long as the weapon was zeroed properly. But that was something he couldn't guarantee. He certainly wasn't confident given the dilapidated appearance of the rest of the ship.

He wasn't willing to risk Laurie.

But he was certainly willing to risk "selling the lie" that he would.

"Vaughan, lower your weapon, or I will shoot. Do it now," Jack shouted.

Vaughan dragged Laurie in closer, his arm wrapped around her neck and shoulders, the side of his head just visible. "I don't think so. You shoot me, you'll hit her. Even if you get me," Vaughan's one visible eye flicked around the room, "the rest of my crew will take you both down."

Damn, but he's cool. Jack thought. His options were limited; he was in a no-win scenario. He knew it, and worse, Vaughan knew it. He needed to change something and fast.

"If you kill us, there's nothing to stop *Ignatius* from destroying this ship and killing everyone on board."

"Jack," Vaughan chuckled before becoming serious again. "How would they know? Besides, when the locus is found to be nothing but a pipe dream, they will know they need this ship. It's the only source of fuel on this godforsaken sea."

Keeping his gun trained on Vaughan, Jack slowly sidestepped around, seeming to be striving to get a better angle for a shot on him. Vaughan tugged Laurie around, keeping her positioned between them.

"That's a fair point," Jack said. "But they don't need you."

Grabbing the mic off the console he was now next to, he pushed the button and shouted, "Fire on *Titan's* bridge. Now."

"What the fuck?" Vaughan roared. At that moment, he stepped slightly away from Laurie, and that was all Jack needed. The shoulder of Vaughan's arm became clearly visible as the bridge crew began sprinted for the exits.

Jack squeezed the trigger, the gun barked, and a red bloom appeared on Vaughan's shoulder. He spun around, both from the impact and a vain effort to flinch away from the pain.

Vaughan fell to the deck on all fours. He scrambled up and ran for the open hatch, Laurie's staggering figure momentarily blocking Jack's sight just long enough for him to get away.

Jack limped as fast as he could to Laurie and dragged her under a console.

***

"Ma'am?" The weapons officer called in response to the radio call.

"Can you hit the bridge accurately?"

"Yes, I thin—"

"Fire," Slater leaned forward.

"Ma'am, the fuel if I miss?"

"I said fire!"

"Shot out."

The Mk-45 cannon roared. The five-inch cannon shell raced up the cannon barrel, erupting from the muzzle at over twice the speed of sound. In a little over three seconds, it reached the top of its arc.

***

Second five-inch projectile fired.
Origin: USS PAUL IGNATIUS
Target
.....
....
....
TITAN
Time on target: six seconds
LaWS active. Engage. Occluded. No Effect.

***

The shell began to arc down, streaking toward the T-shaped bridge superstructure. The *Ignatius* wasn't as accurate as when she was fully operational, but even with her much-diminished capability, she could still hit where she wanted to... roughly.

The shell slammed into the port wing of the Titan's bridge, burrowing through layers of metal before lancing out of the other side. The fuse, designed to detonate the explosives in the shell a fraction of a second after impact, exploded in midair behind the superstructure, flaying layers of metal at the rear of the bridge section.

***

"Fire ineffective. Looks like the round passed through," Donovan cried out.

"Understood," Slater acknowledged. "Adjust fire."

***

Jack shook his head, clearing it before crawling out of from underneath the console Laurie and he had hidden beneath. The port side of the bridge superstructure was wrecked, the shell having passed through from front to back. The explosion had opened a hole in the corner of the bridge, and the sea was visible rushing by below.

A bullet pinged off the console next to him.

"Stay down," Jack shouted to Laurie as he lifted his weapon and fired.

***

Grayson sprinted onto the muster deck he had by chance found himself on, looking left and right.

He was gambling everything on the fact he could use one of the lifeboats to escape. The question was though, could he activate the cranes from the boats themselves?

He saw a lifeboat that was open and clambered inside. Inside he saw the ladder amidships and climbed into the turret-like cockpit. It wasn't complicated within, and to someone with Grayson's maritime knowledge, made sense.

363

He flicked the electronics master switch and with the whirr of fans, the control computer quickly booted up. The central screen activated, showing a number of options. He tapped an icon blinking **DEPLOY**. The screen was replaced with two more options. **CRANE ASSIST** and **FREEFALL**.

"Oh?" Grayson cocked his head, before giving a shrug and tapping freefall.

***

"Fire adjusted, ma'am," Donovan shouted.
"Fire."
"Shot out!"
The Mk-45 Cannon boomed again.

***

From the cloud column of the locus, a gleaming gray dagger-like prow raced out of the mist.

A bulbous turret atop the prow of the strange ship whipped around. The telescope-like fixture emerging from the turret began to track the arc of the five-inch round. The shell began to glow, a visible ember streaking across the sky. With a thud, the heavy shell exploded in mid-flight.

Slowly, the ship revealed itself further as it cleared the base of the cloud column. It was sleek, beautiful, with long graceful tapering lines, only marred by equipment that seemed unceremoniously bolted on. A much bigger radar mast than seemed right sat atop the bridge. Four box-like missile launchers and storage containers covered every available piece of deck area.

Over Maritime Channel 16, a firm voice announced, "All ships. Cease combat operations. Any further fire will be met with deadly force."

To emphasize the voice's point, one box launcher swung and faced *Ignatius*, the other the direction of the approaching pirate fleet.

***

"What the hell is that?" Mack called out.

She yawed the Seahawk around, bleeding off altitude. The locus cloud swung into view. At the base she could see a huge superyacht.

***

Kendricks and Reynolds stood, looking over the strange vista before them. *Ignatius* defiantly stood between them and the pirate fleet. They were confused by this new player, the strange yacht sailing out of the cloud-column and the firm, mysterious voice that had spoken over Channel 16.

"Sir, we have a deployment on Lifeboat 12," Maine shouted.

"What the hell?" Kendricks said, snapping his attention to the bridge officer. "Override!"

Maine looked up. "I can't. It's controlled locally, Captain."

Kendricks glanced at Reynolds and growled, "Grayson."

***

With a rumble, the arms of the crane extended out

from the side of the ship, the lifeboat swinging in the dolly beneath.

"Fasten harnesses, ejection 10 seconds. Mark." A female voice called out loudly.

Grayson struggled into the harness as the crane slammed to a halt. Outside the cockpit, he could see the security officers gathering on the muster deck. One of them pointed a handgun at him and fired. He flinched as the round starred the window.

The arm of the crane attached to the front of the lifeboat gave another push, extending out a little further, leaving the lifeboat pointed thirty degrees out from the hull. With a lurch the whole dolly tilted forward and Grayson felt himself suspended in the harness.

"3... 2... 1. Deploy."

Grayson felt his stomach rise into his chest, as if he was on a roller coaster. With a cry of "Oh shit!" the lifeboat slid out of the harness and plunged the twenty meters to the water.

With a huge splash, the mega lifeboat submerged. The view before Grayson was a cloud of bubbles. Within seconds the lifeboat surfaced and began bobbing in the water.

"Jesus," Grayson muttered, the only pause he was going to give himself. Looking over the controls, he activated the engine and began pulling away from the bulk of *Atlantica*.

***

"What happened to our shell, Mister Donovan?" Slater called out.

"Some kind of misfire, ma'am."

Slater gritted her teeth and stood, staring intently at the CIC master screen which was focused on the mysterious vessel.

Chapter 63 – Day 24

"LaWS is still on auto engage, anything that comes our way will be taken out. We have our Harpoons all locked on the *Ignatius* and the significant assets in the opposing fleet. Say the word and they're all going to the bottom of the sea."

"Thank you, Richard," Conrad Wakefield replied. The bridge of the *Osiris* would have made *Atlantica's* appear primitive. The crew were seated on grey leather chairs facing black glass touchscreen displays.

No expense had been spared. Even before she had been modified for her current purpose, she was one of the fastest vessels for her size with defenses which would give a warship pause. Now, she was immeasurably more lethal and capable.

Sleek, beautiful, and at one hundred and forty meters long, she wouldn't have looked amiss in any billionaire superyacht harbor. Which was fitting, as that was what she was originally designed for. Except now she was equipped with nearly as many weapons as the *Ignatius*. On her flanks were boxy missile launchers containing a mix of lethal Harpoon anti-ship missiles, devastating Tomahawk cruise missiles, and an array of lighter anti-aircraft missiles.

On her superstructure there was a CIWS, just as capable as the *Ignatius's*.

It was what was on her bow that tilted the advantage in the *Osiris's* favor, a LaWS —a Laser Weapon System. A turret-mounted weapon capable of targeting and destroying anything that came her way with its 200kW beam. Quite the coup for the *Osiris's* owner to obtain.

Leaning back in his chair, Wakefield spoke, seemingly into the air, "All vessels stand down. We are more than capable of sinking every last one of you. Oh, and *Atlantica*, our analysis suggests you are acting as fire control for that warship. Shut down your radar or I'll shut it down for you."

***

"Can they do that?" Kendricks looked at Reynolds.

The retired admiral was looking through a pair of binoculars at the column of cloud which had started to lean over in a direction dictated by the wind. Streamers of mist poured off it. At the rate it was dispersing, within minutes it would disappear.

"I... don't know," Reynolds said slowly. "That ship seems to have advanced capabilities. They took out *Ignatius's* shells in mid-flight. That's very high-end military technology. As of when I retired, the Royal Navy was only just getting there and we had years of work before it would become operational."

"If we shut down the radar, Slater will be blind. She won't be able to fight back against that thing," Kendricks said.

"Without her VLS, she would struggle anyway."

***

"We are not going to be the first U.S. warship to surrender since the *USS Pueblo*," Slater growled. "What precisely are we looking at here?"

The weapon systems operator looked intently at his console, trying to divine meaning from the information washing across it.

"I'm hamstrung, ma'am. We've got some kind of EM hitting us. But without the AN/SLQ, I can't tell if it's a weather scanner or an attack radar, but it's strong and focused. I'd go with the latter."

"And what took out our shells?"

The officer could only shrug. "If I didn't know better, I'd say a LaWS. It's the only thing in the inventory that could."

"Can we defeat it?"

"I..." The officer shrugged again. "We can try saturating it with cannon fire. It seemed to take a second or two to cook off a round but..."

We have seventeen rounds left in the cannon feed before we have to reload, but we can only fire every three seconds. They can pick off the rounds as we fire them, unless there's some kind of limit on them cycling the LaWS, Slater calculated furiously.

"I said, shut down the radar. You have five seconds to comply."

Keying her console, Slater said, "*Atlantica*, shut down your radar. We have an attack solution."

"Okay, Heather. I'm closing it down," Kendricks's voice replied.

"Give me Channel 16," Slater said. "If I call for it, empty our damn cannon at them, but hold till I do."

"Aye aye, ma'am. You have Channel 16... now."

"Unidentified vessel, this is Captain Heather Slater of the *USS Paul Ignatius*. At this time, I am unwilling to cease defense of this vessel or the *M/S Atlantica*. I am however willing to talk if the pirate fleet heaves to."

The silence over the radio extended for a long moment. "Captain Slater, that sounds reasonable. All vessels, cease maneuvering."

***

The round pinged off the console Jack and Laurie were hidden behind. The pirates were attempting to take back their bridge, and were firing from both of the entrances.

"Jack, are you hearing this?" Laurie shouted.

Jack popped his head over the console and returned fire at one of the pirates who had darted into the room. With a clunk, the slide on the handgun locked back. He was empty.

"I'm out, Laurie."

"There's someone new speaking on the radio. He got *Ignatius* to stop firing."

"Great," Jack muttered. "Just when this can't get any worse."

Jack looked at his handgun, then at Laurie. She was scared, that much was certain from the wideness of her eyes, the slight tremble to her lips—but what was also certain was the set of her jaw showing her strength.

"So... any plans, Jack?"

"Something's changed out there, Laurie. I'm beginning to think we need to see how this is going to play out."

Laurie nodded. "I think so, too."

Jack reached across and squeezed Laurie's hand. "It's that or go down in a blaze of glory."

"As much as I like the song… no thanks." Laurie smiled. "Would it be too cliché to ask for a kiss at last?"

"Yes it would," Jack said. "But clichés are clichés for a reason."

Jack leaned in and kissed Laurie hungrily. Within seconds, Jack pulled back.

"Let's do this." Raising his voice, Jack shouted, "We surrender. But before you come in shooting. Something has changed. The locus has arrived."

***

Grayson watched the Seahawk circle him, expecting at any moment a stream of hot tungsten to riddle the lifeboat. For whatever reason the helicopter was holding off, postponing a quick but bloody end.

"Come on, come on," Grayson muttered, glancing back down to the horizon, trying to pick the *Liliana* out. The column of cloud seemed to have lost integrity completely, the whole thing tilting away to one side as streamers of mist gently flowed off it.

Finally, he saw the white shape of the *Liliana* heading toward the lifeboat. Within minutes he had pulled alongside, and Grayson unbuckled himself and clambered around the seats within the mega lifeboat to the entry hatch.

As he reached it, it sprang open.

"Welcome back to the fleet," a familiar voice said as a hand reached down.

Grayson took hold of it and felt himself being hauled up.

"Jesus, Urbano, you look like shit." Grayson saw the closest thing he had to a friend in this godforsaken region. His face was covered in cuts and his left arm was bandaged. It was his eyes which were the most different. They had a look that Grayson recognized from his old life. The thousand-yard stare, they called it. The eyes of someone who had had enough fighting. Someone who was battle weary and just wanted out.

"And you," Bautista regarded Grayson up and down with those distant eyes, "look like you've been eating well."

"Get me back to Kristen and James, Urbano." Grayson started climbing up the rope ladder to *Liliana's* deck.

"There might be a problem with that."

Grayson paused and said through gritted teeth, "This better be good."

Chapter 64 – Day 24

"I still don't like this," Slater said quietly to the others. "Perry has orders to smash every ship he can if this goes south."

The RIB roared toward the *Osiris*, the spray washing over those on board—Slater, Kendricks, and Reynolds.

"A good fallback, but this needs to end, Heather," Reynolds replied, huddling into his wax jacket.

"Maybe," Slater looked at the growing superyacht. The RIB curved around to the stern, finally closing on the platform lowered in preparation to greet them.

***

The conference room was, again, even more palatial than anything that *Atlantica* could offer. On one side was Vaughan, wincing in pain, his arm in a sling from the gunshot to his shoulder. Next to him was Jack and Laurie.

As Reynolds entered, Laurie flew at him. Automatically the old man wrapped his arms around his daughter, hugging her so tightly the breath was squeezed out of her.

"Are you okay, sweetie?" Reynolds asked, his voice muffled as he spoke into her shoulder.

Drawing herself back, Laurie said, "I'm fine, daddy."

"You're the one who spoke on the radio?" Vaughan asked with a wry grin. "You must be fairly senior. Typical. If I'd known she was your daughter... Anyway, well played, my dear."

"You shut the hell up," Reynolds barked, pointing his finger at the smug-looking man.

"John," Kendricks laid a restraining hand on Reynolds's shoulder. "Let's find out why we're here."

Glaring at Vaughan, Reynolds finally gave a nod and seated himself at the table.

For a long moment, the whole room was silent, everyone ignoring the rich assortment of canapés and drinks on the sideboard. Surrounding them on the wall was artwork which seemed expensive. Given the opulence of the surroundings, it didn't seem like it would be fake.

"Sucks, doesn't it?" Kendricks said pointedly at Vaughan.

Giving a sharp hiss as he shifted himself to look back at *Atlantica's* captain, Vaughan asked, "What does?"

"Being shot in the arm. The doctor says I'll be suffering for the rest of my life from my own little mishap. "I'll probably have all kinds of aches and pains going on."

"I don—" Vaughan started. The door opened and Bautista entered. The athletic man moved around the table and prowled to a free chair.

Vaughan stared daggers at the man. "You. Running off like that, you little shit."

"Oh shut—" Bautista started to say.

Again they were interrupted as another man walked in. He was silver haired, wearing a navy polo shirt. He was known to many in the room. Conrad Wakefield, billionaire technology magnate and venture capitalist. A man who was known to have his fingers in so many pies that he probably didn't even know where half his wealth came from.

"So," Wakefield said as he walked to the sideboard and looked at it for a moment. Selecting an apple, he crunched down on it before making his way to sit at the head of the table, still chewing. Finally swallowing his mouthful, he casually leaned back in a chair. "Why the hell are you guys shooting at each other?"

"Perhaps," Slater's voice was icy cold, "you can tell us?"

"Perhaps I can," Wakefield smiled, his casual demeanor fooling no one in the room. The burning intelligence in his eyes was too intense. "I'm Conrad Wakefield, you may have se—"

"We know who you are," Slater interjected in a frosty voice. "What we want to know is what the hell is going on here?"

"Very well, but it is a bit of a long story. Everyone eaten?" Wakefield gestured at the sideboard. "No? Okay."

"Cut the bullshit," Vaughan snapped.

"Business before banter, huh?" Wakefield looked around the room, and was greeted with stony silence. He gave a shrug. "As you wish. Tell me, what do you know about the Permian-Triassic event?"

The frost didn't thaw, but frowns of confusion creased the foreheads of several in the room.

"It was one of several large extinction events," Laurie spoke slowly. "Not the dinosaur one. Another, but beyond that my knowledge is a little lacking."

"That's right," Wakefield nodded. "In fact, it was far more serious than the Cretaceous-Paleogene event you are referring to. Actually, out of the six major extinction events, the one that took out the dinosaurs was one of the least destructive to Earth's species overall. That one merely wiped out seventy-five percent of all life. No the P-Tr event was a touch more serious, taking out something in the region of ninety-six percent of marine life, and seventy percent of the terrestrial species."

"Mr. Wakefield, I must admit, I love the film Jurassic Park, but I'm failing to see the point in the history lesson," Vaughan said.

"The point, kinda, is that the K-Pg event would have been a hell of an inconvenience to humanity, on a species level, but it would probably have muddled through, considering our technology, in some form. As for the P-Tr?

Well, the best theory is that one was in fact multiple extinction events hitting the Earth at once. If the human race had been around during the P-Tr, we would be gone, kaput, exterminated. There's no point in preparing for it, as we can't do anything about it." Wakefield took another bite of his apple, crunching away on it, seeming to think about his next few words. "And, if we can't do anything about it, what is the point in telling anyone it's coming?"

The room was silent as the people gathered in it paid rapt attention to Wakefield. Kendricks could feel a sense of dread in the base of his stomach. He knew that Wakefield had a point he was meandering to, but the only resolution that seemed logical, was also unthinkable in its implications.

"In 2012, the Siding Spring Observatory was the only program dedicated to tracking killer comets and asteroids. They had tracked something coming in, a beast of a comet called C/2012 E2," Wakefield gave a wave of his hand. "Those numbers mean something. C says it's a non-periodic comet, 2012 that it was discovered in 2012, E that it was found in the first half of March and 2 that it was the second to be found in that time period. The catchier name for C/2012 E2 was Perses, the Titan god of destruction, no relation to your little tub out there. It was called that as it was heading right for us."

"How…" Kendricks started, then rallied himself. "How could they keep that quiet? How long do we have?"

"This worried people… people in high-up places." Wakefield ignored him. "So they devoted a lot of time and effort into figuring out what was going to happen, and how to stop it. The problem was, there is no stopping a twenty-mile-wide ball of rock and ice coming at high speed. What they did find though was worse, far worse. The location of where it was going to come down. The Pacific Ocean, just to the west of mainland America. Only that created whole new problems. By the scientists' best estimates, it would set off the Yellowstone Caldera. So get this, much like the P-Tr event, we would have not one, but two extinction-level events to face. Humanity might have staved off one of them, though we likely would have been blasted back to the Stone Age. Without a doubt, America would be gone, it would simply cease to be, but other redoubts of humanity might have survived. But two? Not a chance. By the best estimates, we were looking at a ninety percent extinction level."

"Ninety percent? Only one in ten people would survive?" Kendricks said in disbelief.

"No," Laurie said quietly. "He's saying ninety percent of everything living would die."

"That's right, little lady." Wakefield nodded. "And humanity, being a higher lifeform, would have been pretty much on the top of the list to go first."

"So how do we stop it?" Slater asked.

Jesus, Kendricks thought in admiration. *She's heard that and all she can think of is defeating the problem. So that's how someone gets to be commander of a warship.*

"I told you. There is no stopping it," Wakefield said. "Don't get me wrong, a number of programs were instituted and discarded. In top secrecy, NASA tried to come out with a solution—and came up blank. So then it becomes a matter of survival, and let me tell you, there were some pretty hare-brained schemes. Assuming that elements survived the initial impact and eruption, the surface of the Earth would be uninhabitable for dozens of years until the dust and crap settled out of the atmosphere. Meanwhile, the world would be thrust into subzero temperatures as all sunlight would be blocked out, killing most of the surface animals and life. Sea life would take a massive hit."

"So what are these hare-brained schemes you refer to?" Vaughan said, before giving a sharp, pain-laced intake of breath.

"The American government had given up. No one else knew, but a… collective managed to get wind of what was going on through their own confidential sources. A number of projects were instituted. The most glamourous? A scheme to colonize Mars under the guise of a competition. Actually the competition was a little less random than it seemed. One hundred people were selected who would have the genetic diversity and frankly skills to start again on Mars. Problem is, no one had the technology to do it. Nevertheless, the last time I checked in, they were still tinkering away, trying to get the first load up by 2035. Seemed like a dead end to me though, quite literally. One hundred people on a barren world with no support from Earth? Hell, even if they did survive the journey, they'd be dead within a couple of years. There were a few other schemes. Desperately creating shelters, which would mean humans would spend decades underground, hibernation crèches where people could somehow be preserved. None of them were viable for the time we were talking."

"You had a plan though, didn't you?" Kendricks said.

"I did, with the help of some people far brainier than I. The Large Hadron Collider beneath France and Switzerland discovered something very interesting. The Higgs Boson. The so-called 'God Particle'. That thing was fantastic, had all kinds of interesting properties, but that's not what was truly exciting. When a Higgs Boson is created, something called a 'Higgs Singlet' pops into existence as well. These things are temporally unbound, in other words, they can travel in time. With some modification, we figured we could stream these as a beam capable of passing through the Earth itself. When that beam hits a suitable receiver, one of which I happen to have in the back," Wakefield gestured over his shoulder with his thumb, "then it would shift the surrounding area forward in time. And there came our plan, to sidestep the extinction event, bypassing it and coming through on the other end, when the Earth had repaired itself.

"I don't understand though. Surely if something travels around in time, we will just end up floating in space," Laurie said, a confused expression on her face. "I mean, while the object travels in time, the Earth would still carry on spinning around the sun."

"You are a smart cookie." Wakefield seemed genuinely pleased with her. "Can I hire you?"

"We'll see," Laurie retorted.

"The LHC itself would act as an anchor, effectively locking us to the mass of the Earth. There was some risk—what if the sea level rose or lowered significantly? Frankly it was a gamble, but better than the alternative. But this was also the reason why we needed to target only craft on the sea, and in areas where continental drift wouldn't mean that anything that popped through didn't get trapped in the middle of a mountain range or some equally grim end."

"Mister Wakefield," Slater said coldly. "You haven't said it explicitly yet. I need you to, and right now. Are you saying you've sent us into the past or future?"

"Yes, Commander. Welcome to the year 10002024 AD," Wakefield said each number individually, counting the zeros out on his fingers. "Or thereabouts. 10 million years in the future. The nature of the Higgs Singlet didn't give us a lot of choice in when we would pop back into the world; we couldn't fine tune it closely enough to actually pick what point in the future. It was to here or nowhen."

"My…" Slater's voice cracked finally, her bottom lip giving the slightest of wobbles. "I have a daughter. How long…? When did Perses hit?"

Wakefield leaned across the table and grasped the top of her hand. Slater quickly drew it back, as if the billionaire's touch was burning hot.

"She would have had years," Wakefield said quietly. "Twenty of them. And when it happened, they were going to keep it secret. When Perses was visible in the sky, they would have given disinformation that it was going to fly past and harm no one. It would have been over in a blink. No pain. She wouldn't have suffered."

"Send us back," Slater shouted, causing everyone in the room to jump. "I want to go back to her. I want to be with her."

"I can't," Wakefield's cockiness had disappeared in an instant. "This was a one-way trip. Your ships, all of them, were just caught on the outer edges of the Singlet beam. You got pulled through in our wake which, due to the rather bizarre nature of the beam, meant you came through first. That's all by design, I might add. We wanted to save as many as we could."

The room was silent except for the crunching as Wakefield took another bite of his apple.

"Are there others?" Kendricks asked after a long moment. "Other loci, I mean."

"If you mean by loci, the beams?"

Kendricks nodded.

"Yes, a few. The LHC was set to target a number of areas around the world. We needed to give ourselves as good a chance as we could that we would save... enclaves of humanity."

"So, what is your plan now?" Reynolds finally asked.

Wakefield looked at Reynolds for a long moment. "I'm sure you can figure that out. We start again."

Chapter 65 – Day 24

Night had fallen. The soft twinkle of stars glistened down on the gathered ships. Wakefield had wisely chosen to withdraw, allowing the two factions to ruminate, and then negotiate.

"This has to stop," Reynolds made the first overture. "This conflict. Things have changed now and irreversibly so. If we are to survive, all of us, it is only going to be together."

"No," Slater slammed her fist into the table. She stood and leaned over the table, seeming to grow in stature. "My ship was attacked, your ship was attacked. Our people are dead. There will be no ceasefire. I'm not in the business of negotiating with either terrorists or pirates."

"Heather." Kendricks reached over and gripped her arm, gently but firmly. "Your business has changed, all of ours has. We lost people, too."

"We all did," Bautista's voice was soft. "But are we going to carry on losing people? Good people? People who have families, like your passengers, like our community?"

"They are right, Heather," Reynolds pressed. "Both sides in this conflict have inflicted losses. We need to broker a truce at the least, an accord at the best."

"Then I demand reparations," Slater said. "Under my authority as the senior officer, I am going to try and convict the leaders of your fleet.

At the very least that includes you, Vaughan, Bautista here, and that treacherous piece of shit, Karl Grayson."

"I think we can all agree that Grayson needs to be hung by the yardarm," Kendricks said with uncharacteristic venom. "He killed one of my crew, and sabotaged the *Ignatius*."

Jack nodded in agreement.

"The way I see it, we have the most significant resource in the region… in the world." Vaughan smiled condescendingly. "We have a tanker full of oil and the resources to get started again. Now we know there are no more ships coming through, we will leave this area, go somewhere else and never bother you again."

"Eric, that is not going to happen," Bautista said. "Have you heard nothing? Everything's changed. We must work together. I'll not let you just leave and continue your empire somewhere else."

"You don't have a choice," Vaughan hissed, wincing in pain and standing. "I'm done here. I will return to the *Titan*. You can have your people back, but we are leaving."

"Vaughan, if you try to leave, I'll just take your goddamn ship," Slater growled.

"And there we have it," Vaughan smiled. "You're no better than us. This is over. We will clear outside your radar range and then drop off the hostages."

Vaughan stood, and began to walk toward the door. He paused. "Urbano, despite your shitty attitude, you help keep my fleet together. One chance. Come with me."

Bautista looked around the room. His eyes settled

on Jack. The battered soldier gave a slow nod and an unspoken communication passed between the two. Bautista, remained still for a moment, before saying, "Very well, I'll come with you."

"I want Grayson," Slater called after them. The door slid shut behind the two men's backs as they left.

***

"Well, that didn't go well for 'em." Wakefield's feet were resting on his desk, watching the exchange on the huge TV screen on his office wall.

"You want to intervene further?" Richard Hogarth, the *Osiris's* captain, asked. "Commander Slater looks pissed. If this goes south, *Ignatius* looks hurt bad, but I still wouldn't put a bet on that we can take her. She's designed from the keel up to take hits. She only needs to land one good one on us and we're done."

"Nah, screw 'em." Wakefield swung his legs off the desk. "They're just posturing. We have everything we need to start afresh, they don't — not individually, anyway. They work it out or they don't. Them being here is a bonus. We always knew others were going to get caught up in the Singlet beam, it's just that somehow we managed to catch a bunch of real assholes."

"We could always go after the *Titan's* fleet?" Hogarth phrased his statement as a question.

"Richard," Wakefield became deadly serious, switching off the false joviality he had previously showed. "We're here to save the human race. Frankly, we can do without bringing conflict into our brave new world. I'm not going to attack *Ignatius*, *Titan*, or anyone else if I can help it. We have given them information, they can make of it what they will."

Chapter 66 – Day 25

It was past midnight by the time Bautista had returned to the *Liliana*. Grayson stood on the shattered bridge, lost in thought as he gazed at the sleek superyacht alongside.

The luxurious craft was familiar to him. Every line had been burned into his memory, even obscured as they were by the equipment and weapons that had been bolted on. But it was something he had never expected to see again. Not after so many years.

Memories that had been filed away as irrelevant to his current situation were beginning to emerge. Memories that told—

"I'm taking you home, Karl." Bautista had paced quietly onto the bridge and stood alongside Grayson.

Grayson started, before turning to look at his friend. "Home?"

"To the *Titan*, to Kristen and James."

"It's not really our home though, is it?" Grayson said.

"No, and we'll never be going there again. Home is where we make it now."

Grayson listened in dim shock as Bautista explained, as best he could in his ill-educated way, what Wakefield had told him and Vaughan's decision to leave. And he told Grayson of Slater's demand.

Grayson turned and looked at the distant *Atlantica*, brightly lit against the nighttime sky, the smaller speck of the *Ignatius* next to her. "You know Slater will follow us. She wants me; I hurt her ship. And Kendricks? I did something far worse to his ship and to his crew, Urbano. I killed someone on there."

"We've all killed people."

"Yes, but that was battle. Slater gets that, even the crew of *Atlantica,* I reckon. They might not forgive it, but they understand it. No, what I did was cold-blooded murder." Grayson held up two bunched fists. "With my bare hands."

Bautista turned and looked at him, a flicker of calculation behind his battle-weary eyes.

"So to bring peace, they will need a sacrifice on the altar of justice."

"They do, Urbano." Grayson leaned forward on the console. "But not yet. Take me back to my family. I want to see them first. Then we'll do what we have to do."

***

"Shit," Donovan said. The color had completely drained from his face.

A flicker of a smile washed over Kendricks's face. He had expected nothing worse than "Gosh" from Donovan. Slater's summary of events had been concise, to the point, and emotionless in its delivery. Donovan's single word response spoke volumes of his worry.

"So what now, ma'am?"

"I don't know, Perry. I just don't know. But what I am sure of is that it is incumbent on you, me, and the other senior officers to look after the welfare of our crew," Slater said.

These two are soldiers without a country, along with the rest of the crew of the Ignatius, Kendricks thought. He frowned gently at himself. Was he being disingenuous by wondering if they would now exert their authority in a benevolent, or not so benevolent dictatorship? After all, if they wanted anything from the *Atlantica,* they could just take it.

"Your mission," Jack finally said as he reached across to Laurie and placed his hand over hers on the cramped *Ignatius* wardroom table. "Our mission, has not changed. We still have people to protect. People who in turn will provide for us and entrust us. To my mind, the model still works. It's just on a much smaller scale."

"Young Jack makes a valid point," Reynolds broke in. "Heather, the *Ignatius* and her crew still have a purpose in this new world. It's the six thousand people on board we still have to find direction and hope for. And that is something we need to give them."

"And you have an idea?" Slater asked.

"Yes." Reynolds gestured at the bulkhead upon which a screen print of the map from the LEAP was hung. "Mainland America. It's a lot further

away than we expected. But we can make it, quite easily. Once there, we can hopefully renew our farming efforts and, well, begin the process of rebuilding civilization."

"And the pirates?"

"We, and they, have a decision to make. Are we going to move forward together? With each other we'll be far more than the sum of our parts. They must know that."

Chapter 67 – Day 25

The hatch swung open with a creak.

"Dad!" The boy darted away from his mother straight toward Grayson, who was already kneeling to accept James with open arms.

"Hey, little fella." Grayson clutched the boy to him so tightly the child gasped. He hadn't seen him in a month. A month that felt like a lifetime. "You been looking after your mom?"

"Yes he has," Kristen said, wrapping her arms around both of them, squeezing the boy even more tightly between them. "Tell me you're not going away on one of those damn scouting missions again?"

"No, he's not."

Grayson had dimly realized that Vaughan, and two crewmembers who seemed suspiciously muscular, had been in the room. Realized and not cared. Now Vaughan stood and approached the family, reaching out his left hand as he did so, his other in a sling.

"Well done, Karl."

Standing, Grayson regarded the man who had given him a new mission since he had arrived here.

In many ways, being welcomed into the community had been responsible for his meeting of Kristen, and his son's existence.

But Vaughan was responsible for what could best be described as perfecting the piratical system they had adopted, too.

"And, Urbano. Welcome back to the *Titan* as well, I suppose." Vaughan gave a false smile, letting his ignored hand drop. "We will have to have a chat about your actions at the locus later, though."

"Sooner rather than later," Bautista nodded in agreement.

Vaughan gave a frown. "Always good to clear the air."

"Honey." Grayson kissed Kristen on the forehead. Letting it linger there for a moment. "I just have to have a chat with Eric. Then I'll come join you and James."

"Okay." A flicker of disappointment crossed Kristen's face. "But hurry. We're down on deck three. Someone down there will point you in the right direction."

"Thanks, honey." Giving her another kiss, Grayson released his wife and watched his family leave the cabin. He turned to Vaughan. "We have a lot to talk about."

"Yes we do," Vaughan sighed. "Slater and Kendricks want you. I don't think they'll stop until they have you, and that puts us in an uncomfortable position."

"That's an understatement, Eric." Grayson looked around the room. The two crewmembers were leaning idly against the wall. Grayson gave a mental nod to himself as he saw one of them clench and unclench his fist. Their idle demeanor was a show. These two were ready.

"You understand, I don't want to give you to them, don't you?"

"I do."

"And you do know it would be in the best interests of your family if you were to go without any fuss. We can then just sail away into the sunset and never see the *Ignatius*, *Atlantica*, or anyone else who can bother us again."

"The best interests of my family?" Grayson's voice was little more than a whisper. "Are you threatening them again? I thought we'd discussed your motivational techniques before, Eric, and how much I disapprove of them."

The two men stood straight, and from the corner of his eye he could see Bautista moving closer to his left side.

"You know me, Karl. I never like to threaten. But the thing is—"

Grayson snatched the gun Bautista had given him from the back of his waistband. Smoothly but quickly he brought it up, sighted along it, and pulled the trigger. The shot was loud in the confined cabin. A red circle, the size of a dime, appeared on Vaughan's forehead. The bulkhead behind splattered with blood.

As Vaughan sank to his knees, Grayson trained his gun on the crewman to the right, Bautista aiming his own weapon at the other.

"The thing is," Bautista finished Vaughan's sentence, "someone has to pay the price. Please, drop your weapons. There need be no more killing."

The two crewmen had only managed to grip their

own weapons and half draw them from their holsters. Slowly, they knelt down and placed their guns on the deck.

Grayson cocked his head as he looked at the body of Vaughan, slumped on the deck. He felt no sympathy for the man and he suspected Bautista had less. He had wanted nothing more than his own empire, at any cost.

"So, Urbano…" Grayson's weapon was still trained on the crewman. "It's time to ask them if this is a suitable sacrifice for that altar of peace you were talking about."

***

"Message on Channel 16, sir. It's from the *Titan*."

Kendricks turned from where he stood, hands clasped behind his back staring out at the superyacht and pirate fleet beyond.

"Let's hear what Vaughan has to say. Put it through the speakers, Kelly."

"It's a different voice. Not Vaughan."

"Oh? Put it through anyway."

"Captain Slater, Captain Kendricks, and the other man who seems to be in charge," the thickly accented voice said. "We of the *Titan* wish to stop all fighting between us and talk about joining together."

Kendricks blinked in surprise. Why would the tone change so much?

"Identify yourself," Kendricks heard Slater demand.

"I am Urbano Fernandez Bautista. I am now the leader of this community."

"Bautista, this is *Atlantica*. Why the sudden

change of heart?"

"You heard the man on the nice boat. Things have changed. Our leadership has changed to reflect that."

"And where is Vaughan now?" Kendricks asked.

"Vaughan led this fleet into war with you," Bautista's voice, even over the radio, was earnest. Kendricks could tell he wanted to be listened to. "That war killed people on both sides. For that, we are sorry. Justice has been provided. Vaughan is no longer an issue."

So Vaughan's dead, Kendricks thought. He surprised himself. The man of a month ago would have been horrified that someone he had spoken to less than a day before had been executed. Now, Kendricks felt nothing, other than perhaps a glimmer of satisfaction.

"I'm afraid not, Mister Bautista," Slater's voice was cold, cutting across the coms. "We require Karl Grayson to be delivered to us, along with the rest of the leadership of your fleet, and the hostages too, of course. If you care about your people, that will be done."

There was a pregnant pause from the radio speaker. Kendricks looked at the grill.

"Your hostages will be released as soon as we load them onto the boats. This is a gesture of goodwill."

"And the rest of my terms?" Slater asked.

"No. Captain Slater, you are a soldier, no? Grayson was a bullet. Our fleet was a gun, but Eric Vaughan pulled the trigger—"

"I'm not going to debate warrior philosophy with you. My terms or none."

"Then we leave," Bautista said, his voice as firm as Slater's. "But consider this. We have resources, fuel, and enough food to more than last until we reach the coast. *That* we will provide for you in recompense. In return we wish two things, to join your fleet as equal partners and, what is the word? Amnesty, yes amnesty for past actions."

"Wait, out," Slater said.

A moment later, Kendricks's phone began buzzing in his pocket. Pulling it out, he saw it was Slater calling him.

"What do you think?" Slater asked without preamble. "Is he bullshitting us?"

"Heather, I want Grayson and Bautista hung from the yardarm as much as you. Those bastards attacked my ship and killed my crew."

"I sense a but."

"But, you heard Wakefield. We have to start thinking bigger. We might be the only people left. Can we really afford to cut them loose?"

"Liam, I can just take the *Titan*."

"Before they scuttle her or do something equally silly?"

"Possibly," Slater said slowly.

"And how many more would die, Heather?"

"Lots, probably."

"You want to run it past John Reynolds? And Jack Cohen?"

"Yes… no." Slater sighed. "As much as it galls me to say, I can understand Bautista's actions. In his own way, he is a soldier. Grayson is something different. He's an American. How could he have done this?"

"Trust me, I want him as much as you. Could we not say yes and, I don't know, arrest him later?"

There was a silence on the phone before finally Slater spoke wistfully. "That would be the easy solution, Liam, but not the honorable one. I'm an officer. My word is my bond. I would put that bastard in front of a firing squad in a heartbeat as part of either negotiations or a judicial process. I should not, however, lie, kidnap, and then murder him."

Kendricks smiled for what felt like the first time in a long time as his admiration for the woman grew. "I'm very pleased to hear that."

"Liam, *Atlantica's* been wronged the most. You have the largest complement of people to look after. Until we decide otherwise, the model of government works. Your call. You are the taxpayer, after all."

Kendricks could sense her wry smile through the phone. Lowering it, he nodded at Maine to activate the bridge mic.

"Mister Bautista?" Kendricks said formally. "Terms accepted."

"Thank you." The relief in Bautista's voice was palpable.

"But, even if your people and ours become the most bosom of buddies, Grayson comes nowhere near my ship, the *Ignatius,* or our people. If he does, he'll be detained on sight, tried and, if Captain Slater gets her way, executed. Understood?"

"Understood."

"Lady and gentlemen," Wakefield's voice came over the speakers. Kendricks was unsurprised he had been listening in. "I knew you had it in you to come to a mutually acceptable position. Bravo."

What a cocky asshole, Kendricks thought.

Chapter 68 – Day 26

The quiet and subdued—or sullen—passengers and crew of the *Atlantica* filled the promenade in front and behind the span.

Kendricks gave a slight swallow. He had never addressed so many people at once. A mass of people filled the promenade. Nearly every one of the six thousand passengers and crewmembers who could be excused from duties were crowded before and behind him.

Rallying himself, Kendricks started. "Passengers and crew of the *Atlantica*, I have called you here to tell you of the extraordinary situation we have found ourselves in, and what we're doing about it."

Kendricks lowered his head, taking a moment. How did you tell people that everyone they ever knew were gone and long dead? How did you tell them they had found themselves thrust far in the future? It was fantastical, inconceivable... and terrifying.

"I have thought long and hard about how to tell you this news. And if I'm honest, I even considered if I should tell you." A murmur washed over the crowd, the collective reaction to his somber tone.

"The first thing you may be curious about is that Captain Solberg has, unfortunately, been taken ill. For the time being, I am taking on his duties and I fully intend to step up to the plate. Your team is here for you, and you are safe."

Kendricks paused, giving the crowd a moment. "But that is not the most significant news. We have established where we are. Or more accurately, *when* we are."

Once again, Kendricks gave the crowd a moment to take in his wording. This was the bit they had elected to be somewhat sparing with the truth, lest the passengers and crew demand action against the *Osiris* for what they might view as a wholesale kidnapping. "By means we do not fully understand, we have been thrust far into the future, so far it is difficult to imagine. In that time, the world has changed and the continents have moved. That is why we have not been able to locate land. And that is why home, as we know it, no longer exists."

The shouts and cries that erupted created an unintelligible wall of sound. This was the moment Kendricks had feared, and what they had debated for hours. Jack Cohen had been a staunch advocate of simply locking everyone in their rooms and telling them there, over the TV PA system. At least that way, the shattered remnants of the security team wouldn't have a full-scale riot to contend with. In the end, Kendricks had decided that if this new world were to work, it had to be built on trust, and that would only work if he, the captain, made the first gesture.

"Please," Kendricks repeated. "I need you to listen and be calm."

For long moments Kendricks feared violence was going to erupt. He waved Carrie over. "Turn the volume up full, as loud as you can."

Giving a nod, Carrie rushed back along the span and entered the DJ booth that overlooked the promenade. After a moment, she gave a thumbs up.

"PLEASE, I NEED YOU TO BE CALM." Kendricks winced at the volume of his voice thundering out of the speakers, but it broke the mood, and the shouting subsiding.

"We know a few things." Kendricks noted with relief that Carrie was reducing the volume steadily to a more-tolerable volume. "We know mainland America exists still, and that will be our course. We are returning home. What we may find there, we don't know, but that is our destination. We know that the fighting you have witnessed over the last month cannot continue. The pirates were in the same situation as us. Scared, uncertain, and desperate for answers. They have made a choice. They have a new leader, one who wishes to ally with us. They have fuel and supplies, and have offered to share them with us. The man who led them in attacking us has been brought to justice. They are eager to help, and we are eager to accept. We know that the brave sailors of the *Ignatius* will continue to defend us from whatever we face. We know the *Atlantica* can support us for as long as we need. I repeat, you are safe, as long as you are calm, and trust us."

"We know," Kendricks said, letting his voice rise. "That together, we can get through the challenges we will inevitably face. Tomorrow, we will set sail from this place. Tomorrow we are going home to America."

Lowering his microphone, Kendricks looked over the quiet crowd. They seemed, as a collective, mollified that they finally had a destination.

***

"Well said, young man." Reynolds took a sip of his brandy.

"I'm not that young." Kendricks winced from the twinge in his shoulder.

"Everyone's young to me, son," Reynolds smiled.

Kendricks had found the half-full bottle of McDowell's Number One in Captain Solberg's bottom drawer when he had taken over his office, and thought it would be good lubrication for the job offer he had for the old admiral.

"About that," Kendricks said, looking at the man, a picture of calm, reassuring competence. "The passengers are going to need a leader, a spokesperson if you will, and preferably one of them."

"Are you headhunting me?" Reynolds asked.

"Yes. Want the job?"

"I hate politics." Reynolds gave a frown. "And no, I don't want the job, but someone has to do it, I guess."

"That's the spirit."

"And here's me thinking this would be a nice relaxing cruise," Reynolds grimaced as he downed the amber fluid in his glass in one fell swoop.

"You know I was going to suggest a cheers to your new appointment." Kendricks raised one eyebrow.

"That implies a celebration, dear boy."

Chapter 69 – Day 26

Kendricks ducked as the sleek Airbus H155 touched down on *Atlantica's* flight deck. The blast of air from the rotor wash caused him to step back slightly.

One after another, the occupants stepped out. Wakefield, Slater, and Bautista joined Kendricks, Reynolds, and Jack on the landing pad, the billionaire owner of the *Osiris* having done a round robin, picking up the senior members of the fleet.

"Welcome aboard the *Atlantica*," Kendricks shouted over the spooling-down engines.

"Don't think I'm going to be offering this kind of taxi service often," Wakefield shouted back. "Special occasions only."

Gesturing toward the hatch, Kendricks ignored the man's attempt at humor. "If you'd like to come with me."

***

The discussions and negotiations had taken them well into the night. They had batted many things around the table. How to redistribute the remaining food and people around the fleet? What should they do about the wrecked yet mostly untapped resource of the container vessel the pirates had discovered? Which ships should be left behind, and which should be taken with them?

Eventually, the plan came together. Together they would make the expedition home.

***

The meeting had drawn to a close, and small talk had taken over business.

"I feel I must take some fresh air," Reynolds said, standing and stretching out his arms.

Wakefield looked at the man for a moment before saying, "I think I may join you. It's been a hell of a long night.

In silence the two men stepped out of the conference room and walked down the corridor. Reaching a pair of glass doors that slid open at their approach, they stepped out into the fresh night.

Reynolds leaned on the railing and gazed over the moonlit ocean, and Wakefield took up a position next to him.

"You are a hypocritical old bastard, John," Wakefield said after a long silence.

Reynolds seemed to ignore him for a beat, before looking up at the man next to him. "To be honest, I'm surprised you didn't have me bumped off after you cut me loose back in Nassau. You have been somewhat... single minded in this endeavor."

"Ha," Wakefield scoffed without humor. "What were you going to do? Blow our little secret? You may not have liked my methods, but the objective was still sound; the survival of the human race. Even your much-vaunted morals acknowledged this was all for the greater good, and the only way to escape what was coming."

"And for Laurie, it was the only ride out of dodge," Reynolds replied.

"That's right," Wakefield winked. "Well, the only ride you and she could get on."

Standing, the retired admiral looked at the billionaire. "So what are you going to do, Conrad? Tell them I was in on it?" Reynolds inclined his head back toward the door to indicate the others within.

"Why?" Wakefield shrugged. "To what end? They'd just keelhaul you. Besides, it's always nice to have an inside man."

"I don't like swearing, Conrad. But fuck you. I helped you back home, but I'm not your inside man."

"Just remember that keelhauling I mentioned, John." Wakefield's voice became firm. "They won't take kindly to—

Wakefield gave a gasp as Reynolds's hand gripped his throat. "Don't you dare threaten me. My conscience is clear, more or less. You, however, are a murdering bastard."

Wakefield reached up and pried Reynolds's fingers from around his throat. "Yet you find yourself here, with me. Your principles only took you so far, you still wanted on the last train, and you made sure you were on it. Even when you knew what would happen when that train pulled out the station."

Reynolds stepped away from the other man. For a moment he considered giving another retort. Instead, he settled for just shaking his head. "We're here,

Conrad. What more could you want from me?"

"We have to rebuild the human race. That Kendricks guy said you're going to be the mayor or some such shit on this road show. I need you to make sure they stay on course, to make sure things go the way they should go."

"The way they should go? Or the way you want them too?"

"That's the same thing, my friend, that's the same thing." Wakefield slapped the other man on the back, once again jovial and cocky.

Chapter 70 – Day 27

"So, will I get more?" Laurie said as she bumped her shoulder playfully into Jack's side.

"More?"

The two of them stood on the rear deck by the empty waverider, overlooking the motley collection of ships anchored behind the *Atlantica*.

"You know," Laurie winked at him. "Snogs?"

"Ohhh," Jack said, looking in every direction other than at Laurie. "You know that was under pressure. I was vulnerable at the time."

"You were," Laurie pursed her lips and nodded. "Vulnerable. I do admit I took advantage of a moment of distraction caused by a horde of rampaging pirates."

"Yes, you did."

"But maybe, it's time to see how you perform under real pressure."

Laurie grasped Jack's hand firmly and tugged him in the direction of the doors leading inside the *Atlantica*.

***

"Come on, Hank. Put your back into it!" Mack called to her WSO. Her overalls were streaked with grease after she had been lying under the spare Seahawk they were cannibalizing a fuselage panel from.

Together they lifted the heavily armored section, and as gingerly as they could, placed it in a dolly for wheeling to the hanger next door so they could replace damaged parts of her helicopter.

"You know what, ma'am? I'm seriously considering going on strike. Then you'll learn to appreciate us poor NCOs," Hank said, his voice straining with effort.

"You don't mean that, do you, Hank?" Mack gave a roguish grin.

"Pilots!" Hank muttered with affectionate exasperation.

***

"Kelly, how are we looking?" Kendricks turned from the window overlooking the dawn-lit ocean.

"As good as we'll ever be, Skipper."

Kendricks gave a slight smile. To be called Captain was one thing, an acknowledgement of one's rank. To be called Skipper was a respectful, yet affectionate, other. It showed he had been accepted as their leader in heart as well as mind.

"Then please, signal the rest of the fleet and our wagon train we're ready to move. Economic cruise, if you please."

"Aye aye. Ahead at twenty knots, economic cruise."

Kendricks moved around the bridge and settled

into his chair.

Slowly, the huge ship built up its speed, giving the slightest of lurches as the towing cable played out behind the vessel snapped taut.

The wagon train of craft, running parallel to the one led by the supertanker, *Titan,* began moving west. Ahead of the fleet, the *Ignatius* sailed, the flicker of welding torches blinking across her damaged superstructure.

Together, the fleet set a course to the west, in the direction of America.

Epilogue

Slater stood on the deck of the *Ignatius*, gazing up at the battered mast. The breeze from the speed of their journey over the nighttime sea caused her hair, uncharacteristically loose, to whip around. Unconsciously, she was twisting the Annapolis Naval Academy ring on her right hand.

She thought back to the conversation with Kendricks.

"That would be the easy solution, Liam, but not the honorable one. I'm an officer. My word is my bond. I would put that bastard in front of a firing squad in a heartbeat as part of either negotiations or a judicial process. I should not, however, lie, kidnap, and then murder him."

It galled her. Her Millie and Frank—her family— were long dead, yet a man who was a murderer, traitor, and saboteur was still alive and free. Could she let that stand?

She touched a hand to her breast, feeling the locket beneath her coveralls she always wore containing her family's photos. A tear leaked out of her eye and trickled down her cheek.

"Captain?" a figure called over from the hatch. "I

need you to sign off on some repair proposals."

Wiping her cheek, Slater composed herself and walked toward the hatch leading back inside the *Ignatius*.

"Okay, Perry, what have you got for me?"

***

The single cot was deep in the bowels of the *Titan*, situated at one side of a small cabin which was divided in the middle by a thin curtain. The cabin was stuffy, airless, but it was home for Karl Grayson, his wife, and his son—who lay asleep on the other side of the curtain. The space was lit by a flickering halogen lamp. James hated being in the dark, and him feeling safe was more important to Grayson than the sleepless nights the perpetual light caused.

Gently, Grayson pushed Kristen's arm off him and slid off the bed. She gave a moan before turning over.

Standing, he took a few steps and moved the curtain to one side. He spent a long moment looking at his young son and listening to his light snores.

It may not have been much, but this was as good as it got in the crowded spaces of the fleet for them. He wished he could take his family to the comforts of *Atlantica*, but that seemed like it would never be.

Sighing, he let the curtain drop back into place. Padding on bare feet to the corner of the cabin, he saw his suitcase there. The suitcase that he insisted that no matter what, Kristen was to keep with her.

As quietly as he could, he unzipped the case, careful not to disturb his family. Opening it, he dug his fingernails under the tacks which kept the lining attached to the lid, and pulled it away. Underneath the lining was a brown manila folder.

Opening it, his eyes, squinting in the low light, flicked past the eagle and star crest and the words "Central Intelligence Agency—Special Activities Division" and TOP SECRET stamped beneath.

It had been years since he had even thought about the contents of this folder and he scanned it quickly to refresh his memory. Words sprang out—Weapon of Mass Destruction/Unknown Type, Nassau, and Project Elpis.

Turning over sheets, he eventually came to a sheaf of photographs.

The first was an image that had been taken of a group seated in the outdoor area of restaurant. Most of the people had names in black marker scrawled above them, but in the picture, one man could be seen presiding over the others.

Above him was the name Conrad Wakefield.

And beside him, scribbled above another man who was seated at the table: Admiral John Reynolds.

He flipped through the photos until he reached a photo of a ship. It was within a dry-dock hanger, scaffolding all around her. Yet even beneath the barnacles of industrial equipment covering the vessel, her sleek lines were beautiful. And it was the ship he recognized as being the one which had appeared from the locus.

And the name emblazoned on her bow was the *Osiris*.

Stuffing the sheets of paper and photos back into the folder, he slipped it back into the suitcase and zipped it up.

Climbing back into the narrow bed alongside his

wife, Grayson stared up to the ceiling.

Maybe the mission ain't over yet.

The story continues in THE LOCUS SERIES BOOK 2: EXPEDITION.

If you want to receive a FREE eBook copy of EXPEDITION then please leave an honest review for UNFATHOMED on Amazon and send me the link:

Ralphkern1980@gmail.com

Reviews are very important to independent authors. The feedback is invaluable, and they help readers find the books they like.

Author's Note

Reviews make a huge difference for an independent author. If you've enjoyed this book, please leave a spoiler free review on Amazon.

If you want to find more information on my work, including purchase links, please visit my website:

www.ralphkern.wordpress.com

And to subscribe to my spam-free mailing list, which is hosted in partnership with several other indie authors:

http://scifiexplorations.com

You will get a twice monthly newsletter containing great offers we spot, exciting interviews and, of course, keep you updated on our own stuff.

Alternatively, I'm always happy to be emailed or added on Facebook using:

Ralphkern1980@gmail.com

***

I hope you've enjoyed reading *Unfathomed* as much as I've enjoyed writing it.

This was one of those stories where inspiration struck in a surprising way. A few years ago, my girlfriend and I were on a cruise ship in the Caribbean, when it occurred to us just how much of a floating city these vast ships are. What was even stranger was how isolated from the outside world it felt to be on board.

So there we were, in the ship's nightclub talking about this, when the seed of a story began to gestate — what if the whole world had disappeared? What if all that was left was this ship?

As we spoke, the idea grew and grew. Originally, it started out as a kind of whodunit, set exclusively on the ship as the crew and passengers sought to find land while contending with internal threats.

I can't remember which of us suggested it, but pirates became involved, and by that point it was the wee hours and we wandered back to our cabin through the deserted promenade (leading to a scene which is pretty much replicated in the book).

Then the idea got shelved when we returned, while I finished off *Erebus* and started plotting *Endings*.

But my thoughts kept turning back to this and, as my fellow writers might agree — once the muse strikes, you just have to harness it.

So I began plotting and researching what became *Unfathomed*. It was quite surprising how the elements just flowed in and the story began to grow and expand in scope into what you have just read.

As with my previous novels, *Endeavour* and *Erebus*, I have tried to keep as accurate to the real world as possible. All the technology used by *Atlantica* and *Ignatius* exists. For very obvious and completely understandable reasons, obtaining accurate information about capabilities of some of the military hardware depicted is difficult or impossible. Any errors are mine alone or conjecture based on information obtained through open sources.

Printed in Great Britain
by Amazon